THE ANGOLA DECEPTION

DC ALDEN

Also by DC Alden

Invasion
The Horse at the Gates

'It would have been impossible for us to develop our plan for the world if we had been subject to the bright lights of publicity.'

David Rockefeller
Address to the Trilateral Commission

Prologue

'This is it? This is everything?'

Engle blinked behind the lenses of his horned-rimmed glasses as he appraised the government flunkey before him. The younger man was dark-haired and square-jawed, with shoulders that strained at his cheap suit. He looked more like an athlete than a bag carrier for Special Advisor Marshall, and his manner— well, to say it was abrupt was an understatement. The guy was just plain rude.

At sixty-seven years old and Director for Special Projects at the United States Geological Survey, Professor Bruce Engle was unused to being dictated to. Keyes, on the other hand, was a low level bureaucrat, yet he seemed indifferent to Engle's status, or indeed the importance of any of the VIPs sitting around the conference table. Engle glanced at the others, his own indignation mirrored on their faces.

'That's all of it?' Keyes repeated. 'Including backups?'

Engle waved a liver-spotted hand at the piles of folders, tapes and CD-ROM discs stacked at the end of the table. 'It's all there, as requested. And why isn't Marshall here? He should be here.'

'I believe you spoke to him this morning.'

'He called me at five a.m. I was barely conscious, for Chrissakes. I don't appreciate these sudden changes. Of arrangements *or* personnel.'

'Mister Marshall has authorised me to act on his behalf.'

'This is unacceptable,' the professor grumbled.

Frank Marshall was a National Security Special Assistant at the White House, and Engle's only point of contact since the data had been confirmed. He'd ordered Engle to make a list of names of those who knew the whole picture; the security guys from the International Energy Agency, the whistle-blowers from Saudi Aramco, Gazprom and ExxonMobil, and two of Engle's trusted colleagues at the USGS in Virginia. Twenty-three men and women in all, the only people on the planet who knew the brutal truth, now gathered around a grimy conference table in a disused office in Manhattan. Marshall had impressed upon them the need for avoidance of leaks of any kind. Disinformation was to be positively encouraged, at least for the foreseeable future. They'd all agreed, especially Engle; lately his nightmares of crumbling cities and starving populations were keeping him awake at night.

Keyes produced a plastic tray and pushed it across the table.

'I'll need all your identification, please.'

'Is this really necessary?'

'The Secret Service will need to record your personal details.'

Engle tossed his wallet into the tray. Keyes took a moment to examine the driving licences and social security cards, the corporate IDs and passports. Then he handed the tray to someone waiting outside the room.

Two more men appeared, both young and fit like Keyes, wearing the same cheap suits and each pushing a small cart. They began clearing the table, dumping the documents and CD's into the carts. One of them dropped a folder, the computer printout within spilling across the floor.

'Goddamit!' Engle clambered to his feet. With considerable effort he knelt down and retrieved the document, carefully folding the perforated edges together. 'This is sensitive data,' he grumbled. 'Be careful.'

He pulled his cell phone from his pocket and speed-dialled Marshall's number. *No signal*. He approached Keyes, who waited by the open door. He seemed oblivious to Engle's presence, his gaze fixed on his watch, his index finger resting on the lobe of his left ear. That's when Engle noticed the small, flesh-coloured receiver nestled inside. *Odd*, he thought. Perhaps he had a hearing impediment. He cleared his throat.

'Mister Keyes?'

The government man looked up, and Engle saw there was something wrong. Keyes was sweating, his eyes darting over the professor's shoulder, towards the men clearing the table behind him.

'Are you all right?'

'Me? Sure.'

Engle held his cell phone aloft. 'I can't raise Marshall.'

'He's on his way. Step aside, please.'

The men with carts squeezed past him and rumbled

outside. His precious data – all their data – was now in the hands of someone else.

'He's coming here?'

The distant chime of an elevator seemed to startle Keyes. He reached for Engle's hand and shook it. It was clammy, hurried.

'Take a seat. Help yourself to coffee. Mister Marshall will be with you shortly.' Then he was gone, the door swinging closed behind him.

Engle turned to his colleagues and shrugged.

'That's it, then. I guess we wait.'

'They seemed to be in a real hurry,' observed one of the guys from the International Energy Agency.

'I think they call that indecent haste,' Engle agreed.

He flopped into his chair, fatigue compounding his irritation. He understood the need for secrecy but a decrepit office was taking things too far. The furniture was dated, the walls yellowed with age, the brown carpet almost threadbare in places. This office hadn't been used in years.

Overhead, a bank of strip lights buzzed and flickered. Engle slipped his glasses off and loosened his tie. He pinched the bridge of his nose as a painful drum began to beat behind his eyes.

He checked his watch and cursed; 08:32. Where the hell was Marshall? He reached for his cell again. *No Service.*

'Does anyone have a signal?'

Heads shook around the table. Engle got to his feet, swatting the ever-present dust from the seat of his pants. He snatched at a nearby wall phone and jiggled the switch. Dead. He slammed the phone down and marched toward the door.

The Head of Operations from Saudi Aramco got to his feet. 'Bruce, where are you going?'

'To find someone,' Engle growled. He grabbed the door handle and twisted. It didn't move. He frowned, tried again. He turned to the Aramco executive.

'Ahmed, help me please.'

Engle stepped back as the younger Saudi grappled with the brass knob. The door shook but didn't open.

'It's locked,' Ahmed said.

Several of the other men got to their feet. Engle moved aside, anger boiling in his veins. What in hell's name was going on here? He saw the others yanking the handle, working their fingers into the gap above the door, important people, all experts in their fields, now sweating with effort, forced to vandalise the fixtures and fittings. Disgraceful. Suddenly the lock gave way with a loud crack, sending two of them tumbling across the carpet. Engle hurried over and helped them to their feet. He buttoned the front of his sports jacket and marched towards the open door.

'Stay here. I'm going to find out what the hell is going on.'

Outside the floor was open plan, dark, empty. Engle hurried towards the main doors. The lobby beyond was busy with office workers moving back and forth between the elevators and some kind of brokerage firm.

There was no sign of Marshall.

He passed a stairwell. He heard urgent voices inside, then the sound of rapid footsteps quickly fading to nothing. The door had been wedged open. Engle peered around it. Footprints stamped dusty trails on the concrete steps. A door slammed somewhere above, echoing down the vastness of the chamber.

He grabbed the handrail and began a slow climb to the floor above. Puffing hard on the landing, he yanked open the door and stepped inside.

'Hello?'

His voice echoed across the empty space. There were no offices up here, no desks or chairs, no bathrooms, no light fittings, no wall partitioning, not even carpet. It was just an empty space, silent, devoid of life, stripped back to its basic skeleton. Like a construction site. So where were all the workers?

Curiosity got the better of him. There was an air of recent industry about the place. The dust was much thicker here, but not from neglect. The toe of his shoe caught something and he looked down. A heavy black cable snaked across the concrete floor, one of several dozen that trailed away towards the building's massive central supporting columns. He wandered over towards them. The columns were huge, lancing from floor to ceiling like giant redwoods, partially boxed in by large sheets of timber. There were more building materials here, saws and benches, with sandbags piled high against the fresh lumber, the cables disappearing somewhere inside. He saw chalk marks on the wood, seemingly random numbers and roughly drawn crosses and arrows. Nearby, powerful-looking drills and jackhammers lay discarded in an untidy heap on the floor, as if their operators had abandoned them in a hurry. Engle shook his head in disgust. Not even nine a.m. and already on a break. Goddam unions.

A sudden wave of dread gripped him. Maybe they'd been duped. Maybe Keyes wasn't who he said he was, the meeting a ruse to steal their precious data. The Russians, perhaps? Or the Chinese? Both were masters at commercial espionage. Maybe *that* was why the man was so nervous. Why they'd been locked in.

He had to speak to Marshall.

He fumbled inside his jacket for his cell phone; still no goddam signal. He swore and strode across the room to the window. Finally the signal bar crept upwards. He punched Marshall's number and waited, relieved to hear a crackling ring tone. He thrust a hand into his trouser pocket and rocked on his heels as he waited for Marshall to pick up. He glanced out of the window and, just for a moment, forgot about the call.

For all his later years spent behind a desk, Engle never missed an opportunity to marvel at the sheer beauty of the world around him, the wondrous legacy of its violent creation, the land masses formed over millennia that had fused together to form a life-sustaining environment that most people barely appreciated. This was one of those moments.

Beyond the thick glass the sky was a glorious blue, the view breath-taking, the horizon, endless. In all his visits to New York, he'd never once been inside the

World Trade Centre and here, near the top of the North Tower, he could see all the way out to—

The morning sun caught a reflection, light bouncing off metal.

Then he saw it, growing larger by the second as it hurtled across the Manhattan skyline, the rising, screaming whine of jet engines that rattled the windows and shook the floor beneath his feet. For a moment, Engle's higher brain functions refused to process the scene he was witnessing.

The silver airliner filled the window.

His eyes widened in horror, the scream trapped in his throat.

The phone slipped from his hand and clattered to the floor.

The cell in his pocket stopped ringing.

From his vantage point in Jersey City, Frank Marshall swallowed hard as he watched a huge ball of flame engulf the top of the North Tower. Moments later a muffled boom rippled across the Hudson River. All around him people gathered along the boardwalk. He registered the gasps of horror, the frantic phone calls, the shock and fear. Then he made a call of his own using an encrypted satellite phone.

'Go ahead,' ordered a distant voice after a single ring.

'I'm in Jersey. Are you watching this?'

'It just made CNN. Where's our party?'

'Inside.' Marshall watched a young Latina staring open-mouthed at the smoking tower across the water. Tears rolled down her cheeks, her hands cupped around her face, as she swayed in denim shorts and roller blades.

'You're sure?'

'Remote camera showed them still sitting there at eight forty-three. Engle moved out of shot just before. Probably went snooping.'

'Any possibility he took the elevator back down?'

'Doubtful.'

'And you have the data?'

Marshall glanced over his shoulder towards a dark blue Chevy Suburban parked a short distance away. Inside, Keyes and the two 'Secret Service' agents were watching the drama unfold. He circled a finger to indicate that they should start the vehicle. 'We got everything, even a detailed index. It's all there.'

'Good work.'

'What now?'

He was eager to get going, before the next plane reached Manhattan. He didn't want to see that.

'The jet's at Teterboro. Our guy at NORAD can't keep this thing shut down for much longer. Pretty soon the FAA will initiate a ground stop, so get a shake on. We'll see you in DC.'

'Roger that.'

Marshall climbed inside the back seat of the Chevy next to Keyes. 'Let's go.'

'What about the other plane?' asked the driver. He

was crouched over the steering wheel, searching the sky through the windshield. 'D'you wanna wait?'

Marshall glared at the back of his head. 'Sure, good idea. Go grab some hotdogs and a six-pack. We'll make a day of it, you sick fuck.'

The driver took the hint and shifted the SUV into gear.

Marshall stared out of the window as the Chevy circled the lot and headed for the exit. Hundreds of people were now descending on the Jersey shoreline; office workers, construction guys, cops, cooks in chef whites, mothers pushing strollers. They gathered along the boardwalk, their expressions a mixture of horror and disbelief. Some were openly crying, just like the Latina. There'd be many more tears by day's end.

As they headed west on Second he forced himself to take one final look. He'd always believed the operation was necessary but now it was underway he wasn't so sure. For the first time in his professional life, doubt troubled him. If what they'd done turned out to be a mistake they'd all burn in hell for eternity. Marshall's skin suddenly tingled, the hairs on the back of his neck rising: *hell?* He hadn't thought about that concept since he was a boy.

He turned away and focused on the road ahead, folding his arms to stop the sudden, inexplicable shaking of his hands.

Behind him, across the river, a thick plume of black smoke belched from the shattered summit of the North Tower, an ugly stain across the sky on what was an otherwise beautiful September morning in New York City.

Chapter One

The nightmare was always the same.

He was a boy again, lost in a cornfield. He heard his brother laughing, glimpsed a flash of colour, Jimmy's orange T-shirt bright amongst the towering stalks. Roy surged after him, thrashing through the corn, thick rubbery leaves whipping his face.

'Jimmy!'

Only the wind answered, a low hiss that stirred the corn around him. Dark clouds blotted out the sun. He heard his dead parents calling, their voices laced with a shrill note of warning. The corn towered above him in silent, menacing ranks, pressing in on him, seeking to trap him.

Devour him.

Roy charged onwards, his sandals slapping the dirt as he ran, the cornfield morphing into a dark, ancient wood. He heard a telephone ringing, its urgent trilling echoing through the gnarled and twisted trees. He crept deeper into the woods where the shadows were darkest, where the air was still, drawn by the insistent ringing.

The clearing lay ahead, the phone box at its heart, its red paintwork cracked and peeling. Weeds sprouted around its base, its watery luminance dappling the clearing. Roy inched forward and reached for the door handle. He tugged, and the naked figure floating inside jerked wildly.

'Jimmy, it's me. Please come out.'

Jimmy cocked his head, no longer a boy but a man, the gold St Christopher pendant and chain around his neck glinting inside the cloudy waters of the phone box. Roy banged on the glass and his brother's bloodless body twisted like an eel to face him.

His eyes snapped open. He screamed soundlessly in an explosion of bubbles.

Roy screamed too...

He jerked awake, heart thumping like a hammer in his chest. *Bloody dream,* he cursed, fingering the sleep from his eyes. Spooked him every time.

He stared at the ceiling, the back of his skull thumping steadily. He was hung-over, yet he struggled to remember the events of the previous evening. He'd been drinking, possibly in The Duke, but he couldn't be sure. He recalled flashing lights and heavy music, a half-naked girl, a couple of tattooed strangers crowding him in a dark booth. His head pounded and his mouth tasted awful. He didn't even remember getting home.

He took a shower and dried off, taking stock in the mirror. He wasn't in great shape for thirty-eight. His short blond hair was rapidly thinning, his body a little more soft and baggy. Vicky once told him that he looked like the actor Jason Statham, but Roy didn't see it. The truth was he'd grown lazy over the years. *A bag of shite,* he heard Jimmy laugh.

He brushed his teeth and cracked the bathroom window. It was quiet outside. Roy liked this time of day;

most people had gone to work, the kids to school and the rest of the estate was a long way from surfacing. It was a sliver of tranquillity, but Roy knew it wouldn't last. Soon the muffled drone of a TV would filter through the wall on one side, later the jackhammer thump of a sound system on the other, rattling the family photographs in the sitting room. Right now they were still, arranged in a collection of neat frames above the wonky shelf and the fake electric log fire; Roy and Jimmy as children, Mum and Dad standing behind, beaming faces and ice cream cones. Teenage Jimmy in full parachute gear, grinning as he waited to jump from an aircraft ramp; an older, unshaven Jimmy in dust-caked civvies, an assault rifle slung across his chest, a wide smile across a face burned brown by the Afghan sun. And Roy's favourite, the black-and-white ten-by-eight of Jimmy and Max, the toddler suspended in mid-air, his chubby face a mask of delight, Jimmy's strong arms held aloft to catch the boy. Irrepressible Jimmy, Max's forgotten uncle, Roy's rock – gone. And no one knew where or why.

He got dressed in jeans, T-shirt and a navy blue jacket and left the flat. On the balcony outside he heard his neighbour hurling a mouthful of abuse at her brood of fatherless kids. He ducked into the stairwell and vowed for the umpteenth time to get his act together and get as far away from the Fitzroy Estate as possible.

He crossed the road and entered the park opposite, a cold wind whipping at his clothing as he headed for Kingston town centre. An hour later and Roy was trudging up Whitehall, past the long lines of police vans that stretched towards Trafalgar Square. Nelson's famous column loomed ahead and soon he was swept along with a steady stream of protesters.

The demo was a big one, maybe a hundred thousand crammed into the square, a living organism that ebbed and swayed before a huge platform erected in front of the National Gallery. Thousands of flags and banners fluttered in the breeze, and a police helicopter clattered overhead, an angry wasp probing the crowd with its high-definition cameras.

Roy headed towards the media stand erected in front of Canada House, pushing and shoving his way through the throng until he found himself directly beneath the rows of TV cameras, guarded by steel barriers and thick black lines of riot police.

He opened his jacket and produced his folded cardboard sign, insignificant as it was, but he was close enough to the cameras to be noticed. He unfolded it and held it above his head, hoping the news crews might catch the large, block capital words in thick black ink: *Justice for Jimmy Sullivan. Inquiry Now!* He looked towards the stage as the crowd suddenly roared, the noise deafening.

'Here we go,' an ageing protester next to him grinned, rubbing his hands together. The man wore a sheepskin coat with a peace badge pinned to the lapel. He was fired up for the occasion and Roy felt it too, although he was certainly not political. All he cared about was his homemade sign, and the hope that someone, somewhere, might ask, *who is Jimmy Sullivan?*

Onstage, the diminutive figure of Anna Reynolds, the formidable Member of Parliament for Selly Oak, took up position behind a bloom of microphones. Roy craned his neck as the cheering crowd pressed forward and Reynolds's booming voice cut through the chill air.

'It warms my heart to see so many decent, hardworking people here today...'

The crowd roared. She was a pro, Roy had to admit, a bridge across the social divide, privately schooled yet a champion of the working classes, her provocative words and dramatic timing stirring the crowd's emotions. As the minutes ticked by her voice began to rise in pitch and she began stabbing the air towards Whitehall, where police vans had formed a blockade across the road. Even Roy found himself jeering along with the crowd.

'Our world is changing,' Reynolds boomed from the stage. 'Today, less than twenty giant corporations now dominate more than a third of the world's economic activity. One of this government's biggest sponsors is TDL Global, a corporate entity richer than Italy, Portugal and Greece combined, yet the hardworking families of this country are forced to struggle against a tide of rising prices and failing local services. Let them go there,' she cried, 'let them talk to the beleaguered communities, let them try and explain to a pensioner living in a tower block that the lifts don't work because of crippling cuts, greedy banks and government inaction! This cannot, must not, be allowed to happen!'

The crowd thundered its approval, a wall of noise

that made the hair on the back of Roy's neck stand on end. Reynolds was in full flow, like Boadicea rallying her fighters, preparing them for battle. Flags and banners waved manically, and the crowd surged back and forth. Sign held aloft, Roy's arms were beginning to ache.

It was just after the second speaker had left the stage, when the dark clouds had drifted overhead and the first drops of rain began to spatter the crowd, that Roy noticed them. They were forty strong, maybe more, masks and bandanas covering their faces, moving as one through the crowd. They congregated a short distance from the stage, close to Roy and the glaring eye of the news crews.

Trouble, was Roy's immediate thought.

The third speaker took to the stage, a little-known environmentalist. Gone was the inflammatory rhetoric of Reynolds, replaced instead by the dull tones and measured arguments of a stuffy academic plunged into the spotlight. Roy sensed a change of atmosphere, the mood of rebellion unexpectedly tempered, replaced by a tide of impatience that rippled through the throng.

The catcalls started a few minutes into the speech, whistles and jeers competing with the amplified drone from the stage. Someone barged past him, a whip of fair hair, followed by a man with a camera perched on his shoulder. TV people, hungry for good footage, pressing into the crowd. As rain began to slice across Trafalgar Square Roy's eyes were drawn to the speaker onstage. He felt sorry for the man, his thin hair plastered to his head by the sudden squall, the pages of his speech clutched like a wet rag in his hand. *Poor bastard.*

'Shut up, will you? We can't hear him!' shouted the man in the sheepskin coat.

A dreadlocked anarchist twisted around, lashing Roy's face with his dreads. He snarled something unintelligible, then shoved Roy hard in the chest, causing a ripple through the crowd. Roy felt himself pushed forwards, and before he could recover his balance the fists began to fly.

He heard a woman shout, saw the TV reporter being slapped and punched by a masked anarchist. Roy lunged forward and punched him full in the face. The man went down hard and Roy grabbed the woman around the waist, pulling her back through the melee until they were swept up against a barrier.

Missiles arced through the air, a barrage of bottles, stones and paint bombs. People were getting hit, some dazed and bleeding, many more covered in pink and green paint. The riot cops surged forward, unleashing a fusillade of baton blows on the closest demonstrators. Roy clutched the reporter's hand and shoved his way through the throng until they found a break in the barriers. He ducked through and led her beneath the safety of the scaffold stand as the missiles continued to fly. Breathless, Roy sank to his knees.

'Thank you.'

She was thirtyish, slim, with a bob of mousy hair. Her nose was a little bloodied, her shirt ripped at the neck, her face paled by the proximity of violence. Still, she seemed pretty together despite her close call. Roy watched her cameraman squeeze through the gap and join them beneath the stand.

'Thanks, buddy.'

'No worries,' Roy muttered, getting to his feet.

The woman held out her hand. 'I'm Kelly Summers, MSNBC. You kinda saved me back there.'

The cameraman winked at Roy. 'A three-week stint in Kabul and she thinks she's invincible.'

Summers smiled sweetly. 'Fuck you, Art.'

'Classy,' Art chuckled, checking his camera.

Summers asked, 'What brings you here today?'

It took a moment for Roy to realise the opportunity that had presented itself. He produced his placard and launched into his story.

Summers held up a hand, positioned them both in front of Art's camera, and smoothed her hair down. 'You've got ninety seconds.'

As Summers wound up the segment a firework exploded overhead, a huge bang that rained a brilliant shower of sparks onto the crowd below. They panicked like a herd of cattle, and a phalanx of riot police charged into them, armour-plated Robocops swinging their batons mercilessly, their visored faces contorted with delicious rage. The noise was deafening, the chaos complete, the air ripe with body odour and fear.

A barrier gave way and the mob spilled into the media pen, scattering in all directions. Roy found himself swept away on the human tide, clutching and clawing at those around him, desperate to stay on his feet. The historic square had become a coliseum of mayhem.

'Come here, you!'

Roy yelped as a cop's gloved hand yanked his collar. He struggled free, plunging into a tight gap between two outside broadcast vehicles, the familiar dome of the National Gallery looming above him. He burst out of the narrow opening and hurtled straight into a trio of yellow-jacketed policemen, sending them tumbling to the ground like fluorescent skittles. They were on him in seconds, his arms wrenched and twisted into painful locks, stiff handcuffs ratcheted over his wrists.

'You're under arrest, violent disorder,' puffed an overweight plod as he frogmarched Roy toward a waiting van.

His protests fell on deaf ears. He was searched and shoved inside the van, squeezed up against a catch of grumbling detainees. He leaned his head against the mesh-covered window, bumping and swaying with the motion of the van as they headed along Pall Mall. His little interview, his one real chance of telling Jimmy's story, would be swallowed up by the riot, the mayhem played out again and again on every TV and news channel across the country. Who'd care now about a missing Brit in Iraq? The opportunity had passed. He wouldn't get another one like that.

The van raced along the Mall and turned hard right into Horse Guards Avenue, passing the famous parade square, the Cabinet War Rooms, the bronze soldiers on their granite plinths. His thoughts turned to Jimmy and the dream, the pain it represented. When his parents had died their loss had been heart-breaking, yet he'd got over that eventually.

But not Jimmy.

Despite the passage of time there was still no peace. His brother haunted him, and Roy was scared.

He peered out through the grimy Perspex window as the van howled through the busy streets of Victoria. He watched the crowds as they swept past, saw the anxiety in their faces, their nervous flight towards bus stops and train stations, escaping the city before the violence spread. Roy felt their fear too, a sense of trepidation that plagued his dreams, a growing apprehension that made his mouth dry and his heart beat fast inside his chest.

Something was coming.

Something dark and terrifying.

Chapter Two

Reverend Clarence Hays was halfway through his sermon when he noticed the man with the red ponytail seated in the rear pew. He'd seen him before, several times in fact, but he stood out simply because he was white, and it was unusual for a white man to be a part of the congregation at the Calvary Southern Baptist church on West 131st Street.

Not that Hays minded of course; all were welcome in God's House, even here in Harlem, where white folk were scarce and usually only seen behind the windshields of police cruisers.

Yet the man intrigued him. Hays recalled the first time he'd walked in, midway through a Wednesday evening service. He'd loitered at the back of the church, hands in the pockets of a black winter coat, baggy pants gathered around a pair of scuffed shoes, a few days of carroty growth on his face. At first Hays presumed he was homeless, seeking temporary shelter from the winter storms, but lately he'd re-evaluated that assessment. He didn't possess that beat down quality that bent the backs of most unfortunates. This man had bearing.

Hays finished his sermon and the first notes of the piano began to echo around the hall. Soon the swaying choir were in full voice, the achingly sweet sound of James Pullin's *He's Faithful* filling the room. Hays watched the white man bringing his hands together and mumbling the song's words. There was a strange intensity about him, his lips playing catch-up with the lyrics, his clapping hands trying and failing to keep the simple rhythm, the expression on his face far removed from the beaming joy of his fellow worshippers. Hays had seen that look before, in the faces of the sick and the dying, the Death Row inmates back in Kentucky. It was a look of desperation.

He knew he didn't have long. As the hymn filled the rafters, Hays slipped out into the corridor at the back of the church. He grabbed a black felt homburg and overcoat from his office then threw the bolt on the rear door. Out in the alleyway he popped the collar of his coat up against the chill and made his way to the street, a thin crust of frozen snow crunching under his shoes. As he reached the end of the alleyway he saw the white man trotting down the steps of the church. He stopped beneath the red neon cross, zipping up his jacket and tugging a Yankees beanie over his head. The street was empty, silent, the temperature hovering somewhere just below zero, crystals of snow drifting through the light of the streetlamps.

They were alone.

Reverend Hays wasn't a large man, but behind his lectern he felt as big as a mountain. He felt that same strength now, an instrument of God's work. He held up a hand as the man headed towards him.

'Excuse me, sir.'

Immediately the man veered to his right, large hands springing from the pockets of his coat. He moved out into the street, watching Hays but saying nothing.

'I don't mean you any harm. I'm Reverend Hays, from the church.'

Hays smiled and raised his homburg, allowing the light to reveal his ebony face. The man hesitated. A distant siren wailed on the cold night air.

'What do you want?'

Hays smile widened. 'I have everything I need. It's what *you* want that I'm interested in. Can we talk?'

The church was empty, the congregation long gone. Settled in the warmth of his cramped office, Hays poured two coffees into chipped black mugs with *Christ is Lord* emblazoned in swirly gold lettering. The stranger sat in the shadows, out of the glow of the gooseneck lamp on Hays' desk. He eased himself into his creaking chair and studied the stranger as he sipped his coffee. He was a big man, six-four, wide-shouldered, and there was some meat on those bones too, though not as much as there should be. Probably played some football in college. He was thinning on top, a dusting of freckles on his scalp, his remaining red hair tied into a thin ponytail that dangled past the frayed collar of his shirt. Those deep-set eyes missed nothing, Hays was sure of that. They roamed the walls, the floor, the dusty bookshelves, the ancient laptop that whirred quietly on his desk. Most of all they studied Hays, his face, and especially his hands. The stranger tracked them as Hays moved, as he scratched the grey curls of his beard and drank his coffee. The man was stretched tighter than a snare drum. Maybe he was a fugitive from the law, although on second thoughts Hays doubted it. White men didn't exactly blend in Harlem.

'It's just us,' he soothed. 'Please, try to relax.'

'I'm fine.' His voice was deep, resonant. There was authority there, but Hay's couldn't place the accent.

'My name is Clarence. What do I call you?'

'Frank will do.'

'Okay,' Hays smiled, rising from his chair. 'Well, Frank, let me officially welcome you to our humble church.'

His guest hesitated, then took the offered hand. He had a strong grip, and clean fingernails too, unusual for a man on the streets. Frank retreated back into the shadows.

'Without sounding like a bad movie, I'm guessing you're not from around these parts.'

Frank twisted the beanie in his lap with those big hands. 'I like the singing,' he said. 'Reminds me of when I was a boy.'

He's from Boston.

'Well, we sure like to sing around here,' Hays chuckled. 'Prayers are mighty fine of course, but I truly believe that people connect with the Lord on a different level when they sing. Cleanses the soul, wouldn't you agree, Frank?' His guest said nothing. Instead he slurped the dregs of his coffee. 'You want another?'

'Got anything stronger?'

Hays' face clouded. 'I'm not in the business of

feeding a man's vices, Frank.'

The man smiled, for the first time. 'I'm no alcoholic, Reverend, though for a time I tried my best to become one.'

He had good teeth, Hays noticed, clean, even, and the eyes, unclouded by the ravages of liquor or drugs. This was no bum.

'Too much coffee makes me edgy,' Frank said. 'I tend to smooth it out with the occasional drink.'

Hays reached into the bottom drawer of a battered filing cabinet and produced a bottle of Old Crow Reserve and two glasses. 'Made in my home state of Kentucky. Not the finest, but not too shabby either.'

He poured a couple of shots and watched Frank take his glass without lifting it to his lips. Okay, so he wasn't a drinker. Hays' instincts were right about this man. He had a story, one of pain and loss that would be as desperate as the thousands he'd heard in thirty-five years of being a minister. All Frank needed was someone to tell it to. Hays leaned back in his chair and sipped his own liquor. The computer hummed faintly, the alleyway outside deserted, silent.

'It's not just the singing, am I right, Frank? There's another reason why you came to us.'

The big man nodded, staring into the untouched contents of his glass as he swirled it around in small circles. When he spoke he did so quietly, eloquently, without hesitation.

'I grew up in a children's home in Southie, a Catholic one. I remember taking confession as a boy, and I'd sit there in the dark and the priest would promise me all kinds of eternal tortures in the fires of Hell if I didn't stop my sinning. I was ten years old, for Chrissakes. At that time the most sinful thing I ever did was use a curse word or two, but those images of damnation kept me awake most nights.'

Hays watched him take a small sip of bourbon. He'd had ex-Catholics through his doors before, most burdened from a young age with a misplaced sense of guilt, their spirits broken by the withering gaze of a spiteful God who was quick to judge and relished the punishment of sin. That certainly wasn't the Lord that Hays knew and loved, no sir. Frank would come to see that.

'That priest told me it was a sin to take your own life,' Frank continued, 'but God has to understand that sometimes people just can't live with themselves anymore.'

'Is that how *you* feel, Frank?'

'I used to, Reverend. There was a time when I'd wake up and promise myself I'd seen my last sunrise. I've stood on top of buildings and bridges, I've waited on subway platforms and closed my eyes when I've felt the rush of an oncoming train...'

Frank's voice trailed away. He tipped the rest of the bourbon down his throat.

Hays said nothing, allowing the poison to flow, the layers of guilt to peel away and reveal the pain beneath. Across the room Frank hung his head, the beanie wrung like a rag in those strong hands. When he looked up his eyes were moist, his voice a whisper.

'But I couldn't do it, Reverend, because dying would be the easy way out. I have to live, to be reminded of the pain I've caused, the families I've destroyed. I have to suffer.'

Frank crushed his face into his beanie.

Hays got to his feet. He was troubled, and not simply for the man's soul. He had blood on his hands. Two scenarios sprang to mind; either Frank was a murderer, in which case he would have to somehow steer him towards the authorities, or he was a veteran. Hays had met plenty in his time, men haunted by their experiences on the battlefield, those battles continuing long after the last flags had been waved and the homecoming bands had packed up and gone home. He'd have to tread carefully here.

He walked around the desk and crouched down in front of Frank. The tears flowed freely, coursing down his hollow cheekbones, catching in the red growth on his chin. Hays took his hands in his own.

'We've all made mistakes, Frank, each and every one of us. You carry this burden with you like Atlas with the world on his shoulders, but it's time to let go. Jesus brought you to me, I can see that now, and together we'll—'

Out in the corridor, the back door rattled violently.

Frank sprang from his chair, sweeping the lamp onto the floor. Hays felt a powerful hand shove him to the carpet. He lay there, frozen, watching the gun in Frank's hand sweeping the room. He heard a muffled curse from the alley outside, saw shadows flash by the frosted glass, the sound of laughter and running feet. Then silence.

Hays' voice soothed in the darkness. 'It's just kids, Frank, fooling around. Happens all the time.'

He picked himself up, retrieved the lamp from the floor, tinkered with the bulb. Soft light flickered, glowed. Frank was in shadow, his face ashen, the gun gripped in both hands and pointed towards the window. Hays moved closer.

'It's okay. Please, put down the gun.'

He raised his hand, laid it on the sleeve of Frank's coat, felt the limb beneath, rigid, like rock, He applied a little pressure, felt no resistance, saw the barrel of that big, ugly automatic tilt towards the worn carpet. 'This is God's house, Frank. There's no danger here, only refuge.'

Frank lowered the gun. He stood there in silence, his ashen face hovering like a ghost in the shadows.

'We want to help you,' Hays whispered. 'Me and Jesus, we've got your back, Frank.'

'I've done terrible things—'

'We'll get to that, son. Right now it's what's in your heart that matters.' He reached down, took Frank's free hand in both of his own. 'I believe Jesus has brought us together this night. He guided you to me, and He did it for a reason, Frank—salvation. Yes sir, salvation lies right here, in this church tonight. Let me help you, son. Please.'

The gun clattered to the floor. It was only after Frank had sunk to his knees, after the big man had wrapped his arms around Hays and buried his face into his sweater that the pastor realised he was sobbing like a baby.

As Hays comforted the troubled soul who clung to him so tightly he whispered a quiet prayer of thanks, for the abundance of God's love, and for the strength to guide this broken man along the path to redemption. As he breathed that quiet litany Clarence Hays felt another, deeper rush of emotion, of compassion, of joy, and realised that God was with them both, right there in the room.

Frank woke from another deep, dreamless sleep. Above him the ceiling was adorned with heavenly clouds and a flock of multiracial cherubs. He shifted beneath the thick eiderdown, the small army-issue cot creaking beneath his body. He felt safe here, as Reverend Hays had promised he would. Memories of that first night came flooding back.

He'd gone to pieces.

Yet it was here, in this rundown church in Harlem, that Frank discovered that the remorse that ate him like a cancer was nothing more than the affirmation of his own humanity, the spiritual declaration of a good soul determined to right a wrong. Guilt can be assuaged, Reverend Hays had assured him. It's why Jesus had died for them. Frank remembered asking how, and the pastor had smiled and spread his hands; *signs,* he'd replied. Apparently there were all around, you just had to be receptive to them.

He kicked off the eiderdown and stood, working the blood back into his muscles. He retrieved the Beretta from under the cot and slipped it into the back of his trousers. Outside, the morning sun barely penetrated the alleyway. The air was heavy and silent, muffled by an overnight snowfall. He let the curtain drop back into place and went into the washroom, throwing water over his face and drying himself with a towel. He was contemplating shaving when he heard a tap on the door. He reached for his gun and held it low by his side.

'Yeah?'

Reverend Hays poked his head around the frame. 'Morning, Frank. You decent?'

Frank tucked the pistol away. 'Sure. Come on in.'

Hays carried two mugs of steaming coffee over to a battered table in front of the equally battered sofa. 'Here you go. Black, no sugar.' He straightened up, pulled his Mets sweatshirt down over his large belly. 'You sleep okay?'

'I did, thanks.'

Frank sat on the battered sofa, cradling the coffee in his hands. 'I thought I might start on the hallway today. Paintwork's a little tired and there's a few loose boards underfoot.' He'd fix them all in due course, except the boards outside his room, the ones that creaked when someone approached the door.

'The work isn't compulsory, Frank. You can stay as long as you like.'

'I gotta earn my keep. I've been here nearly two weeks.'

'And the church is better for it,' Hays admitted, his eyes wandering around the recently painted walls. 'Oh,

I have something for you.' He reached into his back pocket and held out a crumpled leaflet.

'What's this?'

'A support group. It's run by veterans, right across the river in Brooklyn.'

Frank smoothed out the leaflet and gave it the once over. A soldier on the cover, his head in his hands, silhouetted against the Stars and Stripes, the letters PTSD liberally sprinkled throughout the text inside. It was close enough to the truth.

'Thanks,' Frank said, and he meant it.

Hays got to his feet. 'I'll leave you be.'

'I'll see about that hallway, if it's all the same.'

'I'll be in my office if you need me.'

Hays pulled the door closed and Frank snapped on the TV, the screen glowing into life as he located his socks and sneakers. On the screen a MSNBC anchor stared earnestly into the camera as he ran through the headlines at the top of the hour. As usual it wasn't good news: the economy was back in the toilet, there was civil unrest in Europe, and a massive cyclone in Bangladesh had made tens of thousands of people homeless. The stark images reminded Frank of the early seminars, where the speakers had likened humanity to a plague of locusts, devouring, laying waste. He fingered the faint scar on his right shoulder, a natural reaction whenever he thought about *them*.

He ran the hot tap in the bathroom and shaved. Raised voices drifted in from the TV, the muted roar of a large crowd.

A reporter barked into her microphone, then another voice cut in, the dull, nasal tones of a working-class Brit.

'—Working for TDL Global in Iraq. Officially my brother went missing in Baghdad but the Iraqi authorities claim they have no knowledge of the incident in question—'

Frank's hand gripped the edge of the sink, the razor frozen in mid-air.

'That was three years ago. No one cares any more, not the British government, not TDL, not even my local MP. How can a man, working for a giant corporation like TDL, simply disappear without trace? And why won't anyone hold an inquiry?'

Frank stepped out into the room, chin lathered with foam.

TDL Global. A huge building block in the pyramid of power. Frank had run black ops under the banner of their Security Division for years. Including the Iraqi operation.

'What is it you hope to achieve by coming here today?'

The reporter thrust her mike beneath the guy's mouth. The man with the homemade sign looked tired, beaten. He watched him turn away from the reporter and stare into the camera.

Into Frank's eyes.

'If there's anyone out there who knows what happened in Iraq, please come forward. My brother's name is Jimmy Sullivan—'

Frank jolted as if he'd been Tasered. He reached for the medallion around his neck, felt the smooth metal between his fingers, remembered that young face frozen in death.

Jimmy Sullivan.

He found the TiVo remote and rewound the segment. There was desperation in the Brit's words. He was seeking the truth, swimming against a tsunami of bureaucracy, lies and disinformation. He paused the segment, the Brit's face frozen on the screen. The man had no idea what he was up against. The evil that had taken his brother was unchallenged, unstoppable—

Frank's legs felt weak and he sagged onto the sofa. It was so clear now, like sunlight bursting through the clouds.

This wasn't a coincidence.

This was a sign, the kind Reverend Hays had spoken about.

That was his redemption, right there on the TV screen, a man adrift, battling against an unseen evil, his desperate plea a last throw of the dice. And his brother Jimmy, the seed, the genesis of it all.

Frank grabbed a pencil and paper from the table and scribbled some hurried notes. Then he gathered his things.

Ten minutes later he was standing in Hays' office. The pastor was packing tinned goods into a large cardboard box.

'I think I've found a way,' Frank said.

Hays paused, a large can of franks 'n' beans in his

hand. 'You're leaving?'

'Yes, sir.'

'That's a mighty quick decision, Frank.'

'It's hard to explain. There's a man I can help. He doesn't know it yet but I can ease his suffering.'

Hays put down the can. 'You know this person?'

'In a way. I think God spoke to me, through him. I need to find him. Save him.'

'I understand you need to right some wrongs, Frank, but this is kinda sudden, don't you think?'

Frank shook his head. 'It feels right. I have to do this.'

'The path to salvation can be a long and difficult one. Evil is out there, watching and waiting, looking to foul things up for righteous men.'

'I know all about evil, Reverend. We go way back.' He handed over the Beretta, wrapped inside its harness. 'Could you take care of this for me? For the record, I've never used it. I took it off a kid in Phoenix one night. A desperate kid.'

Hays hesitated. 'Okay,' he said, placing it in the filing cabinet. 'You need money? I don't have much but—'

'Thanks, I'm good.' Frank pulled his beanie hat over his ears, tucking his ponytail up inside.

Hays walked around his desk and held out his hand. 'Good luck to you, Frank. Never forget that Jesus will be with you every step of your journey. And we'll be praying for you too, right here in Harlem.'

'I appreciate that.'

'Wait a minute.' Hays walked over to the coat stand in the corner. 'I want you to have this. It's my personal travel Bible. I've had it since I was a young preacher.'

'I can't,' Frank protested, turning over the small, leather-bound book. 'This is too personal.'

'Nonsense.' Hays tapped a finger on his chest. 'The word of God is right here, in my heart. Take it, Frank. It'll be there for you on your journey, like it was on mine. My card's in there too, in case you need to talk. Call me anytime, day or night.'

'Thank you.' Emotion squeezed Frank's throat.

'Come back to us, when you're ready to start your life again.'

Frank nodded. 'I'll do my best.' He stepped forward and gave the pastor a warm hug. 'Goodbye, Reverend. God bless you.'

He left without another word, through the back door and out into the alley, passing Hays' shadow behind the frosted window. The cold air felt good on his skin, the sound of fresh snow crunching underfoot as he reached the street.

He paused a moment, taking a breath to steady his nerve, then he turned south, towards Manhattan.

Frank Marshall was back from the dead.

And back on the grid.

Chapter Three

He woke in a cell inside Belgravia police station.

He swung his legs off the mattress and stood up, blinking beneath the harsh strip light. The chaos of the previous day was a distant memory, the slamming of cell doors, the stomp of standard-issue boots, the shouts, the slamming of cell doors. All he heard now was the drip of the stainless steel toilet pan in his cell and the faint rumble of early morning traffic out in the street.

Then he heard footsteps in the corridor, the measured stride and jangle of keys outside his cell. The inspection flap scraped open.

'Take a step back, chum.'

Roy did as he was told. The door was unlocked.

'Duty sergeant wants a word,' said an overweight gaoler. He pointed to Roy's feet. 'You can put your trainers on.'

A few moments later Roy was standing in front of the custody desk, his personal possessions sealed in a clear plastic bag in front of him.

'It's your lucky day,' the sergeant said, pushing the bag across the counter. 'You're being released without charge. No case to answer.'

'That's because I didn't do anything.'

'You say so. I'll need your autograph.'

Roy signed the necessary paperwork, slipped his belt on, and was escorted off the premises. He was glad to be out in the fresh air. He found a coffee shop near Victoria Station, bought a latte and a paper, the first few pages splashed with lurid pictures of yesterday's riot. He pointed to the TV in the corner and asked the waitress if they had MSNBC. She mumbled something about management and moved on. He finished his coffee and headed for the station.

Roy was back on the Fitzroy by mid-morning. He dropped his clothes in the washing basket and stepped into the shower, soaping away the memory of his overnight accommodations. He changed into sweatpants and a T-shirt, and fired up his laptop. He scoured the internet for his segment but found nothing. He collapsed onto his bed, frustrated. He read his paper.

He dozed.

The musical chime of a text message woke him from a deep slumber.

In future, don't make promises you can't keep.

Roy rolled off the bed. *Shit*. Max's football match.

He hurried into the hallway, hopping into his trainers and tugging on a jacket. He was out of the door in less than a minute, wheeling his decrepit racing bike down the stairs and pedalling for the main road.

The school was a private one, a couple of miles to the west of Kingston town. It had walled grounds and impressive spires, and a boating club with private moorings along the Thames. Roy whizzed through the wrought-iron gates and headed towards the green chessboard of sports pitches at the rear of the school. He bounced onto the grass, skirting the half dozen rugby fixtures in progress, and headed for the soccer match at the far edge of the playing fields.

He propped his bike beneath the branches of a large oak tree and took a moment to catch his breath.

Two teams of energetic kids chased a football up and down the nearby pitch while a group of well-heeled adults shouted encouragement from the touchline. Roy spotted Max almost immediately, and not because he was on the pitch impressing the others with his skills; instead he played alone, clumsily kicking a ball around behind the grown-ups, his small body swamped in oversized shorts and shirt, his mind lost in a world of its own.

Roy hesitated.

No one had seen him yet. He could turn around and head home, send a text, make some sort of excuse. As he wrestled with his options he saw Vicky peel away from the touchline and march across the grass. *Busted.* She came to a halt in front of him, her pretty face furrowed in anger.

'You made a promise.'

'I know, I—'

'He's six years old. What's wrong with you?'

'Nothing.'

She looked great. Dark brown hair expensively styled, tanned skin and perfect teeth, a smart black overcoat with a silver faux fur collar, black knee-length suede boots. A long way from the cute graduate he'd met way back when. He felt long buried emotions stirring, then reminded himself that Vicky wasn't that same person anymore.

'A real father wouldn't desert his son like this.'

'Here we go.'

'It's not Max's fault.'

'I've told you before, it's not about Max.'

'Liar.' The wind ruffled the collar of her coat in tiny silver waves. 'It doesn't have to be this way, you know.'

Roy raised an eyebrow. 'Meaning?'

Vicky stared at her boots. 'Nothing. Doesn't matter.'

'Where's Clark Kent?'

'Nate's working.'

'*Nate*,' Roy muttered. 'Stupid name.'

'Grow up, Roy. Go say hello to your son.'

He watched her stamp off towards a clutch of designer-clad women, their cold eyes appraising Roy's rusted bike, his mud-speckled sweatpants and British Army combat jacket. He could read it in their faces; he was *that* Roy, Vicky's mistake, poor Max's indifferent father. The loser. He gave them a sarcastic wave.

Max was toe-poking the ball around, floppy brown hair bouncing as he ran. His movements were clumsy, his tongue protruding between his lips as he focused on kicking the ball at his feet.

'Hey, Max!'

Roy squatted down and spread his arms wide. The ball ran past him, quickly followed by an oblivious Max who puffed after it. Roy caught his arm and scooped him off the ground. He held him in a gentle embrace.

'Sorry for being late, Max,' he whispered in the boy's ear. 'Daddy had a bit of trouble.' The child didn't respond, a faint whine of protest building in his throat, a rag doll in Roy's arms. Defeated, Roy let him down. 'Go and play, then.'

He heard the rustle of dry leaves behind him, heavy footfalls beating the ground.

A flash of grey hair swept by, coat tails flapping, the ball scooped from under Max's feet then dribbled around him with enviable speed and dexterity. Max squealed in delight.

'Come on, son, show us what you got!'

The man turned this way and that, running proverbial rings around Max who chased him with unbridled joy. Then he took a big swing and hoofed the ball into the distance. Max's little legs pumped after it.

'That's it, son, go get it!'

The man turned around and Roy's stomach lurched.

'Jesus Christ.'

'Not exactly.'

Sammy French smiled, watching Max chase the ball across the grass. 'Look at him go. Like shit off a shovel.' He turned back to Roy. 'You ever watch them Paralympics? I saw a Chinese mong bench press six hundred pounds once. Fucking amazing.'

He held out his hand.

'Been a long time, eh Roy? I'd say you look well, but I'd be lying.'

The handshake was less than fleeting.

'What are you doing here, Sammy?'

Roy regretted the question instantly. Sammy

French was six years older and four inches taller, with long grey hair that swept back from his suntanned forehead and nestled in gelled curls over the collar of his coat. He had ice-blue eyes and a sharp, angular face that men thought dangerous and women ruggedly handsome. His smile was unnaturally white, his athletic build always wrapped in expensive clothes. Even today, on a windswept playing field, Sammy French looked like he'd stepped out of the pages of an Armani winter catalogue, uber-cool in a fawn trench coat, designer jeans and brown suede shoes. He had the looks, the money, property, power, and a dangerous reputation. He was everything Roy wasn't. No wonder some of Vicky's friends eyed him from the touchline.

Sammy cocked a thumb over his shoulder. 'How old's the boy?'

'Six.'

'A spastic from birth, eh? Must be tough.'

Roy bristled. 'He's got a few learning difficulties, that's all. Development issues. He's getting treatment. We don't say spastic anymore.'

Sammy's face darkened. 'Do I strike you as someone who gives a fuck about political correctness?'

'No, I—'

'That's what I thought.'

Max puffed back towards them, chasing after his ball. Sammy brightened.

'Here he comes, little twinkle toes.' He trapped the ball beneath his shoe then kicked it into the distance. Max spun around and chased after it.

Roy cringed as Sammy moved closer and laid a hand on his shoulder. 'I was sorry to hear about your brother.'

'Thanks.'

'A gobby little fucker as I remember. Shame what happened to him.'

'No one knows what happened. Officially he's still missing.'

'So's Lord Lucan, and he ain't coming back either. I'll say one thing about him—Jimmy had bottle. I could've used someone like him, ex-Para and all that. Went missing in Baghdad, right?'

'He wasn't in Baghdad. That's all bullshit.'

'Poor bastard. That's one place you don't want to go walkabout.' He turned his collar up against a fine mist of rain that swept in across the playing fields. 'Anyway, it's you I need to speak to.'

'Me?'

'Correct. I need a favour.'

'A favour?' Roy paled. It'd been years since they'd spoken, although Sammy was a regular face around Kingston, flitting between his many businesses in a white convertible Bentley. Sammy French lived in another universe compared to Roy, so what the hell could he want from him? Whatever it was, Roy had a feeling it wouldn't be legal.

'It's a real bad time at the moment, Sammy. I've got a lot on my plate.'

'Haven't we all.'

The final whistle shrilled, signalling the end of the

match. Roy watched the mud-caked boys on the pitch shake hands, a signal for the parents to hurry en masse for the car park as the fine mist strengthened into a steady rain. He saw Vicky pop up a Burberry umbrella and call to Max.

'I've got to go,' Roy said, backing away from Sammy's glare. 'Sorry I couldn't help.'

Vicky was tugging a sweatshirt over Max's head. He smoothed the boy's hair down.

'Hey, Max, you did really good today.'

Vicky sheltered them both with the brolly. 'He's soaking. I have to get him to the car.' She glanced over Roy's shoulder. 'Who's that?'

Roy saw Sammy waiting a short distance away, oblivious to the rain.

'No one. An old friend.'

'He looks upset.'

Roy leaned over and kissed Max on his head. 'I'll see you soon, Max. I promise.'

Vicky forced a smile. 'We won't hold our breath, will we, Max? Say bye-bye to Daddy.'

He watched her hurry away.

Between him and his pushbike Sammy stood immobile, hands thrust into his pockets, shoulders damp from the rain. As Roy approached Sammy produced his BlackBerry and speed-dialled a number. 'Start the car, Tank. I'll be there in five.'

Roy swallowed hard. Sammy wasn't going to let it go. They faced off in silence, in the rain, until the playing fields were empty. Then Sammy closed the gap between them.

'That was a bit naughty, walking off like that. You didn't even hear me out.'

'Listen, Sammy, I don't—'

The blow sent him staggering backwards, dumping him on the wet grass. Roy flinched as Sammy grabbed the collar of his combat jacket and dragged him beneath the shadow of the tree. He yanked him up and kicked him hard, sending him careering into the pushbike. Roy fell to the ground in a painful heap, bike wheels spinning on top of him. Sammy grabbed it and threw it to one side. He wasn't out of breath, his face showed no signs of anger; this was Sammy French, taking care of business. He slapped the dirt from his hands.

'I don't like being disrespected, Roy.'

'Jesus Christ, take it easy, Sammy.'

He touched his lower lip, muddy fingers red with blood.

Sammy loomed over him. 'Like I said, I need a favour. It's not a request.' He squatted down and pulled a hankie from his pocket. He handed it to Roy, who pressed it to his lips. Blood blossomed. Sammy spoke.

'I might've earned a few quid over the years, moved up to the big house, but I like to keep my ear to the ground, find out what the old Fitzroy faces are up to, who's been banged up, who's dead. Who's working, what they do.'

Oh shit.

'You work at Heathrow, Roy. Terminal Three, right?'

Roy shook his head. 'I won't do anything dodgy—'

Sammy whipped his arm back and cracked Roy around the face with an open-handed slap. He grabbed him by the collar and twisted the material in his large fist.

'You'll do as you're told, you little cunt. Understand?'

Roy nodded, withering before Sammy's icy glare. The big man suddenly thawed, veneers like pearls in the gloom.

'In the meantime don't do anything stupid, like change your job or go on holiday. Business as usual, got it?'

Roy nodded again.

'Good boy. I'll be in touch.'

Roy watched him duck under the branches and head across the playing fields in long, loping strides. He pulled himself up, swatting the wet grass and mud from his clothes. His lip stung and his hand shook when he dabbed his mouth. He never imagined he'd cross paths with Sammy French again.

And he was frightened.

He wheeled his bike from under the tree and headed across the grass towards the distant gates. His legs felt too weak to pedal. When Sammy wanted something, he got it. Roy's immediate thought was drugs; Sammy must be sending a mule through customs, and Roy would have to turn a blind eye. What else could it be? And what if it went wrong? Arrest, a lengthy prison sentence, his security clearance gone forever, which meant no job and no future worth thinking about. He'd be trapped on the Fitzroy forever, scraping by on benefits. He thought of Jimmy, longed for the comfort of his brother's company, his wise counsel.

But Jimmy was gone. Roy had no one to turn to.

The wind picked up, rain lancing across the playing fields in cold, silver sheets. He mounted his bike and pedalled out through the main gates. He barely noticed the weather, the passing traffic, the clouds of cold, fine spray. As he neared Kingston town centre the traffic began to snarl, brake lights blooming, windscreen wipers beating off the rain. Roy weaved through it at speed; with any luck someone would jump the lights, or maybe he'd slide on a manhole cover and break a leg.

No Roy, no favour.

Then he thought about the pain he'd have to suffer, the potential for serious injury, disability, or even death, and that scared him more.

He kept moving, heading for the grimy cluster of tower blocks that loomed in the distance.

Chapter Four

Located thirty miles east of Denver, the Golden Gate Canyon State Park is an area of breathtaking natural beauty, comprising rugged mountains, pine forests and lush meadows covering over twelve thousand acres of pristine real estate.

For the average visitor there's plenty on offer; hunting, fishing, trekking, and when the snows sweep down from Canada in late November, a whole host of winter sports, triggering the seasonal stampede to the Rocky Mountains.

Just over half a mile northeast of the park's visitor centre on the Crawford Gulch Road, a hard-packed dirt road intersects a gentle curve in the blacktop. The large metal sign by the entrance warns: *Private Property—No Trespassing.* Beyond that, the road runs straight for a hundred yards then bends right into a narrow, steep-sided and densely wooded valley.

Josh Keyes knew that from the moment he turned off the blacktop and passed that sign his approach was being monitored. As he powered the Grand Cherokee Jeep up the first mile of the twisting mountain road he knew he'd already passed at least a dozen cameras. In fact the whole mountain was sown with motion sensor systems, thermal imaging, pressure pads, optical beams and ground radar. To back up the technology, a security team of former Special Forces contractors remained on permanent standby to ward off any trespassers. But it hadn't always been like that.

As he rounded another bend high above the valley, Josh recalled the first and only breach, back when building had just begun. A moderately influential conspiracy blogger had turned his spotlight on the heavy construction underway at Blue Grouse Peak. He'd encouraged his followers to ask questions, apply pressure, to find out why the FAA had issued a Prohibited Airspace order above the area. The blogger himself had hiked up through the forests and went to work with his video camera and long lenses for two days before a security team rumbled him. His body was eventually discovered sixty miles away, at the foot of a popular mountain trail. An autopsy found traces of cocaine and marijuana in his blood stream. A search of his home computer uncovered hundreds of pornographic images of children. The story soon died.

The Committee didn't screw around.

But the episode had frightened them. That's why security was paramount, why they kept the legend of Bohemian Grove alive, the annual frat party in the Californian woods that attracted the attention of every conspiracy nut in the country and drew attention away from Blue Grouse Peak. Smoke and mirrors, Josh smiled. The Committee were masters at it.

Another bend, and then the plateau opened up before him, a wide, snowy meadow dotted with Scots pines that sloped up towards the magnificent lodge built beneath the jagged bluffs. Josh was always impressed, not just by the architecture or the way the facility blended in with the surrounding landscape, but by what lay behind those thick granite walls.

He followed the road until it dipped beneath the building into a huge underground parking lot. It was almost empty and would remain so until closer to the Transition. That's when they would come, to escape the cities. He parked the Jeep, passed through the security cage, and took an elevator to the complex above.

The lobby of the Eyrie reminded Josh of the Park Hyatt in Chicago, all polished floors and thick rugs, expensive furniture, discerning artworks, and long-drop light clusters hanging from the cathedral-like ceiling. One wall was all glass, offering a spectacular view of a snow-dusted valley. And that was just the lobby.

The Eyrie boasted a hundred lavish suites, a restaurant, a bar, a cinema, a gymnasium and health spa, and a host of other luxuries. There was a state of the art communications centre, conference rooms, a barracks for the security force and two, all-weather helipads. It was more than a luxury retreat; it was a redoubt, a command and control hub, one of several dotted across the globe, built by the Elites, for the Elites. Or it would be, once the Transition began. Right now, it was pretty empty.

As he cut across the lobby Josh recognised a couple of faces; the current Defence Secretary, the Chinese wife of a billionaire computer mogul, a Nobel prize-winning geneticist, a British blue blood. No one paid Josh any attention, except for the uniformed desk clerk behind the sweeping reception desk.

'Good afternoon, Mister Keyes. They're expecting you in conference room three.'

'Thanks.'

He took the elevator back down a couple of levels. His smoothed his neatly trimmed black hair, a legacy of his quarter Navajo ancestry.

The lift stopped. The doors swished open. He walked along a granite corridor to conference room three. He paused outside the door and cleared his throat.

A man and a woman waited for him, both middle-aged and suited, trusted advisors of the most senior Committee members. And both were pissed off.

No words were exchanged as Josh took a seat. He produced a memory stick and inserted it into the tablet waiting for him on the table. The lights in the room dimmed. CCTV footage began to play on the room's huge projection wall.

'These are the latest images of Frank Marshall,' Josh began.

On the wall Frank was seen from several different camera angles entering a bank, crossing the lobby, speaking to an employee.

'Where was this taken?' Freya Lund inquired in her lilting Swedish accent. She was a severe-looking broad, snow white hair swept back off a thin, tanned face, wrinkled neck protruding from a starched white shirt beneath a black suit jacket. She reminded Josh of a Quaker. Probably hadn't been laid in decades.

'Yesterday, nine oh two am, Bank of America,

Manhattan. He accessed a personal deposit box in the vault.'

'Why didn't we know about it?' the man next to her barked. His name was Beeton. Beeton's boss was once a blue-collar guy too, his construction business growing from a single mall in Cincinnati to one of the world's largest commercial construction empires. It was the billionaire's company that had built the Eyrie. His consigliore, Beeton, with his gnarled hands, shaved head and flattened nose, was a man not unfamiliar with physical violence, a Teamster leg-breaker in his younger days. Or so the rumours went.

'I guess he never declared it,' Josh said.

Lund tutted. 'This is a clear breach of policy.'

'Yes, ma'am.'

'How did we find him?'

'He used a fingerprint reader to gain access to the vault. The bank's system is interfaced with the Homeland Security network and we got a hit. A security team was scrambled but Frank was back on the street and gone in less than ninety seconds.'

Lund scribbled notes on a yellow legal pad. 'Do we know what was in the box?'

Josh shrugged. 'Hard to say.'

'Humour us,' Beeton growled. He played the city detective, tie askew, sleeves rolled up, thick forearms folded in front of him; the sort of guy who would enjoy beating out a confession.

'Knowing Frank, I'd say cash, credit cards, a passport or two. Rainy day stuff.'

'The box is not the problem,' Lund said. 'It's Marshall himself. He's been on the ground since TWA eight hundred. He has intimate knowledge of our organisation and its operations. Especially Messina.'

Beeton slapped a gnarly hand on the table. 'Why in God's name haven't we picked this maniac up yet?'

Because Frank Marshall is a smart guy, Josh didn't say. He glanced at the footage looping on the screen, saw Frank push his way through the bank's revolving doors out onto the street, a large black holdall slung over his back. The sidewalks are packed with commuters, a sea of umbrellas tilted against a heavy rainstorm. Frank pulls on a cap, unfurls a plain umbrella and plunges into the human tide. Within seconds he's lost. *Smart.* His former boss looked pale and thin, and Josh found the ponytail faintly amusing, but looks could be deceptive. Frank Marshall was one of the best, totally ruthless.

Or had been.

'What about the city's surveillance network? The MTA systems?'

Josh shook his head. 'Nothing yet.'

Beeton ran a hand over his shaved head. 'Help me understand all this, Keyes. One of our most senior security guys bolts from a highly sensitive installation, flies back to the States, disappears in Texas and then stages his own suicide. A couple of years later he waltzes into a downtown bank, helps himself to the contents of an undeclared strongbox, then disappears like a ghost. Two questions; how did he stay off the grid that long and why is he back?'

'I've no idea.'

'Real helpful.'

Lund said, 'Tell us about Marshall's suicide.'

'Three days after Frank landed at San Antonio, his clothes, wallet and driving licence were found on the shores of the Amistad Reservoir. His RFID implant went cold about the same time. He was presumed dead after the subsequent investigation.'

'You failed to notify your superiors that Marshall had absconded from his post in Iraq. Why?' Lund tapped her pen on the table like a schoolmistress. 'His seniority and deep involvement with Messina should have prompted your immediate action.'

Josh shifted in his chair. 'Like I told the inquiry, ma'am, Frank was upset. I figured he'd calm down, call me from Kuwait. It was a mistake.'

Lund brought the lights back up and scribbled a few more notes on her pad. Then she leaned back in her seat and fixed Josh with cold eyes. 'I'm finding it difficult to understand how we got here, Mister Keyes. Specifically, how you were unaware of Marshall's mental state prior to his disappearance.'

Josh glanced at the wall, at the frozen image of Frank Marshall. The compound at Al-Basrah was the last place he'd seen Frank, alone in his office, mumbling incoherently, cuffing tears from his eyes. While Josh had wrestled with his conscience Frank had left Iraq without warning.

'I worked closely with Frank Marshall for many years. In all that time his conduct and behaviour never gave me any reason to doubt his mental health. In my view he was a highly professional, dedicated and respected leader. I trusted him completely.'

Lund arched a pale eyebrow. 'A misguided trust, it would seem. Perhaps you were *too* close.'

Josh recalled the impossibly blue sky, his pale reflection in the elevator doors as it transported him far above the streets of Manhattan. 'I was twenty-eight years old when I was assigned to the New York office. My second op put me in the North Tower on the morning of Nine-Eleven. I was in a washroom on the hundred and seventh floor when we got word the planes had gone dark. The truth? I was terrified; every fibre of my being screamed at me to get the hell out of that building. But Frank was in my ear, coached me all the way. He got me through that morning, and every operation after that. Do I feel a sense of loyalty towards Frank Marshall? Sure I do. Does that loyalty extend to covering the ass of a man who has betrayed me? Who has undermined The Committee's confidence in me? No, ma'am, it does not.'

Lund made a *hmmm* sound. 'Is there anything else about Marshall you can tell us? His motivations, intentions, anything?'

Josh shook his head. 'No, ma'am. If Frank Marshall had secrets he didn't share them with me.'

Lund put down her pen and leaned into Beeton's ear for several moments. Beeton, his eyes never leaving Josh's, nodded in agreement.

'Marshall's intimate knowledge of Messina poses a

considerable risk,' Lund announced.

'I doubt Frank would do anything to expose us, ma'am. In my estimation—'

Beeton rapped his knuckles on the table. 'This isn't a debate, Keyes. We're not asking for your opinion here.'

'Your concern is noted,' Lund continued, 'but Marshall has the potential to hurt us.'

'With all due respect, ma'am, how? He can't stop the Transition.'

'You're missing the point, Mister Keyes. Before or after the Transition, it doesn't matter. What is troubling is the message that Marshall's continued liberty sends to others in our organisation. Word has spread— we've lost a senior figure, a man who has intentionally deceived us, who has managed to avoid detection and capture for some considerable time, despite our vast resources. He has challenged our authority and in the process made us look vulnerable. This is unacceptable. Do you understand?'

Josh did. 'Yes, ma'am.'

'This is a critical period for our organisation. As the Transition approaches some people may begin to question their faith in Messina, their role in its implementation, or indeed their very humanity. These are natural reactions, but doubt and uncertainty can do great damage to us. What is needed now is stability and, more importantly, unswerving conviction in the path we've all chosen. We must be as one, Mister Keyes. Marshall's continued autonomy jeopardises that.'

Lund gathered her notes. 'You are to track Marshall down and return him to us for evaluation.'

Josh raised his eyebrows. 'You want him alive? All due respect, I don't think —'

Lund silenced him with a raised hand. 'Marshall's capture will send a strong message. Fears will be calmed, faith restored.' She tapped her notes on the table. 'A replacement has been found and your FEMA workload reassigned. A field team, plus any additional resources, will be made available to you. Is this understood?'

Beneath the table Josh balled his fists. This was a demotion, plain and simple. He was out of the loop. He wanted to punch the walls. Instead he remained poker-faced.

'Of course.'

Beeton leaned forward in his chair. 'You know the sonofabitch best, Keyes. We don't care what you have to do, just find him. Right now Marshall's a goddam tumour that needs cutting out. Quickly.'

'I'll take care of it,' Josh assured them.

'Do that. And after he's been wrung dry you can drop the bastard back into that goddam lake. Is that clear?'

'Crystal.'

'Good. The clock's ticking. Any more fuck ups and it's on you.'

Lund picked up a telephone, signalling the end of the meeting.

Josh got to his feet and headed straight for the car

park. He had to swallow his anger, focus.

Outside the sun had set, the eastern slopes shrouded in a cold grey blanket. Josh steered the Grand Cherokee down the twisting dirt road, headlamps slicing through the mist. Did they really think Frank would be picked up that easily, confess his crimes and cheerfully place a noose around his own neck? The Committee wasn't stupid, no sir, but they had to know that an experienced field operative like Frank would be an extremely hard target to hit. And where to begin? Like all operators Frank's real identity had long been erased; birth certificate, medical records, even his social security number. Frank Marshall did not exist, period.

In fact, there was never any Frank Marshall in the first place.

Nor a Josh Keyes.

What *was* real—and wholly dangerous—were the lies he'd told to Lund and Beeton.

He'd not only respected Frank Marshall, he'd felt a deep sense of loyalty to the man. Frank had taken him under his wing from the very beginning, fast-tracking his career, promoting him to trusted lieutenant, anointing Josh with authority, responsibility, praising him to others in the organisation. He owed Frank everything.

Later, when the anxiety attacks began, the secret boozing and erratic behaviour, Josh had covered his boss's ass as much as he could. He'd pleaded with Frank to get help, got him prescription drugs, cleaned up his puke, dry-cleaned his suits and faked his emails and text messages. Yet even in his darkest moments

Frank had never confided in him, not once. Josh figured it was some kind of delayed post-traumatic stress. Whatever it was, it had turned his former mentor from a stone-cold killer into a pussy-ass cry baby. If Josh delivered him to Lund and Beeton in one piece, Frank would probably spill his guts about his breakdown. They would discover the extent of the lies and cover-ups that Josh had committed to save Frank's drunken ass. If that happened, Josh was finished. The Committee demanded loyalty from its people. Anything else was simply unacceptable. And unforgiveable.

And there was something else too, something that Frank was keeping from everyone, something that made them all nervous.

He recalled the surveillance footage, the field craft that had fooled the cameras, that familiar posture, the loping stride, the resolve in those watchful eyes. Whatever mental hellhole Frank had descended into, he'd managed to claw his way out, and now Frank was back.

More than that, Frank was on a mission.

Before Josh killed him, he would find out what it was.

Chapter Five

'Sit down,' Roy mouthed through the glass partition.

'Please, boss, my brother, he wait for me in Arrivals. Give him message, yes?'

'That's not possible. Take a seat. Someone will see you shortly.'

He waved the man away and flopped down into a chair. Beyond the security glass the holding room was populated with seventy or so new arrivals seeking refuge in Britain. Roy knew that most would now be rehearsing stories of torture and persecution for his colleagues in the processing team, but he didn't blame them. He'd probably do anything to escape whatever Third World shithole they'd flown in from, a recent and vocal observation that had earned him a written warning.

The blot on his copybook had worried Roy; there wasn't much work out there, and the irony was if he ever lost his job he'd probably end up competing with someone on the other side of the glass. He'd done well to get this far, Assistant Immigration Officer. He just had to tread a little more carefully.

He thought of Sammy and checked his messages. Nothing. There'd been no contact since their run-in at the school. Maybe there'd been a change of plan. Whatever the reason, Roy was glad. As each day passed he began to relax a little.

Another new arrival tapped on the security glass.

It was a woman this time, Somali or Sudanese Roy guessed, wrapped in a red and green silk gown. There was a vague beauty about her, the light brown eyes, the high cheekbones, perfect white teeth. She held a screaming child up to the glass like a trophy. 'Baby sick,' she mouthed.

The kid wailed like a banshee. Roy punched the intercom button. 'The doctor will be here soon.'

'Baby sick,' the woman repeated.

'Won't be long,' Roy smiled, ending the conversation.

The woman stared at him for a moment then turned away, heaving the child onto her hip. He heard the door behind him click and he sprang out of the chair. His team leader Yasin marched in. He raised a suspicious grey eyebrow at Roy.

'Any problems?'

'Possible sick child. The woman in green.' Roy pointed through the glass.

'Okay.'

Yasin clutched a sheaf of folders to his chest and walked along the row of interview booths, placing one at each station. Roy trailed behind him, eager to please. The stench of his written warning followed him like a bad smell.

'Need a hand, Yas?'

'No.'

Yasin snapped on booth lights as he went, creating a stir on the other side of the glass. He doubled back along the booths, tapping microphones, straightening chairs. A young Asian man approached the glass. Yasin raised his hand and leaned into a microphone. He spoke rapid-fire in one of his many dialects. The man hesitated, then stepped back. Yasin nodded his thanks.

Roy was impressed. That's why Yasin was a team leader; a stickler for the rules and the command of several tongues ensured his rapid rise up the promotion ladder. His appearance helped too, the bald dome and large grey beard a magnet for those of the faith who felt they might get a sympathetic ear. Instead they got the same rigorous interrogation that everyone else got, regardless of race or religion. Yasin was an equal opportunities bastard, but the man was tough on his troops too. They'd been sort-of friends once, during probation.

The door opened again and a line of tired-looking immigration officers filed into the room. They took a booth each as Yasin briefed them. Roy's phone chimed and he stepped out into the corridor. Vicky was downstairs, in Arrivals. Could they meet? Roy frowned; she never texted him unless it was to berate him about something, usually Max. He ducked back inside the interview room.

'Yas, can I take my break early? My ex-wife is here.'

The team leader glowered at him. 'I told you before, it's Mister Goreja. Remember, you're already on a warning. You want to return to the ramps?'

Roy shook his head. He'd worked airside at Gatwick for several years, loading and unloading baggage in long, backbreaking shifts and in all weathers. He'd hated it.

The older man checked his watch. 'Thirty minutes, no more.'

Roy mumbled his thanks and tapped out a reply to Vicky. He took a back staircase down to the Arrivals concourse.

The coffee shop was tucked between a newsagent and a currency exchange kiosk. Roy ordered a white coffee. He searched for a table and swore under his breath when he saw another colleague sitting nearby. Colin Furness was in his early sixties, a widower, and a heartbeat away from retirement. Any conversation with the terminally dismal Colin depressed Roy. He didn't want to end up like that, miserable, embittered by his job yet fearing the emptiness of retirement. The older man saw him and waved.

'Hi, Colin.'

'Roy. What brings you over to the dark side?'

'Meeting the ex. You?'

'Chemist. Bowels are playing me up something chronic today.'

'Sorry to hear that,' Roy smiled, moving all the time. 'See you later.' Colin looked disappointed.

He found a table at the back of the room and sat down. He sipped his brew and watched a gaggle of new arrivals filing past the shop. Many were loaded with luggage and duty-free bags, and almost all of them were woefully underdressed for the March weather waiting for them.

He saw Vicky approaching and waved. She bought

a coffee and weaved through the maze of tables towards him. She wore a fawn raincoat belted tightly around her waist, her dark hair heaped stylishly upon her head, a pair of expensive-looking sunglasses clamping it all in position.

'Are you sure you don't want to sit in the storeroom?' Vicky chided, dropping breathlessly into the chair opposite Roy.

Roy bristled. Even her accent had changed, far more cultured than it used to be.

'I'm on a break and I don't want to get hassled. What are you doing at Heathrow?'

Vicky looped her laptop bag over the back of her chair and swiped a few stray hairs off her forehead. 'I'm doing a human-interest piece, a working mum who happens to be a pilot.'

Roy chuckled. 'Not exactly the investigative journalism you imagined, is it? Still, I guess it's the best you can hope for at that rag of yours.'

'The *West London Herald* has a circulation of over a hundred thousand. That's hardly a rag, Roy.'

'Whatever.'

Roy simmered. Unlike him Vicky was ambitious, determined. She'd just got her degree in journalism when they'd first met, during that long, hot summer of love. A year later and they were married, with Max already on the way. Roy was happy. Vicky, on the other hand, had begun to regret her recklessness. Five years on and Vicky had her Masters, a good job, and a smart flat close to the River Thames. They were worlds apart, always had been. Roy knew that from the moment he'd met her. He was still in love with her, he knew that too, but her success intimidated him. And when Roy felt worthless he usually went on the attack.

'I thought you were a senior reporter? Isn't that the sort of fluff they give to a work-experience kid?'

'Everyone mucks in at the *Herald*. George needs copy for the online edition. I said I'd cover it.'

'Hardly the big break you're looking for, is it? Must be killing you.'

Vicky sipped her coffee, wiping lipstick marks off the rim of her mug. 'It'll come. One has to be patient, that's all.'

'One does,' Roy mocked. 'Then again there's always Jimmy. There's a story, right there.'

Vicky hesitated. 'Please, not again.'

'That's it, just keep ignoring it. It never goes away for me.'

She glared at him. 'I don't need reminding, Roy. It's what broke us, remember?'

'I don't get you. It's an important story with local interest. Right up the *Herald's* street.'

'It would smack of a personal crusade.'

'It is.'

'Yes, for you.' Vicky sighed, nursed her coffee. 'Maybe you should face the truth. Jimmy's been gone for three years. No one comes back alive after that, especially in Baghdad.'

'How many fucking times do I have to say it? He wasn't in Baghdad. You heard his voicemail.' He took a breath, swallowed his frustration. 'Jimmy was working at some installation near the coast when he went missing. The only thing I can find on the Internet is the ABOT, the Al Basrah Oil Terminal, where they load the tankers. It's a story, Vicky, a big one. You could speak to George, get the *Herald* to demand answers. No one's talking to me anymore.'

'Lots of people go missing in Iraq, Roy. Not just westerners.'

'So use that angle then.'

Vicky didn't answer. Instead she finished her coffee and scraped the cup to one side. 'I need to talk to you about something else, Roy. Something important.'

'More important than Jimmy?'

She gave him a hard stare. 'At this moment in time, yes.'

Roy bit his tongue, checked his watch. 'Make it quick. I've got to go soon.'

Vicky cleared her throat. 'Well, as you know things between Nate and me are going well. We're serious about each other. And he cares about Max, too.'

Roy boiled with jealousy. Nate Anderson, a big shot hedge fund manager, son of a wealthy New York financier. Roy had taken an instant dislike to the man, not just because he was sleeping with his estranged wife, but also because he was taller, better looking and infinitely more successful. He had lots of money, nice cars, and a penthouse apartment that overlooked Hyde Park. Vicky had once said the view was magnificent. Roy had remarked that the view she was probably more familiar with was that of Nate's bedroom ceiling. *He's better at that too,* Vicky had smiled.

Touché, bitch.

The truth was the American hailed from a different universe and Vicky had been drawn into his orbit. In a short time they'd gravitated towards each other like two shining celestial bodies, their compatibility written in the stars. By comparison, Roy felt like an insignificant lump of moon rock. No, more like an alien turd *on* a lump of moon rock.

Vicky's words pulled him back to the table.

'Things have changed, Roy. Nate's been offered a position, a senior one.'

Roy responded with a sarcastic handclap. 'Congratulations. Remind him to take the silver spoon out of his arse before he sits on his new throne.'

'It's in New York. He wants Max and me to join him.'

Roy's face dropped. 'Say again?'

'He wants us all to go to New York. His family is very influential, so visas and employment won't be a problem. Max would be taken care of too—'

'He's asked you to marry him,' Roy realised.

Across the table, Vicky took a breath. 'Yes. Once things are settled between us.'

'Settled? That's cold.'

'It's a wonderful opportunity, Roy. There's a special school for Max in Connecticut. We're talking the very best in care and facilities.' She reached inside her laptop bag. 'Here, I printed out their prospectus. That's for you, to keep.'

Roy skimmed the pages. It was all ivy-covered buildings and state-of-the-art amenities under a cloudless Connecticut sky. 'You could come and visit whenever you like,' he heard Vicky say. 'We'll pay your airfare of course.'

Roy swiped the prospectus to one side. Damp rings of coffee soaked through the paper. 'That's all well and good, but as you rightly pointed out, we're still married. I'm Max's father. I have rights.'

Vicky plucked a tissue from her pocket and blotted the prospectus. She avoided Roy's sullen gaze. 'We wouldn't do anything without your permission, Roy. Nate has a family lawyer. This could all be done with the minimum of fuss and at no expense to you. You can meet him if you want. I really think—'

'On what grounds? The divorce, I mean.'

'We've been apart for two years, so a no-fault separation would work. I'm not interested in blame.'

'Sounds like the paperwork's already been drawn up.'

'Nate is taking up his position in the next few weeks. He wants us to travel together. As a family.'

Roy sat in silence for a while. She'd wounded him, but in doing so she'd also handed him a little power. And he intended to use it. He checked his watch again. 'I've got to get back. I'm late already.'

Vicky reached across the table. 'Please, Roy, we need to discuss this.'

He shook her hand off his arm. 'I don't have to

do anything.' He stood up and pushed his way past the table. Cold coffee slopped across the prestigious Connecticut school. He leaned over her.

'You've got some nerve, Vicky. You were never there for me, so why should I help you? As for divorce, well, a courtroom might be a good place to get everything out in the open. Like a missing brother-in-law. Someone might actually sit up and take a bit of notice.'

Vicky shot out of her chair. He could see the pain in her eyes, the angry twist to her mouth.

'Don't do this, Roy—'

'Tough shit. Max stays here. You don't like it, I'll see you in court.'

He dodged between the tables, flushed by his rare victory. He swerved towards the counter and ordered a coffee to go. He heard Vicky's heels clicking angrily from the coffee shop and the satisfaction of his triumph quickly faded. Vicky wanted a new life, that was all, but still Roy found it difficult to forgive her. In the early days she'd been sympathetic about Jimmy while Roy had chased shadows. They'd talked, and argued, then fought, long and hard. Bitterness had turned to poison. Vicky left, taking Max with her. She'd joined the *Herald* but still she shied away from the story for fear of getting burned by her personal involvement. Roy hated her for it, but deep down he knew she was right. Jimmy was gone. A newspaper story, if there was one, wouldn't bring him back. She'd broken his heart, twice. All he wanted now was revenge, and she'd given him the opportunity to exact it. Yet surprisingly, it didn't make him feel any better. At that moment he wasn't sure whom he disliked more, himself or Vicky.

Out on the concourse he took a detour to the men's toilet. He threw his half-finished coffee into a waste bin. He urinated then washed his hands. He dried them on a fistful of paper towels that followed the coffee into the bin.

The radio on his hip crackled. He left the toilet.

Not once did he look in the mirror.

At that exact moment, a hundred feet away, Frank Marshall was moving through the Arrivals hall towards the exit.

He'd passed through customs without incident, using one of the passports taken from his personal strongbox in Manhattan. In this case it was a Belgian one in the name of Doug LeBreton, and although Frank's face had changed since the original photo was taken, it hadn't changed that much. Gone were the ponytail and the scruffy clothes; now Frank wore a grey suit and blue tie, a black raincoat draped over one arm, a leather carry-on in his other hand. He looked like a businessmen, not the first-class type but more of a travelling salesman, an eighty-hour-a-week guy who lived for commission and would travel anywhere to get it. Generic. Forgettable. Like the rest of his fellow passengers on the American Airlines red-eye flight he looked a little beat, having endured a bumpy ride east in the grip of a fast-moving jet stream. The aircraft had landed on time.

Now he had a thirty-minute window, maybe less, to get clear of the airport.

Overhead signs pointed him to subways and bus stops. Frank kept moving towards the cab rank beyond the terminal doors. Outside the air was cold and damp, the grey sky already darkening, the roar of distant aircraft competing with the black snake of taxicabs rattling in front of the terminal. He spied the cameras overhead, the faces of the crowd around him, the cars that loitered nearby. He had fifteen minutes now, maybe less. Soon the phones would be ringing in a dozen agencies across Europe, Doug LeBreton's mugshot broadcast to police, security services, Interpol and others. He kept his head low and shuffled forward to the head of the line. A black cab squealed to a stop and Frank ducked inside.

'Where to, mate?'

'London. The West End.'

The cab pulled away. Frank spun around in his seat, swiping the condensation from the rear window. He watched the traffic behind them, saw no wild movements, no sudden acceleration or changes of direction. They joined the freeway into the city. As the driver answered a personal phone call Frank shoved the now-useless Belgian passport deep behind his seat.

Just before they reached the sprawl of Hammersmith, Frank ordered the driver to pull over. He paid the man in cash and disappeared into the darkness of a nearby park, emerging onto a busy high street on the other side. He checked a route map and mingled with a group of shoppers clustered beneath the shelter of a bus stop. He waited ten minutes and boarded a bus towards southwest London.

An hour later he checked into a modest hotel on Richmond Hill. The lobby was empty when he arrived and he paid cash, in advance, for two weeks. For an extra hundred the manager was persuaded to overlook the formalities and Frank was given his key. The room was clean and comfortable, and the view beyond the window provided a glimpse of the river Thames at the bottom of the hill.

He took a long shower, switched the lights off, and stretched out on the bed.

For the first time in forty-eight hours he could relax a little. As his breathing slowed and sleep beckoned, Frank clutched the dog-eared travel Bible to his chest and thought about the path of redemption he'd chosen. He was a ways down that path now, his sights set on another who was lost, who mourned a loved one and sought closure.

Frank would deliver that closure, and more, before the demons, both real and imagined, caught up with him again.

And when they did, Frank, with Jesus's help, would destroy them all.

Chapter Six

The bus rumbled to a stop outside the Fitzroy Estate.

Roy shuffled off with a dozen others and trudged beneath the concrete archway, a fine mist falling through the yellow wash of streetlamps. On nights like these the estate reminded him of a prison, dull grey concrete blocks surrounding the exercise yard, the long balconies stacked on top of each other like tiers of cells. Only this prison had no guards, no watchtowers or lockdown. There were no bars or fences either, but Roy felt trapped within its walls just the same.

At the top of the stairs two men loitered on the landing. They were draped over the balcony, the pungent smell of cannabis drifting on the air. Roy recognised one of them, his neighbour's latest boyfriend. Dwayne, or something. He seemed oblivious to the cold, wearing only jeans and a white singlet. A comb with a black fist handle poked out of his unkempt afro. The other man was better dressed for the weather, a New York baseball cap pulled low over his brow, a black hoodie over that, black jeans and trainers. The street robber's uniform of choice. They stopped talking as Roy approached.

'Evening,' Roy muttered, fiddling with his key.

They didn't answer, and neither did Roy expect them to. This was the Fitzroy, after all.

He shut the front door behind him.

He kicked his shoes off and made a cup of tea in the kitchen. He used the rest of the water to stir up a curry-flavoured Pot Noodle and retired to the living room. He slumped onto the couch in front of the TV. He ate. He channel surfed. He was bored, and tired, but not enough to go to bed. He toyed with his phone, and thought about texting an apology to Vicky. He decided against it. She was probably with Nate.

He stretched out on the sofa, found a late night movie on the TV, one about a kid who could jump through time and space just by using the power of thought. He wished he could do that too.

He fell asleep.

The phone trembled on the coffee table. Roy bolted upright, startled. He cuffed saliva from the corner of his mouth and fumbled for the remote. The time jumper was gone, replaced by a man and woman kissing in soft, black and white focus and speaking in ridiculously posh voices. He snapped the TV off. He scooped up his phone; almost one in the morning. He didn't recognise the number. He thought it might be Vicky, a new phone maybe, but calling him wasn't her style. She was a texter, her messages sharp, disapproving.

'Hello?'

'Open the door, Roy.'

Oh shit.

'Sammy?'

'Open the door. Leave the lights off.'

The phone went dead. Roy sprang off the couch. He dropped the bolt on the front door, eased it open, peered along the landing. Deserted, the prison silent, slumbering like a dormant volcano. Then he heard movement in the stairwell, footsteps, the rustle of clothing. He retreated back down the hallway. A familiar shadow loomed in the doorway—Tank, Sammy's long-time driver and minder.

'In the sitting room,' she commanded.

Tank's voice was as deep as a man's. She was a former cage fighter, and used to work the door at one of Sammy's nightspots. She was tall, just over six feet, and had one of those dreadlock Mohawks that was woven into a thick clump at the back of her head. She was probably the butchest, most intimidating woman Roy had ever met. He slapped the light off.

'Pull the curtains.'

Roy scraped them together.

He heard the front door close, the bolt slide into place. His legs felt hollow.

Two men entered the sitting room. The light came back on. Sammy's face was shrouded in an expensive designer hoodie.

'Jesus Christ, Sammy, you scared me to death.'

Roy cursed himself for uttering the word. He didn't want to put ideas in anyone's head.

Sammy flicked his hood off and smoothed his grey mane. 'Shut up.'

Roy complied. Then glanced at the other man in the room, the one dwarfed between Sammy and Tank, a little older, fifties, carrying a black sports bag and wearing a dark coat and jeans. His balding grey hair was shaved close, his broken nose spread wide across his deeply lined face. He sat down on the couch and kicked his trainers off. He produced a packet of cigarettes from his coat pocket and lit one. Sammy broke the difficult silence.

'Roy, this is Derek. He's going to be staying here for a while.'

'He's what?'

Derek nailed him with a malignant stare. 'Put the kettle on, son. I'm dying for a cuppa.' He was a Scot, his accent thick and harsh.

Roy's feet were rooted to the carpet. 'What was that?' he stammered.

Derek glanced at Sammy. 'Forrest fucking Gump, this one.' He sniggered, but the humour never made it to his cold grey eyes. 'Tea. Now.'

Roy willed his legs to move and headed for the kitchen. He filled the kettle, grabbed a mug from an overhead cupboard. Sammy trailed in behind him.

'What's going on, Sammy?'

'Derek needs to lay low for a while.'

'He can't stay here.'

'Yes he can. You live alone, rarely go out, no girlfriend—wait a minute, you're not a poof, are you, Roy?'

'Course not.'

Sammy smiled. 'Just checking. Like I say, you live alone, no regular visitors. You and Derek are a good fit.'

Roy's mind raced. 'There's no room.'

'Really? Far as I can tell you've got two bedrooms in this shoebox.'

'Yeah, mine and Max's.'

Sammy's smile disappeared. 'Don't lie to me. That kid hasn't stayed here for over a year. The mums down at the school, they like to gossip. Seems you're not pulling your weight as a dad, ignoring the kid. Still, I can see why; when the fruit of your loins turns out to be a window licker I guess it's hard to connect on an emotional level. And your ex, she thinks you're a loser. The word is, she wouldn't let him come within a thousand yards of this shithole. Smart girl.'

He took a step closer, looming over Roy. 'Derek stays. And a word of advice—him and me go back a long way, so it would be advisable on your part to pay him the appropriate level of respect.

'Course,' Roy mumbled, pulling open a drawer and fishing for a spoon. There was no point in arguing. His life had just gone up a few notches on the shit-o-meter. Or down. Whatever. 'How long will he be here?'

'A few weeks. Six, tops.'

Roy's eyes widened. 'Six weeks? Jesus Christ, I've got a life here, Sammy.'

'All evidence to the contrary.'

Sammy produced a thick roll of fifty-pound notes from his pocket and peeled several off. 'That's for Derek's keep. He likes a drink, but he's a punchy drunk, so stay out of his way.' He slapped the wad onto the counter.

Roy stared at the money, more cash than he'd held in his wallet for longer than he could remember. He had a sudden mental image of himself at the airport, squeezing into a window seat, flying off to the sun,

Sammy's cash stuffed into his pocket. Never coming back.

The image melted away as a cold sweat prickled Roy's skin. 'This is about my job, right, Sammy?'

'Bingo.'

'I can't do anything illegal. They don't just sack you, they prosecute.'

'You'd best be careful then.'

Roy felt like a panicked animal, a pigeon desperate to escape a lofty room. He wanted to charge past Sammy, fling open the front door, run until his lungs burst. Coarse laughter drifted in from the room next door. 'Don't make me do this,' Roy whispered. 'You know I'm straight, always have been. I just want a quiet life. I can't afford to get mixed up in—'

Sammy grabbed Roy around the throat and slammed his head against a kitchen unit. Pain flashed and crockery rattled. Sammy's strong fingers dug into his neck. Roy wheezed.

'Sammy, please—'

The kettle whistled, filling the kitchen with steam. Sammy grabbed it with his free hand.

'You ever watch the History Channel Roy? I saw this programme once, about the Roman Empire. Back then they used to pour molten lead into people's mouths as a form of execution. Cruel fuckers, eh?'

He held the kettle close. Roy could feel the heat on his cheek.

'We can work things out a couple of ways, Roy. Tank wanted me to use violence. She gets off on it, crazy fucking bitch.'

He lowered the kettle and dropped his hand.

Roy coughed and spluttered.

'I said no. I told her, I've known Roy Sullivan since he was a kid. Violence would work, sure, but I'm going to cut him some slack, for old time's sake. No rough stuff, just these.' Sammy handed over his BlackBerry. 'Scroll through them. There's some good ones there.'

Roy took the phone. He jolted as if he'd been stung. The picture on the screen was of him, seated in a booth in an unfamiliar night spot, a drink in one hand, giving the camera the finger with the other, a stupid grin plastered across his face. He swiped the screen; a topless girl straddled across his lap, platinum-blond hair falling down her back, voluminous breasts thrust in Roy's face. *What the hell?*

'Keep going,' Sammy urged.

Roy did as he was told. With each image the mood darkened; clinking glasses with two hard-looking men, one shaven-headed, the other lank-haired, both suited, both tattooed, dead eyes and expensive wristwatches. A serious Roy in deep conversation with same. Roy doing a line of coke.

The last picture was the worst—the lap dancer, staring into the camera, her face ashen, eyes blackened, a deep cut across the bridge of her nose. Dried blood caked her hairline, her lips. Sammy snatched the phone from Roy's trembling hand.

'That's Tank's handiwork. Sofia didn't mind too much, though. You know what these Russian birds are like, hard as nails. She got well paid too. In any case, she'd swear in court that it was you who did that.'

'Me?'

Roy was suffering from system overload. It looked like him in the photos but he didn't remember any of it. He must have a double—

'It's you,' confirmed Sammy. 'You made it easy, leaving your glass on the bar while you popped to the Ladies. I bet you don't even remember leaving The Duke.'

'The Duke?'

'Anyway, I don't think a night on the gear with a couple of jailbirds would go down too well at work. As for the sexual assault on poor little Sofia—'

'I didn't touch her. I've never seen her before in my life.'

'The camera never lies, Roy. Your fingerprints are all over her arse.'

Sammy flicked through the images again.

'Yeah, some cracking shots there. Oh, she reported it to the police, by the way. Made a statement, gave a description—of you, in fact. Not an accurate one, not enough to get you lifted, but she'll pick you out of a line-up if she has to. You see where all this is going, Roy? You're at a crossroads, and you've got two options.'

He waved his BlackBerry in Roy's face.

'Option one; you fuck things up for me and this little photo shoot will find its way into the hands of the law. Then, after you've done your bird and you're rebuilding your shitty little life, I'll be there to remind you how you fucked things up. And that'll never stop, Roy. Ever.'

Sammy leaned against the counter, folded his arms.

'By the look on your face I'm guessing you're going for option two.'

'What do you want?' Roy finally managed to croak.

'Derek's going to catch a plane. I'll let you know which one when the time comes. All you have to do is get him onto that plane, avoiding the usual formalities. You know, stuff like customs and security checks. Walk him through the terminal unmolested and get him to the gate. That's it. Simples.'

Despite the danger, Roy almost laughed. Smuggle someone onto a plane? Was that a joke? Then he realised Sammy was still talking. He forced himself to pay attention.

'All the time Derek is here you mustn't have a single visitor. Not one. No one comes through that front door unless it's Tank or me. I don't care who it is—gas man, electricity, Jehovah's fucking Witness. No one gets in. No one sees him. Got it?'

'I got it.'

'Good.' Roy flinched as Sammy patted his cheek. 'Now fix him his tea.'

Sammy disappeared into the sitting room.

Roy held onto the counter. He wanted to urinate but was afraid to move. He was in deep with Sammy now, deep enough to have serious, life-threatening consequences. He heard the front door close, saw two shadows pass by the window.

He was alone with Derek.

He forced himself to focus.

He made tea and carried it into the sitting room. Derek was stretched out on the sofa, a cushion behind his head. He kicked his legs off and rummaged in his sports bag. He produced a small bottle of Scotch and poured a stiff measure into his tea. He sparked up another cigarette, the smoke swirling around the room. Roy moved to open a window.

'Leave it,' Derek ordered.

'I had bronchitis as a kid. I can't be around cigarette smoke.'

'Do I look like I give a fuck?'

Roy let the curtain drop back into place. 'I'll go make up the bed.'

'You do that. And make sure you get plenty of food in. If I'm staying here I want to eat well. I'll leave you a list.'

'I've got to work in the morning.'

'Well, you'd better set your alarm then.'

Derek took a deep pull of his cigarette and exhaled in Roy's direction. The Scot's hard eyes bored into him.

'What time do you finish?'

'I should be back by half-seven.'

Derek waved at the DVD's stacked beneath the TV. 'Your movie collection is shite, all romances and stuff. Get some more. And pick me up a paperback or two. I like to read. Crime, murder, that type of thing.'

Murder?

'Sure.'

Derek stretched out and reached for the TV remote.

Roy made up the spare bed and retreated to his bedroom. Then he dragged a chest of drawers inch by silent inch across the carpet until it blocked the door.

He climbed into bed and lay beneath the quilt for a long time, staring up at the bars of light that stretched across the bedroom ceiling. He listened in the darkness, to the sound of the TV across the hall, to the pad of feet on the carpet outside, to the echo of Derek urinating in the toilet; and much later, the sound of the spare room door closing. A short while after that, Derek's snores filtered through the wall between them. They were long and loud, and seemingly never-ending.

Red digits hovered in the darkness—3:19. An early rise meant less than three hours' sleep. A black cloud of despair settled over him. His flat, his private sanctuary, had been invaded by another, a man in hiding, belligerent, dangerous. Hiding from who was anyone's guess but Roy assumed it was the law.

Six weeks, Sammy said. All he had to do was tough it out until then. After that, he'd be free.

Or would he? Would Sammy ever let him go? Would he use this episode as blackmail, demand favour after illegal favour until one day the police kicked his door in? Or would Roy outlive his usefulness and have boiling water poured down his throat? He shivered in the darkness.

He'd managed to avoid the displeasure of Sammy French for most of his life. As kids, both he and Jimmy had been tolerated, allowed to hang around the playground while Sammy and his gang ruled from their fortress of monkey bars. As the years went by Jimmy joined the army, Mum and Dad passed away and Roy was left alone, a permanent fixture on the estate where new gangs had taken over and the football pitch had been converted into a basketball court. Sammy had gone too, the law finally catching up with him.

He'd resurfaced a few years later, a different man. Gone was the wildness of youth, replaced by a ruthless ambition for legitimacy. But for those who knew his past, the stench of gangland hovered around Sammy like a cloud of flies. Despite the nightclub and restaurants, and the big house that overlooked Richmond Park, those who knew him were convinced. Sammy French was, and always would be, a dangerous criminal.

And now Roy was fixed on his radar.

For the first time in his life he considered running. He could pack a bag, grab his passport, empty his paltry savings account and get the hell out. The question was, go where?

So the problem remained; he lay ten feet from a psycho stranger. He was obligated to a gangster who'd ruin his life if he didn't help in a criminal enterprise that would surely see him nicked and sent down. Roy felt like crying. He was trapped, the walls of his bedroom pressing inwards. Panic ebbed and flowed.

The bars across the ceiling faded and the sky outside paled.

He thought of Jimmy and realised what the dream meant; it was a warning, an omen of bad things to come, personified by Sammy and Derek, brutal prophets of doom about to ruin his life.

Frightened, Roy snuck out of bed and rummaged at the bottom of his cupboard. He found Jimmy's old army daysack, retrieved the Gerber combat knife from inside and wedged it beneath his mattress. He climbed back into bed, his fingers finding the tough black plastic of the hilt, reassured by its proximity.

But sleep evaded him, and his thoughts turned to the airport, to the task that lay ahead. As the sun crept above the horizon, Roy realised that he was about to face the most dangerous challenge of his life.

The next few weeks would decide if he made it through to the other side.

Chapter Seven

Josh tugged his seatbelt a little tighter as the Gulfstream G650 dipped her nose towards the distant lights of RAF Northolt. He felt the undercarriage lock home with a solid thump, and watched the rise and fall of the port wing as the aircraft levelled for landing.

Beyond the wingtip, patchwork fields surrendered to the grey urban sprawl of outer London. Josh was a native of Arizona, born and raised beneath the warmth of its eternal sunshine. By contrast, the view outside looked cold, damp and miserable. Despite this being his first trip to the UK, Josh decided it was another reason not to stay a minute longer than necessary. The plane would be kept on standby. The hunter team would do their job.

They were scattered around the cabin now, six former Special Forces guys and two Marines from Force Recon, all of them with extensive operational experience in a wide variety of countries. The Marines were communications specialists who'd served with the JSOC Signals Team. They would be juiced into a myriad of global surveillance systems, acting as Josh's eyes and ears. Like the rest of the guys, they were primed and ready to get the job done.

The Gulfstream returned to earth with a gentle bump and a muffled roar of reverse thrust. It taxied around the apron and veered inside a private hangar where it jerked to a stop and shut down its engines.

Josh was out of the aircraft first. Two men waited at the bottom of the steps. He didn't recognise either of them.

'Mister Keyes?' said the well-groomed collegiate type wrapped in a smart overcoat and scarf. 'Mister Beeton sent me. My name is Fisher. I'm from the embassy in Grosvenor Square.'

They shook hands and Fisher reached inside his coat. 'These are your temporary passports, all bearing official stamps of entry. I'll need those back before you leave the country.' Fisher was younger than Josh, well-scrubbed and impeccably dressed, probably a rising State Department star, cutting his diplomatic teeth at the Court of St James. He was confident, authoritative, and brandished Beeton's name like a baseball bat.

Josh fanned the Canadian passports like a hand of cards. He saw stamps and mugshots and pseudonyms. He nodded his approval and pocketed them.

The man standing next to Fisher was older and taller, forties, with wide shoulders and receding grey hair that was cut short to a scalp that sported several pale scars. He had a lived-in face that was heavily lined around sharp eyes, and a square chin that sprouted a couple of days of pale growth. He was dressed casually, jeans and a roll-neck jumper, a black North Face jacket. He greeted Josh with a rough, calloused hand.

'Dave Villiers.' His voice was deep, the accent London, heavy.

'Mister Villiers is SIS,' Fisher announced. 'He'll act as your point man.'

'Good to meet you. Where are we headed?'

'Mister Beeton has arranged for a house in Chelsea,' Fisher said.

'Then let's go.'

Three vehicles waited nearby, black Audi Q7's, doors and tailgates open. Villiers slipped behind the wheel of the nearest one and Josh got in back. Fisher rode shotgun next to Villiers. The hunter team squeezed themselves and their gear into the other two. They left the airport in a tight convoy and headed into central London.

Josh didn't talk and Fisher was distracted by his email inbox. Villiers remained silent, steering the big Audi through the heavy traffic. Josh checked his BlackBerry. There was nothing from Beeton or Lund. All of his FEMA responsibilities had been handed over, his own inbox empty, except for a reminder, a National Advisory Council meeting at the end of April. Not the whole council of course, just the key players who'd been selected for the continuation process. Josh cursed under his breath; another crucial meeting he would miss because of this goddam reassignment.

Fifty minutes later the Audis turned into a quiet street in Chelsea. Expensive properties crowded the narrow road on either side. Villiers swung the wheel into an open driveway that dipped beneath a luxurious period house into an underground parking lot.

Fisher led them inside and up to the first floor reception room. The heavy drapes were drawn, the giant wall-mounted TV muted. Pots of coffee and plates of sandwiches waited on a long sideboard. The hunter team ignored the refreshments, piling their gear against the wall and waiting in silence for instructions. Josh and Villiers sat down on the large sofas grouped around a wide glass coffee table. When everyone had settled, Fisher addressed the room.

'Welcome to London, gentlemen. This house will be your main base of operations while you're here in the UK. No doubt you'll have questions, many of which will be answered by the briefing packets left in your rooms. Please familiarise yourselves with them, and the details of your Canadian passports too, should you fall foul of local law enforcement. This eventuality is also covered in your briefing packs. Bear in mind I have no knowledge of your operation and neither do I need to know. Deniability, gentlemen, is essential. Remember that when you're outside these walls. Understood?'

Josh nodded. He guessed Fisher was a product of The Committee's covert executive programme, its secretive alumni liberally sprinkled across every branch of government. While people like Josh and his hunter team got their hands dirty, Fisher and his kind fought a different and infinitely more complex war, in the chambers of Senate and Congress, in front of TV cameras and microphones. Everyone had a role to play, even those who were oblivious to what was really happening around them.

He was reminded of George W. Bush's visit to the elementary school on the morning of Nine Eleven. He recalled the President's face, the bewilderment, the incomprehension, when he'd heard about the hit on the Trade Centre. He'd been rooted to his chair, dumbstruck. Frightened. That shit couldn't be faked.

The conspiracy theorists were all over it, though—Bush was complicit, the good ol' boy routine masking a sinister, Machiavellian personality. They couldn't have been more wrong. Some of his administration, sure, but Bush? Not a chance. Every president after Eisenhower had been vetted, groomed and selected. Most had no clue about the power that existed behind the throne. The truth was, it really didn't matter who was president.

The Committee held true power, because they controlled the global media. They'd fought a secret war for decades, to sanitise and trivialise the news, to disengage the population from the ideas and principles of democracy, to shift focus from the dull grey world of politics to the shining lights of a celebrity culture that dazzled and entertained.

Four Americans butchered in Benghazi? The White House complicit? Screw that, Kim Kardashian is trashing her sister's boyfriend on Twitter, y'all!

The Committee's war on reality was almost complete. It was a twenty-four-hour news cycle now—scandalous headlines, salacious gossip, reality TV, the ethnic cleansing of morals, values, traditions, culture, all clearing the way for the Transition, when everything would be wiped clean. Humanity, reprogrammed, rebooted. Josh couldn't wait.

But killing Frank Marshall came first.

He heard Fisher talking, and refocused his thoughts.

'—is a highly secure, mission-capable facility with a secure command suite situated in the basement. Where are the comms guys?'

Josh's Eyes and Ears stepped forward.

'We have hard-wired, piggy-back feeds routed via the embassy into all major stateside intel hubs,' Fisher explained, 'plus encrypted voice and data access to TDL Corporate and our Executive and Legislative sponsors in DC. I suggest you familiarise yourselves with the equipment as soon as possible.'

Eyes and Ears looked at Josh.

He nodded.

The men grabbed their shockproof cases and left the room.

'That's it,' Fisher said. 'Any questions?'

Josh shook his head. 'Okay, your confidential briefing package has been pre-loaded on to the AV system. I have to get back to the embassy. My number's there.' He snapped a business card onto the glass table and left the room.

Josh worked the controls of the huge LED TV. Two blown-up images of Frank Marshall filled the screen, one in front of the bank in Manhattan, the other a much clearer shot from the immigration desk at Heathrow.

'This is the target. His name is Frank Marshall, a former TDL senior security executive. I know some of you know Frank and have worked with him in the past, in which case you don't need me to tell you that he is an extremely dangerous individual with extensive knowledge of our organisation and its objectives.

Frank's gone rogue, people. The Committee want him located and terminated fast.'

Josh swallowed, conscious of the lie. There was no going back now.

'Twenty-one hours ago Marshall passed through Heathrow's Terminal Three using a Belgian passport in the name of Doug LeBreton. The last confirmed CCTV shot we got of Marshall was outside the terminal waiting for a cab. Dave?'

Villiers drained the dregs of his coffee and got to his feet. The screen divided into multiple frames, the Heathrow taxi rank, stills from Automatic Number Plate Recognition systems, street maps of west London.

'CCTV shows Marshall boarding a taxi outside Terminal Three. The driver was detained, the taxi searched, and the passport recovered. He confirmed Marshall was dropped off in a layby near Hammersmith.'

Villiers blew up the street map to full-screen.

'He entered this park at eight oh seven pm yesterday evening. The only other exit is directly across the park, which empties onto Chiswick high street. We've checked footage from there with a fine toothcomb but we've failed to get a hit. We think we know why. Directly adjacent to the park entrance is a row of sheltered bus stops with limited camera coverage. The routes are varied, mostly heading west or southwest. My guess is that Marshall crossed the park and boarded a bus here, out of view of the CCTV. There are several bus companies that operate from that location and we've pulled last night's footage from their vehicles, but reviewing it will take some time. There are a lot of routes, a lot of stops.' He turned to Josh. 'Any ideas where Marshall could be headed?'

'None. His record shows he's visited the UK before, but only on a layover. He's never been to London. We need that footage.'

'We're working as fast as possible.'

'Good. Tell me about your set up.'

'The investigation is being run out of Vauxhall under the banner Operation Talon. A confidential FBI file has been generated at your end and that's been picked up by Interpol and fed to SIS and Scotland Yard. Marshall is wanted under international warrants for illegal banking practices and money laundering. We've also thrown in connections to terrorist organisations in Europe and Pakistan to beef up inter-agency cooperation. Frank's profile has been circulated on the Met's intelligence briefing system as a wanted individual and I've got two mobile surveillance teams on standby for the legwork.'

'Sounds good.'

'Can I make a suggestion? Marshall will want to remain anonymous, keep his head down. That means frequenting less affluent areas of the city.'

'If he's still in town.'

'True, but until we've established otherwise, we have to assume he is. So he'll be staying in cheap accommodation, paying cash for everything. A man like that will stand out, especially an American. Once we've established his destination I'd recommend distributing his profile to local hotels and B&BS. The tactic's worked before.'

Josh hesitated. 'Frank knows he's being hunted. If he gets a sniff of the dogs he'll bolt. We may never find him.'

'He has to stay somewhere, and low-rent establishments like cash payers. It's your call but trust me, whenever we offer a substantial cash reward for information these hotel managers become dedicated surveillance operatives overnight. That money also buys discretion.'

Josh considered it for less than five seconds. 'Okay, do it. Anything else?'

Villiers shook his head.

'In that case we'll wrap it up for now.' Josh got to his feet and approached the contractors. 'Get prepped and ready to deploy. When you're done, hit the racks. Unless we get any hard intel the next briefing will be at seven am.' They filed out of the room.

'Heavy-looking team,' Villiers observed. 'I was told this would be a bag job. A rendition.'

'Things have changed.'

Another lie.

He handed Villiers a file. 'Frank has an extensive background, both military and as an ops commander with TDL. If he wants to bring it, he will.' Josh helped himself to another coffee, stirred in cream and sugar. 'There's no room for complacency on this one, Dave. I'll coordinate the intel, authorise whatever assets we need, but locally I'll need you to keep things tight. We locate him, box him in, then take him down clean. I can't afford a single fuck up on this one.'

'I understand.'

Villiers fingered the intelligence packet, withdrew the black and white still of Frank leaving the bank in Manhattan. 'I'm guessing you two know each other. Can you tell me something about him? Something personal?'

'He's a former Navy Seal, extremely smart and highly capable. If he sniffs you out, he'll end you. That's all you need to know.'

'What's he done?'

'That's not important. What's important is finding him.'

Villiers got the message, got to his feet. 'I'll crack the whip. Anything comes through I'll be in touch.'

The Brit left the room and Josh drained his coffee. He was tired and edgy, the last seventy-two frantic hours taking their toll. He needed sleep, but it was a race against time now, and the clock was ticking.

He crossed the room and peered through the heavy drapes. The street below was devoid of life, no cars or pedestrians, just empty roads and sidewalks. Even though they were in the heart of London it felt as if the Transition had already passed. What would it be like, he wondered, after the clean-up, after the regeneration? The thought had consumed him when he'd attended his first orientation seminar at Turner's private ranch in New Mexico. Those first few nights troublesome ones, the enormity of what lay ahead denying him sleep, the knowledge that the civilised world simply had no choice. Now the only thing keeping him up at nights was Frank Marshall.

But why England? Why now?

So many goddam questions.

Josh let the curtain drop back into place. He had to file a report to Beeton, the first of his daily dispatches to Denver. One a day, until Marshall was caught and rendered unto Caesar.

He headed down into the basement. Despite the pressure he was under, part of him was looking forward to the hunt. Frank had to be flushed from his bolthole, and once he was out in the open, Josh would unleash his dogs.

When that happened, Frank Marshall wouldn't have a chance.

Chapter Eight

It was just past noon when the insistent tapping on the hotel room door woke Frank from a deep sleep. His eyes snapped open and he grabbed the hand-held CCTV monitor on the nightstand. The tiny screen glowed, a high-definition image of a white-shirted waiter outside the door, a tray balanced on the palm of one hand, the other raised to knock again.

Behind him the hallway was empty.

'Be right there.'

Frank rolled off the bed. He removed the chair wedged under the door handle, unlocked it.

'Your midday call, sir.'

'Thanks.'

He gave the guy a bill in exchange for the tray. He kicked the door closed, set the tray on the sideboard and rechecked the monitor. The waiter was retreating down the corridor, shoving the five-pound note into his pocket. The mini wireless CCTV system was a smart move. It bought him a little peace of mind, and the tiny remote camera, secured to a ceiling tile a little further along the corridor, gave him with a clear picture of movements outside his room.

Frank's stomach growled with hunger. He demolished the scrambled eggs and toast and washed it all down with juice and coffee. He took a shower and got dressed into jeans, baseball cap and a dark waterproof jacket. He left the hotel without passing anyone in the lobby.

He'd spent the last three days familiarising himself with the area, walking the streets, the narrow lanes, the path along the Thames that led into central London. He'd walked the main street once, cap and scarf obscuring his features, using the cover of other pedestrians to avoid the CCTV cameras. He'd bought some clothes, running shoes, a torch and several other items he thought he might need, including a hair dye that had transformed his recently trimmed red fuzz into some kind of chestnut brown. Or so the label had promised. He traded with cash. He had plenty of that.

Physically, Frank felt revitalised, but spiritually he was restless. As he headed for the towpath that ran alongside the Thames he reached for the travel Bible in his pocket. It felt good to touch. Comforting. The same hand crept towards his armpit, felt the sheathed knife secured in its holster there, upturned for immediate and deadly use. That felt reassuring too. He'd bought it in a camping shop over the river in Twickenham and that was where he was headed today. He'd found a church on the hotel's Internet PC, a Baptist one, where he could sit and pray, and maybe listen to an afternoon service. He needed a spiritual fix, before his mission truly began.

As he put Richmond behind him the towpath changed from tarmac to hard-packed dirt. A freshening wind stirred the river, the trees around him. It was hard to believe he was so close to London. There wasn't a soul around.

He recalled the dark days, the loneliness he'd felt after escaping into that Texas night, the umbilical cord that had bound him to The Committee for the whole of his adult life finally severed. He knew they would come for him, knew they'd never stop looking, so he'd faked his death. He had to take other precautions too, drastic measures that would set him free, allowing him to continue on his journey unmolested...

He'd found her in a homeless shelter in Odessa. She was a former army medic, an Afghan vet who'd become dependent on drink and drugs. She'd performed the procedure on the promise of two bottles of vodka, using a stolen key to enter the hostel infirmary after dark and removing the RFID chip in Frank's shoulder by flashlight. She did a decent job, never asking about the chip nor curious as to why it was implanted in her patient's body. All she cared about was the booze. Frank gave her five hundred dollars instead.

From there he travelled north, crossing the state border into Arkansas then Tennessee, travelling light, staying in remote trailer parks and cheap hostels. He drank heavily but found no answers. Every move took him further north. Frank knew why, even if he was too scared to admit it—he was heading back to New York, where the tear in the heart of the city still lay exposed, where the tourists came to take pictures and the bereaved to remember. He was drawn to that wounded city as surely as a thirsty man staggers toward a distant oasis. He was desperate to unload the weight that was crushing him.

He needed closure, redemption, something.
Frank believed he'd find it in New York.

He stiffened as a dog bounded towards him along the towpath, feet scrabbling on the gravel as it circled Frank's legs and raced back towards his owner. Frank studied the man as he approached; sixties, wispy grey hair, small frame lost in a bright red parka. Threat assessment, zero. Frank nodded as they passed each other.

The river flowed around a small island. It was thick with tall trees, its banks clogged with reeds and rushes. A slender-necked bird peered above the vegetation, eyeing Frank as he passed.

He recalled the first time he'd laid eyes on the island of Manhattan since that terrible morning...

The snowstorm was tracking across the eastern seaboard when he rode the bus from Edison to Jersey City. The air was frigid, the streets thick with snow. He'd stamped along that same boardwalk, the one where he'd stood all those years ago and watched the North Tower burn. He'd stared across the black waters at the hole in the New York skyline and trembled, not from the cold but from fear. He wasn't ready to venture across the water, not yet.

The need to talk to someone, anyone, was building. There would be others out there just like him, real citizens, still grieving, still confused and angry. Frank needed to hear their stories, to be able look them in the eye and not flinch.

The Nine Eleven victims' group was located in the nearby city of Hoboken. It took him three attempts before he finally summoned the courage to enter the public library building on Park Avenue. Outside the meeting hall a middle-aged man in an NYPD T-shirt called him 'brother' and gave him a leaflet. Frank took a seat at the back. He remembered his heart pounding, the dryness of his mouth, as the speakers were introduced. He was in a lion's den of pain. Sweat ran down his back. He made ready to bolt from the hall.

It was a girl called Rachel that kept him in his chair. He remembered the wide smile that battled the sadness of her eyes, the love for her dead brother, a firefighter who'd made it up to the sixty-eighth floor of the South Tower before it was brought down. She remembered him with a love and pride reserved for one who'd died saving others. His blown-up portrait in fireman's blues stared right back at Frank as she spoke of a man she'd never speak to again, a man whose empty plate was set at every Thanksgiving and Christmas by parents still mourning his loss. Nine Eleven had devastated her family. Her words were like knives in Frank's heart.

He'd approach her when the meeting broke for coffee. He told her about the fear, the guilt, about the never-ending nightmares. She'd been confused, her smile fixed, her eyes uncertain. She'd been about to walk away when he'd grabbed her hands. Then he was begging her for forgiveness, for her brother's death, for the grief he'd inflicted on her parents. His hands shook and Rachel had snatched hers away. She'd demanded to know what he meant. Her voice had risen. Heads had turned. She'd searched his grief-stricken face, finally understanding the terrible truth of his words.

And she knew.

He'd barged his way through the crowd. He'd heard her shout, her voice echoing down the fire escape, chasing him across the snowy parking lot, the angry calls of the men who spilled into the lot behind her.

He never went back.

The following weeks were long and torturous. Rachel had robbed him of redemption. Guilt plagued him, beckoning him to rooftops and bridges and subway platforms. Somehow he'd resisted the whispers that urged him to join them in the abyss.

It was a blustery January afternoon when he'd stood on the corner of 7th Avenue and West 135th. He'd been unsure where he was headed, only knowing that he had to keep moving. As the traffic rumbled by he saw the poster flapping on a light pole beside him, an African villager bent double beneath a huge sack that dwarfed his tiny frame. The man's face said it all—pain, not just physical, but a soul encumbered by the sheer hardship of life. Beneath the image the swirly text read, 'Come to me, those who labour and are heavy laden, and I will give you rest' - Calvary Southern Baptist Church.

It had been instinctive. A moment without hesitation.

And quite possibly the smartest move he'd ever made.

The rusted iron footbridge carried Frank over a

foaming weir and into Twickenham.

His path was clearer now, that burden partially lifted, enough to allow him to finish what he'd begun. Today he would pray for the continued strength to right the wrongs, to save the lives that could be saved. Everyone else was in God's hands.

The air felt sharp and the sky threatened rain. He found the church after twenty minutes, a red-bricked building with a small steeple squeezed between a row of convenience stores and a gated park. There was no afternoon service but the pastor was happy for Frank to stay. He took a seat in the front pew and spent an hour or two thumbing through his Bible, thinking, praying. South Whitton Baptist Church was a lot smarter than the one in Harlem. The walls were brightly painted, the wooden pews polished, the altar bedecked with fresh flowers. There was money here, an affluent congregation that donated to the church's upkeep. He wished he could say the same for Reverend Hays' place. That was a different world altogether.

It was late afternoon when he left the church. He stood on the steps and zipped his coat up against the cold, feeling much stronger than when he'd first arrived. The sky above was darker, and streetlights had flickered into life. He turned towards the river, taking a circuitous route back to the footbridge, passing the convenience stores where several hooded youths had gathered outside, swilling sodas and pulling on smokes. Before he knew it he was moving through them, through the pungent clouds of cannabis, his arm brushing against one of the teenagers.

'Sorry,' he mumbled.

'Watch where you're going, prick.'

There were a few laughs, then a can sailed through the air and exploded at Frank's feet, spraying him with sticky soda.

'Real smart,' he clapped, walking backwards, 'real clever.'

He kept moving, angry at himself for rising to the bait. He heard a shout, then the sound of running feet. Frank turned.

There were five of them, black and white kids, and they wanted trouble whether Frank liked it or not. They were young though, fifteen, maybe sixteen. They would be unaware of the value of psychological combat, inexperienced in the use of applied violence. Frank had to end this quickly, without causing serious harm. The first kid came running towards him, unafraid.

'Who the fuck do you—'

Frank's open-handed slap cracked across his face, sending him careering into one of his buddies. He used the momentum of another to hurl him to the ground and buried his fist into the belly of a third youth, all the while screaming at the top of his lungs. The kids scattered, bruised and shaken by the unexpected attack. Frank moved fast in the opposite direction, twisting and turning the length of four full blocks before slowing his pace. He cursed his stupidity; a grown man beating on a few kids would bring the cops in no time.

He'd lost his bearings. He cursed again, and kept

moving. Ten minutes later he found himself passing a warren of shabby social housing. He saw a sign for the river, pointing down a dead-end street with an alleyway beyond, boxed in by orange-bricked houses that had surely seen better days and prouder, cleaner occupants. Beat up vehicles lined one side of the street and trash tumbled this way and that on the wind. He was halfway towards the alley when he heard the sound of a fast-approaching vehicle.

A dark saloon car shot past the street. He heard the screech of tyres and the whine of a vehicle reversing at speed. The car rocked to a stop and Frank saw a finger stabbing in his direction. He broke into a run but knew he wasn't going to make it. He ducked between two parked cars as the vehicle roared past him. It slewed to a stop with a squeal of rubber, blocking his path to the alleyway. He turned to see another vehicle barrel around the corner and brake hard. Now he was trapped.

He stepped out into the road as car doors flew open. Several men piled out and formed a wide half-circle around him. Frank recognised one of them, the black kid he'd dropped with the body shot.

'That's the motherfucker!' he yelled, his young face twisted with rage.

His companions were older, heavier, and clearly more experienced in the ways of street violence. They fanned out around him, six of them, their faces covered with bandanas and scarves. All held weapons in their gloved hands; a couple of short wooden bats, a screwdriver, three knives. As they inched closer Frank smiled—this was the evil that stalked him, manifesting itself into physical form, determined to stop Frank from doing God's work. He would not allow that.

'He's laughing at you!' screamed the black kid. 'Fuck him up!'

'Don't do this,' Frank warned. 'It's not going to end well for you.'

'Shut the fuck up!' bellowed the largest man in the group, a twenty-something black guy with a lock knife clutched in his fist. 'You fucked up, bruv. You messed with my peoples.'

'It's *people,* singular, you dumb fuck.'

The man scowled, his yellowed eyes devoid of humanity. 'Gonna cut you bad, bruv.'

'He's a Yank,' said another, confused eyes above a red bandana.

'Who gives a fuck! Do him!'

They were close now, ten feet and closing. Frank guessed they were used to people running, begging for their lives. That wasn't Frank's way. He reached for the weapon beneath his jacket and waved the six-inch hunting knife in a wide, well-practised arc, his eyes watching, waiting.

One of the bat carriers hesitated.

The other one screamed something unintelligible and threw his club at Frank.

The bat flew past him.

Frank dropped into a fighting stance.

They attacked.

The first man in was the leader, fearless as a leader

should be. Frank blocked the knife aimed for his chest and sunk his own blade deep into his attacker's thigh. The man dropped to the ground screaming in pain. Frank brought his leg up and stamped on his face, feeling the crunch of teeth beneath his sneaker. He moved to his right, putting the casualty between him and the others, launching himself at a snarling kid armed with a screwdriver. Frank parried his blow, smashing his fist into the man's jaw with his knife hand then sinking the blade into his shoulder in one fluid motion.

Two down, one of them the leader.

Adrenalin powered through his system.

The survivors shimmied around him, angry, hesitant. Another mistake. Frank sprang towards them, cutting the face of one and nicking another. Weapons clattered to the ground and they scrambled away, one kid pressing a flap of loose cheek against his blood-soaked face, the other surging past his injured buddy in an Olympian bid to escape.

The remaining two kept their distance, their defiant curses silenced. The cries of the wounded echoed around the houses.

'Walk away, while you still can,' Frank warned them.

He was breathing hard, blood pounding in his ears. The two men spun on their heels and raced towards the waiting cars. The vehicles reversed out onto the main road and sped off.

Suddenly the street was quiet.

Frank strode over to the leader. He was lying on his

back, hands clamped around his leg. There was a lot of blood but none of it arterial. He hadn't lost his ability to wound with discretion. He'd fought well here today, but now he had to move quickly.

The black man turned his head, looked up at Frank with pleading eyes.

'Help me, bruv.'

He could barely form the words, his speech hampered by a mess of broken teeth and punctured lips.

'Give me your hand.' The man raised his bloody paw and Frank grasped it. 'Promise me you'll turn your back on evil. Promise me you'll never do violence to another human being again.'

'Yeah, bruv, whatever,' the man spluttered, 'just get me a fucking ambulance.'

'Good, because the Lord is watching. And I'll be watching.' Frank glanced at the man's crimson-wet fingers. 'This is your knife hand, right?'

He turned the wrist over and wrenched it as hard as he could, feeling the snap of multiple bones, the hollow pop of the shoulder joint as it detached. The man's head came off the ground, his eyes bulging wildly. He screamed, then slumped unconscious.

Frank dropped the shattered limb and looked around. The others were dragging themselves away from the madman in their midst. Frank ran for the alleyway.

In its shadows he shoved the baseball cap in his pocket. He flipped the reversible windcheater inside out and tugged a brown watch cap over his head.

Emerging on the other side he slowed his pace, conscious of the blood on his jeans and sneakers. He saw folk carrying bags of groceries, kids in school uniform. He kept his distance, criss-crossing the street.

He heard the faint wail of a siren.

A description would be circulated—white male, American accent, black baseball cap, dark coat, jeans. Frank was now dressed in a tan coat, brown hat, but the jeans were a giveaway.

He thanked God when found the footbridge over the river. On the other side he scanned the towpath in either direction. Halogen lights winked in the darkness, a lone cyclist, avoiding the rush-hour traffic. He whirred past at speed, oblivious to the man in the shadows. Frank followed him, towards Richmond town.

Fifteen minutes later he was safe behind the door of his hotel room. He pulled off a refuse sack from a roll, undressed, and dropped everything into it. The knife he kept, secure in its holster. He took a shower, ordered room service, then lay on the bed and channel-surfed. There was nothing on the TV news.

He decided to lie low, stay in his room. Later he'd drop the sack in a dumpster behind the hotel. It wasn't clean but tomorrow morning he'd be gone. If anything the incident across the river had only served to speed up his timetable, which was okay with Frank. He was fully rested and acclimatised.

Now it was time to go to work.

He spread a map of the UK across the bed. The

target installation was seventy miles away, deep in the countryside. He'd been there before, a favour for their guy in Iraq. He'd need transport, a car, something reliable. He had no UK documentation but the second-hand car market would offer up a few deals, made all the more attractive with Frank's considerable supply of cold, hard cash. Afterwards he'd need another bolthole, a deeper, darker one.

He traced his finger along the map; there was another town to the south, one that hugged the river like Richmond, only this one was bigger, with a large mall, and lots of potential escape routes if things got tight.

It would suit him perfectly, because Roy Sullivan lived in the same town. And soon he would know the truth of his brother's disappearance.

Chapter Nine

Roy stood outside his flat and cursed.

It was cold. The TV had warned of a weather front moving down from Scandinavia. Roy didn't care; his own depression front had moved in a while ago and showed no signs of moving on anytime soon. That's why he cursed. These days, he hated coming back home.

He let himself in, swearing again as he snapped off the lights in the hallway and bathroom. The flat was hot too, the radiator by the front door ticking on full blast. As well as electricity, Derek was also burning through Sammy's money. Soon Roy would have to ask for more, a conversation he wasn't looking forward to.

The smell of fried food filled the flat. Roy's stomach groaned with hunger.

He found Derek watching TV in the living room, a tray on his lap, a delicious mess of chips and fried eggs on his plate. Roy loitered in the doorway, the juices running inside his mouth. All he'd eaten today was an overpriced tuna and mayo sandwich and a Coke in the staff canteen.

'You're out of eggs,' Derek mumbled between mouthfuls, his eyes never leaving the TV screen. 'Tea bags too. Put 'em on the list.'

'Eggs and tea bags. Anything else?'

'Yeah. Get me a fresh one.' He tapped his empty whisky glass with a yolk-stained fork.

Roy went out to the kitchen and his heart sank. Filthy pans and crockery crammed the sink. The cooker was spattered with grease. Teabags spilled over a saucer on the sugar-dusted worktop.

Roy turned on his heel and marched into the sitting room, kicking the tray from Derek's hands. He fell on top of him, raining blow after blow into the pleading Scot's face until blood poured from his nose and mouth—

'Where's ma drink?' Derek barked from the sitting room.

'Coming.'

Roy gave him a silent finger and flipped open a cupboard. He grabbed a fresh bottle of Scotch, Derek's third in less than a week. Roy was worried about the drinking, the way it was affecting Derek's behaviour. As well as being up half the night watching TV, he'd chat endlessly on the mobile phone Sammy had given him, his raucous laugh leaking through the walls. Roy was exhausted. And becoming increasingly unnerved.

He took the bottle into the sitting room and plopped into a chair. Derek was watching a documentary about a prison that was supposedly one of America's hardest. Roy thought the Scot looked like a prisoner himself, dressed in a white vest and navy trackies, his arms and shoulders covered in blue-ink tattoos that looked like they'd been drawn by an illiterate, semi-blind drunk. Roy could only take a wild guess at what they meant, except for the word 'MAM', inscribed on his right shoulder. She must be so proud.

'Derek, can I have a word?'

'What about?'

'I just wanted to ask, you know, if you, er...'

Derek stopped chewing. 'Spit it out, son.'

'Well, any chance you could turn the lights off around the flat when you're done? Maybe knock the heat down a notch? I'm thinking about the bills, really. The electricity meter's spinning like a bloody roulette wheel.'

His attempt at levity didn't work. Derek stared at him for several long, uncomfortable moments. 'I'm a sufferer,' he finally announced. 'SAD.'

Roy frowned. 'You mean you're depressed?'

'SAD,' Derek barked, 'S-A-D, Seasonal Affective Disorder, ya thick twat. Means I can't stand the winter, the long nights, no fucking sunshine. Sends me into one of ma moods.'

He swallowed a final forkful of soggy chips before sliding the tray across the coffee table. He lit a cigarette, exhaling a contented column of smoke towards the ceiling. 'I'm surprised you don't have it yourself. It's like a fucking tomb in here. What are you, son, a fucking bat?'

'No, it's just that the bills are—'

'Sammy's taking care of things, sort it out with him.'

Derek twisted the cap off the bottle and poured himself a large Scotch. He took a deep swallow and smacked his lips in satisfaction. He waved his cigarette over Roy's shoulder. 'What's with the shrine?'

Roy checked the montage of photographs above the fireplace. All there, unmolested.

'Nothing. Family stuff.'

He was worried by Derek's growing curiosity. At first the Scot had been distant, barking orders then lapsing into silences filled with movies, newspapers and books, but things had changed. Derek was getting impatient, his restlessness manifesting itself in a variety of ways. At first it was a flurry of physical activity, jogging in the living room, push-ups and crunches, wild bouts of shadow boxing that left him breathless and sweating. That lasted a week, maybe two. Then Roy began to notice the long periods of inactivity, the channel surfing that continued until sunrise, the pacing of the flat, the heavy drinking. Sammy had warned him about that. Derek was chugging the booze to excess.

Roy was scared. He was living with a ticking time bomb, and now he'd begun poking around Roy's personal stuff. As if on cue, Derek got to his feet, inspecting the photos above the fireplace.

'You were a fat wee bastard when you were a nipper.'

Roy kept quiet as Derek peered at the pictures.

Who's the squaddie?'

'My brother Jimmy. He went missing in Iraq, three years ago.'

Derek leaned closer, smoke leaking from his mouth in a blue cloud. 'What was he doing in Iraq?'

'He was a security contractor.'

'Missing, my arse. Your brother's dead, son.'

Roy stiffened. 'Actually, no one knows what happened.'

'Bullshit. Someone knows. Someone always knows.'

'Well, I've heard nothing in three years.'

'Probably got his head hacked off in a Baghdad basement. Fucking animals.' He sucked on his cigarette with a sharp intake of breath and crushed it out. He stood in front of Roy, rocking on his bare feet, his bony fists jammed into the pockets of his trackies. He had egg yolk on his vest, a greasy sneer on his thin lips. 'What's happening at the airport?'

Roy forced a smile. 'I'm working on it.'

'Well work faster, ya wee prick. I can't stay cooped up in this shithole for much longer.'

Roy didn't like the dangerous edge to Derek's voice. He pushed himself off the chair. 'I'm going to make something to eat. D'you want anything?'

'You've no time. Tank's picking you up in ten minutes at the bus stop downstairs. Sammy wants a progress report.'

Roy tried and failed to smother his irritation. 'I've just got in, for Chrissakes. I'm bloody starving—'

Roy flinched as Derek shoved him against the wall, rattling the photos above the fireplace. He poked Roy's chest with a stiff finger, the stink of booze and cigarettes on his breath. 'You'll do as you're fucking told. And why didn't you mention the drug dealer living next door?'

'Who, Dwayne?'

'You know who I'm talking about then.'

'Dealing? I didn't think—'

'He's at it,' Derek spat. 'A fucking blind man could

see that. Now get yourself downstairs pronto. Sammy's not happy.'

Roy beat a hasty retreat to the hallway. He pulled his coat on and stamped downstairs to the bus stop, cursing the day that Derek had darkened his door. If work wasn't risky enough right now, he had to come home to a brooding maniac.

He waited for fifteen long, cold minutes before Tank pulled up in a dark Range Rover. Roy climbed in back, grateful for the warmth. A soulful R&B track beat rhythmically through the sound system.

'Evening, Tank.'

Sammy's minder said nothing. Instead she hit the accelerator and powered away from the kerb. They drove in silence, the dashboard lit up like the flight deck of an aircraft, casting deep shadows across Tank's chiselled features. Conversation was clearly off the menu.

Roy's mind drifted back to the MSNBC interview. He'd found it on the net, tucked away on the 'World News' page and already nearing the bottom of their Featured Videos list. The piece had been heavily edited with other voices, other opinions, quick fire sound bites that merged into one. His was a lone voice in an ocean of voices. Jimmy's plight was ancient history. Other people went missing every day, women, children, babies. The news was a bottomless chasm of tragedy. The fight was fast leaving him. When it finally did, he hoped Jimmy would forgive him.

The traffic slowed as they funnelled down Putney Hill before turning left onto the Upper Richmond Road.

Sammy's place was called The Old Fusilier, a huge, expensively renovated Victorian building that dominated the corner it stood on. As soon as Roy climbed out of the Range Rover he could feel the thump of music from behind the blacked-out windows. A queue lined the pavement behind a thick red rope, eyed by a cohort of wide-shouldered doormen wearing long coats and earpieces. Tank cut the line and no one complained, the bouncers parting like the Dead Sea as Roy followed her through a set of heavy doors.

Inside the noise hit Roy like a wave, a bass-binned punch to the stomach. The crowd was packed wall-to-wall, a sea of faces lit by machine gun bursts of strobe lighting. They queued four deep at an enormous bar that took up half the club, a posse of curvaceous girls behind the brass pumps snatching money and cards from waving hands with practised efficiency. Business was booming.

Tank ushered Roy through a guarded security door and suddenly the madness of the club was left behind them. He followed her up a wide flight of stairs to a dimly lit passage that ended at a large door. Above, a camera eyed them in the gloom, red light winking suspiciously. A buzzer sounded. Tank shouldered the door open.

Roy was impressed by Sammy's private office. It was all copper potted palms and brass lamps, dark wood furniture and oriental rugs. A red-coated soldier in oils watched him as he crossed the room to stand in front of Sammy's impressive desk, as big as a snooker table and probably twice as heavy. Roy felt like a native, summoned to the governor's office in some far-flung corner of Britain's former empire. Sammy waved him into an antique chair that was far more comfortable than it looked.

He studied the huge painting behind Sammy's head, a nineteenth century soldier posing against a backdrop of red hills.

'*A light infantryman of the Royal Regiment of Fusiliers,*' Sammy recited from memory. 'That's Afghanistan, back in the day. No comfy boots or Oakley shades back then. No cushy air bases or Domino's Pizza. They were hard bastards, fighting a real war.'

Roy smiled crookedly. He studied Sammy's desk, the letters and papers scattered across its wide surface, the stack of receipts on a spike, a plate with a half-eaten sandwich. A MacBook glowed. A neat row of mobile phones lay within easy reach of Sammy's fingers.

'So, tell me about Dwayne,' he began. He was dressed casually, an open-necked blue shirt, jeans, a gleaming silver and gold Rolex on his wrist.

'I've never seen him dealing, I swear.'

He heard Tank chuckle behind him. Roy felt very uncomfortable. He had his back to a professional neck breaker.

'If Derek says he's dealing, he's dealing.' Sammy said.

'I had no idea.'

'So you said. The fact is, all this has made me look a bit of a mug. Implies that I don't know my own manor. Derek feels his safety has been compromised. That's put a lot of pressure on me.'

Roy raised a hopeful eyebrow. 'Maybe you should move him, just to be on the safe side?'

'Not an option.'

Sammy tossed a folded newspaper across the desk. Roy picked it up, smoothed it out on his lap. It was a Scottish newspaper, the *Daily Record*, and staring back at him from the front page was a police mugshot of:

Derek Niven, 62, a Paisley businessman, escaped from a prison van while travelling from the high court in Saltmarket, Glasgow, where he'd been remanded in custody on charges of attempted murder and conspiracy to supply Class A drugs. Niven used a concealed knife to threaten his escort then escaped into surrounding streets. A nationwide hunt is still underway. Police sources have confirmed that Niven has links to criminal gangs across Scotland, and should not be approached by members of the public...

Roy felt the blood drain from his face.

'Now you know,' Sammy said. 'I first met Derek when I was banged up in Bedford. He was well connected back then, took a shine to me, funded several deals that got me started. That man has put a lot of money in my pocket over the years, but he got careless in his old age. Understandable I suppose, what with retirement just around the corner. Brief says he's looking at eighteen to twenty-five. Derek can't do that sort of bird, not anymore.'

Sammy took a slug of mineral water and smacked his lips.

'Derek's been on his toes for a while now, but he's running out of options. That's why he came to me. Jock plod has turned over every cave and mud hut north of the border and now they're looking south, at previous addresses, past contacts and associations. There's a possibility that somewhere down the line my name might crop up. I can't have that, Roy. Our friend needs to be long gone before the Old Bill start sniffing.' Sammy folded his arms and leaned on his desk. 'So tell me about your plan.'

Roy swallowed hard.

'It can't be done, Sammy. You're talking about Heathrow airport, armed coppers, CCTV, metal detectors—'

'I told you before, you need to bypass all that shit. Derek's a wanted man. Can't have him waltzing through customs.' One of Sammy's phones warbled softly. He scooped it up, ended the call.

'I can't just hold a door open and let him in. He'd need a kosher ID card, a security swipe. Those doors are monitored.'

'That's your problem. You've already screwed things up by failing to mention the dealer and now I've got an uber-paranoid Derek on my case twenty-four seven. I can't have the aggravation, Roy. Just get it done.'

Roy could see it now, the two of them walking through the terminal, the Scot wheeling a large suitcase behind him, the drum of boots, the barked orders to freeze—

'All due respect, Sammy, I don't think you understand the security involved. Why can't you get him out another way? A seaport, a private airfield or something. Why Heathrow?'

'It's all about who you know,' Sammy explained. 'For example, I know you, my man on the inside. Derek knows a man in Dubai, one who's got bent officials on his payroll and will help him disappear. You're right, we could get him out a dozen other ways, but the more checks he goes through the more chance he stands of getting caught. Derek wants to get to Dubai in one easy hop, not wander around Europe like a fucking student on a gap year.'

'But even if I got him airside, how will he get on a plane? He'll need a passport, a valid boarding pass and ticket—'

'That's being taken care of.'

'If he's got a clean passport he could go through check-in like everyone else.'

'He can't. He's taking cash with him, a lot of it, plus some other bits and pieces. Anyway, none of that is your concern. You've got the credentials, a backstage pass to the whole fucking terminal. All you need to worry about is getting him to the gate.'

Roy's skin prickled with fear. His face felt paler than the sour-faced Fusilier hanging behind Sammy's head. 'Please don't make me do this, Sammy. I don't want to go to jail—'

Sammy slammed his hand on the desk. 'Stop your fucking whining. I know a mob over in Feltham making a fortune ripping off cargo out of Heathrow, so don't tell me that place is like Fort Knox. It's wide open.'

'Why don't you use them?' Roy pleaded.

Sammy shook his head. 'Jesus Christ, you really do go out of your way to avoid responsibility, don't you? To answer your question, those Feltham boys are Indians, all good lads, but Derek wouldn't trust them and quite frankly neither would I. So, now I know your piece-of-shit neighbour is dealing, it's time to move the plan up a gear.'

'Can't you just lean on him? Dwayne, I mean.'

Sammy shook his head. 'Kids don't listen these days, especially the blacks. Right, Tank?'

'Right,' she echoed behind Roy.

'It's a cultural thing. They revel in all that American gang bullshit, guns and hoes, get rich or die trying. Getting nicked is a lifestyle choice for those idiots, so no, I won't be having words with your mate Dwayne. Here.' He rapped a long, thin paper tube on the desk and handed it Roy. 'These are architectural plans of Terminal Three, including all the airside spaces. Derek's a stickler for detail. It'll give him something to focus on.'

Sammy picked up his sandwich and took a bite. Roy sat rooted to his chair, weighing the drawing in his hands. When he spoke his mouth was so dry he had to force the words out. 'Listen, Sammy, I want to help, really, but I just don't think it's possible.'

Sammy finished off his sandwich and wiped his mouth with a napkin. He took a long slug of mineral water and screwed the cap back on.

'I know what you mean, Roy, but it's not about you anymore. I know your ex hates your guts — the kid would too if he had a brain instead of a walnut — but they're the only family you've got left. I'm guessing you've still got a soft spot for them, am I right?'

Sammy flipped a photograph across the desk. It was a colour ten by eight of Vicky and Max, a recent one, mother and son sat at a table eating lunch in a busy shopping mall. Vicky was toying with her phone while Max was absorbed in a colouring book, a fat crayon grasped in his chubby fist, sandwich cartons and balled up napkins on the table between them.

'That's a nice shot,' Sammy observed. 'Just the two of them, enjoying a bit of lunch. Take a good look.'

Roy frowned, studied the photograph again. He saw Tank seated behind them, sucking on the straw of a soft drink, her soulless eyes hidden behind dark glasses. He dropped the photo back on the desk as if it were burning his fingers.

'Need I say more?' Sammy snatched at the photo, his suntanned face darkening. 'I'll take her life apart, piece by piece. That job of hers at the *West London Herald*? Gone. Maxi's posh school, the one you don't pay for? I'll make sure the kid gets turfed out. And the

Yank boyfriend, the banker? Once I'm finished he'll drop Vicky like she was a crack addict with AIDS.' Sammy raised an eyebrow. 'What, you think I wouldn't know? Silly boy. Bottom line is, you fuck things up and your family's lives go down the toilet. And trust me, I'll make sure that Vicky knows it's your hand pulling the chain.'

Sammy leaned back in his chair and swung his feet up onto the desk, expensive brown loafers and no socks.

Roy was rooted to his seat, frozen by the weight of Sammy's threats. He tried to open his mouth to speak but failed.

'What is this, Madame Tussauds? Get the fuck out.'

Roy flinched as Tank pulled him out of the chair. She walked him downstairs. Roy was oblivious to the music, the clamour of the club. Outside on the pavement he gulped the sharp night air like a beached fish. He saw Tank lean into a taxi window, hold the back door open, gesture to Roy with a scowl. Roy climbed in, a fifty-pound note thrust into one hand, the drawings in the other.

He stared out of the window as the cab motored back along the A3 towards Kingston, seeing nothing other than the desperation of his situation. This was karma, plain and simple. He'd cursed Vicky for her ambition, Max for his physical and emotional detachment. Now, because of Roy, their lives were threatened. And they were good lives too, decent, shaped by patience, love and hard work, the very traits that Roy had lacked or discarded, his inadequacies masked by the futile quest for his brother.

If Roy failed and Sammy made good on his threats then Vicky's life would come apart. And she would know why, her final judgement of Roy complete, the sentence eternal. In his mind's eye he could see Jimmy shaking his head.

Jesus, Roy, what a mess.

Roy squeezed his eyes closed to blot out the image of his brother's mocking smile. 'Leave me alone,' he whispered. 'You're dead.'

The cab driver glanced in the rear view mirror. 'You say something, mate?'

Roy shook his head. It was the first time he'd said it aloud, and he felt ashamed. He reached for the drawing, twisted the thin tube in his hands. If he couldn't go back then he had to move forward. He needed Derek gone, the debt to Sammy repaid, before Vicky and Max could be free. Maybe then Roy could start his life over again.

And when he did it would be far away from the Fitzroy, from Kingston, and from everything he knew.

Chapter Ten

Josh drummed his fingers on the conference table, trying and failing to calm his mounting frustration. Alone in the basement war room he decided to give vent to it, cursing loudly and swatting a pile of reports onto the rubber-tiled floor.

A week had passed and the trail had run cold. Beeton had burned up the secure line, berating Josh as if he were some slack-jawed cherry, threatening to pull him if he couldn't get the job done. Josh had assured him he could, that Frank would be located soon, but Josh's words had sounded hollow. His early confidence had waned, in the mission, in his own ability. Sleep evaded him.

Frank Marshall was a ghost.

The deep background check had turned up nothing. The Chiswick CCTV had been treble-checked, so unless aliens had abducted Frank, he must've boarded a bus. They had some partials pulled off routes that ended in places called Hounslow, Kingston and Ealing, but the stills were inconclusive; nondescript clothing, a pale sliver of a cheek here, a shadowy face there. And if Frank had picked a bus here the cameras were screwed, well, that was needle and haystack territory. If that was the case Josh was fucked.

He studied the partials again, four of them, pinned to the giant board that covered an entire wall of the war room. His eye kept returning to one in particular, a grainy image of an individual tucked into a corner seat on a bus. He wore dark clothing, his face hidden by a large black woman in front of him for much of the journey, or buried in a newspaper for the rest. The footage was poor quality, the camera hood scratched and smeared by kids with keys and knives and fat felt marker pens. It could be anybody, but Josh kept coming back to it anyway. In the past he would have trusted his instincts, but with Beeton breathing down his neck he had to be sure. Wild goose chases were not advisable.

Josh ducked under the table and scooped up the mess of his frustration. Villiers loomed in the doorway.

'We might have something.' The Brit held up a sheaf of paper.

Josh clambered to his feet. 'What's that?'

'An incident report, suspected gang fight in Twickenham a couple of days ago. There were several casualties.'

'So?'

'It was one against six. The six came off worst.'

Josh snatched the report from Villiers' hand. The casualties had suffered a variety of wounds, lacerations and broken bones, but nothing life threatening. A surgical strike.

'Witnesses?'

'One.' Villiers handed him another sheet of paper. 'That's her statement.'

Josh skimmed it. His heart beat fast.

'Show me exactly where this happened.'

Villiers pointed to a spot on the wall map. 'Right

here. A thirty-minute drive, give or take.'

Josh traced the nearby bus route overlay. It wasn't far from the scene of the brawl. 'Tell the guys to saddle up. Meet me in the parking lot in five.'

He crossed the corridor to the command suite. Eyes and Ears were there, crabbing around on wheeled chairs in front of a dizzying array of communications and surveillance systems that stretched the length of the basement. He slapped the incident report down on a table.

'This just came in. Feed key words into SENTRY, get them red flagged.'

'Already done. We're also patched in to law enforcement comms and local municipal CCTV.'

'Is the short wave up?'

'Affirmative. Encrypted handsets are in their chargers by the basement door.'

'Good work, guys.'

Josh turned on his heel. Five minutes later Villiers was steering one of the Audis along the Fulham Road. Behind Josh, two of his contractors rode shotgun, Glock automatics beneath their jackets. The other two Audis followed behind, staggered in traffic. Beyond the windshield it was a clear day, sunny and fresh. It felt good to be doing something.

Villiers was almost right; it took just over thirty minutes to get to Twickenham. The housing project was a collection of scruffy dwellings and dead-end streets, with peeling paint and trash cans that spewed crap across the pavements. Police tape twirled in the wind across one street. A patrol car loitered nearby. Josh radioed the other Audis to keep their distance. Villiers pulled into the kerb. He got out, had a brief conversation with the police officer, then climbed back inside the Audi.

'Forensics are almost done and inquiries have reached a dead end. They're keen to notch it up to gang violence.'

Josh nodded. 'Let's go see our witness.'

He climbed out, ordering the contractors to stay put. The property stood out from its neighbours. New windows, swept pathway, a few tubs of flowers arranged around a neatly tiled front garden. Villiers went to the door and flapped the letterbox. The door opened on a chain, a round black face peering around the gap.

'Yes?'

Villiers held up his warrant card. 'Mrs Kalu? Can we can have a word?'

She scraped the chain back and invited them in. Josh took a look around. Everything was clean and citrus fresh, the small living room decorated with black leather furniture. On the walls, African masks carved in wood competed for space with several photographs of beaming young men and women in colourful tribal clothes. Another framed picture of two young boys in green blazers stood in pride of place on a sideboard. She offered them tea. They declined.

'We'd like to discuss what you saw the other day,' Villiers said.

'I made a statement.'

'Did you know any of the kids that were hurt?'

The woman nodded. 'One of them. He lives with his mother a few doors down. Always hanging around with some other boys. Always trouble.' She almost whispered those last words, as if they could be heard through the walls.

'You work at home, is that right?'

'Yes. I'm a bookkeeper.'

Josh looked around. 'Where do you work? Upstairs?'

The woman stared at him for a moment, then said, 'You're American.'

'This case may have international implications,' Villiers explained.

'Is that why you're here? Because the man they attacked was American too?'

Josh's heart beat a little faster. 'You're sure about that?'

'I heard him speak. A churchgoer.'

'Excuse me, ma'am?'

'Come. Follow me.'

She led the way up the stairs, her huge bottom swaying in front of them, puffing loudly as she reached the landing. A small bedroom had been converted into an office, with a desk beneath the window. A dated computer and printer squatted on top. There was a grey metal filing cabinet against one wall and another small table piled high with folders and spread sheets.

'It gets a bit stuffy in here, with the computer, so every now and then I open the window.'

Josh peered through the blinds, over the Kalus' well-kept garden to the cul-de-sac behind the houses.

'I heard the cars first, racing down the street. There was a lot of shouting. They had that poor man surrounded, like an animal. It happened very fast after that.'

'What did he say?' Josh wanted to know.

'He warned them, told them they would get hurt, but they seemed determined to harm him. I was very scared. After it was over he spoke to one of the injured ones. I heard him say something about evil, about the Lord. Then he hurt him again.'

Josh smiled. That was Frank, for sure. He reached inside his jacket for the photograph, Frank passing through Terminal Three at Heathrow. 'Is this the man you saw?'

Mrs Kalu traced a finger across the image. 'Yes, that's him. His hair is much darker, but it's definitely him. Is he a bad man?'

'The worst,' Josh confirmed.

'My God, what has he done?'

'Unspeakable things—' Josh noticed a dog-eared photograph of the Kalu boys in shorts and T-shirts stuck on the computer screen. '—mostly to children.'

'Which way did he go?' asked Villiers.

The woman jabbed the air with her finger. 'Like I told the other policeman, he went down the alleyway, at the end of the street. That's the last I saw of him. Running like the wind.'

'Where does that lead?'

'Another street. There's nothing much between here and the river, just houses. If you want to get to the shops or the buses you have to go the other way.'

'The river?' Josh echoed.

'Yes. Over that way.' She pointed again.

Josh smiled. 'Thanks. You've been a great help.'

He took the stairs two at a time. The hunt was on again and Josh felt the thrill of the chase. He had a shot now, something to aim at, and suddenly that obscure partial on the wall of the war room made sense. It *was* Frank. He made a call to the house in Chelsea, fired his orders down the line—concentrate on Partial Two, find out where he got off the bus then trace his movements via CCTV.

Villiers got behind the wheel of the Audi and they circled the block until they found the alleyway. It didn't take them long to find the footbridge over the river. Josh and Villiers got out and crossed to the towpath on the opposite bank. It was quiet, Josh noted. The towpath was empty in both directions, bordered by a thin strip of woodland. At night this place would be very dark and very deserted. Frank would've scoped this route out for sure.

'You reckon he came this way?' Villiers asked.

'No CCTV cameras between here and the site of the brawl, good access across the river, low foot traffic. Almost certainly.'

Villiers pointed to a cluster of lights in the distance. 'That's Richmond up there. An American tourist would fit right in. Lots of hotels and guesthouses, good transport links to the city. Heathrow too.'

'If he was here he would've skipped town by now. Check all the local cameras. And do your thing with the hotels, find out where Frank stayed. We need to get inside his head, work through the problems a man like him would face in staying off grid. I need scenarios and options and I need them fast.'

'Got it.' Villiers was already speed-dialling a number on his phone.

'Pick me up in town.'

Josh needed to think, so he started walking towards the distant bridge at Richmond. At least he had something to report to Beeton now. He checked his watch as he neared the bridge; almost six o'clock. It was getting dark and lights glowed from buildings overlooking the river.

The town centre was busy with shoppers and commuters. Traffic crawled. Streetlights popped on. Josh backed into the shadow of shop doorway. He watched the crowds, trying to locate Frank, knowing it was futile. The man would be long gone by now, destination unknown, but Josh had a feeling he wouldn't be far away. Frank had come to Richmond for a reason. He had business across the river in Twickenham, maybe somewhere else close by. He would order a thorough evaluation of the area; sensitive installations, key personnel, addresses, phone numbers. There had to be a link somewhere.

Frank was a closed book. In all their time together he'd never really spoken about his past. What he *did* know was almost a mirror image of his own life. Orphaned at an early age, lost in the system until his above-average intelligence brought him to the attention of the Harvesters, the specialist educators that searched for likely candidates in public schools and child care systems, candidates who would benefit from privately funded education and scholarship programmes in secure, and often remote, institutions dotted across America. Frank's was in Nebraska if Josh remembered rightly.

There he would've undergone the same selection process as Josh did in South Dakota, the advanced curriculum that encouraged and identified academic, vocational and physical skills. It was true what they said, everyone had a talent for something; Josh had seen his fellow tenth-graders strip truck engines, hack secure computer networks and handle weapons with the same speed and dexterity as seasoned combat veterans.

Like Josh, Frank's natural abilities saw him enter the Field Team programme, culminating in a fast-track entry to Annapolis. That's when the government took over; Frank went Marines, then Navy Seals, his true allegiance not to the flag but to The Committee that had plucked him from a life of children's homes and foster care, of failed schools and unrealised potentials. They'd been taught that while governments came and went, only The Committee prevailed, bestowing a sense of purpose on those that served its needs, providing the kinds of challenges and rewards that most people could only dream of.

So how, Josh tried to reason, could Frank possibly want to betray them, to spit in the face of the very organisation that had found him, nurtured him and set him on the path to...*righteousness?*

Josh frowned. The idea of a spiritual Frank seemed absurd. They'd all been taught from day one that religion was nothing more than a stone-age tool of control and manipulation. Maybe Frank had been simply trying to scare those kids into thinking he was some sort of Bible-thumping nut-job? Maybe. Frank had never hinted at any kind of spirituality whatsoever. Was it the breakdown that had reprogrammed Frank's consciousness to consider the existence of some omnipotent being? Josh shook his head; it was laughable, a man like Frank Marshall believing in —

Wait.

It came to Josh like a bolt, a half-remembered conversation during a late night bar sitting, in the days before Frank went loco. He'd been a late entrant to the programme, at maybe ten or eleven years old.

Before that he was in a children's home in South Boston.

A *Catholic* one.

Josh tugged his radio out of his pocket, ordering Villiers to pick him up. As he waited in the shadows Josh realised it made sense. Frank had suffered a breakdown, a genuine one, therefore it was reasonable to speculate that that episode had sparked the reawakening of his faith. Stranger things had happened. And there was something else too. He remembered Frank wearing a chain during those last few months, a pendant of some sorts. Josh had asked but Frank didn't want to talk about it. So, maybe Frank *had* found God. How did that affect their mission? And what was Frank's agenda, *if* it involved some religious context? Josh was baffled; the scenario threw up more questions than answers.

The Audi pulled into the kerb and Josh climbed in. 'Get your people to go door to door with Frank's picture in local churches. Start with the Catholic ones, then everyone else. And find out if there's anything like that near the fight scene. Maybe Frank was in this Twickenham place for that very reason.'

While Villiers made the call Josh stared out of the window. He felt good about the mission now, a sense that Frank would soon be located, captured. Religion was a weakness, and it could prove to be Frank's Achilles heel.

Josh watched the busy sidewalks, the myriad of faces ebbing and flowing past them. What a fool Frank was, to turn his back on The Committee. They were the real gods, the real power on this earth. And in their wisdom they'd decided that humanity must be steered away from the path of self-destruction it was taking.

Josh was comfortable with that.

After all, he was one of the Chosen.

Chapter Eleven

Professor Jon Cohen hated cyclists.

In fact, he hated people in general, but cyclists he harboured a particular disdain for; their lurid clothes, the way they clogged up country roads in large, sweating groups, the grating tap dance of their ridiculous shoes as they invaded quiet rural pubs. Such a flock now hampered Cohen's journey to the facility, a dozen or so gaudily coloured riders choking the lane ahead, a *Tour de France* of buffoonery. He leaned on his horn as he gunned his Lexus saloon past them, smiling as he registered the angry faces and obscene gestures in his rear-view mirror.

He continued east through the Wiltshire countryside until he reached the entrance to the facility. He turned into the narrow lane, steering the Lexus along a strip of black tarmac bordered by thick woods until he reached the security gate. The weather-beaten sign sported the standard TDL logo, Romanesque initials suspended over a bronzed globe, the wording beneath a complete fabrication: *TDL Global – Business Services Authority.* The electronic gate hummed upwards.

More woods, more turns, then the main building loomed before him, a sprawling Victorian manor house. From the outside it appeared to be a tired edifice, one that never caught the sun, the moss that clung to its black iron gutters and the greenish tinge to its faded brickwork testament to over a century spent in the damp gloom of the encroaching woods. And like the sign, just another façade.

He parked the car and swiped into the building, waiting for the heavy inner security door to swing open with a vacuumed hiss of welcome. When it did, the diminutive, lab-coated figure of Doctor Ros Wyman was waiting for him.

'Hello, Jon. Sorry you had to be paged.'

'What's the problem?'

'Not a problem, exactly. Let's walk.'

He followed his senior associate into a cargo lift that rumbled below ground. The doors clattered open and he stepped out. The harsh lighting and whitewashed walls made him squint. He heard the hum of the HEPA systems filtering the air. He saw the robotic vacuum cleaners sucking dust particles from the microbial resistant rubber flooring. Everything in the sub-surface laboratory appeared normal.

'So what is it, Ros?'

'It's a couple of things.' Wyman's hands were stuffed into the pockets of her lab coat as she marched along the corridor on short, stout legs. 'The first is subject fourteen. He expired forty-seven minutes ago.'

'Isn't he the last of his trial group?'

'Correct. Exposed to batch seven-one-alpha six days ago. Two have already expired, two remain healthy.'

Cohen's pulse raced. He'd fought almost all of the nastiest infections nature had to throw at mankind for many years, from battling contagious diseases in some of Britain's most deprived areas to managing disease control programmes for the World Health Organisation in sub-Sahara Africa. *Creating* a deadly virus, however, had been a challenge, like nothing he'd ever experienced before. It was exhilarating. 'We must be close.'

Wyman nodded, unable to contain the smile that cracked her lined features. 'I think we are.'

'Take me to him.'

They passed through the Entry/Change Area and emerged in their personal protective equipment; sterile facemask and Perspex visor, full body gown, overboots and latex gloves. They moved through a pressurised lobby then on to the infection ward itself.

The unit reminded Cohen of a high-tech cellblock, which was fitting really, given the demographic of most of their subjects. There were twenty isolation treatment rooms in all, each protected by a transparent Trexler curtain. As his overboots squelched along the rubber matting Cohen glanced left and right, noting the condition of each subject. Most were comatose, their vitals monitored by beeping equipment. Others writhed and twitched beneath sweat-soaked sheets. Only two subjects were still conscious, indistinct shapes secured to their beds beyond the thick plastic screen. One of them called out to Cohen in a strong Merseyside accent.

'Hey, mate! Help us, will ya? Why won't someone talk to us? You can't keep us here, for fuck sake!'

Cohen smiled and moved on.

Wyman snatched a clipboard from a wall-mounted holder. 'Here we are. Subject fourteen, Lithuanian male, thirty-one years old. Aerosol dose administered six days ago. He presented four days later with a high fever, pain behind the eyes and stomach cramps. He became comatose twenty-four hours later.'

Cohen unzipped the transparent curtain. The single bed was cocooned inside a tent of clear plastic sheeting. The monitors beside the bed were powered down, silent, the UV line disconnected. Two orderlies waited nearby, both wearing pressurised bio containment suits.

Wyman ordered the plastic curtains removed.

'This one was exceptionally strong, hence the longer period of illness. Cause of death, respiratory failure.'

Cohen stepped forward. The corpse lay naked on a black rubber mat, eyes closed, the skin paling as lividity set in. The shaven head was heavily indented with scar tissue and the muscular body sported the same. Beneath a colourful array of tattoos Cohen searched for physical symptoms of a viral presence. He didn't find any.

'Turn him over.'

The victim's muscular back was hairless and unblemished. Cohen checked the armpits and folds of the neck while Wyman inspected the buttocks and legs.

'Nothing down this end,' she reported. 'No pustules, no signs of confluent petechiae. He's clean.'

'Likewise.' Cohen examined the corpse once again. 'This is excellent work,' he said through his mask. 'A thorough post approval study and we should be able to sign off. We're right on schedule. The Committee will be very pleased.'

Wyman turned to the orderlies. 'Prep him for disposal and have the unit deep cleaned.' Out in the corridor she re-zipped the plastic curtain. 'We're expecting five new subjects this evening, three from homeless shelters in Gwent and two from a youth offender facility in Devon. None have any next of kin. They'll be infected with seven-one-alpha on arrival.'

'Thank you, Ros. And what was the other thing?'

Wyman frowned behind her plastic face shield. 'The other thing? Oh yes, you have a visitor. An American, from Security Division, just flown in. Says he knows you. He's waiting in the canteen.'

'Well, I need a cigarette anyway. Let's go and meet him.'

They passed through decontamination and took the lift up to Cohen's first-floor office. It was far removed from the controlled environment below ground, a large space with high ceilings, the intricate cornice work so favoured by the Victorians now yellowed by Cohen's addiction to Marlboro Lights. He waved Wyman into a seat and settled behind his desk. He scooped up the telephone.

'Dana, would you have my visitor shown in? And send up some refreshments, please.'

A grey-coated orderly appeared a few minutes later and set down a tray of coffee, tea and biscuits. Dana framed the doorway, the visitor at her side. Cohen got up and held out his hand.

'Professor Cohen.'

'Frank Marshall.' He held up an ID card for inspection.

Cohen glanced at it then offered him the chair next to Wyman. His guest shook himself out of his overcoat and sat down.

Cohen wasn't impressed by what he saw. His visitor wore a cheap suit, creased and ill fitting, and a tie that had been tugged from its collar. A reddish chin fuzz jarred with the noticeably dyed hair. He stared at Cohen with a strange intensity and the professor reminded himself that Marshall was Security Division. A strange breed to be sure, professionally paranoid, always assessing threats and suchlike. And comfortable with violence. He forced a smile.

'Tea? Coffee?'

'Coffee's good. Cream, no sugar.'

Cohen did the honours and handed his guest a bone china cup. He picked up a pen and scribbled a note, offering it to Wyman.

'Ros, would you take this to Alan? Ask him to get back to me?'

Wyman read it, frowned. She got to her feet. 'Of course.' She closed the door behind her.

Cohen lit a cigarette and exhaled a cloud of blue smoke. He fixed his guest with a smile, waving the Marlboro between his fingers. 'You don't mind?'

'It's your funeral.'

'So, Mister Marshall, what can I do for you?'

'You don't remember me, do you?'

Cohen studied his guest again. He shook his head. 'I'm afraid you have me at a disadvantage.'

'We met before, a couple of years ago. I picked up a package for Quinn in Iraq.'

Cohen's cigarette froze near his lips; there *was* something vaguely familiar about his guest but recognition still escaped him. So he lied.

'Yes, of course, now I recall. How is Doctor Quinn?'

'Still at Messina, I guess. I haven't seen him for a while.'

The American stirred his coffee, fixing Cohen with a stare that appeared faintly challenging. He stubbed out his cigarette. 'What is it I can help you with?'

Marshall pointed to a tower of small boxes with colour-coded stickers stacked against the wall. 'Are those the latest viral batches?'

'Yes. How did you know?'

'I recognise the labels. I provided security for the dispersal team at the Central Prison in Luanda during the initial field trials. How's the testing going, anyways?'

Cohen felt faintly irritated. Marshall may have been involved from the beginning, however he wasn't prepared to engage with him as an equal. He lit another cigarette and leaned back in his chair, aiming a thin plume of smoke at the ceiling. 'The programme is on track,' he offered.

'So when does Messina go into full production?'

'Soon. I won't trouble you with the details.'

Marshall got to his feet. He crossed the room and picked up one of the colour-coded boxes. Without asking, Cohen noted. *Where the hell was Ros?*

'Is everyone in the programme protected against the latest strain of yours?'

'Of course.' Cohen huffed. 'Prevention was always the priority when the pathogen was engineered. When were you immunised?'

'Before the African trials.'

Cohen couldn't help himself. This was the pinnacle of his life's work and he was proud of his achievements.

'There have been some modifications since, but the anti-viral you were administered with contains all the necessary corticosteroids, protease inhibitors and monoclonal antibodies required to create and sustain cellular resistance. We're talking state-of-the-art technology in preventative medicine. Mister Marshall. If we went commercial it would be a major game changer in health care. Of course, the downside would be vastly increased rates of survivability, which pretty much defeats our purpose here, no?' Cohen snickered at his own aside. 'In any case, modifications to Angola have always been benchmarked against the antiviral. You're protected, so please don't concern yourself.' He tapped his cigarette on the edge of the ashtray.

'What about the immunisation programme?'

'It's complete. There will be unexpected high-profile fatalities of course, but these will only serve to reinforce Angola's neutrality. Rich, poor, young, old, white, black—the virus is wonderfully indiscriminate.'

A quiet computer *beep* had Cohen twisting in his chair, his fingers tapping out a reply to the incoming email. He clicked the *send* button, turned around, surprised to see the American staring out of the window behind him. How did he get there so quickly? And so quietly? Marshall started tapping the glass with a forefinger.

'What's that out there?'

Cohen sighed and pushed his chair back. He was tired of playing host now. Outside the sun had dipped beyond the treeline. His eyes searched the grounds below, the vague humps of the ventilation units sprouting from the lawn, the huge, trailer-mounted incinerator unit that squatted beneath the camouflage netting at the edge of the woods. White smoke drifted from its filtered chimney. That would be subject fourteen. Nothing untoward. He took a pull of his cigarette.

'What am I supposed to be looking at here?'

Vice-like fingers grabbed his neck and crushed his face against the glass. Smoke exploded from his mouth.

'What the hell do you think you're doing?' he rasped. Then he felt something cold and sharp prick the skin of his neck. He stiffened.

'Shut the fuck up,' the American hissed in his ear. 'Where are the antivirals?'

'Antivirals?'

Marshall leaned in close. 'Stall or lie once more and I'll gut you like a fish. The antivirals, where do you keep them?'

'Down in the lab. There's a small supply.' He heard Marshall swear under his breath. He had to keep him calm. *Where the hell was Ros?*

'What was on the note?'

'The what?'

Cohen felt the blade dig a little deeper.

'Don't fuck with me, professor. The note. What was on it? Quickly.'

'It was nothing, an equipment request. Please, let me go.'

He felt the blade drop, the hand lifted off his neck. The smell of burning reached his nostrils. He looked down to see his cigarette smouldering on the carpet.

Marshall's arm circled his neck, the pressure immediate and terrifying.

He tried to scream but his throat was pinched shut, the hard muscle and radius bone crushing his windpipe, his fingers scrabbling at the material of Marshall's suit. He glimpsed his attacker's reflection in the glass, a face contorted with savage effort, and suddenly Cohen knew he was going to die.

The room swam. His fingers felt numb. Darkness crowded his vision.

He felt the pressure increase on his windpipe, felt his eyes bulging, and then the darkness was complete...

Frank heard two sounds.

The first was the faint hum of Cohen's computer. The second, his own laboured breathing.

He counted to ten in his head, crushing the Brit's neck with all of his strength. He hadn't killed with his bare hands for some time and he'd forgotten how much effort it required. The knife would've been easier but way messier.

He lowered Cohen to the floor and hurried across the room. He swiped Cohen's computer mouse, keeping the screen active. He snapped on the desk lamp and inspected the indentation of Cohen's hastily written note—

Ask Alan to run background on our guest.

No time to lose.

He fished in his pocket for the USB key drive and plugged it into Cohen's computer. The professor's security access was up in the Gods. Frank's fingers danced across the keyboard. He trawled Cohen's data share, copying the vast, well-organised file structure in its entirety. Then he backed up the professor's secure mailbox, every email, every electronic conversation, every official communication going back over eighteen months. Frank watched the progress bar crawling towards its completion; there would be names, dates, times, locations, shipments, manifests, meetings, orders, instructions, plans, doubts, fears, accomplishments, developments, triumphs, goals and dreams. Everything. Gigabytes of decrypted data filled the key drive.

Beep.

Copy complete.

Frank's heart raced. He put the key drive in his pocket. He snapped Cohen's ID lanyard from around his bruised neck. He dragged the body across the room and onto a sofa against the wall. He shaped Cohen into a foetal position, dressed a blanket over him, took off the well-polished shoes and arranged them neatly on the floor.

He tugged his overcoat on.

Cohen's phone warbled.

Frank waited, frozen. The ringing stopped. Something caught his eye among the clutter of Cohen's desk, a white card with gold piping around its edge. He shook it free, saw the embossed pyramid, the numeric strings below, the date and grid reference. An invitation, like the one he'd been given all those years ago. *Holy shit*. He shoved it in his pocket.

He scanned the room.

He saw the fireplace, the unlit gas fire, the small brass pipe. He opened the valve, heard the hiss of escaping gas. He lit a couple of Cohen's Marlboros and left them burning in the ashtray. It was crude, but what the hell.

Time to exfil.

He moved towards the door, talking loudly.

'Well, thanks again, Jon—' he pulled open the door '—a real pleasure. Yes. I'll tell her. Goodbye.'

He closed the door.

Dana saw him, unplugged her earphones.

'The professor has requested not to be disturbed for thirty minutes.'

'Very well.'

He smiled, said goodbye and headed out into the hallway. He fought the urge to run down the stairs. As he reached the entrance lobby he heard laughter from the security office. Wyman was sitting in a chair, a mug in her hand, sharing a joke with a man in a dark, military-style jumper. He had a phone clamped to his ear.

He was on hold to someone.

Someone who was checking Frank Marshall for red flags.

Frank swiped Cohen's card.

The door hummed and clicked. Wyman's head turned in his direction. The smile slipped from her face. She said something to Webber.

Frank hit the button release in the lobby. He flinched as an alarm klaxon echoed around the building. Then he ran.

The eight-year old Mercedes estate was twenty feet away, unlocked, the key in the ignition. Frank fired the engine into life. In the rear view mirror a couple of guards spilled out of the main door, Webber and Wyman trailing in their wake. Frank dropped the car into drive and roared away as the guards fired several pistol rounds. Two heavy thumps hit the bodywork and then he was screeching around a bend in the woods. Ahead loomed the main gate. He floored the accelerator and ducked as he smashed through the barrier in a shower of sparks and a screech of twisted metal. More shots echoed around the woods. He fish-tailed around another bend.

In his rear view mirror, nothing but trees.

He kept his foot down.

'What's your emergency?'

'I heard shots fired, people shouting.' Frank panted

in his best English accent. He blurted out the address of the Copse Hill facility. 'I think someone's been killed—'

He replaced the receiver, moved through the lobby and left the hotel. He walked towards Andover town centre a half mile away. He found a taxi rank and hopped one to Basingstoke station, where he boarded a fast train to Clapham Junction in southwest London. When he arrived he avoided the cab rank outside, conscious of the CCTV cameras. He walked for ten minutes then hailed a passing one.

He stretched out in back as the cab headed south. It had been a long, stressful day and his hostel bed called, a cheap establishment on the edge of Kingston town with an anonymous and transient population of mainly eastern Europeans. He knew the hunt would be focussed out west now, the Mercedes found and traced, his movements caught on CCTV, but right now whoever was leading the chase would have more questions than answers. Frank hoped it would stay that way, for the next twenty-four hours at least. After that, all bets were off.

Cohen's death would send a ripple of panic through The Committee. He imagined the frantic phone calls, the angry voices. They would feel vulnerable, and Frank smiled at the thought. The Transition couldn't be stopped, he knew that; in fact, his actions today would probably bring the timetable forward, but at least the world would know how it started. And who started it.

He reached into his pocket, for the stiff white invitation card with gold piping. Frank smiled. He decided he would head east, target the evildoers where they least expected him to be. Once upon a time Frank excelled at chaos.

It was time to get reacquainted with it.

He ordered the driver to pull over near Richmond Bridge. He waited for him to drive away before crossing the road and heading towards the river. He found the unlit towpath that twisted along the banks of the Thames and followed it south, towards Kingston.

The path was empty, the river still, silent.

Moments later Frank was swallowed by the darkness.

Chapter Twelve

'Where is he?'

'They.'

'What?' The police inspector had to shout above the roar of aircraft engines.

'*They.* There're four of them. One's dead. Hypothermia, probably.'

'Dead?' The inspector snarled. 'Jesus Christ, my bloody paperwork just tripled.'

Roy stood beneath the nose of an Emirates Boeing 777 watching the exchange. He was wrapped in a high-visibility yellow parka, his hands shoved into his pockets, and he stamped his feet in defiance of a bitter wind that barrelled across the flat expanse of Heathrow. He smiled as he watched the fat cop's face redden with anger. Next to the cop, Senior Immigration Officer Piper offered a sympathetic shrug.

The flight had recently arrived from Jordan. Cargo handlers had made the grim discovery, the refugees huddled together in a dark corner of the hold, staring wild-eyed at the world beyond the gaping hold door. Someone said they were Pakistani, which was why Yasin was here. Roy had tagged along for the experience. Seeing the refugees first hand, he was amazed they'd survived the journey at all.

Now both he and Yasin were relegated to bystanders, loitering beneath the Boeing while Piper and the police inspector shouted above the noise of taxiing aircraft. The inspector was a real miserable bastard. Roy heard him shouting about poor security, a hand clamped on top of his service cap that the gusting wind threatened to snatch away. He noticed Piper had no such concerns, his long, thinning comb-over dancing on top of his sparse dome like the flames of a fire. That made Roy smile.

A hydraulic flatbed was raised and the stowaways unloaded, destination a miserable, bulging detention centre somewhere around the country. Still, it was probably better than where they'd just come from.

The show finally over, everybody headed for the terminal building. Roy lingered, watching Yasin stride away, deep in conversation with Piper. Ground crew busied themselves around the aircraft, hoisting, unloading, coupling and decoupling. Lights flashed and warning beepers battled against the wind and the roar of aircraft. Yasin and the others had disappeared inside.

Time to go.

He strode back to the terminal, swiping into the airside access corridor. He kept moving, conscious of the all-seeing black orbs that tracked his progress. Not too fast, not too slow, the iPhone poking from his coat pocket recording everything. His heart thumped inside his chest.

He stowed his airside gear in the locker room and headed for the staff canteen. Roy made himself a coffee and sat down away from the handful of people enjoying a break. He checked the footage he'd just taken. It was the last time he'd take such a risk, because he was pretty sure he'd found a way to get Derek through to Departures.

Sammy had been right, the architectural drawings had helped to keep Derek focused. The Scot had snatched at the tube when Roy brought it home. He'd spread the drawings across the kitchen table, his finger tracing the entrances and exits, the stairways and concourses, like a general surveying his battle maps. Later Roy had pinned the drawings to the living room wall, adding photographs to it so Derek could visualise the corridors, the swipe readers, the signs and uniforms. It was all coming together.

But the weak link was Derek himself.

The man was getting more impatient, more volatile, with each passing day. He'd become fixated on Dwayne, watching him through the kitchen blinds, muttering under his whisky-laced breath. The pressure was building. Roy wanted him gone, before something erupted.

He pulled out his phone. Time to update Sammy—

'Who are you calling?'

Roy's head snapped round. Yasin stood over him, a radio in his hand.

'Excuse me?'

'You're calling your criminal friends?'

Yasin's thick eyebrows were knotted together, his bearded face dark with thunderous outrage. He wagged an accusing finger in Roy's face. 'Why did you not return to the terminal as ordered?'

Roy swallowed hard, his face burning with guilt. He

struggled to find a satisfactory answer.

'I was looking for an old mate out on the ramp.'

'Liar. Come with me.'

Roy followed Yasin towards the glass wall at the far side of the canteen. *Criminal friends?* How could he possibly know? Next stop the duty manager's office, and from there it would all fall apart. Roy was ready to bolt from the room. Beyond the glass, aircraft whined and rumbled along taxiways. They were out of earshot from the rest of the canteen. Yasin held out his hand.

'Give me your phone.'

Roy gripped the device a little tighter. 'No. Why?'

'I know what's on it. Give it to me. Or do you want to do this upstairs?'

'That's my personal property.'

Yasin smiled. 'Okay, then perhaps you can explain to Mister Piper why you're taking pictures of airside areas, hmm? Are you a terrorist? Are you part of a cell?'

'Don't be stupid,' Roy blurted, 'I'm not even a mus—' He stopped short.

'A Muslim? You're racist too?'

'That's not what I meant.'

'Give me that phone.'

Roy tried to calm his voice. 'Okay, I took a little footage. For personal interest.'

'You like corridors? And security gates?' Yasin took a step closer. 'I've been watching you for many days, Mister Sullivan. You are a liar and a criminal. Give me your phone, now. Last chance.'

Roy's heart pounded in his chest. Why didn't he

wipe the files once he'd saved them to his computer? *You stupid, stupid, idiot!*

'I can't, I—'

Yasin snatched the phone from his hand. He scrolled through Roy's camera roll. It was stuffed to the gills with images and video, all covert, all deeply incriminating. Yasin tutted several times then waved it in Roy's face. 'The police call this hostile reconnaissance. It is my duty to report it.'

The fight left Roy. His legs felt hollow. This was all going to end very badly. He looked beyond Yasin to the apron below, saw a group of yellow-jacketed ground crew clustered around a low-loader, chatting, laughing. Roy cursed the day he'd decided to leave that world behind. Back then Jimmy was a phone call away, the emotional iceberg that was Vicky Hamilton still far over the horizon. Life had been good.

How did it all come to this?

'Do what you've got to do,' he told Yasin.

He should run, warn Sammy, get Derek out of the flat, but Roy simply didn't have the energy. It was all over. What was it Jimmy used to say? *Hope for the best, prepare for the worst.* Yeah, well the worst had arrived. He was finished.

Then Yasin did something unexpected. He slipped the phone into his pocket.

'I'm going to keep this for a while, give you the opportunity to reflect on your deeds.'

Roy frowned. Why wasn't he being marched off to Piper's office? Yasin took a step closer, his eyes roaming the canteen.

'These crimes, these accusations, I can make them go away.'

Roy pulled a face. 'What?'

'You help me, I help you. Then we move on.' He wiped his hands together, like a street trader making a deal.

'What sort of help?'

'I want twenty-five thousand pounds, in cash. This is what it will cost to get your phone back. For all this to go away.'

Roy's jaw nearly dropped open. 'Say that again?'

'You heard me,' Yasin hissed. 'Twenty-five thousand. For this you don't go to jail.'

Roy's shoulder slumped. His boss was a crook, just like Sammy. His relief was palpable. He hung his head and let out a long, slow breath.

Yasin mistook it for something else. 'Good, we have an understanding. You pay ten thousand first, the other fifteen by the end of next month. Plenty of time to get the money together.'

Roy shook his head. 'Listen, Yas, you don't want to do this, trust me. Whatever it is you think I'm doing, you're mistaken. Those pictures, they mean nothing.'

'So you admit to taking them? Okay, we'll talk to Mister Piper, let him sort this problem out.'

This time it was Roy who stepped in closer. 'Wait, Yas—'

'Mister Goreja.'

'Whatever. Look, take my advice, just give me

the phone back and drop the whole thing. I won't say anything if you don't, okay? Let's put it down to a bad day at the office and move on.'

Yasin shook his head. 'Not okay. The deal is twenty-five thousand. Or we take a walk upstairs. Yes, we may both be suspended, maybe our houses searched. I have no problem with this. Mister Goreja is an honest man, they will see. But what about Roy Sullivan? What secrets will they discover at *his* home?'

Roy had a sudden mental image of the police piling through his front door, discovering an escaped prisoner sprawled on his couch, the drawings pinned to the wall.

'It's not just about me,' Roy warned. 'There're other people involved, heavy people. The kind you don't mess with.'

Yasin laughed. 'You try to scare me? Where I come from, Taliban make the law. Not the army, not Islamabad, Taliban. And when they come to my village even the goats shit themselves.'

'I'm not fucking around, Yas. These are serious—'

'Twenty-five thousand, then you can have your phone back.'

He spun on his heel and marched away, whistling as if he didn't have a care in the world.

Roy called after him. 'I'll need a few days off. I need to get a new phone, make some calls.'

The older man stopped, considered the request. 'Send me a leave form.'

'Bullshit. Cover for me.'

Roy headed for the locker room. He was in deep

now, the stakes piled high, the consequences hanging over his head like the blade of a guillotine. Roy could've called his bluff, but it was Yasin they'd believe, and the whole thing would quickly fall apart. He had to let his supervisor think he was getting his money, and that meant talking to Sammy.

An hour later Roy was tapping on the glass door of a cafe on the Upper Richmond Road. Tank unlocked the door and waved Roy over to a booth. Sammy was sat next to a suited Indian man, one hand leafing through a stack of spreadsheets, the other tapping away at a large calculator, a pair of black designer glasses perched on the end of his nose. He didn't look up as Roy hovered by the table.

'So, what's the big emergency?' Sammy said, scrutinising some sort of financial printout.

'It's about the lodger.'

He gave Roy a look then tapped the Asian on the forearm. 'Take a break, Jay. Go out back, get Paulo to knock you up some pasta.' The accountant vacated the table and Roy slipped into the booth.

'I'm busy, so make it quick.'

'It's about the airport,' Roy began. 'There's been a complication.'

Sammy took his glasses off. 'Speak.'

So Roy did.

When he'd finished, Sammy said, 'Twenty-five grand, that's it?'

Roy nodded.

'And it won't affect the thing with our friend?'

'Not if we move quickly.'

'Tell me about the plan.'

Roy took a breath. 'Okay, I've gone over it again and again. The hard part is getting Derek airside, and for that I need a uniform and an airside pass. Now, there's an older guy, Colin, a work colleague. He's got IBS.'

'What?'

'Irritable Bowel Syndrome. Every day Colin takes his break in Costa Coffee, on the landside. He likes to watch the crowds. He always takes his ID off and puts it in his coat pocket over the back of his chair. Then he normally uses the toilet. Sometimes he's gone for a couple of minutes, sometimes ten. If I'm with him he'll ask me to watch his stuff. The day you give the green light, I'll go for the usual coffee, distract him, and then put liquid laxative in his brew. Bingo. He'll be on the throne for ages, during which time I'll borrow his coat and swipe card.'

Sammy chewed the arm of his glasses, staring at Roy for several moments. 'So, let me get this straight— your well thought-out plan depends on some old geezer taking a shit, is that right? You're not inspiring me with much confidence, Roy.'

'Look, once Colin's out of the picture Derek slips his coat over his travelling clothes, and together we'll swipe straight through to airside. Once we're there, Derek goes into a toilet cubicle, stuffs the coat in a bag and loses himself in the duty-free shops. I take the bag and the swipe, head back to landside and wait for Colin. If he's already out of the toilet I'll say I took his stuff because I got called airside and didn't want to leave it. Then I'll head back and shadow Derek until he boards his flight. Job done.'

'What about CCTV?'

'I've got an official cap that Derek can wear. Him and Colin are about the same build. No one will take any notice as long as Derek keeps his cool and sticks to the plan.'

Sammy leaned back in his seat. 'Sounds like you've done your homework, Roy. I'm impressed.'

'I just want this to be over, Sammy. What about Yasin?'

'Yeah, I'll need his details. Name, address, shift pattern. And a picture. Can you do that?'

'I've got one at home, a group shot from our induction course.' Roy hesitated. 'The thing is, I need a new phone.'

'Use the one I gave Derek.'

Roy hesitated. 'I don't want to ask him, Sammy. He's on that thing twenty-four-seven and I—'

Sammy held up a hand. 'He's what?'

'He hammers it, day and night. Non-stop.'

Sammy's knuckles turned white. 'Who the fuck is he talking to? Jesus, I told him not to—'

He stopped himself. He pinched his nose and flexed the fingers of his right hand.

Roy had never seen Sammy like this. He'd seen the anger, but this was something else. He was rattled. Roy almost smiled. *Welcome to my world.*

Sammy reached into his pocket and pulled out a

thick wedge of cash. He peeled off several crisp fifties and handed them over. 'Get a BlackBerry on pay-as-you-go. None of that iPhone shit, got it?'

'Got it.'

Roy scooped up the cash. Sammy's arm snaked across the table and grabbed his wrist like a vice.

'Listen to me carefully, Roy. If plod kick your door in anytime soon you'd better make sure my name stays out of it. Understand?'

Roy paled. 'You think they're going to?'

'Just focus on keeping your mouth shut.'

'Okay.'

'And get me that info on your mate.'

Roy hesitated. 'What are you going to do? Have a quiet word or something?'

'You worry about your end. Leave the rest to me.' He reached for a printout, signalling the end of their meeting.

'Sure, Sammy. Whatever you say.'

Roy left the cafe in a hurry, the door chiming as it swung shut. He headed for the nearest bus stop. He stood in the cold, rubbing his wrist.

He imagined the cold steel of a police handcuff clamped over that very same joint and shivered.

Chapter Thirteen

The longer Josh loitered in Professor Cohen's office, the harder it was to decide what offended him more; the lifeless body at his feet or the lingering stench of charred carpet and wood. Probably the corpse, he decided.

He looked down at the dead professor, his hair singed, the blanket that covered him scorched. Frank's crude IED had worked, kind of. The blast should've been much bigger but somehow they'd got lucky. A flash fire, a few windows punched out. Thankfully the viral packs stacked against the wall were undamaged. That was the upside. The downside was the sheer level of heat he was catching from Beeton and Lund.

He winced, recalling the video link back in Chelsea. Lund still played the ice maiden while Beeton did nothing to curb his temper. He'd bawled at him, promising to break his career unless Frank was found. He hadn't had a tongue lashing like that since West Point, and it infuriated him. Josh hadn't hunted men in this way before. He wasn't a cop, for Chrissakes. On the other hand he could understand Beeton's anger. Frank had strolled into one of The Committee's most sensitive facilities on the planet and killed a very, very important guy. Not only that, he'd got away scot-free. The mystery of Frank's mission remained just that. He'd warned them back in Denver that it wouldn't be easy. Like they gave a shit what Josh thought.

The sound of scraping wood interrupted his thoughts. Across the room Villiers struggled to open a cracked window, hefting it up in short, jerky movements. Then the night air swept in, banishing the smell of burning and the pungent odours that were leaking from beneath the blanket. Josh briefly wondered whether Cohen had shit his pants during strangulation or afterwards.

Villiers was bent over the carpet by the window. 'Got a crushed cigarette butt and a burn mark here. I'd say this is where Frank put the choke on Cohen.'

'Figures. Probably distracted him.'

Josh picked around the blackened and overturned desk, the piles of scorched and burned paper, the cracked and partially melted computer. Broken crockery crunched under his feet.

'Looks like the desk took the main hit.'

'We got lucky,' Villiers said.

'No, lucky would be Marshall lying dead at our feet. Ask Doctor Wyman to step in.'

He squatted down and sifted through the wreckage of Cohen's desk. There had to be *something* here. He righted an overturned chair and wondered if Frank had sat in it only a few hours ago. He winced again. Local records confirmed that Frank had been here before, an unscheduled detour made while transiting back to Iraq. That's why the visit hadn't been recorded in Frank's personnel jacket. Another glaring oversight. Copse Hill was a key installation. He should've checked.

He stood up as Doctor Wyman entered the room. She was a small, middle-aged, stick-thin woman. She stiffened when she saw Cohen's body.

'Jesus Christ, poor Jon.' She looked away, saw the open window, a night breeze plucking at the paperwork scattered across the floor. 'Shouldn't this all be sealed off? I thought this was a crime scene.'

'You want to call the cops?'

'That's not what I meant,' Wyman bristled. 'All this is very sensitive. We don't want a stray lab report drifting on the wind, do we?'

'Of course not.' Josh reminded himself to be careful. Cohen's death meant that Wyman was now in charge. He signalled Villiers to close the window. 'What can you tell me about Frank Marshall?'

'I only met him briefly, the first time in reception and again in this room. A strange man. Rather intense, I thought. He said he knew Jon.'

'Did the professor know him?'

'I don't think so. They shook hands like strangers.'

'Did he say what he wanted?'

'Not to me. We don't get many visitors here but when we do they're normally people directly attached to the Messina programme.' Her eyes narrowed. 'If Marshall was on a threat list, how did he get through our security?'

'He was buzzed in,' Josh told her. 'He had a Security Division pass but he didn't swipe it. He timed his entrance to coincide with the arrival of another member of staff. CCTV shows him entering the secure lobby with a female and signing in. She swiped, he didn't. You waved him through.'

Wyman shuffled her feet. 'I came down in Jon's absence. He greeted me as if he knew me. I thought I—'

'Don't let it trouble you, doctor. Marshall knew that swiping his card would've sent this facility into lockdown. So, what happened after that?'

'I left him in the canteen. Shortly after the meeting began Jon passed me a note. He wanted Alan to run a background check.'

Josh had already spoken to the erstwhile head of security, now locked in an interview room downstairs. He'd pleaded his innocence but it wouldn't make any difference. Webber was done.

'What did they talk about?'

Wyman chewed a knuckle, shrugged. 'I don't know, I'd left the room by then. The atmosphere seemed cordial enough. We were in good spirits because we'd made a breakthrough today.'

Josh raised an eyebrow. 'Oh?'

'A significant one. The Transition is now on the horizon.'

Josh felt a flush of excitement. 'That's great news, doctor.'

'We're not there yet but we're very close. The Committee has been informed.' She glanced at the charred grey lump on the sofa. 'Poor Jon. It's so sad that he won't get to see the culmination of his work. Still, he knew we'd achieved our goal. We must take comfort in that.'

Josh bit his lip, his elation snatched away by a

cold wind of disquiet. If Frank was still on the loose when the Transition began then Josh would be stuck in England. He didn't want that. He wanted to be back in his rightful place, at FEMA, managing the crisis that would quickly engulf the globe. There was so much to do; the preparation of the detention camps, the public health incinerators, the military mobilisation orders, the deployment of Homeland Security troops. Josh *had* to be there, *had* to be a part of it.

But first he had to find Frank.

'What about the police?' he asked.

'They came to the main gate but they didn't linger. You think Marshall made the call?'

Josh nodded. 'Traced to a hotel in Andover. He was trying to sow a little distraction.' Behind him he heard Villiers clear his throat. He turned around. 'What is it?'

The Brit tapped his earpiece. 'They've found the car.'

'Where?'

'About six miles east of here. They're sending me the grid reference.'

'We're moving in two.'

Josh zipped up his jacket, pulled an Arizona Cardinals baseball cap over his neatly combed black hair.

'I have to go, doctor. You'll supervise the clean up?'

'We have a team en route. If they find anything out of the ordinary I'll let you know immediately.'

'Yes, anything at all. And please remind your staff

that this facility remains in lockdown until you receive word from Denver. Webber's deputy will head up security for now.'

Wyman folded her arms and nodded at the covered corpse. 'What about Jon?'

'He goes into your incinerator. Cohen's wife has already been informed of his death. She's in the programme, so she'll understand. Webber goes with him. That's straight from Denver.'

'Of course.'

He shook her bony hand. 'Thank you, doctor.'

'I hope you catch the bastard,' she called after him.

The Audis waited in the darkness outside, engines purring, doors open, the contractors forming a loose cordon around the vehicles, automatic weapons held ready, night vision equipment scanning the shadowy woods. Within seconds they were mounted up and powering along the access road. They passed the security hut, its shattered gate lying twisted by the side of the tarmac, and Josh saw a Land Rover move into a blocking position across the road behind them.

Six miles east took them across a major highway and back into the countryside. When they got to the location the local cops had the road sealed off. Villiers' SIS warrant card got them access and the Audis pulled to a stop beside a wooden gate wedged between two hedgerows. Overhead a helicopter clattered around the sky, searchlight probing the nearby wood. Uniformed cops gathered around the gate. Villiers had a huddled discussion with two locals. This would be a big deal for them, Josh figured, a team from London, an operation with global terrorism implications. They'd be tripping over each other to help.

Blue and white police tape formed a path that led from the gate into the wood. The Mercedes estate was parked beneath the trees, front end crumpled, wheels caked in mud, tailgate open. Josh picked at Frank's discarded suit, the worn shoes, the cheap blue tie that lay coiled like a snake in the folds of a beige overcoat. He moved around the vehicle, fingering the bullet holes in the bodywork. He slipped behind the steering wheel. He ran his hands over the worn plastic, caught a whiff of burned metal. He popped the glove box. No map, no personal junk, not even a candy wrapper on the floor. He climbed out. Villiers loomed in the dark.

'The locals found some footprints, heading that way.' He pointed towards the inky darkness between the trees. 'Map says there's a road through there, a hundred yards or so.'

Another car. Or worse, an accomplice.

Josh swallowed a momentary jolt of panic. 'You think he had help?'

'I don't think so. Take a look at this.'

Villiers shone his torch inside the trunk. He fingered a dark, circular stain.

'That's oil. There's another spot, just there. The spacing suggests a pushbike. Looks like Frank got changed here, carried the bike through the trees and cycled away.'

'Right.' Josh exhaled, a little reassured by the

deduction. Formidable though Frank was, working solo had its operational limitations. 'Did you run the plates?'

'Yes. The vehicle's registered to a car dealer in Putney. Marshall bought it with cash two days ago. Physical description checks out but everything else is a dead end.'

'Figures.'

The helicopter hovered overhead, harsh white light washing the scene, flickering through the trees.

'Stand that chopper down,' Josh ordered.

He followed the trail until he came to a wooden stile. He climbed over and found himself on a narrow country lane that stretched into the darkness in either direction. Across the lane was a wide field of tall grass, bordered by shadowy woods. Josh took a few steps out into the middle of the blacktop and looked east. Frank would've cycled that way, towards Andover, stopping at the hotel, using the lobby phone to call the police.

Then he'd disappeared.

Overhead, the earlier cloud cover had scattered before a freshening breeze, exposing a dark blanket of sky dusted with stars. The wind stirred the trees around him, swirling through the field in hypnotic waves. Josh took his cap off and closed his eyes, allowing the breeze to wash over his skin, cleansing him, clearing his mind. He absorbed the serenity of the moment, imagined a similar peace that would transform huge tracts of the globe once the Transition had passed. The vision thrilled him.

He heard the snap of twigs underfoot. Villiers

clambered over the fence behind him.

'Anything from this Andover place?' Josh asked.

'I'm pulling the CCTV for all routes out of town. Checking the rail and bus feeds too.'

'What about the local cops?'

'I've briefed them about Operation Talon. They'll stand down after tonight.'

'Good.' Josh cocked his chin towards the east. 'My gut says Frank's gone back to London. Whatever mission he's on seems to be focused around Richmond, maybe somewhere close by.'

'I agree.' Villiers' phone beeped with a message. 'The low loader's here to remove the Merc. I'm having it shipped to a secure warehouse in Wandsworth, get a team to go over it again, properly.'

'Okay.'

Headlights glowed in the distance, blooming and fading as the approaching vehicle negotiated the twisting lane. Josh slapped his Cardinals cap back on his head.

'Let's wrap it up here. We'll head back to Chelsea, start collating the new data. We need something concrete, and fast.'

Josh took one last along the deserted lane, at the field of swaying grass, at the stars that glittered in the night sky. Over the rise to the east the headlights grew brighter, the sound of the approaching car drawing ever nearer, carried on the night air.

He climbed the fence and disappeared into the trees.

Chapter Fourteen

'Here we go, Max. Hold on tight.'

The child gripped the roundabout with pudgy hands, feet dangling as Roy spun the ride. He gave Max a reassuring smile, but his son began to whine after a couple of turns, his chubby face screwed into a mask of fear. He raised his arms, begging to be plucked to safety. The roundabout spun full circle. Roy lifted him off.

'Jesus Christ, Max, it's only a roundabout.'

The child clung to him, watching the spinning ride as if it were a medieval instrument of torture, the whine reduced to a throaty grumble. Josh gave him a squeeze.

'Mummy wants to take you away, to a big school across the sea. You don't want that, do you, Max? You won't be able to see daddy then, will you?'

He heard a shout, saw a bunch of kids running across the road. There were five or six of them, early teens, swaggering towards the playground. A few of the mums eyed them warily, calling their kids close. The teenagers headed for the swings, chains rattling as they slouched in the low plastic seats, lighting cigarettes and roaches. The smell of cannabis drifted on the cold wind. Roy cursed the Fitzroy.

'C'mon, Max, let's go kick the football.'

He swung his daysack over his shoulder, took Max's hand and left the playground behind. He found an empty park bench some distance away and sat down. He rummaged in his pack for a chocolate bar and wagged it in Max's face. His son's eyes lit up, a goofy smile splitting his rosy cheeks. Roy held it out of his reach.

'Promise you won't tell Mummy? Our little secret, right, Max?' He peeled back the wrapper and Max snatched it from his hand. 'Nothing wrong with your motor skills, eh?'

Roy smiled as his son took a big bite. The boy bounced up and down on his little legs, school shoes squelching in the mud. Roy fixed his scarf and adjusted his bobble hat. He rolled a football out onto the open grass. Max gave it a mechanical kick, his focus on the sweet that had already painted his lips and chin a dark brown.

Roy settled on the bench, hands deep in the pockets of his parka, chin nestled in the folds of a thick scarf. It was cold today, a biting wind that whistled through the trees. The park stretched away before him, curving down towards the distant town and the steely glint of the River Thames. Not a soul to be seen, and Roy was glad of it. He needed time to think, because things had taken a turn for the worse at home.

Last night Derek had hit him.

Not a punch, just a sharp slap around the back of the head, but it was an escalation none the less, and Roy was now officially scared. He wasn't sleeping properly, lying awake in the dark of his bedroom as Derek prowled around the flat, jabbering into the mobile phone that Sammy now regretted parting with. Things were coming to a head. Roy could feel it.

Derek had to go.

He checked his new BlackBerry. Nothing. Yasin was too shrewd to call or send a text. If Derek got away before Yasin made good on his threats his team leader wouldn't have a leg to stand on. Roy had already started building a cover story. Entitled 'My Job at Heathrow', he'd created a rough video diary using the movie software on his laptop, overlaying the covert video he'd shot with text about his working day at Terminal Three. It was crude, but someone might just buy it. After that, Yasin could whistle for his twenty-five grand. Roy would be in the clear, free. He hoped.

Max bounced towards him, face smeared with chocolate, empty wrapper clutched in a sticky hand. 'Good boy, Max.' He dug inside his daysack for a packet of wet wipes, cleaning his son's hands and mouth. Max didn't struggle, just stood there obediently, eyes closed, dark lashes fluttering as Roy worked the wipes across his face. Even after Roy had finished the boy stood there, immobile. He was a good kid, beautiful. Roy felt a rush of emotion. He would miss him terribly.

'Go on, then. Go play.'

Max clapped his hands and skipped after his football.

Taking him out of school was a good move. If everything went bad Roy would go down for years, and Vicky would never bring Max to visit him. This might be his last chance to spend a little alone time with his son, maybe reconnect with him on some level. He didn't hold out too much hope but he was enjoying it anyway. And maybe Max was enjoying himself too.

His phone trembled in his coat pocket. As he reached for it a voice said, 'Roy Sullivan?'

Roy spun around. A man loomed behind him said, tall, wide. Menacing.

Roy twisted off the bench. 'Max, come here.'

The boy ignored him, puffing across the grass after his ball. Roy placed himself between them. His phone rang again and he thumbed it silent.

'I'm sorry, I didn't mean to startle you,' the man smiled.

A yank? Maybe Nate had sent him, some sort of intimidation attempt. No, he decided. Vicky's fiancé wasn't the type. Sammy, definitely. Not Nate.

'What do you want?'

Max trotted over, the ball at his feet. Roy swept him behind his legs. He felt Max's arm wrap itself around his thigh. He couldn't help himself. He looked down, smiled.

'That's a nice kid. How old is he? Five? Six?'

'None of your business. What do you want?'

'I've come a long way, Roy. I've been rehearsing this moment in my head for a long time. Now I'm here, well...'

Roy scooped up his daysack and looped it over his shoulders. 'You've got five seconds, then I'm gone.'

The big man nodded. 'Fair enough. My name is Frank Marshall. Your brother James worked for me in Iraq.'

Roy froze.

'What do you mean?'

'Exactly that. We both worked for TDL Global.'

Roy's mind raced. There'd been a few over the last three years, timewasters, cranks, even a journalist who'd quickly moved on to other things, but he'd never met anyone in person. Until now.

'How did you find me?'

'Through your website domain name. I saw your interview on MSNBC.'

'Really? Where?'

'New York.' The man smiled, his eyes taking on a faraway look. 'I remember the exact moment when I heard your brother's name. Hit me like an electric shock.'

The eyes refocused.

'Your brother didn't disappear in Baghdad, Roy. He was stationed at a secure compound inside the Al Basrah Oil Terminal on the Iraqi coast. That's six hundred kilometres south east of the Iraqi capital.'

Roy's eyes widened. The man knew about the ABOT. He remembered the voicemail, the anxious note of his brother's voice.

'...I'm working down on the coast, Roy. Something's not right down there. Something weird going on...'

'How d'you know Jimmy was at the ABOT?'

'Like I said, he worked for me.'

The man reached behind his neck, removed something, and curled it into his hand. He offered it to Roy. 'He would've wanted you to have that.'

Roy stared at the St Christopher in his palm. Then he turned it over.

Safe travels. All Our Love, Mum, Dad, Roy.

Emotion surged, threatening to choke him. The medallion in his hand mesmerized him, reconnecting him to his brother, an invisible bond that stretched across time and space. But the spell was quickly broken. Suddenly the St Christopher weighed heavy in his hand. It told him something else, a truth he'd shut out for so long.

'Jimmy's dead, isn't he?'

The baseball cap bobbed up and down. 'I'm afraid so.'

Roy slumped onto the bench, winded. He scooped Max up and held him close. It wasn't a shock, not any more, yet it still felt like a punch to the guts.

'When?'

'Three years ago. At the ABOT facility.'

Dead, this whole time. 'How?'

The man held out a plain brown envelope. Roy fixed the pendant around his neck and shifted Max onto his other knee. He took the envelope and turned it over in his hand. It was unmarked, unsealed.

'What's this?'

'The classified report into your brother's death.'

Roy weighed the envelope in his hand, his eyes flicking between it and the man standing before him. 'Who are you exactly?'

The stranger sat down next to him. When he spoke he did so quietly, his eyes scanning the landscape in all directions.

'I worked for TDL Global for many years, running

covert operations for their Security Division. SD is a private army, the biggest in the world, made up of the best ex-military contractors money can buy. Your brother was assigned to a special project, his tasking to provide security at a TDL subsidiary called Terra Petroleum on the Iraqi coast. He didn't like what he saw there, tried to do something about it. It cost him his life.'

Roy was stunned. Denied the information he'd craved for three years, he forced himself to take it slowly. One step at a time.

'It's Marshall, right?'

'Frank.'

'You knew Jimmy?'

Frank shook his head. 'Not personally. I managed the security operation for the programme he was assigned to. It's all in the report.'

Roy weighed the envelope in his hand, the pill that would banish the pain of uncertainty. A restless Max reached for it, trying to grab it with his chubby fingers. Maybe Max wanted to know what happened to his uncle too. So be it.

He took a deep breath and thumbed open the envelope. He extracted two plain, neatly typed pages of text.

No corporate headings, no logo.

Roy turned the pages over and back again.

'This is it?'

Frank nodded, watching the world over Roy's shoulder.

Roy began to read...

CONFIDENTIAL
SUBJECT: JAMES SULLIVAN/UK NAT/CL5
CONTRACTOR/DECEASED//
REF: FMSDMS2177/TKANE/281133//
DIST: /CL 1-2/EYES ONLY/MESSINA//
* *

JAMES SULLIVAN (63176311) was a UK National contractor assigned to the MESSINA programme. Sullivan was a member of BAKER TEAM and worked a 28/5-day shift/ R&R pattern, rotating between the TERRA PETROLEUM corporate compound in Baghdad and the Al-Basrah Oil Terminal, southern Iraq. As per SOPs, Baker Team was tasked to provide shore based and mobile escort duties for shipments and key personnel, transiting to and from MESSINA as part of—

'What's Messina?'

'Just keep reading.'

Roy complied. There was much that seemed irrelevant, military speak and logistical stuff. It was the second page that made Roy's heart pound.

--During the course of Baker Team's fourth rotation to ABOT, Sullivan was observed taking clandestine photographs of marked shipping crates. His actions were reported and a local surveillance operation was authorised. Sullivan was observed undertaking several illicit activities over a period of three days, culminating in a nocturnal trespass at the compound offices. Sullivan was challenged by a security patrol and found to be in possession of several classified documents. He was shot while attempting to escape. Sullivan's personal cell phone was found to contain twenty-nine images of classified materials and eight external shots of the MESSINA facility itself. Tech team have confirmed that these images were not transmitted in any form or downloaded to any other digital device. A search of Sullivan's personal possessions and subsequent interviews with Baker Team personnel proved inconclusive. Sullivan's body has since been removed from site and disposed of. In conclusion--

Roy scanned the cold text several times. Finally he said, 'What happened to him?'

'He was laid to rest at sea, out beyond the offshore facility.'

'Laid to rest?' Roy scoffed. 'With military honours and a brass band?'

'I wish that were true. He deserved it.'

'Why did you keep his St Christopher?'

Frank touched the skin around his neck. 'I was

going through a breakdown. Your brother's courage made me feel ashamed. I took it, to remind me what he'd risked. To remind me what a worthless piece of shit I was.'

Roy sat in silence, his emotions tumbling like washing in a machine. He held Max close. Jimmy was dead, and Roy had never given up on him, not until the pain of reality had begun to invade his sleep. Now the dream made sense. His brother had spoken to him from beyond his watery grave, and that gave Roy a strange sense of comfort. He felt something else too, a stirring resentment directed at the man next to him, a man who'd suddenly stiffened. He stared over Roy's shoulder.

'Do you know a woman, mid-thirties, dark brown hair, five-eight?'

Roy frowned. 'Why?'

'Because a lady of that description is headed straight for us. And she looks mad.'

Roy spun around.

Vicky.

He stood up, swinging Max to the ground. Vicky marched towards them, high-heeled boots clicking on the path, a rain mac belted around her waist, designer handbag slung over her shoulder. Roy braced himself for the storm. He wasn't disappointed. She opened up from ten paces away.

'What the hell do you think you're doing? How dare you take him out of school!'

'I needed to see him—'

'Liar!' she seethed, snatching at Max's hand. She bent down, pulled the bobble hat off his head, smoothed his ruffled hair. She held his hands and cooed in his ear.

'Stop panicking. He's fine.'

Vicky pulled the hat back on, adjusted Max's scarf. She grasped his hand.

'How dare you do this? I've called you a dozen times, for Christ's sake.'

Roy reached for his phone, saw the string of missed calls. 'I'm sorry. I just needed to spend some time with him, that's all.'

'Why? Max has always been a chore in the past. What's so special about now?'

'Nothing. I needed to see him.'

'On a school day? And what's this rubbish about taking him to a specialist?'

'I made that up, just to get him out. I was going to have him back by lunchtime.'

'Thank God one of the other mums saw you.'

'They should mind their own business,' he snapped. Then he shook his head. 'Look, I'm sorry. It's hard to explain.' He held up the report, the wind plucking at the pages. 'I've got some news about Jimmy. This is Frank, by the way.'

The big American lifted his cap. 'Ma'am.'

Vicky looked bemused, suspicious eyes flicking between Roy and Frank. 'What about him?'

Roy hesitated, fingering the chain around his neck. Maybe now wasn't the time. 'I'll tell you later.'

Vicky held his gaze for a moment longer. 'Max

needs to get back to school.'

Roy knelt down, gave Max a hug, felt his tiny lips on his cheek. 'I think we've bonded a bit,' Roy said.

'I'm glad.' Her words sounded hollow. 'Say bye-bye to Daddy.'

Max did, a silent wave of farewell.

'Don't ever do this again,' she warned. 'Next time I'll call the police.'

Roy held up his hands. 'I promise.'

She scooped Max up and hurried away towards the park gates. Roy and Frank watched her go. It was Frank who spoke first.

'You let that one get away?'

'Stupid, right?'

'Very.'

Frank turned to face Roy. 'Look, I know this news isn't what you hoped for. Your brother was a popular guy, well liked and respected by his peers. Brave, too. I hope you can find some comfort in that truth. Closure, perhaps.'

Roy folded the envelope into his pocket.

'Why was he taking pictures? What's Messina?'

Franks eyes wandered around the horizon. 'I came here because it was important to me that you knew the truth about James. I also came to warn you, to give you a chance to save yourself from what's coming. I hope to God you take it.'

'What are you talking about?'

Frank took a step closer. 'Pretty soon the news is going to get bad and it won't get any better. Before that happens you should find a place to live, far from any city, and learn to be self-sufficient. Liquidate your assets, buy gold, a gun too if you can, and stock up—water, tinned food, dried goods, fuel. Buy some good books on survival, food production, basic medicine. And stay away from people. If you do that, you and your loved ones will probably see it through. After that, I can't say. But short term, you'll live.'

Roy didn't answer straight away. Instead he scrutinised Frank for the first time. His face was thin, dyed hair peeking beneath his baseball cap, dark clothes, running shoes. He was a strange one, and Roy sensed an air of danger about him. If he was Jimmy's boss then he was probably a Special Forces type, and that made the danger real, yet Roy didn't feel threatened at all.

'You came here to help me, right, Frank?'

'I did. I hope I have.'

'Look, I know *how* Jimmy died. I need to know *why*. What's TDL doing in Iraq that's so bad it got my brother killed? He called me you know, before he went missing. He was scared.'

The American popped his collar up as a light rain began to spot the pathway. 'It doesn't matter, now. The clock is ticking, Roy. Leave town while you still can, before martial law is declared and the streets fill with the dead.'

Roy paled. 'What the hell are you talking about?'

'I'm talking about Messina. What I know will get me killed. I don't want you caught in the fallout. Neither would your brother.' He snapped his arm out, checked a high-tech digital wristwatch. 'Just remember what I said. Save yourself, and your family. And good luck.'

Frank tried to walk away and Roy sidestepped into his path.

'You can't just leave it like that.'

'I must. There're things I have to do. People are coming after me.'

'What people?'

'Bad people. Anyone who gets in their way will die. I won't put anyone else in danger, Roy. I have to keep moving.'

'You said you were compelled to come here, right?' Roy dug into his pocket, flapped the report in the American's face. 'And this is all I get? This and Jimmy's chain? I need more than that, Frank. You owe me, and you owe Jimmy.'

Frank looked away, shook his head. 'There's no time.'

'Then make time. You said Jimmy was brave, that his actions made you feel ashamed. Jimmy had a story, Frank. He'd want you to tell it to me. Please.'

The wind whipped around them. Frank swore under his breath. 'Is there somewhere quiet we can sit, get a coffee?'

'There's a cafe, down the hill.'

'You go there much?'

'Hardly ever.'

Frank checked his watch again. 'Okay, let's go.'

They walked in silence across the park. Roy's life

was already spinning out of control and now it was about to go faster. He had that feeling again, stronger now, that events were coming to a head. Jimmy still had a voice, something to reveal from beyond the grave, and Roy was about to find out what it was.

He shivered as the wind picked up and the rain began to fall.

The storm that rumbled over the horizon, the one that had troubled Roy for so long, was about to break.

Chapter Fifteen

They crossed the park to a quiet, tree-lined avenue, its quaint shops and gentrified houses a world away from the grey mass of the Fitzroy.

The cafe was wedged between an upmarket wine shop and an estate agent. The interior decor was pastel painted, the fittings, floor and furniture all fashionably distressed. Classical music played in the background. A tattooed girl smiled at them from behind a glass counter filled with cold pastas, meats and salads. Her nose stud winked under the hanging copper lights. She took their order. They took a seat in a quiet corner. Two young mums chatted at a table by the window. Babies bounced and gurgled on their knees. Frank watched them, watched the door, the street outside. The girl brought their drinks, two mugs of dark coffee.

'Enjoy.' She smiled and walked away.

Roy folded his arms on the table. 'So, tell me about Jimmy.'

'He was a brave kid. Stupid too.'

'Excuse me?'

Frank smiled over at the mums. 'Lower your voice. Your brother was stupid only because he underestimated the ruthlessness of his employers.'

'What's Messina all about, Frank? And why the bullshit story about him going missing in Baghdad?'

'Initially you made some noise. Questions were asked. TDL wanted to avoid an investigation. The public

203

don't have much sympathy for hired guns, right? A man wears a uniform, takes a bullet, he's a hero. The same guy swaps his uniform for Five Elevens and a corporate pay cheque, suddenly he's a mercenary. No one cares about those guys. Missing or dead, people lose interest fast. The tactic worked.'

'Jimmy was a pro. He'd never do anything stupid like leave the Green Zone by himself. I didn't believe it from the start.'

'Death is easy to cover up in places like Iraq.'

The door chimed and an elderly couple shuffled inside, bulging shopping bags clutched in their hands. They fussed around a window table, unwrapping coats and scarves. Tattoo girl hurried over.

Roy sipped his brew. 'What's Messina, Frank? Why did it get Jimmy killed?'

Frank's eyes wandered around the cafe before settling on Roy.

'Your brother's service jacket was impressive, that's why he was hired by TDL. For a while he did the standard stuff; pipeline security, close protection duties, but he was flagged as a potential candidate for Messina because he possessed three crucial qualifications— professionalism, dedication, and most of all discretion. He passed a battery of psych tests and got reassigned to Terra Petroleum, down on the Iraqi coast. Terra is a front for Messina. He got well compensated, eight thousand dollars a week—'

'Jesus,' Roy blurted, 'why so much?'

'Discretion and loyalty cost money, Roy. Messina

is highly classified and compartmentalised, so much so that your brother and his team were unaware of its true purpose. Hundreds of tons of construction and laboratory materials were shipped into the country via the Terra facility at ABOT. Your brother's team would provide armed escort for those shipments to and from the Messina site, a disused drilling platform out in the desert, about a hundred clicks southwest of Baghdad. From the outside it looks just that—disused, fenced off, but below ground it's a different story. Your brother was there when they were fitting out the sub-surface labs. He saw the biohazard equipment, the military spec security systems, and joined a couple of dots. He asked questions, took pictures, broke into the program offices. That's what led to his death. Now, three years on, Messina is fully operational. And production is about to begin.'

'Production of what?' Roy murmured. He found himself mimicking Frank's conspiratorial tone, his furtive body language. The story that rolled off the American's tongue had an air of unreality about it, like the plot of a Bond movie. All that was missing was a gorgeous bad girl with a European accent. Roy realised Frank was still speaking.

'Sorry, say that again?'

'The Angola virus,' Frank said.

'What about it?'

The American leaned a little closer. 'That's what they're about to start manufacturing at Messina.'

Angola.

The word had become synonymous with death. Roy recalled the outbreaks that had wiped out the populations of two prisons in the country of the same name. There were other epidemics too, in South America, China, Eastern Europe, sparking a world health scare that killed thousands and faded as quickly as the SARS panic a few years before.

Roy frowned. 'Did you say they were *making* the Angola virus?'

'That's exactly what I said. They've been developing it for years in secure labs across the globe, testing different strains on vagrants, drug addicts, runaways, people with no kin. Those outbreaks in Africa and other parts of the world were early field trials. Now it's ready and Messina is where they're going to mass produce it. That's what your brother stumbled on. It's why he was killed.'

Roy stared across the table at Frank. 'What do you mean it's ready? Ready for what?'

Frank spread his hands. 'Worldwide distribution. So they can eliminate over half of the planet's population. That's why they called the program *Messina*. It's a port in Sicily, where the Black Death was introduced into Europe back in the fourteenth century. That outbreak killed sixty per cent of the world's population too.'

Roy sat back in his chair. A smile played at the corners of his mouth. 'You're joking, right?'

'You think Jimmy's death is funny?'

The smile vanished. 'Don't be stupid.'

'You said he was scared. Did he scare easily?'

'No.'

'Then ask yourself, why would a guy earning the biggest dollar of his life risk everything to find out what his employers were doing out there?'

Roy didn't respond immediately. He watched the mums, the older couple, chatting, smiling. Music played quietly in the background. It was peaceful, ordinary. What Frank was talking about was pure fantasy. Yet Jimmy had died because of it. Frank was right, his brother's death was no joke. So he had to pay attention, *really* listen. Then he would decide whether Frank was the real deal or not.

'Okay, Frank. Let's say Jimmy died because of Messina—'

'He did.'

'And Messina is where they're going to manufacture Angola?'

'Pretty soon. And distribute it.'

'So they can wipe out half the human race?'

Frank nodded.

'So you're telling me Jimmy was working for terrorists?'

'The biggest on the planet.'

'You mean ISIS? Al-Qaeda?'

Frank shook his head. 'I'm talking about an organisation that transcends any terrorist group you've ever heard of. One that hides behind an intricate facade of legitimacy, accountability and normality. They're everywhere, and they hide in plain sight because most people are blind to them.'

Roy pushed his empty mug to one side. 'I hate to keep repeating myself, Frank, but what the hell are you talking about?'

The American finished his coffee and did the same. 'It's better if I start from the beginning. But bear this in mind, Roy—you've been conditioned to reject what I'm about to tell you. It'll seem implausible, but try and stay with me, okay?'

Roy nodded.

Frank settled into his chair.

'Back in the nineties a group of people from some of the world's biggest energy companies got together to voice their concerns about oil production. This group—we're talking top executives, eminent geologists, engineers—they believed that the world had already passed the point at which total global oil extraction had been reached, and that we'd entered the very first stages of terminal decline. They met secretly, and eventually they compiled a report confirming their findings. They had a truckload of data too, and their objective was to go public with their conclusions and begin preparations for a planet that could no longer rely on fossil fuels as economic bedrock.'

Tattoo girl drifted by their table and took their empty mugs. Frank waited until she was out of earshot.

'I read their report. The short-term projections were sobering enough; gas rationing, restricted public travel, phased brown and blackouts, soaring food and energy prices, crippling unemployment. And that would just be the beginning. The long-term picture was much, much worse—we're talking full global economic collapse, poverty, starvation, riots, martial law. It would be a crisis so bad it would make the Great Depression seem like Thanksgiving. As the lights went out around the world, governments would crumble and democracy would fail, and the resulting resource wars would consume every nation on the planet. The clock of human progress would be dialled back a hundred and fifty years. Pretty soon we'd be standing on the edge of the abyss. But it didn't turn out that way because we had a guy on the inside.'

'Who's *we*?'

Frank held up a hand. 'Just hear me out. Our guy was a senior executive at Saudi Aramco, one of the world's leading oil producers. His engineers were reporting that thirty per cent of the product being pumped out of their biggest field at Ghawar was water. It all went into the report. But our guy also informed The Committee.'

'Who?'

'Let me ask you a question, Roy. You ever hear of the New World Order?'

Roy shook his head. 'I don't think so.'

'It's an urban myth, pandered around by conspiracy theorists for decades. It goes something like this; the world is actually being run by a secretive group of elites with a globalist agenda who plan to seize ultimate control by replacing sovereign nation states with a single world government. One that will control everything, and everybody.'

Roy shrugged. 'No, never heard of it.'

'Most people haven't. Sounds crazy, right?' Frank leaned a little closer. 'It's not. It exists. And it is very, very real. That's The Committee.'

Roy waited to see if Frank's stony face cracked a smile. It didn't. Instead he pulled a pen from his pocket and drew a rough triangle on a napkin, which he divided into three sections.

'The Committee believe that global power takes the form of a pyramid, one made up of tiers of influence. Everyone on the planet falls into one of these tiers.' He tapped the napkin with his pen. 'This bottom section, the biggest, that's tier one. Tier one represents the bulk of humanity—the poor, the destitute, the street-sweepers, factory workers, the billions who survive on minimum wage. Tier two constitutes what most would call the middle classes, people with professional jobs, working for established institutions like governments and major corporations, and entrepreneur types, employing tier one people, helping economies grow, contributing to the system. That's the second tier. Tier three, well, now we're talking serious people with serious money. Bubbling to the top of that tier is the wealthiest one per cent of the world's population. Do you know how many billionaires there are in the world, Roy?'

'No idea.'

'Two thousand, give or take. Most of them make up that one per cent. But there's another group—' Frank drew slow circles around the tip of the pyramid '– right here, at the very summit. The people who form this capstone group number around a hundred, and they are the richest, most influential people on the planet. These are the super-elites, a group of mega-wealth individuals and dynastic families who between them own eighteen of the twenty biggest multi-national corporations in the world. A group who, by corporate extension or financial interconnections, directly influence almost every other major conglomerate on the planet across a whole range of industries—we're talking energy production, banking, finance, communications, transportation, healthcare, manufacturing and the biggest of them all, the military-industrial complex. Their worldview is global, unrestricted by political affiliation, national sovereignty or physical borders, and in utmost secrecy they influence the agendas of governments, NATO, G7, G8, the G20, the World Bank and the World Trade Organisation among many, many others. Their power flows not just to each other but also to powerful and influential individuals in the tiers below them, forming a collective, where members think and act in unison to preserve their economic domination. The Committee's ultimate goal is to consolidate that growing power, to sweep away the chaos of national self-interest, to dismantle governments and the myriad of international organisations and replace them with a single entity, a global corporate body that will oversee and govern every resource and every human being on the planet. *That* is *The Committee*, Roy. Are you still with me?'

'I think so,' Roy stuttered. It was difficult to accept what Frank was saying but the man was on a roll, becoming more animated as he spoke, the words tumbling from his mouth. It was a confession, Roy realised. And he wasn't done yet.

Frank's eyes narrowed. 'But it goes deeper, and far darker. Their multinationals consume smaller companies like a whale swallowing plankton, divvying up billion-dollar contracts to hundreds of other companies eager to suck from the teat. It's a corporate labyrinth of Byzantine proportions, and at the centre of that maze is The Committee, pulling the levers, like Oz behind his curtain. And it's not just the corporate world. They have key people everywhere; governments, the military, federal agencies, academic institutions, public policy groups, global media, PR and marketing. All the bullshit on TV, the mass entertainment, the news, it's all about distraction and distortion, about maintaining illusions and deflecting blame from the ruling classes when times get tough. Less cash in your pocket? Blame the banks, or climate change, or the goddam immigrants, right?'

'Right,' Roy mumbled. It felt like he was on a rollercoaster ride, hanging on by his fingertips as he plummeted up and down. Then suddenly the ride slowed. Across the table Frank seemed to catch his breath.

'But they're not finished yet. Remember the whistle-blowers? Well, their findings terrified The Committee. A world without oil, with billions fighting for control of dwindling natural resources, that kind of chaos isn't in their playbook. So the wheels were set in motion.

They reached out to the whistle-blowers, swore them to secrecy, duped them into thinking they were about to get the backing of the US administration. Finally, when all the pieces were in place, they were lured to New York where they handed over every scrap of their precious data. Once The Committee had it, they drove a plane into the building. That was the North Tower of the World Trade Centre. That was Nine Eleven.'

'You're kidding,' Roy blurted.

Frank shook his head. 'You know the rest. Events ran their course, giving The Committee what they wanted—unrestricted access to Iraq's massive oil and gas reserves. They've been stockpiling it ever since, in huge storage facilities all over the world. Afghanistan was part of it too, but they needed time to get the military infrastructure in place. Once they did, the geologists went in. I've seen their reports; the country is a gold mine, literally. We're talking huge mineral deposits— natural gas, copper, gold, cobalt, lithium—so much of it that years from now Afghanistan will resemble one giant quarry, the biggest and most productive mining facility in the world, with the Afghans themselves providing the labour. Well, those that survive the Transition.'

'The what?'

'The Transition.' Frank's finger tapped the table. 'Look, you have to see things from The Committee's perspective. They've secured vast amounts of natural resources for future consumption, that's all good. As an added bonus, the whistle-blowers might have got it wrong; new exploration and extraction technologies have opened up previously undiscovered energy fields in East Africa, Asia and the South Atlantic. And then there's the whole fracking thing too, tapping into more resources than they previously thought possible. So now The Committee is sitting on these huge reserves and the new fields are coming online and everything's rosy, right?'

'I guess,' Roy shrugged.

'Wrong, because now you've got a much bigger problem.' Frank's face darkened. 'The world's population is seven billion plus. In a few years' time, thanks to rising living standards and falling mortality rates, it'll be eight billion. In twenty years it'll be over ten. So whatever reserves we think we've got now, it's never going to be enough. I told you already, The Committee wants to govern the world under the banner of a single corporation, controlling the future and managing natural resources. How you gonna do that with ten billion people and rising, all demanding food, water, fuel, technology, consumer goods, healthcare, living space? That's why they're going to initiate the Transition, an event that will wipe out over half the population of the planet. After that, the numbers will be strictly controlled. They're looking at a figure of two, maybe three billion tops. In their own sick way they're the ultimate environmentalists.'

Roy shook his head. 'This can't be real.'

'It is. A lot of very important people have discussed population control in the public forum for decades, but the masses are generally too distracted to notice. That's the corporate media at work, doing what they do best. It's real, Roy. And it's headed straight for us.'

That's when Roy's penny finally dropped. 'Messina.'

'Exactly. The delivery method of choice is hand dryers, the public washroom variety. For the past couple of years a TDL subsidiary has been fitting specially modified units in airport washrooms, right across the Middle East—'

'Why there?'

Frank shrugged. 'It's a tactical decision. The Committee have always been uneasy about Islam. Religious fundamentalism continues to spread across the world, and those guys can't be bought or bargained with. The plain truth is, wherever Islam goes, violence follows. You take Islam out of the equation and suddenly the world is a considerably less violent place. That's why they're targeting the Middle East first. There're dispersal units in Latin America and the Far East too.'

'Dispersal units?'

'Yeah, the hand dryers. At some point in the very near future small, pressurised containers of the Angola virus will be slotted inside these modified dryers. After that, a measured dose will mix with the normal blast of hot air every time someone punches the button. Angola is airborne too, so by the time the container is empty the air in those washrooms will be highly contagious. Thousands will be infected, and they'll be travelling all over the globe. It'll spread so fast that the world won't be able to react in time. And it kills half the people it infects. Don't ask me how, it's all done on a genetic level, like the way mosquitoes bite some people and not others. Billions will die.'

'Holy shit,' Roy breathed. 'Isn't there a cure or something, an antidote?'

'Sure. Everyone in the programme is immune, plus millions of ordinary people too, although most of them don't realise it.'

'You mean I could be immune? Max, Vicky?'

Frank shook his head. 'Doubtful. You've heard of Kansas, right? Kansas is America's biggest producer of wheat. For the last four years selected state water supplies have been treated with the antiviral, like adding fluoride. The big grain producers, the farmers, suppliers and distributors, most of them will live. It's the same with other critical industries, like energy supply, military bases, major hospitals, educational communities, and a heap of other people and institutions that are vital to The Committee's interests. They've been marked, Roy. Some won't make it, that's been factored in, but many key personnel will survive. As for the rest, they'll die in their billions. That's the Transition, and one day soon the only thing they'll be talking about on the news is Angola.'

Frank laid a hand on Roy's coat sleeve. 'I tried to get you the anti-viral, Roy, but things didn't work out. That's why I'm urging you to get as far away as possible. You can survive this. You've got enough time.'

Roy glanced over his shoulder. The old couple were packing up to leave, the mums and their babies gone. The tattooed girl was standing outside, smoking a cigarette. Everything was still normal, business as usual. Just Roy and Frank, contemplating the End of Times. He turned back to Frank.

'And you work for these people, right?'

Frank shook his head. 'Not any more. I'd been sliding towards a nervous breakdown for some time when your brother was killed. He would've known he was in danger, yet still he tried to uncover the truth. I'd seen too much death, Roy. Jimmy's was the final straw. I made a decision, went missing. I was lost in the dark. God showed me the light again.' He saw the look on Roy's face and said, 'Sure, laugh that up if you like, but He saved me. He also crystallised my thinking. What we face now is a straight fight between good and evil. I'm going down swinging.'

He dug into his pocket, pushed a small USB key drive across the table.

'That's full of highly sensitive data from a black site here in the UK. There's a bunch of stuff on there, names, dates, references to Messina, shipping manifests— we're talking reams of classified information that The Committee won't want anyone to see, even those of us in the loop. I want you to take it with you, Roy, make sense of it, tell your boy that the history they'll teach him in their schools will all be a lie. That the people that rule them are nothing more than godless murderers. You need to make sure the next generation knows the truth.'

Tattoo girl breezed in from outside, the scent of cigarette smoke trailing in her wake. She smiled at Roy and disappeared behind the counter. He weighed the drive in his hand.

'Why not go public with it? Blow the whole thing out of the water.'

Frank shook his head. 'On the outside chance that someone might believe what I just told you, it would take months, even years, to verify the data. And even if someone did, somebody else higher up the chain would hear about it and squash it. Then they'd silence you permanently. But it won't matter because the Transition will be underway long before then. No, it's up to future generations to make a stand.'

Frank got to his feet. 'I can't stay. I've stirred up a hornets' nest already and they'll be coming for me.' He scribbled a number on a napkin. 'You can reach me there for the next twenty-four hours. After that, I'm gone. You need anything, clarification, whatever, call me. And if you do, be smart—use a payphone.' He came around the table, placed his hand on Roy's shoulder. 'I'm guessing you've got a couple of months, six at the outside, before it starts. Get out, Roy. While you still can.' He gave his shoulder a squeeze. 'Good luck, son. God bless.'

The bell above the door chimed, a cold draught gusting around Roy's legs. He stared at Frank's empty chair and realised he'd been distracted by talk of conspiracies and biblical prophecies. It wasn't Frank's fault, Roy had pressed the guy, but in the process he'd lost focus, away from Jimmy. He should've asked about practical stuff, like personal effects, and wills and bank accounts. He imagined someone clearing out his brother's locker, dumping it all into a rubbish bag, Jimmy's life scattered on an Iraqi rubbish tip.

Roy cursed and pushed his chair back. Outside a cold rain was falling as his eyes searched the pavement, the empty road, the damp green sweep of the park beyond the iron railings.

There wasn't a soul to be seen.

Frank Marshall had disappeared.

Chapter Sixteen

Roy trudged back across the park towards the Fitzroy.

The wind whipped his clothes and rain drummed his head, but it did little to clear his thoughts. He tried Frank's phone again. It rang, unanswered again.

Get out, Frank had warned. Roy did the calculation, realised his assets would barely stretch to a decent set of camping gear. The flat was rented, and he had little savings. If he needed to run he could probably find somewhere cheap, but that would be it. There'd be no budget for supplies, for fuel or generators. As for gold, well, Frank was having a laugh there.

Even if he did have the resources, how would he convince Vicky to leave everything behind, drag Max out to the middle of nowhere? To wait out a crisis that may never come?

He felt for the USB key buried in his pocket as he trotted up the dank stairwell. Okay, so Jimmy *was* inquisitive, always asking questions, reading up on stuff. Roy imagined him at this Messina site, taking pictures, rifling through drawers, wondering what he'd gotten himself involved in. That part of Frank's story was credible. As for the rest, well—

'Where the fuck have you been?'

Derek's rough bark startled Roy as he closed the front door. The Scot was in the hallway, his bloodshot eyes narrowed, dark shadows trapped in the hollows of his stubbled cheeks.

'I was in the park. I had my son this morning.'

Roy tugged off his coat. Derek was in a foul mood. He was a mess too, his Celtic T-shirt spattered with food stains, his grey tracksuit bottoms the same, the nails untrimmed on his pale, bare feet.

And the blood.

Roy pointed. 'I think you've cut your foot.'

Derek said nothing, ignoring the claret that squelched between his toes. A cigarette dangled between his lips and he screwed a flinty eye as he took a long, glowing drag. Ash tumbled to the carpet.

Roy forced a smile. 'I'll get the vacuum cleaner.' He tried to squeeze past. The Scot blocked his path.

'The fuck are you going? I'm talking.'

Compliance, that was the key, the only way to deal with his unstable squatter.

'Sorry, Derek. I've got a lot on my mind, that's all.'

'You think I give a fuck about your problems? I've been ringing all fucking morning. Your phone goes straight to voicemail.'

Roy slapped his forehead. 'Dammit, I forgot to tell you. I've got a new one.' He pulled the BlackBerry from his pocket and held it up.

Derek stood immobile, blocking the hallway, bony hands dangling by his side. 'You get a new phone and don't tell me?'

'I forgot.'

'You forgot. You're a stupid cunt, you know that, son? I'm sick of seeing your stupid face, and I'm sick of staring at the walls of this fucking shitebox too.'

Roy swallowed nervously. Derek's cabin fever had got a lot worse. Roy had Googled the syndrome at work, disturbed by Derek's deteriorating moods. He'd read about isolation and claustrophobia, about chronic restlessness and a distrust of others. And outright hostility. Derek was a ticking time bomb. Sammy had to get him out, one way or another, before he went off.

'Look, you'll probably be on your way any day now. Sammy should have some news soon.'

'Don't fucking baby me, son. And that prick doesn't answer his fucking phone either. I'm tired of this shite.'

Jesus, he was really starting to lose it. 'Can I make a suggestion, Derek? Don't take this the wrong way but why don't you, er, clean up a little?'

'What?'

'You know, for when we get the go ahead. Have a shower and a shave.'

He smiled, hoping he'd chosen his words carefully. Lately he'd imagined a surly, unkempt Derek, trailing behind him through the airside corridors, muttering under his whisky-fuelled breath and giving passers-by the evil eye. That was unthinkable.

'Are you calling me a soap dodger?'

Derek flexed his fingers.

Roy took a subtle step back.

'No, not at all. A lot of people will be watching us as we move through the airport. We've got to look the part, that's all.'

Derek stared at Roy for a moment then grinned, baring his yellowed teeth.

'Ya cheeky wee gobshite. Trying to teach me the game, are ya? Mugging me off, is that it?'

'For Christ's sake no,' Roy protested. 'Look, just have a think about it, eh?' He squeezed past Derek. 'I'll put the TV on. I've rented a couple of movies that—'

He stopped dead in his tracks.

The living room had been trashed.

No, not just trashed. Completely and utterly wrecked, like a bomb had gone off. His disbelieving eyes roamed the empty walls, his pictures smashed and splintered. The curtains had been dragged from their tracks and pale foam bled from the wounds of his sofa. His flat-screen TV lay on its back, impaled with the tube of the vacuum cleaner. The floor at his feet was ankle deep in the detritus of domesticity; the DVD player in pieces, discs broken, ornaments and cutlery shattered, the architectural drawings shredded. A pile of Roy's clothes, all soaking wet. Urine, he guessed. Even his bike had been vandalised and hurled on the heap, the wheels twisted, the spokes buckled. He caught a glint of brushed silver, his laptop, the screen viciously separated from the keyboard. He stared open-mouthed, unable to comprehend what his eyes were telling him.

Then he spotted something else, a shard of glass, a twisted gold metal frame. He dropped to his knees and scrabbled amongst the debris, found the photographs he treasured most, the family in Cornwall, Jimmy and Max. Or what was left of them. Along with the others they were torn to pieces, maliciously destroyed by the man who watched him from the doorway.

Roy rubbed a gentle thumb over Max's toothless grin, the faded, headless bodies of his parents, distinguishable only by their dated clothes. He couldn't find Jimmy at all.

Derek stepped into the room, another cigarette jammed in his fist. 'This is what happens when I get ignored. When wee pricks forget to tell their guests about new phones.'

Roy knew he should've kept his mouth shut. He should've just cleared up and bided his time until he could ring Sammy, then beg and plead with him until Derek was gone.

But he didn't.

Instead he got to his feet, letting the shreds of his dead family flutter to the carpet.

'What the fuck is wrong with you, Derek? What sort of mental case does something like this?'

The Scot took a pull on his cigarette, exhaling tiny circles of smoke with loud clicks of his jaw. 'Be careful, son.'

'Be careful? Really? You've trashed everything I own. Pissed on my clothes too, judging by the smell. And all because I forgot to tell you about a new phone?'

Derek sniggered, and the anger surged through Roy. He was going down, he knew that, so fuck it, he might as well go down in flames. He felt the red mist enveloping him, and embraced it for all it was worth.

'Oh, you think it's funny. After all I've done for you. Shopping, cooking, washing, cleaning, waiting on you hand and foot—I mean, short of wiping your arse, I've practically been a slave in my own home.'

'What's your point?'

Roy folded his arms and drummed his fingers on his chin. 'Hmm, let me see. Oh yeah. My point is this— you, Derek what-ever-the-fuck-your-name-is—are a rude, dirty, ungrateful, self-centred, ignorant fucking pisshead. That's right, and I can't wait for the day you walk out that door for good because I am sick to death of you being here. You're a fucking parasite.'

The venom in his own voice surprised Roy. And it felt really good.

Derek stared at him, his grey eyes unflinching. 'Finished?'

'The truth is, I hope somewhere down the line you get nicked, Derek. It's what someone like you deserves. I hope you end up in some Third World prison, where you get arse raped every fucking day. I hope you sink slowly into a black pit of despair, and realise living is too much trouble. And one day, with any luck, they'll find you hanging by your scrawny little neck in your cell. Because you are one nasty, horrible piece of human shit, Derek, and I hate your fucking guts.'

Roy was panting now, his anger spent, the red mist blown away by the cold wind of reality. He knew then he'd gone too far. An icy ball began to form in his stomach.

Derek smiled and said, 'Well, I guess we know where we both stand.'

He flicked his cigarette with well-practised

accuracy, the butt exploding in a shower of sparks in Roy's face. The Scot closed the distance between them with the speed and agility of a seasoned street fighter, a bony fist crashing into Roy's skull. He stumbled backwards, threw an instinctive punch. It cracked off Derek's cheek but the Scot never flinched, his hands a blur of bone and knuckle. Roy went down hard and Derek kept coming. He straddled his chest, raining blow after blow, grunting with effort. Roy felt his lip burst, tasted blood. He tried to grab Derek's arms but they were like pistons, pummelling him. A punch landed below his ribs and the air left his body with a loud *oof!* He rolled onto his side but Derek wasn't finished. He stood up, rummaging through the debris, his hand finding a leg of the coffee table.

Roy saw it and suddenly he thought he might die.

He tried to crawl away, clutching his stomach, blood dripping from his mouth, his face. He felt a blow to the back of his head, a hollow crack that detonated a million pin pricks of light behind his eyes. His legs and arms buckled.

He heard Derek standing over him, the panting of his breath, the rasp of wood in the Scot's hand. Any second now the makeshift club would be raised and the end would come.

Roy closed his eyes and the blackness was complete.

Yasin Goreja cursed his brother-in-law. Again.

He'd cursed him as he lay in bed that morning.

He'd cursed him on the bus to Heathrow, cursed him for most of the day at work, and now he cursed him as he made his way home from the bus stop. Then Yasin cursed himself.

How stupid he'd been to trust Amir. Secretly he'd always been jealous of his wife's younger brother, his designer clothes, his boastful inventory of done deals, the two-year-old Mercedes he drove between his many businesses. Amir holidayed in Florida twice a year. Yasin took his brood to his cousin's caravan in Derbyshire. And he especially resented the thick roll of cash Amir always pulled from his pocket whenever he visited the house, peeling off a note or two for Yasin's five girls and two boys. Yasin always felt insulted, shamed by his children's squeals of delight, the fawning esteem his wife held for her sibling.

He'd hit her once, for her lack of respect. She'd remained silent of course, and Yasin had been plagued by guilt, a guilt that had faded far quicker than his wife's blackened eye. And soon the jealousy had returned.

Yasin felt shackled by his inadequate salary, the cost of his growing family. Amir had dangled the carrot of a lucrative business venture. Against his better judgement, Yasin had taken the plunge. He cursed himself again.

Now Yasin was desperate. The money he'd sunk into the deal, the one that involved the calling cards and a fast food outlet, had disappeared. Twenty thousand pounds, squeezed from the equity of his meagre three-bedroom property, was gone. Amir had shrugged;

solicitors' fees and agents and a string of other debtors had swallowed up the money. Yasin had begged and pleaded. Then he threatened to involve the police. Amir had countered with his own threat, the exposure of Yasin's fiscal irresponsibility. The damage to his status would be permanent, his standing in the community undermined, his name sullied at the local mosque. His family shamed.

It was enough to silence Yasin's tongue.

But the bills kept mounting, and Yasin's nights grew ever more sleepless—until the day he'd seen Roy Sullivan on CCTV taking pictures with his phone. He'd watched him for a week, building the case against him. He had no idea what the man was up to, nor did he care. All he saw was opportunity. The bank was calling him daily, the recent interest rate rise plunging him further into debt. Someone had to pay. It wouldn't be Amir, of course—that bastard had taken his family away again, this time to Pakistan for a wedding. Lately Yasin had begun to suspect that there was never any deal in the first place. It was all a scam, retribution for striking Amir's sister. What a fool he'd been.

And now his own plan was starting to backfire. Sullivan had not buckled like Yasin thought he would. Instead he'd gone absent from work, forcing Yasin to cover for him, fuelling his growing sense of impotence. He felt inside his coat for Sullivan's iPhone. A few days ago he felt assured of its lucrative potential. Now it burned like a hot coal in his pocket. Whatever mistakes he'd made in the past, none of them could compare to his recent stupidities.

He passed a parade of shops and cut down a narrow alleyway. He contemplated his own arrest and imprisonment, and the thought filled him with dread. He was well respected, a pillar of the community, his word trusted, his advice often sought. Now he ran the risk of being exposed as dishonest, a blackmailer and debtor. Yasin shook the vision from his mind, raindrops flicking from his beard. Once again he cursed his brother-in-law.

Ahead the alleyway was in shadow, the streetlights still lifeless despite the darkening sky. He saw someone approaching him, a hooded figure, but Yasin took no notice. The path narrowed, a lifeless lamppost forcing the gap. The man was approaching quickly, hands in his pockets, face obscured by a dark hood. Yasin made way.

He caught a sudden hand movement, felt the blow to his groin, a pain so sharp and so deep that it robbed the breath from his lungs. He doubled over, grabbing at the hand, at the serrated knife that glinted as it buried itself deep in his stomach. Yasin tried to scream and failed, the sound trapped in his throat as the blade rose again and again, slicing through his hands, his clothes. He fell forward, pulling at the man's hood, his fingers slippery with blood. He felt the blade enter his side this time, and he dropped to his knees, gasping. He looked down, saw his coat and trousers soaked with blood.

'Please stop,' he rasped.

He felt his attacker's hands snake beneath his armpits, dragging him over a drooping wire fence and onto the waste ground beyond. He had no strength left, unable to stop his body being rolled beneath a stand of twisted shrubs. He knew his life was about to end.

His attacker loomed over him and he was surprised to see it was a woman. She worked fast, rifling his pockets, burying him beneath a mound of split and filthy bin liners, his nostrils filled with the stench of rotting rubbish, his hands warmed by the ceaseless flow of blood.

Yasin Goreja wondered many things as the life ran out of his body; he wondered how his wife would cope, how his young children would survive, and how they would remember him. He was desperately sorry for what he'd done. He hoped that somehow, someday, they would forgive him.

As his lungs inflated for the last time he saved his final breath for one more curse. As it left his lips he prayed it would carry on the wind, would travel over land and sea, would find his brother-in-law Amir and ruin his life as surely as his own.

Roy cracked open a cautious eye.

The room was in semi-darkness, the glow of the estate washing over his naked walls. Night had fallen. He wasn't dead. The blow he'd been expecting, the one that would crush his skull, hadn't come. He was alive, and right now that was the best he could hope for.

Slowly, very slowly, he dragged himself upright, resting his back against the slashed sofa. His head swam and his eyes lost focus. He inspected the back of his skull with careful fingers. There was a small lump there, but the skin was unbroken. He held up his lacerated hands, the dried blood black against his skin. He reached for the St Christopher around his neck. Still there, thank God.

He got to his feet, holding the wall to steady himself. He made it to the kitchen and found the first aid box. He washed four aspirin down with a glass of water and gripped the counter until his head cleared.

He staggered along the hallway. The door to Derek's room lay open, everything beyond wrecked. A foul stench told him that the Scot had emptied his bowels somewhere inside. He slapped the light off and closed the door, too exhausted to do anything about it. In the grand scheme of things it was a small price to pay. Derek was gone, and Roy doubted he'd be back.

He bolted the front door and headed for the bathroom. He inspected the damage to his face; a split lip swollen like a raw sausage, a black eye, numerous cuts, scrapes and swellings. He dabbed his wounds with cotton wool and antiseptic and retired to his own room. Derek had trashed that too but thankfully the Scot's bladder and bowels must've been empty. His mattress was intact and Roy lay down in his clothes, wrapping himself in his shredded quilt. Feathers drifted on the air. Relief consumed him. Despite everything, Roy felt safe inside his own home for the first time in weeks.

He lay in the darkness, skull thumping. Today was proving to be one of the worst of his life, ranking right up there with the crash that killed his parents, the news that Jimmy was missing, the day that Vicky had walked out on him. How Sammy would react to Derek's departure was anyone's guess, but Roy had the feeling that he wouldn't be entirely exonerated of blame.

He turned over, curling into a ball and dragging the quilt over his head. His hand brushed against his jeans and he felt it again, the USB drive inside his pocket. It meant nothing to him now. His problems were more immediate and they wouldn't be ignored. He buried himself a little deeper, wishing he could hibernate, and wake again in six months' time when the world had moved on and taken his troubles with it.

But he knew that wasn't possible.

He knew that with the coming of dawn the whole, terrible merry-go-round would begin again.

Chapter Seventeen

'A murder investigation was launched today after the body of forty-seven-year-old Yasin Goreja was discovered behind a row of shops in Hounslow, west London—'

Roy's toothbrush froze in mid-air. He winced as toothpaste leaked into his split lip. He spat a pink swirl down the plug.

'—family have since been notified. Mister Goreja's body was discovered by a passer-by at eight-thirty yesterday evening, and police have yet to confirm or deny reports that Goreja had been assaulted. A post-mortem will be carried out in an attempt to establish the cause of death. In other news a—'

He snapped off the radio and stared at his reflection, his battered face drained of colour. Sammy had killed Yasin, or had had him killed. And it was Roy's fault. He leaned on the sink to stop his hands from shaking; blackmail notwithstanding, Yasin didn't deserve this.

Jesus Christ, his phone! Would the cops have it? His stomach churned. He thought about running, like Frank told him to, but with Yasin dead, that would make him a prime suspect. No, he had to stay calm, think. Tough it out.

He checked his Blackberry for messages. Nothing. Derek was probably with Sammy right now, stoking his dangerous mood. Roy was in a world of shit. He touched the purple puffiness around his eye and winced. At least he had physical evidence of Derek's lunacy. Maybe he should take photos of the flat too.

His body ached as he dressed. He found the USB drive and Frank's number in his pocket and pinned them to the corkboard on the kitchen wall, along with Jimmy's report. Right now he had bigger problems—

Bang! Bang! Bang!

The front door shook with a force that echoed through the flat. Roy's heart leapt into his mouth. It had to be the police. He peered through the blind—no uniforms, just the angry whip of a dark ponytail.

Vicky.

He threw the bolt, swung the front door open.

'Jesus Christ, you nearly gave me—'

'Where is he?' she yelled, barging past him.

Roy slammed the door. He trailed after her as she checked the kitchen, about-faced into the hallway, then marched into the living room. Like Roy, she also stopped dead in her tracks. Then she spun on her heel, pushing him out of the way.

'Max!' she yelled, heading towards the spare room. She flung the door open, gagging as the smell hit her. She slammed the door shut, marched into Roy's room. More damage. He could see the emotions raging behind her large brown eyes, anger, fear, and now confusion. She closed them, took a deep breath and regarded Roy for the first time.

'I'm only going to ask you once. Where is he?'

'You mean Max?'

He flinched as Vicky took a step towards him.

'Don't play games. You've got five seconds to tell me where he is or I'm calling the police.' She fumbled in her handbag, brandished her phone in Roy's face. 'Four seconds—'

'Vicky, I have no idea what you're talking about.'

'Three—'

'I mean it. He's not here. I haven't seen him since yesterday, I swear to God.'

Vicky stared at him, searching for lies. 'The Head called me. She said a woman from social services had taken Max away, just after I dropped him off. She had paperwork, a court order—'

'A what?'

'I know you want to hurt me, Roy, but this isn't about us. It's Max's life you're playing with.'

Roy reached out and held her arms. 'Look at me, Vicky. I didn't do this. I've just got out of bed for Christ's sake. Now tell me, was this woman alone?'

Suddenly there was doubt in her face. 'I don't know.'

'What did she look like?'

'The Head said she was mixed-race, thirties.'

Roy's hand covered his mouth. *Tank.* 'Oh shit—'

'What is it? Tell me, for God's sake!'

'I know where Max is.'

'Where? Tell me!'

'Sammy's got him. Sammy French. He was at the school that day, when I was late for Max's football match.'

'Sammy French, that's his name?' She dialled a

number and held the phone to her ear.

'Who are you calling?'

'Who d'you think? The police, of course.'

Roy slapped the phone from her hand. He scooped it off the carpet and ended the call.

'What the hell are you doing? That man has our son.'

'You can't call the police.'

'Don't be stupid! Max has been kidnapped!'

'Keep your bloody voice down!' He flicked the hallway light on. 'Look at my face, Vicky. Look at the state of the flat. They've taken Max for a reason.' He bit his swollen lip. 'You can't call anyone. It's down to me to sort it out.'

'You?' Vicky slammed him against the wall surprising force. 'What have you done, for God's sake?'

'Nothing. For once in my life I've done nothing.'

Vicky looked past him, into the shattered living room. 'What happened here?'

'A lunatic happened. The woman who took Max, she works for Sammy. He'll be fine. They won't touch him.'

'Why are they doing this?'

'Look, let me make a coffee and—'

'I don't want a bloody coffee! Get this Sammy person on the phone, Roy. Explain to him that Max isn't like other little boys. Tell him Max is special. That he needs his mummy...'

Her face crumpled and she buried herself into Roy's chest. He hesitated, then he held her close, her tears damp on his T-shirt, her arms wrapped about his waist. Roy closed his eyes, captivated by the familiar scent of her skin, her hair, the warmth of her embrace. Right then he missed her so much his chest ached. Then he thought about Max and his mood turned dark.

'We'll get him back, Vicks. I promise. It's leverage, that's all.'

She looked at Roy with bloodshot eyes, fat tears rolling across the delicate rise of her cheeks. 'Why is he doing this?'

'Come with me.'

He took her hand and led her into the kitchen. He sat her down at the kitchen table, where Vicky had once decided they would eat their meals, where Roy had sulked because he couldn't watch TV with his food on a tray. Vicky had won that battle. Vicky always won.

He boiled the kettle, poured two mugs, and placed one in front of her.

'I told you, I don't want coffee,' she sniffed.

Roy didn't argue. He settled in the chair opposite, sipped his brew.

'That day at the school, that was the day all this started. I hadn't seen Sammy for years but he came looking for me...'

Roy told her everything—well, almost everything. He left poor Yasin out of it. That would only make things worse. By the time he was finished twenty minutes had passed. Vicky grilled him for another ten. It was then she asked about Frank.

'No, Frank's got nothing to do with it. He came to

tell me about Jimmy. About his death.'

'What?'

'I was right, Vicks. Jimmy didn't go missing in Baghdad. Look.' He showed her the St Christopher around his neck. 'He was killed down on the Iraqi coast. It was all covered up. Frank said he was working at some secret place out in the desert but I'm not—'

'Roy, wait.' She reached out, laid gentle fingers on his hand. 'I'm sorry about Jimmy, but we have to focus on Max. That's our immediate priority, okay?'

'Yeah, of course.'

'So, what do we do now?'

'You should go back to work—' He caught the look on her face. 'Okay, home then. I'll go see Sammy, pick Max up. He'll be home by teatime, I promise.' Roy nearly gagged on his own lie but he had to buy some time, just in case things got messy. Across the table Vicky closed her eyes and took a very deep breath.

'Okay, Roy. We'll play it your way for now, but if Max isn't home by six I'm calling the police. Tell your friend this isn't Brazil or Colombia; we don't snatch children off the streets here. And let him know I'm a journalist. I won't be intimidated.'

Her blood was up, the fury of a lioness deprived of her cub. But Sammy was the man with the rifle, the big game hunter.

'I'll tell him. And don't say anything to anyone until you speak to me. Not even Nate.'

'Christ, if he found out—' She twisted the straps of her handbag, the blood draining from her knuckles.

This time it was Roy who reached out.

'Hey, we'll get Max back. I promise.'

He could see she wanted to believe him but the doubt lingered. She got to her feet.

'I'm going home. Call me the second you have news.'

Roy watched her from the balcony until she'd disappeared off the estate. There was no way Vicky would last until six. And when normality returned, he doubted she'd ever let him alone with Max again. It wouldn't matter anyway. After this, America would be the best place for all of them.

He grabbed a coat and slammed the front door behind him. For the first time in Roy's life he had absolutely no idea what the next few hours, or days, or weeks, had in store for him. He was scared, not for himself, but for his son, and for Vicky too. He'd been a poor husband, a distant father. This time things would be different.

This time he wouldn't let them down.

'Focus, Keyes, focus.'

Josh heard the snapping of Beeton's fingers, his gravelly voice filling the soundproofed war room.

'I'm sorry, please continue,' he mumbled.

He was seated alone at the conference table, a deer caught in a truck's headlights as Beeton's angry scowl filled half the wall-mounted TV screen. The other half was taken up by the icy visage of Lund, a high-definition tag-team ragging on Josh's ass. There were others there too, shadows in the background, a sense of intense activity humming down the dark fibre from Denver. The Transition was drawing closer. Then he saw Beeton's eyes narrow, his thick black eyebrows knitting together.

'This situation is completely unacceptable, Keyes. You've had every resource made available to you and yet Marshall is still on the loose. Not only that, now he has this.' He shook a sheaf of papers in a large fist.

Josh studied his own copy of the technical incident summary spread out across the table in front of him. It had been spat out of the room's big laser printer just a moment ago. The pages were still warm, smooth beneath his fingertips. Most of it didn't make much sense but what it symbolised was the ass-fucking Frank had given him. His forced his mind to focus, his finger tracing the text on the page.

'Okay, so he used Cohen's account to get in. His PC was probably unlocked when Marshall killed him.'

'The technicians have confirmed this,' Lund said. 'Professor Cohen's email account was backed up and copied to an external drive. Those emails go back almost two years. In addition he copied the professor's data store, over forty gigabytes of the most sensitive data, much of it referring to the Messina program. Committee members have been directly referenced. Do you comprehend the severity of the situation, Mister Keyes?'

Even over a scrambled line and nearly five thousand miles away, Lund's voice was like an ice-cold shower. Her thin face was expressionless, her body clothed in her customary uniform of tailored black suit and white buttoned-to-the-collar shirt. Auschwitz chic, Josh decided. Next to her, Beeton's fist thumped down onto the table.

'That son-of-a-bitch now has proof of Messina. He's got names, dates, locations, every goddam thing.'

Josh wanted to fire back, to vent his own frustration. He wasn't a cop, or an investigator. This assignment should never have been given to him. He thought Beeton and Lund might be getting some heat too, but not the kind that would see them demoted to a burial detail in Queens, or watchtower guard at a FEMA camp. That would be Josh's fate, if this thing didn't get resolved. His eyes roamed the tech report, the jargon about port interaction and processor spiking, about key drives and network packets. Cohen's computer was a melted heap of junk when he'd seen it. The fact that Frank might've hacked it and stolen data didn't register with him or Villiers. They were hunters, and their quarry was in flight; they didn't have time to sift through the charred remains of Cohen's office. Someone had thought about it though, probably Doctor Wyman. An IT forensic team had been alerted, a myriad of systems analysed, the final report spread across the table in front of him. Josh cursed the security team at Copse Hill. Frank had breezed in, killed Cohen, stolen data, and escaped right under their noses. Fucking amateurs. He hoped Webber was still alive when they'd thrown him into the incinerator. Beeton's voice interrupted his murderous vision.

'Keyes,' he barked, 'are you listening?'

'Sorry, the feed broke up there for a moment.'

'Well make sure you hear this. The Committee is deeply troubled by the incident over there. A decision has been made. An investigation team will fly to London in the next couple of days. You'll remain in London with your team and hand over to the senior investigator on arrival. You'll take your orders from him and provide muscle until this business with Marshall is finished. Is that understood?'

'Yes.'

'Good. In the meantime, keep looking.'

'What about the data?'

'That is not your concern, Mister Keyes. Your only function now is to assist others. That is all.'

The screen went blank.

Josh felt a ball of cold fear forming in his gut. An investigation team, probably made up of former federal agents. They would do the job right. They would hunt Frank down in that methodical cop way, find him, deliver him alive. Then Frank would be squeezed for every scrap of his story. If that happened, it was game over for Josh. He had a mental image of uber-efficient FBI types packing their gear, hurrying en masse towards a waiting aircraft. The clock was ticking. Josh was running out of time.

He left the war room. In the basement kitchenette he made himself a coffee. He wasn't that hungry—the videoconference with Beeton and Lund had robbed him of his appetite—but he considered eating something to keep his energy levels up. He opened the refrigerator, looked inside. The trays were filled with fresh food but none of it appealed. He swung the door closed. Ears stood in the doorway.

'What's the word from Denver?'

'Standard brief,' Josh lied. There was no point in undermining his own authority just yet. Not while there was still a chance. 'Anything on the wires?'

'Nothing that interests us.'

Josh felt like punching the walls. Or Ears. Anyone would do. He had forty-eight hours, seventy-two tops, before the G-Men got here. Then it was over.

Ears remained in the doorway, watching him.

'Don't let me keep you. We still got a target to find.'

The former Marine stood his ground. 'I wanted to bring something to your attention.'

For the first time Josh noticed he had a sheaf of papers in his hand. 'What is it?'

'A while back you ordered a thorough evaluation of the Richmond area; sensitive installations, key personnel, all within a ten mile radius.'

'And?'

'We came up with nothing.'

Josh felt like hitting him again. 'Thanks for the reminder.'

'I did a little more digging, sir. I made a request to access TDL's employee databases, focussing on Security Division records. They're regularly groomed for security reasons so I had the tape backups retrieved from storage and—'

'Just get to the point,' Josh growled.

Ears held out the papers. 'I got a hit on a zip code. A former military contractor of ours had a transfer facility set up from his TDL payroll account to a bank in the Kingston area. That's not far from Richmond. I did some more digging; turns out the guy was assigned to Terra Petroleum in Iraq. A James Sullivan, deceased. Frank Marshall wrote the report into his death. It's all there.'

Josh tore the pages from the man's fingers. He scanned the text, his heart racing. Sullivan was a Brit, shot while trying to escape the Terra compound. Frank had ordered an investigation into a potential security breach. *Holy fucking shit.* It rang a bell rang somewhere inside Josh's head, an incident that occurred while he was on leave Stateside. He checked the dates; Frank had gone AWOL a short time later. He devoured the pages. James Sullivan's next-of-kin address sang to Josh like a chorus of angels.

'Get Villiers down here now.'

Back in the war room Josh pulled up a map of southwest London on the big screen. He entered the zip code and zoomed in on a cluster of apartment blocks. Villiers marched in and stood beside him. He squinted at the map.

'The Fitzroy Estate? What's this about?'

'Fresh intel. You know this area?'

'Vaguely.'

Josh scribbled on a Post-it note. 'Get surveillance

up and running on that address. Do background checks too, occupants, financials, landline, Internet usage.'

'You think Marshall's there?'

'It's possible. Priority number one is to lock this Fitzroy place down and find out who and what's going on inside that apartment. Get your guys moving.'

Villiers left the room. The next report Josh filed had to be the one announcing Frank's death. Failing that, he was a dead man himself.

But part of Josh was intrigued. What business did Frank have with a dead Brit contractor? The guy had been shot and killed while gathering intelligence on Messina. Fast-forward three years and Frank is doing the same thing at Copse Hill. How were they connected? Was Frank a part of it? Is that why he was so fucked up back then?

Josh pondered it for a moment then decided he didn't care. Whatever business Frank had with Sullivan it had to remain just that, a mystery. Hundreds of contractors had worked on Messina and associated programs over the years. Some had died, victims of accidents, firefights, health issues, so Sullivan's premature death was not unusual. Except for the circumstances. Sullivan was spying. Frank was a spy. Josh had been tight with Frank for many years. Josh couldn't—or wouldn't—find Frank. Go figure.

The can of worms had to be buried deep. He had to locate Frank before the investigators arrived in the UK.

Then he had to kill him.

Fast.

Chapter Eighteen

When Roy got to Sammy's nightclub the heavy black doors were closed.

He jammed his finger on the intercom button and left it there for a good ten seconds. A voice crackled from the speaker.

'What?'

Roy peered into the camera lens. 'I'm here to see Sammy.'

There was a short delay before one of the doors was yanked open. A man motioned him inside. He was rock band thin, with shoulder-length hair and a goatee beard. He wore a retro T-shirt with 'The Who' emblazoned across the front. Roy trailed behind him until they reached the stairwell at the back of the club.

'You know where you're going?'

Roy nodded.

He puffed upstairs and paused outside Sammy's office, steeling himself for what was going to be a difficult confrontation. It swung open and Tank gestured him inside with a flick of her braided Mohican.

Sammy was in the far corner of the room, watering a palm with a brass can. He wore jeans and a yellow Ralph Lauren polo shirt, a chunky silver watch hanging like a bracelet around his wrist, no shoes on his feet. When he saw Roy he smiled.

'There he is. I was wondering how long it'd take before you put it together.'

Tank motioned Roy to raise his arms and gave him a pat down.

'Can't be too careful,' Sammy explained. 'Emotions running high and all that.'

'Where's Max?'

'He's safe. For now.'

'Please, Sammy, you don't have to do this.'

'Don't I?'

Sammy's tone signalled caution. Riling Derek had been a bad idea. Doing the same to Sammy would prove fatal. He kept his mouth shut as Sammy sat down behind his desk. He leafed through the morning post, inspecting each item as if he were a forensic scientist at a crime scene. Above Sammy's head, the cold, indifferent eyes of the Fusilier met his own. Roy cleared his throat.

'Please, Sammy. He's six years old. He's very fragile.'

Sammy ignored him. He inspected the contents of several envelopes before leaning back in his chair and eyeing Roy.

'I had a visitor yesterday, here at the club. He made quite a scene at the door, shouting my name for everyone in a three-fucking-mile radius to hear. Guess who that mystery caller was?'

'Listen, it wasn't my—'

Sammy cupped a theatrical hand over his ear. 'Not your fault? Is that what you were going to say?'

Roy felt the sweat beginning to form under his baseball cap. He whipped it off, cuffed his brow. 'Derek trashed the flat, Sammy. He wrecked everything, smashed my TV, ripped up all my family pictures, bashed me up. Look at my face, for Christ's sake. He even took a shit on the floor.'

'He should've charged you for home improvements.' Sammy shook his head slowly. 'All you had to do was keep him sweet. Babysit him.'

'I tried. I did everything you asked. I waited on him hand and foot. Look, I don't want to get out of line here, Sammy. I know he's your friend but...' Roy lowered his voice, as if the man himself was somewhere nearby, watching, listening. 'Well, the thing is, Derek's lost it. I mean he's gone proper nuts. When I tried to stop him walking out he attacked me with a lump of wood. I thought he was going to kill me, Sammy. He lost it because he couldn't reach me on the phone. You know, the one that Yasin took.'

Roy dropped his eyes, fiddled with the cap in his hands. He'd broached the subject in the only way he knew how, working his story just so he could mention Yasin's name. Sammy didn't bat an eyelid. Instead he tossed a brown envelope across the desk.

'The plan's changed. Here.'

There was a brand new UK passport inside. Roy flicked to the picture and Derek's clean-cut image stared back at him, his head and cheeks neatly shaved, clothed in a crisp white shirt and dark tie. A different person entirely.

'Look, Sammy, I'll help get Derek out, but I have to get Max back first. Vicky is beside herself with worry, and if I don't get him back—'

'You'll what?'

Roy twisted his cap with sweaty palms. 'He needs his mum, Sammy. He'll be terrified, and Vicky's not a patient person.'

'Meaning?'

He hesitated, just for a moment. Then he said, 'If I don't leave here with Max she's going to the police.'

He let the words hang there, praying Sammy would think twice.

Across the desk Sammy smiled and shook his head. 'Now, now, Roy, you of all people should know that threatening me is a *very* stupid thing to do.'

'I'm not, Sammy, I swear. All I'm saying is that Vicky's headstrong. Max is her life.'

'Well she needs to understand that talking to anyone could be extremely detrimental to her health. A phone call, that's all it would take. Then one day she'll come home and there'll be a couple of crack heads waiting for her. And they'll go to work, Roy, big style. They'll rape her first, that's a given, every orifice violated. Then they'll cut her, that lovely face of hers, then her tits, her legs. You know what crack heads are like, Roy, there're enough of them on the Fitzroy. Animals, for the most part, and they'll do *anything* for a rock. So try to imagine what they'll do for fifty. Or a hundred. And after it's all over, well, Vicky will be a mess. Physically of course, but more importantly she'll be head-fucked for life. It'll never let up either. Once she's recovered from her ordeal she'll be followed in the street, felt up on the Tube, spat at, dirty phone calls at home, at work, scumbags ringing her doorbell all hours of the day and night until one day it'll all be too much for her and—well, I'm sure you get the picture.'

Sammy swivelled back and forth in his chair as he spoke. There was a glint in his eye, a brutal smile twisting the corners of his mouth. He was enjoying himself, Roy realised.

'And as for that spastic kid of yours, well, I know someone up north who'll take him off my hands for a few quid. The sort of bloke who gets a hard-on driving by playgrounds. The kid will disappear, Roy. You'll never see him again, not until you get the call to identify his brutalised little corpse. That's how it'll go, if that slag wife of yours goes to the police.'

Roy stood rooted to floor, every vicious word, every horrific promise a slap to his face. He heard Tank sniggering behind him and wondered what sort of person would find any of that funny. He swallowed hard then spoke.

'Vicky won't say anything, I promise. Just let me take Max home. Please.'

Sammy swivelled to a stop. 'Brace yourself for some bad news.'

Roy felt the blood drain from his face. 'What d'you mean?'

'Calm down,' Sammy grinned. 'The kid's fine. The thing is, I haven't got him. Derek has.'

It took Roy a moment to digest what Sammy had just told him. 'Derek?'

'That's right. Insurance, he said. Insisted I hand your boy over. For some reason he's a bit concerned that you might not hold up your end of the bargain. Actually, the arrangement suits me. I didn't want the kid drooling all over the Persian anyway.'

Roy heard Tank laugh again. 'Where is he?'

'He's holed up with some friends out near the airport, ready for his big getaway.'

'Where?'

'A travellers' site in Iver.'

Roy's stomach lurched. 'A gypsy camp?'

'Correct. A smart move as far as Derek's concerned. No one likes gypsies. Everyone gives them a wide berth, including the law.' A phone on Sammy's desk warbled softly. He checked the display, muted the ring. 'Derek knows 'em from way back. I know their top boy by reputation, a bloke called Jim Connor—*Big* Jim Connor, to give him his full title. Used to be a champion bare-knuckle fighter, ran a lot of nightclub doors in Berkshire. Huge fucker, wild too. And therein lies the problem.'

Sammy tapped a finger on his desk.

'I can't afford to have a disgruntled Derek knocking about with Connor for the next few days, getting liquored up and gobbing off about me and my business. The fact is, if Jim gets a sniff of opportunity the first place he'll head for is here, and I can't go to war with that lot, you understand me, Roy? So I told Derek that everything was ready. The plan's on for tonight.'

Sammy's words faded. All Roy could think of was Max, surrounded by strangers, becoming more withdrawn with each passing hour, desperate for his mother, for anyone who knew him and loved him. Maybe even Roy.

He glanced at his watch; almost eleven. Max had been gone for two hours already. 'So what happens now?'

Sammy grinned. 'Enthusiasm, I like it. You'll pick Derek up tonight—'

'Tonight? No, that's—'

'Shut your mouth. When you get to the camp, give Derek his passport and tell him that the ticket and boarding pass are waiting at Heathrow. Then you'll take him to meet Tank at the Holiday Inn near Heathrow. It's the one right on the M4 junction. When you get there, drop Derek off outside then drive to the furthest, darkest spot in the car park and wait. Derek will go to Tank's room, take a shower, and change into fresh clothes...'

Roy's head was starting to throb again, a dull ache at the back of his skull. Maybe he was hurt after all. He should probably go to the hospital, but that could wait. Max needed him. He heard Sammy's voice, refocused.

'Once Derek is presentable Tank will escort him to the car. Derek will sit in the front, next to you. You'll start the engine, and when Derek fastens his seatbelt, that'll be the signal.'

'What signal?'

'The signal for Tank to strangle our little friend to death. Once he's departed this world Tank will tell you where you need to go. Questions?'

Roy stared at Sammy, expecting a laugh, a smile,

anything to indicate it was a joke. But he knew it wasn't.

'You're going to kill him?'

'Like you said, Derek's become a liability.' Sammy kicked a bare foot onto the desk and scratched his sole. 'I thought the midnight phone calls were a bit weird at first. Then it was every night, rambling for hours on end. After smashing your place up and reaching out to Connor and his crew, I've decided enough is enough. There'll be no tearful farewell. No flying off into the sunset.'

Sammy swung his foot off the desk.

'The fact is, Derek isn't the man I once knew. Sooner or later that crazy fucker will get himself nicked, and when he does he'll be staring down the barrel of a sentence that'll probably see him off this earth. He won't like that. He'll do a deal, start talking. And I can't have that, Roy. In any case, the ticket and boarding pass proved to be a bridge too far, even for a man of my means. Fucking Muslims, eh? Bottom line is, Derek's got to go.'

Roy stood in stunned silence. When he finally opened his mouth to speak, he didn't recognise the sound of his own voice. 'You want me to take part in a murder?'

'You're just driving. Tank will do the wet work.'

'I can't do it.'

'Course you can. You've done it before.'

Roy frowned, baffled by Sammy's response.

'Don't be modest, Roy. Here, let me remind you.'

Sammy opened a drawer and produced a clear

Ziploc bag. He held it up, like a goldfish won at a fairground. Roy stared at the blood-smeared plastic, at Jimmy's infantry knife inside, his iPhone. 'That's your workmate's claret all over that blade. Bit of your DNA too, I'd imagine. Derek found it when he first got there, stuffed under your mattress. Gave him a good laugh. He told me about it, so I thought I'd take it, just in case it came in handy one day. It certainly did the job on your mate. And your phone, full of pictures of the airport. Gonna be tough to explain all that away.'

'You didn't have to kill him.'

Sammy dropped the bag back into the desk drawer. 'He was a threat.'

'He had a family, kids—'

'Boo-fucking-hoo. Besides, he was blackmailing you. The fuck do you care?'

Roy wilted into a chair. 'Jesus Christ.'

'Even Jesus won't save you if you balls this up. Here.' He tossed a key fob across the desk. 'Your wheels for tonight. Pick it up from here. ID is in the glove box.'

Roy took the Post-it note from Sammy's hand. 'What about Max?'

'You stay focused on Derek. I'll text you the postcode of the gypsy site later, and some flight details. Derek's bound to ask for that. You can sort the kid out tomorrow.'

Roy came off the chair. 'Max won't last the night. He'll be traumatised already. I'm begging you, please, just tell them to let Max go with—'

'Fuck your kid!' Sammy barked. 'You've never given

a shit before. Now you want to be Father of the Year? You fucking hypocrite.' Sammy's face flushed red, the sinews of his neck like rope. 'You fuck this up, Roy, any of it, and it's over. For you, the slag reporter, *and* the spastic. From now on you're going to do exactly what I tell you, without question. Got it?'

Roy nodded.

'Good. Get the fuck out.'

Roy headed for the door without another word. He was back on the street in less than a minute, grateful to be out in the fresh air. It did little to stem the panic building in his chest. How would he tell Vicky that Max was being held prisoner in a gypsy camp? That they wouldn't get their little boy back for another twenty-four hours, maybe more? What he'd told Sammy was true; a trauma like this could send Max so deep he may never resurface.

Once he told Vicky, she would go to the police. That was a certainty.

Roy headed for the bus stop that would take him north over Putney Bridge. The clock was ticking. He needed to get home, change into his uniform, then get round to Vicky's and break the news. From that point on they'd both be in uncharted territory, but the only thing that mattered now was Max.

He boarded a bus and took a seat upstairs as it rumbled over the bridge. He looked down at the choppy grey waters of the River Thames and considered his options. Sammy, Derek, Connor and his gypsies; he was no match for people like that, and he certainly couldn't go to the police. That meant he *had* no options. He'd be locked into Sammy forever, the constant threat of buried bodies and bloodied knives hanging over his head. Maybe it'd be better if he *was* nicked, but Roy realised that the ordeal would simply continue in prison. He remembered the pictures Sammy had showed him, his unknown drinking companions, villains, ex-cons, whatever they were. In or out of prison, Sammy would find him, would send men like that after him.

He squeezed against the window as a rotund woman laden with shopping bags dropped into the seat next to him. Come the dawn he'd be tied to two murders. His life was floating in the toilet bowl with Sammy's hand on the chain. Things couldn't get any worse, but the strange thing was, Roy didn't care.

All he could think of was little Max, held captive in a squalid gypsy camp, alone, terrified. Desperate.

Roy would gladly kill them all to get him back.

Chapter Nineteen

The Toyota Land Cruiser was parked outside a car wash business just off the Fulham Road in west London.

When he arrived two African men in coveralls and wellington boots were polishing off the vehicle's dark bodywork. The Toyota was only a year old, glossy black paint reflected in the water pooled around the large, gleaming wheels, a set of chunky roll bars wrapped around the front grill. Roy wondered if it was stolen, then decided it wasn't. Sammy wouldn't risk tonight's enterprise on a nicked motor.

He climbed inside. The door closed with a solid *thunk*, the muffled interior smelling of citrus. He leaned over, checked the glove box. Inside was the fake ID, the registration document, a paid council tax bill, an HSBC debit card. He started the vehicle, guided it up towards the main road and eased out into traffic.

Once he got the feel of it he gunned the Toyota all the way to Kingston. He parked at an outlet store, hid the key behind the front wheel, and walked the half mile or so back home. He thought about witnesses and fingerprints, DNA and all the other CSI stuff that could get a person convicted.

He thought about Derek. The Scot was going to die tonight, strangled to death less than three feet away from him. Roy tried to imagine what he would see, the sounds he would hear, and wondered if he could cope with it. It would be nothing like the movies, where a few seconds of mild effort and a soft gurgle was all it took to snuff out a life. No, tonight would be brutal—kicking, screaming, Derek's throat sliced through, blood and bile. Roy decided he would look away, turn up the radio, anything to avoid the spectacle.

He skirted a parade of scruffy shops, the beating heart of the Fitzroy. He shivered as a bank of dark cloud suddenly blotted out the spring sunshine. Shadows crept across the estate, filling the stairwells and the voids between the towering grey buildings. It was an omen, Roy decided, and not a good one.

He ducked into his own stairwell, twisted up the first flight of stairs. A man blocked his way, a big man, grey crew cut, dark coat, jeans. He had a hard face, cold eyes and a square jaw covered with thick grey stubble. Roy mumbled an apology and tried to go around him. The man shoved him hard against the wall. Then there were two others, crowding him, pinning his arms to his sides. Experienced hands went to work, searching him.

'No weapons,' one of them said.

The big man leaned in close to Roy's ear.

'Don't say a word, don't make a sound.'

Grey Beard smelled of soap and cheap cologne, and spoke with a heavy London accent. Roy thought he was about to die right there in the stairwell. That's when he saw the small, flesh-coloured radio receiver lodged in the man's left ear.

Police.

'I'm going to ask you a couple of questions. You'll answer by nodding or shaking your head, do you understand?'

Roy nodded several times.

'Good. Is your name Roy Sullivan?'

A nod.

'Is there anyone in your flat at this moment?'

Roy shook his head. *They've come for Derek.*

'Give me your phone and your door key.'

Roy felt the pressure ease off his right arm and he dug into his pocket.

Grey Beard drilled him with those cold eyes and whispered, 'We're going upstairs now. You'll walk ahead. You'll see two men approaching you from the other end of the balcony. Ignore them. When you get to your front door you'll unlock it and go inside. You'll take three paces—just three—then lie down on the floor. You will make no sound at all and you will not move until you are told. Do you understand?'

Roy nodded again. The man handed him his key, mumbled something into a radio. Then he ordered Roy up the stairs with a pointed finger.

Roy reached the landing on shaky legs. Two men approached him from the other end of the balcony, their hands moving beneath their jackets. Roy thought he caught a glimpse of a sling, the barrel of a gun. *Jesus Christ.* He swallowed hard, tried to ignore them.

He got to his door, fumbled with his key. The men flanked him on either side, three of them crouched low beneath the kitchen window, two in Dwayne's doorway.

Roy began to sweat, scraping the key around the lock, willing it to slide in.

Then it did, and he marched inside, counting—*one, two, three*—he was halfway to the carpet when the men moved past him with barely a sound. He heard a door open, a snort as the smell of shit filled the hallway, then the whispered words, different voices; *clear, clear, clear.*

The tension seemed to drain from the air after that. Roy stayed on the ground for maybe five more minutes as people stepped over him, the front door opening and closing several times, the conversations around him low, urgent. Finally, a pair of scruffy desert boots stopped inches from his nose.

'On your feet.'

Roy did as Grey Beard commanded. Every man around him had a gun in his hand, either a pistol or an automatic weapon. He heard the faint crackle of radios. 'In there,' Grey Beard ordered. Roy entered his wrecked living room, watched by two silent, armed men. Grey Beard righted the sofa.

'Sit.'

Roy complied. Any way he looked at it, it was over. They'd come for Derek, and Roy was glad he wouldn't have to watch a man die, but Sammy's plans were about to come apart and Max was caught in the crossfire. He had no choice. He decided to tell them everything.

The men guarding him wore civilian clothes, but the equipment beneath their jackets looked military-spec, black chest rigs, side arms, extras magazines, radios, the sort of hard-core gear he'd seen Jimmy wear during his Afghan days. Roy was no expert, but they didn't look or act like police.

Then another man stepped into the room. He was wearing jeans, a dark blue jacket with lots of pockets and a black baseball cap embroidered with a bird logo and the words *Arizona Cardinals*. He had dark hair and olive skin, and he radiated authority. He stood directly in front of Roy and unfolded a sheet of paper with a printed mugshot.

Not Derek.

Frank Marshall.

'Do you know this person?'

Roy frowned. The man was American. Then he remembered Frank's voice, the cold warning of his words in the park...

'*People are coming after me.*'

'What people?'

'Bad people. Anyone who gets in their way will die.

Roy forced himself to focus. He had to tell the truth, or a version of it. Enough to convince whoever these men were that he knew nothing. He cautioned himself to keep it simple, to stick as close to the truth as possible. That's what the refugees and asylum seekers did when they arrived in the UK. He had to do the same.

The American waved the picture in his face again.

'Answer me. You know this man?'

'Yes,' Roy replied.

'How do you know him?'

'He said his name was Frank. He came to see me a couple of nights ago.'

Baseball Cap righted an armchair and pulled it close. He sat down on the wide arm, elbows resting on his thighs, his hands clasped together.

'It's Roy, right?'

Roy nodded, the fear rising again. *They knew his name.*

'I'm Josh, with the Federal Bureau of Investigation in the United States.' He pointed to Grey Beard who lingered by the door. 'My colleagues are with the Metropolitan Police.'

Roy smiled and nodded. No last name. No warrant card or ID. He saw a broken coffee mug lying on the floor, repeated the mantra in his head; *Keep Calm and Carry On...*

'We're part of a task force hunting Frank Marshall. Marshall is a very dangerous individual, which is why my men are armed. Do you understand?'

'Of course,' Roy nodded as gravely as he could.

'Good. Where is Marshall now?'

'I don't know. Like I said, he turned up out of the blue.'

'What did he want?'

'He said he had information about my brother Jimmy. He went missing in Iraq three years ago.'

'What information?'

'He wouldn't say. Said he'd bring me proof. I threw him out.'

Josh waved a hand around the room. 'Did he do this?'

'This? No,' Roy forced a chuckle. 'I had a party at the weekend. Things got out of hand.'

'Is that how you got that face?'

'That's right. You should see the other bloke.'

'No time to clean up?'

'I'm waiting for the insurance assessor. You know how long they take.'

'And you live alone?'

'Yes.'

His words sounded hollow. Any minute now this Josh character would slap his face, or punch him, or something. And that would just be the start of it.

'You want a cup of tea? The kettle still works.'

'Not right now,' Josh said. 'What else did Frank say?'

'Not much.'

'Walk me through it. From the first time he made contact.'

Roy massaged his temple, as if summoning up the memory. He imagined the doorbell ringing, a shadow behind the glass, Frank standing in his doorway. 'It was about eleven-thirty at night when he knocked on the door. He said he had information about Jimmy. They both worked for a company called TDL Global. You heard of them?'

'Sure.'

'Anyway, I made him a cup of tea. He struck me as being a bit jumpy, you know, on edge? He started talking, said he knew my brother, but when I asked him to describe him he couldn't. Then he started rambling about Jimmy working out in the desert at some factory.' Roy shook his head. 'I didn't believe a word of it, and he kept going on about God all the time, said we were all sinners and we had to repent. That's when I asked him to leave. I've met a few like him before, you know, nutters, attention seekers. They're all the same, full of shit.'

Josh looked bemused. 'I've seen your website, Roy. You don't believe the official story of your brother's disappearance either.'

Roy felt the blood flush his cheeks.

'I didn't at first. I mean, who leaves the Green Zone on his own, with all them nutjobs running around? But I've spoken to a lot of people over the years, and I think it boils down to the fact that my brother made a single, stupid mistake, that's all. What's he done, this Frank fella?'

'That's not important.'

He could smell Roy's lies, his fear, could probably hear his guts churning. He had to give him something. 'He said he'd be back, said he'd bring proof. Some sort of report.'

He saw Josh's head cock to one side, heard a sudden tension in his voice. 'When?'

'Soon, he said. You're going to protect me from this bloke, right? I don't want him coming back round here.'

'Sure we will.' The American got to his feet. 'Wait here.'

Josh steered Villiers into the cramped kitchen. He peered through the blind, at the deserted balcony, at the second floor apartment in the opposite block that now housed a surveillance team.

'Frank's been here, no doubt. You get anything from the neighbours?'

'They say someone else has been living here recently. Blinds and curtains are always drawn and they've heard chatter through the walls. I wouldn't say they were reliable witnesses but then again this isn't a courtroom. My gut says they're telling the truth.'

'Could be Frank. The time frame fits.'

Villiers shook his head. 'The voice they heard was male, heavy Scottish accent. Yesterday they heard that same voice, shouting and swearing. One of them saw Sullivan's mystery lodger leave. I showed him the picture. It wasn't Frank Marshall.'

'Figures. Taking a shit in some guy's bedroom isn't exactly Frank's MO. So, Sullivan's lying. Why?'

Villiers shrugged, inspecting the contents of the kitchen drawers. 'He lives a quiet life, employed, pays his bills. Separated, no girly bits and pieces in the bathroom. Maybe he's gay. Maybe this Scottish guy was a lover.' He closed the kitchen drawer. 'Who is this Sullivan kid, Josh? What's his connection to Marshall?'

Frank was close, Josh could feel it in his bones. He could also sense the Brit's frustration. He needed Villiers' absolute cooperation now. He closed the gap between them.

'Listen to me, Dave. There are things about to happen that you can't imagine, events on a global scale that'll change everything. Very soon I'll need to call on people, people I can trust —'.

'You can trust me,' Villiers cut in.

Whatever Josh was selling, Villiers already had his hand on his wallet. He wanted in. Badly.

'Your CV's impressive and you've performed well. If I decide to bring you on board it'll mean a move to the States, involvement in some serious operations. It'll also mean personal loyalty to me and the utmost discretion.'

'Whatever it takes,' Villiers said.

'That's good, because if this operation goes bad it will jeopardise future opportunities for both of us. What you see and hear now, you can never repeat to anyone, understand?' Villiers nodded several times. 'Good. You back me up on this, help me terminate Frank, I'll open up a whole new world for you.'

Villiers' eyes shone. 'What do I need to know?'

For the next few minutes Josh explained the link between Frank, Jimmy and Roy Sullivan, making sure he left out the part about Messina. That particular pill would need a little sugar-coating. When he'd finished, Villiers began processing the information.

'If Sullivan is working with Frank, or protecting him in some way, why mention him at all? Frank would know that that kind of information could get a man killed.'

'Good point. And Sullivan said Frank kept mentioning God. The pastor and the witness in Twickenham both confirm the religious angle.'

'So maybe he really has flipped?'

'It's looking likely.'

Did that make Frank more, or less, dangerous? Josh speculated. He glanced at the corkboard on the wall, fingered the utility bills, the fast-food flyers, a USB key drive. 'Still, something's not right with this Sullivan kid.'

Villiers extracted a large kitchen knife from a block on the counter. He ran the blade across his palm. 'I could go to work on him. He doesn't strike me as the type who'd last long.'

Josh shook his head, 'No, let's wait. He said Frank was coming back. When he does we need to be ready. Let's get surveillance up on Sullivan, covert tail, GPS phone track, the works. And we'll need the local cops to back off, in case Frank gets spooked. Can you fix that?'

'I'll get an op order flashed, keep the neighbourhood teams out of the way.'

'Okay. In the meantime we cut the kid loose, see which way he runs. If he's lying about Frank we'll know in the next couple of hours. If that happens, you can get medieval on him.'

Roy thanked Grey Beard for returning his phone. Josh offered him a card.

'That's my direct number. If Marshall makes contact, call me immediately.'

Roy flipped the plain white card over in his hand. The name said *Josh Keyes,* a mobile number scrawled in biro beneath.

'What happens if he turns up at my door again?'

'Act normal. Let him in. Help will be on its way.'

'Okay.'

The men left the room, stepping over the debris. When the last man had gone, Roy ducked into the kitchen. The USB was still there, along with the report, pinned behind a special offer from Domino's Pizza. He flopped into a chair, heart pounding, his thoughts swirling like a sink full of draining water.

Frank was telling the truth.

He *was* being hunted. And the men hunting him, they weren't police. Did that mean the rest of Frank's story was true? If that was the case, Sammy was the least of his problems.

He changed into his work clothes and pulled on a coat. He paused by the front door and looked around. It didn't feel like home any more. It had been violated, fond memories banished like exorcised ghosts. Not that it mattered. All that mattered was Max.

He closed the front door behind him. Dwayne and his friend were on the balcony, smoking cigarettes instead of the usual weed, no doubt mindful of Roy's recent houseguests. He wondered if any of them had spoken to Dwayne. When Dwayne gave him a respectful nod, he guessed they had. Dwayne cocked his chin over the balcony.

'There's two of 'em down there, in a grey Mondeo. Walk to the stairs, duck down, then double back. Works every time.'

Roy mumbled his thanks, did as instructed.

A minute later he was jogging across the estate, trying hard to resist the urge to look behind him. He entered the Fitzroy's bustling convenience store, striding towards the counter at the back. Behind it, three Asian men of varying ages served a steady stream of customers, bagging purchases, printing lottery tickets and reaching for alcohol or cigarettes in the display behind them. One of them, a slick-haired man in his twenties, smiled when he saw Roy.

'More Scotch, my friend?'

Roy glanced over his shoulder. 'I think someone's following me, Raj. You got another way out of here?'

He led Roy through a fly strip curtain and into the storeroom beyond, twisting through a maze of bottled water, tinned goods and pet food until they reached the back door. Raj hit an alarm code and pushed the door open. 'Who's after you?'

'Don't know. A couple of dodgy-looking blokes have been hanging around the block. I think they're watching me.'

There was a van parked in the narrow alleyway outside, its red paintwork faded, bodywork dented in a dozen places. Raj tugged the side door open, waking the man behind the wheel.

'Manish will take you off the estate.'

The bearded Manish bolted upright in his seat.

'Thanks, Raj.'

'Come back and see us,' he smiled. 'Doing a special on Johnny Walker this week.'

The van grumbled into life and drove out of the alleyway. Roy stayed low in the back. It stunk of petrol and rotten vegetables.

Manish eyed him in the rear view mirror. 'Where to?'

Roy told him, and a few minutes later he was crossing the outlet car park and climbing into the Toyota. He drove to Kingston and parked in the multi-storey car park beneath John Lewis. He made a call from a public phone at the train station then switched his Blackberry off. From there it was a brisk ten-minute walk along the river to Vicky's smart apartment block. He pushed the buzzer and waved at the video camera.

He held his breath.

The gate hummed and swung inwards.

Chapter Twenty

When the lift doors rumbled open, a desperate Vicky was waiting for him.

'Where's Max?'

'There's been a complication—'

She spun around and marched back to her apartment. Roy went after her as she crossed the open plan living area. She was moving quickly towards the mobile phone sitting on a glass dining table. Roy got there first. He snatched at it and held it behind him.

'No police, Vicky.'

'I'm not playing this game again, Roy. Give me that phone!'

Her eyes were raw and bloodshot, and when she held out her hand it trembled. Roy guessed she'd probably spent most of the morning crying. So he lied.

'Max is okay. I spoke to him. But we can't involve the police. I've been warned.'

'What d'you mean you spoke to him? Where is he?'

Roy hesitated. 'He's okay, Vicks, that's all I can tell—'

'Where is he?'

She screamed the words so loudly that Roy flinched. Then she flew at him, her hands slapping at his face, his arms. Roy managed to grab her wrists and spin her around, catching her in a bear hug.

'Let me go!' she cried, twisting and squirming in his arms. Then she was still, her breath coming in rapid gasps. 'Let me go, or so help me I won't stop screaming until the police get here.'

Roy released her, picked the phone up off the floor. 'He's my son too, Vicky. I'd lay down my life for him, but we can't call the police, because—' He checked himself. If he told her the real reason he didn't think he'd be able to stop her. 'If we do, Sammy will never let up. He'll never stop chasing us. Is that the life you want?'

'I just want him back,' Vicky whispered, and then she broke down.

Roy held her as she sobbed. They stayed that way for several minutes, until Vicky's tears were spent and Roy finally, reluctantly, released her.

'C'mon, sit down. I'll make us a coffee.'

He flipped the kettle on and rummaged around the cupboards. Vicky perched herself on the arm of the couch.

'So what happens now?'

As Roy opened his mouth to answer a melodic tone filled the apartment. He saw the video entry system on the wall light up, a face partially hidden beneath the peak of a baseball cap.

'I don't know, but this man might be able to help us.'

Vicky got to her feet. 'Who is it?'

'A friend. Buzz him in.'

A minute later Roy was making the introductions.

'You're the man from the park,' Vicky sniffed, squeezing her nose with a tissue.

The big American swept the baseball cap off his head. 'Frank Marshall, ma'am.'

Roy made more coffee and they settled around the dining table. He spent the next few minutes telling Frank about Sammy and Derek, the blackmail, the airport plan. And about Max.

'You've met him, Frank. He's a special boy, vulnerable. We have to get him back.'

'What is it you want from me?'

'Yesterday, in the cafe, I wasn't sure if you were telling the truth. It's a lot to take in.'

'I understand. And like I told you, I shouldn't be here. I could get you killed.'

'What?'

Roy held up a hand. 'Just wait, Vicks.' He turned back to Frank. 'After you left I went home. There were some men waiting for me. At first I thought it was the police, but then I realised they were the people you talked about, Frank. And they were looking for you.'

'A hunter team,' Frank said.

'They scared the shit out of me. They had guns, radios, the lot. The one in charge was an American, FBI he said. He gave me his number, in case you showed up. Said you were wanted for all sorts of stuff.'

Roy slid the card across the glass table.

Frank flipped it over. Sat back in his chair. 'Josh Keyes. Son of a bitch.'

'You know him?'

Frank nodded, slipped the card into his pocket. 'He worked for me for many years. Makes sense to put him on the team. Tell me what he said.'

Vicky's fist slammed down on the glass, rattling the coffee mugs. 'Enough!' she yelled. She looked at each of them in turn. 'We have to get Max back, that's it. Nothing else matters. D'you hear me?'

Roy held up his hand. 'Take it easy—'

'Don't tell me to take it easy! I swear to God, Roy, if you don't stop your bullshit and focus on Max, I'm going straight out that door to the nearest police station.'

Roy saw the pain, the fear in her eyes. He felt it too.

'Listen to me, Vicky. If you go to the police we may never see Max again.' He turned to face Frank. 'I need to know if it's true—'

'If what's true?' Vicky said.

Roy ignored her.

'I need to know if everything you said—about Angola, about Messina and the Transition—is true. I need you to swear it, Frank, because if it's real then none of us can run, not until Max is back with us safe and sound. And if we don't get him back then Jimmy's death, your journey here, your mission, will have been for nothing. Or you can tell me it's not real, and I'll pick up the phone and take my chances with the law.'

Frank stared right back at Roy. 'Everything I said is real. You've got six months, at the outside.'

'Are you married, Frank?'

The American looked at Vicky, shook his head.

'Any children?'

Another shake.

'I didn't think so. Because if you did you'd know

something about the pain of a child ripped away from you. If you did you wouldn't be sat here discussing God knows what else because none of that would be important by comparison.' She leaned a little closer, cuffing the tears than ran freely down her face. 'My son has been kidnapped, do you understand that? I want him back. I *need* him back. That's all I care about, getting my little boy—'

Her face crumpled again and she buried it into her folded arms.

Frank shifted in his seat, cleared his throat. 'I know this is tough but Roy's right, ma'am. Calling the cops will merely complicate things and jeopardise all your lives. Okay, so we get your boy back. After that you have to run.'

Vicky looked up. 'You mean from this Sammy person? I don't care, I just want—'

'No,' Roy interrupted. 'Whether we save Max or not—'

'Don't say that!'

'You're not listening, for Christ's sake! Something terrible is going to happen. The people hunting Frank, they're the same people who killed Jimmy, who killed all those people in the World Trade Centre on Nine Eleven. And they're not finished, Vicky, not by a long shot. Millions are going to die.'

'Billions,' Frank corrected.

Vicky shook her head. 'Wait, stop. What are you both talking about?'

Frank pulled his chair closer to the table. 'Have you

ever heard of the New World Order?'

'Of course I have.'

Roy screwed up his face. 'Really?'

'It came up at uni a few times. There were lots of discussions about it, conspiracy theories about totalitarianism and shadow governments, except they didn't call it the New World Order. I think they call it the Transnational Class, or something like that.'

'Transnational *Corporate* Class,' Frank said.

'That's it.'

Roy stared at Vicky with newfound respect. 'How the hell do you know all this stuff? I'd never heard of it.'

'You won't find it in *Nuts.*' She turned back to Frank 'What's all that got to do with Max?'

So Frank told her.

As he spoke, Roy watched Vicky's face mirror his own reactions to Frank's story; disbelief, doubt, and ultimately, a dreadful acceptance. She asked questions that Roy never thought of asking, about global trade agreements, the destabilisation of governments, hidden agendas. He recognised some stuff, names, newsworthy events, but most of it went over his head. He watched Vicky become animated, challenging Frank, forcing him to quantify his arguments. It was like watching two chess grandmasters do battle, but when it was finally over, when Vicky had expended her journalistic energy, it was clear that Frank had her in checkmate.

'It can't be true,' she whispered. 'They can't do that.'

'They can. And they will.'

'That's why we can't involve the police,' Roy said. 'The investigations will tie us up for months. They might even involve social workers, and you know what'll happen then. They'll try and find ways to take Max from us —'

'I get it,' Vicky said, holding up her hands. She propped her elbows on the table, rubbed her face. 'So, what do we do?'

'We get your boy back,' Frank told her. He looked at Roy. 'Where is he?'

Roy held out his palm, showed Frank the biro scrawl. 'Sammy texted me the postcode.' He glanced at Vicky, steeled himself. 'It's a travellers' site, not too far from Heathrow airport.'

Roy cringed as Vicky jolted in her chair. 'He's where?'

'He's okay, Vicky.'

'Jesus Christ, a gypsy camp? Oh my God, Roy.'

Frank raised an eyebrow. 'What's a gypsy camp?'

Roy explained. Frank nodded, made notes on a pad. 'Where's the data? Is it safe?'

'Here.' Roy dug into his pocket, pushed the USB drive across the glass.

'What's this?' Vicky asked, picking up the small black device. Frank told her. 'Jesus Christ, Frank, why not go straight to the media, the authorities?' Frank told her that too. She held it in the palm of her hand, like a precious stone. 'We'll deal with this later. Now, can we *please* talk about Max?'

Frank Googled the postcode of the travellers' site on his phone. He studied the map for several minutes, then addressed Vicky, 'I'm going to need you to go out, make a few purchases.'

'Like hell. I need to be here, in case someone calls.'

Roy held up his phone. 'No one's going to call, Vicky. It's turned off.'

Vicky was horrified. 'Well turn it on, for God's sake! What if Max—'

'He can't turn it on,' Frank cut in. 'They're monitoring his signal.'

'This is ridiculous.'

Frank rapped his knuckles on the glass. 'This isn't a game, Vicky. If you want to get your boy back I'm going to need your help. Whatever I tell you, whatever I ask, you and Roy must accept it without question. All our lives depend on it.'

Vicky held Frank's gaze for a long time. Finally she said, 'Promise me you'll bring him home safe, Frank. Just promise me that.'

He reached out, squeezed her hand. 'As God is my witness I promise.'

He checked his notes, tapped a pen on Roy's lifeless Blackberry. 'Okay, right now Josh will be trying to reacquire your cell phone signal. The fact that you've shaken a potential tail and gone offline will make him highly suspicious. Vicky, I need you to go into town, where it's busy, and switch Roy's phone back on. You don't need to make a call, just leave it on. Wait ten minutes and switch it off. They'll think that Roy has a problem with his battery or maybe there's an issue with the local repeater towers. It's not unheard of, so it'll add to the confusion. Then I need you to make some purchases and get back here as soon as possible. Roy and I will be going over the plan.'

Roy raised an eyebrow. 'You've got a plan?'

'A seed of one.'

'That doesn't sound too reassuring,' Vicky said.

Frank smiled at her. 'Trust me, it'll be okay. Here, take this.' He tore a page out of his notepad and handed it to Vicky. 'And find a bolthole for the three of you. Somewhere out of town, a rental, a busy hotel, a place none of you has ever been before. We'll rendezvous there in three days, when it's all over and the dust has settled a little. Book it for a month at least. And tell no one.'

Vicky looked horrified. '*A month?*'

'Correct. Use cash and a false name to make the booking. And buy a couple of burners.'

Roy and Vicky shared a look. 'Burners?'

'Cell phones, the throwaway type.'

'You mean pay-as-you-go?'

'Whatever.'

Vicky pushed her chair back without another word. She tugged on an overcoat, stood in front of the hall mirror, checked her face, her hair. 'I'll see you in a bit.'

Roy stood behind her, gave her arm a reassuring squeeze. Frank opened the apartment door and checked outside. Empty.

'Remember, turn the phone on in town and not

before. Wait ten minutes, then turn it off again. Grab the stuff on the list and get back here pronto. Piece of cake.'

Vicky took a deep breath. 'I got it.'

Frank closed the door behind her and led Roy back to the table. They sat down.

'There's something you're not telling me,' Frank said.

Roy was impressed. 'How did you know?'

'I'm good at this.'

'It's about my boss and this guy Derek. One's been murdered, the other's about to be. I didn't want Vicky to know.' Roy spent some time filling in the details while Frank asked questions and made more notes. 'Have you really got a plan?'

Frank put down his pen. 'The primary objective is to get your boy. The secondary objective is to deal with the potential repercussions. After tonight, no one can come after you. No cops, no hunter team, no one. You need to be in the clear, be free to make preparations before the Transition begins. It also occurred to me that I could use this situation to throw The Committee a curve ball of my own. Does Vicky have a computer? A printer?'

'I guess.'

'Good. We need to copy that data. Now, what I have in mind is audacious. There'll be no room for hesitation or compassion. People are going to die tonight, and you might have to do some killing. Can you handle that?'

Roy's eyes narrowed. 'Max is all I care about. Fuck everyone else.'

'That's my boy,' Frank smiled. He checked his watch. 'Okay, we don't have long. We need to go over a couple of things before Vicky gets back. The details may not sit well with her.'

'Don't underestimate Vicks. She's tough.'

'I get that, but let's keep things simple. Now, pay attention...'

It was another two hours before Vicky returned. She dumped several shopping bags on the dining table. 'I got everything,' she puffed.

'Excellent. What about the phone?'

'I did as you asked. It rang several times while it was on. I didn't answer it.'

'Good work.'

Vicky emptied the bags out and Frank began picking through the items that spilled across the glass. He inspected the ski masks and torches, the compasses and dark clothing, the cheap mobile phones and several other items. Then he saw the Ordnance Survey map and spread it out across the table. 'Beautiful,' he purred, 'exactly what we need.'

Roy sat in silence while Frank worked, drawing lines on the map, converting distances on his notepad. He made several phone calls, some bizarre, others that had Roy and Vicky trading worried looks. Eventually Frank nodded and said, 'this might just work.'

'It has to,' Vicky said.

'Both of you will have to stay very cool. Especially you, Roy.'

'I'll be fine.'

Vicky weighed a small canister of spray adhesive in her hand. 'So what's all this stuff for?'

Frank ignored the question, spun the map around. 'Okay, time for a mission brief. This is a detailed map of the terrain surrounding the gypsy camp. As you can see the target is bordered by woods and fields, a couple of farms, but luckily for us, the extended area is criss-crossed with several roads. Now, this is how it's going to go down...'

By the time the briefing had finished, Roy could feel the fear bubbling in his stomach. It was obvious that Frank had done this before, and Roy wished that Jimmy were here to help them. This was his world, one of operations and tactics, and Roy wasn't sure if he shared Frank's confidence in him. Vicky, on the other hand, seemed focused. The colour had returned to her cheeks and there was a determination about her that made Roy feel a little inadequate. He was scared too. Yes, he would do anything to save his son, and if that meant hurting others, then so be it. But everything depended on him tonight; once the pieces were in place, the plan had a single point of failure, and that was Roy. The pressure made his stomach churn and the strength leak from his legs.

This is the most important night of your life, he told himself. *Whatever you do, don't fuck it up.*

The sky darkened.

Brake lights burned red in the heavy traffic. In the front seat of the Toyota, Roy pointed through the windshield. 'There he is.'

Vicky slowed the vehicle and pulled into the deserted bus stop in Staines. Frank, a black rucksack thrown over his shoulder, climbed into the back.

'Go,' he ordered.

Vicky pulled out into the rush-hour traffic. Roy noticed that Frank had changed into his own dark clothing. The American rubbed his hands together.

'Just like old times,' he grinned. 'Did you make the calls?'

Roy nodded. 'I phoned Sammy ten minutes ago, told him I was on my way to pick up Derek. Straight after that I called Josh. He grilled me but I told him my phone was playing up, that you'd called, wanted to meet. I didn't say where.'

'Good. What did he say?'

'He seemed excited.'

'Nice. Your cell's off, right?' Roy nodded. 'Yours too, Vicky?'

'Yes,' she confirmed, glancing in the rear view mirror.

'Did you recce the farm?' Roy asked.

Frank nodded. 'I did.'

'You think it'll work?'

'Mission confidence is high.' He leaned over, laid a hand on Vicky's shoulder. 'Drive nice and steady to the RV point. While we do that, let's go over everything one more time.'

Roy listened carefully, mentally rehearsing his forthcoming movements, his actions. He checked his gear, going through each item with Frank, its intended use, which pocket to keep it in, the physical methods of covert approach. He was scared, sure, but the closer they got the more that fear was tempered by a strengthening resolve. He had to focus on Max, channel his son's terror and confusion for his own purposes. Frank had said that people would die tonight. Roy had to make sure it wasn't any of them.

Outside, night had fallen. Traffic ebbed and flowed around the roads to the west of Heathrow airport. Roy looked towards the distant horizon where the setting sun had left a thin red band across the sky, and wondered what the world would look like when it next rose again. Whatever happened, the life he once knew was behind him.

What lay ahead, unknown.

Chapter Twenty-One

The narrow lane was dark, empty.

Vicky stepped on the brakes and brought the Toyota to a halt. Wild hedgerows closed in on either side. Lights were extinguished and doors closed quietly. Roy saw the rusted signpost, the public footpath beyond, a pale ribbon of dirt stretching away into the darkness. He felt a hand on his on his shoulder.

'Time to move.' Frank went ahead, into the gloom.

'Wait.'

Vicky came around the vehicle, her hair covered by a rolled-up ski mask, her black coat zipped to the chin, her face a pale oval hovering in the dark. Then she was hugging Roy, strong and tight. She stayed like that for a second or two, then laid a gentle hand on his face.

'Bring him back, Roy. Bring our son home.'

'I will.'

He wanted to say more, so much more, but she was already climbing back inside the Toyota. Maybe later, when things had settled, he would tell her how he still felt. How he would always feel. The vehicle pulled away, quickly swallowed by the night.

He followed Frank across the empty field, a black silhouette against the night sky, moving easily across grassy hillocks and muddy furrows. Roy stumbled and cursed in his wake. Then Frank held his arm up in a tight fist. Roy walked right into him.

'Sorry,' he whispered.

Frank grabbed the back of his neck and pulled him low to the ground. 'You want to see your son again, start thinking about what you're doing. There'll be no second chances.'

'Take it easy, Frank.'

'Make the call.'

Roy pulled the BlackBerry from his pocket and powered it up. He dialled Josh's number. It answered on the second ring.

'This is Josh. Tell me where you are, Roy.'

'I'm on a road called Lark Hill Lane. It's to the west of Iver, in Buckinghamshire.'

'Is Frank there?'

'Not yet, but he just called. He's freaking me out, to tell the truth. And he mentioned something about *Messina.* Does that mean anything to you?' Frank nodded in the darkness, a smile cracking his rugged face. 'Hello, Josh?'

'I'm here. Exactly where and when are you meeting him?'

'In an hour, at a caravan site on Lark Hill Lane—'

Roy heard a muted discussion at the other end of the line, then Josh came back on.

'Roy, I need you to send me the number Frank called you from.'

'I can't, it's blocked.'

A muffled curse.

'I'll send you the postcode of the travellers' site though.'

'Do that. What's the problem with your phone?'

'God knows. It keeps switching itself off. It's brand new. Must be the battery or something.'

'Okay. If Frank calls again tell him you're running late. That'll give us a chance to get our people into position. If your phone goes dead again, wait near the camp entrance. Someone will find you.'

'Thanks, Josh, and please hurry. I don't trust this—'

Roy powered off the phone before Josh could answer.

Frank slapped him on the back. 'Nice work.' He checked his watch, a faint green glow in the dark. 'Josh now has good intel, a grid reference and a target. That's all he needs. We need to move quickly.'

Roy followed him across the field, until the footpath ended at another deserted country lane. Frank crouched in the shadows. The wind gusted suddenly, rippling along the hedgerow that hid them. Roy felt a raindrop on his hand, another on his face. A low grumble of thunder echoed across the sky.

Frank smiled, his eyes raised to the heavens. 'Thank you, Lord.' He leaned into Roy's ear. 'Okay, this is it. You know where you're going, what you have to do?' Roy nodded. 'Any questions?' He shook his head. Frank gripped his hand. 'The storm will give you some cover. See you at the rendezvous in three days.'

'Okay,' Roy croaked, his throat suddenly dry. He moved to the end of the hedgerow. The lane was empty in both directions. He rolled the ski mask over his face and loped across the asphalt.

Heart pounding, he plunged into the darkness of the woods.

Frank lay hidden beneath the hedge for a full thirty minutes, impervious to the strengthening wind and rain sweeping in from the east.

He checked his watch, waited another five minutes, then rolled out from cover and got to his feet. He brushed himself off and raised his face to the sky, letting the rain wash away the dirt and stiffness, energising him for the task ahead. Lightning flashed across the horizon like distant artillery, followed by rolling thunder. The storm was a sign, Frank decided, and the knowledge that the Almighty had taken a divine hand in this mission filled him with a righteous strength. He smiled. Such was the joy of rapture.

He hit the road and turned south along Lark Hill Lane.

It was a brisk ten-minute walk to the camp entrance. There was no sign, just a badly potholed road cut into the trees, the ditches on either side littered with weeds and rubbish. Frank headed down it, his eyes roaming the adjoining woods. Twenty yards ahead a stationary Range Rover waited, engine silent, rain drumming off its roof. Beyond that, the trailer park was lit beneath tall pole lights. As Frank neared the camp the Range Rover's doors creaked open and four men climbed out, large silhouettes against the lights of the camp. He squinted as a torch beamed in his face. A voice growled above the wind and the drumbeat of rain.

'State your business.'

'I'm here to see Derek.'

'Are you Roy?'

'Roy couldn't make it. I'm Frank.'

'Let's see your hands, Frankie boy.'

The unmarked Mercedes van turned off the lane and into the car park, crunching to a stop in the wet gravel.

Josh climbed out, boots squelching in the puddled ground. The car park was empty, the dog walkers and ramblers gone for the day, the surrounding woods dark and silent.

Another Mercedes van pulled in, stopping alongside Josh's command vehicle. Rear doors were opened, equipment unpacked. Minutes later, assisted by two trees and a stiff bungee cord, a Desert Hawk miniature UAV shot across the car park and climbed skyward, quickly swallowed by the darkness. Josh ducked into the back of the command vehicle. Eyes was piloting the UAV, its high-definition signal filled with static. Villiers settled into the chair next to Josh.

'How's it looking?'

Josh pointed to the monitor. 'Nada.' He keyed his radio. 'Bravo leader, stand by.'

Through the side window Josh saw his team assembling in the rain. They were geared up in woodland camouflage jackets, military-spec helmets, and NVGs over black Nomex hoods. Each man carried a Heckler and Koch 416 with holographic sight and suppressor, as well as a several grenades. With the storm blowing, Josh thought they might just get away with using them.

'Video is up,' Eyes announced.

Josh peered at the screen. He glimpsed a collection of trailers, then lost them as the UAV swung away towards a distant stand of trees.

'Strong easterlies,' Eyes said. 'She'll self-correct in severe weather. I'll programme her with a GPS fix right above the trailer park.'

'You still think Sullivan is being straight with us?' Villiers asked.

Josh shrugged. 'Maybe. His cell signal confirms he's around here somewhere.' Josh didn't want to get his hopes up, not until Frank was lying dead at his feet with a dozen bullet holes in his chest.

'What d'you want to do with him? Sullivan, I mean.'

'Frank is our only concern here. If the kid catches a bullet, so be it.'

'Back online,' Eyes confirmed.

Josh saw the trailers, a dozen vehicles parked haphazardly, the Star Safire imaging system capturing the park in high-definition shades of black, white and grey. The camera zoomed in and out again, the cross-hair receptacle jumping across the screen.

'Looks like only two of those trailers are occupied,' said Eyes, pointing to the heat blooms on the thermal imaging feed. 'There're a couple of minor heat sources, probably animals. The rest of the park is empty.'

'Perfect,' Josh said.

The killing fields were clear.

The trees swayed around him, the rain lancing down in cold, blustery waves, yet despite the conditions Roy was sweating.

He'd reached the edge of the wood. Ahead of him was open ground, an untended paddock, the grass tall and wild. Beyond that, the camp itself. Roy counted eight caravans, all squatting on concrete stands. There was no life to be seen but what scared him was the light. The camp glowed under harsh white floodlights mounted on tall poles. Power cables swung lazily between them, the rain falling in steady sheets through the cones of light.

Roy took a breath and headed out into the paddock, keeping low, climbing the fence on the other side. He lay immobile in the long grass, his eyes moving left and right through the narrow slit of his ski mask. The nearest caravan was six feet away, but Roy couldn't hear any noise from inside. He got to his feet, thankful for the wind and rain cover.

He crept toward the access road, rolled beneath another caravan, waited, listened…

Voices.

Movement.

Roy lay on his belly, peered around a tyre. Three men stood outside a brightly lit caravan across the access road. He saw Frank and swallowed hard, frightened for him, for both of them. The door swung open and a chorus of voices spilled out into the night air, rough banter, coarse laughter. Frank and his escort disappeared inside and the door slammed shut.

The wind barrelled through the camp, rain bouncing off the puddled road. Roy was about to move when he heard it, tacked onto the end of a long ripple of thunder, the sound cut short by a muffled curse of a woman's tongue. Roy rolled over onto his back, peered at the rusted undercarriage above him, felt the caravan creak as someone moved inside. Then he heard it again. A frightened wail.

A child's wail.

Roy's heart rose into his mouth.

Max.

'Who the fuck are you?'

Frank stared at the giant sprawled across the bench seat in the trailer's large lounge. Big Jim Connor, the bare-knuckle fighter that Roy had warned him about. He had a chiselled face, his oily black hair receding heavily and falling to the wide shoulders of his short black leather jacket. Tattoos crept up his neck and a blue ink tear fell beneath one eye. He reminded Frank of one of those TV wrestlers. Only bigger.

Connor was holding court, surrounded by several other men, tough-guy types, leather jackets, earrings, tattoos. They eyed Frank with palpable hostility. Bottles of liquor crowded the table in front of them, the air thick with cigarette smoke. His two escorts stood behind him, close enough to lay hands on if they had to. Frank did a quick head count. Seven in front, two behind—

He heard a toilet flush and another man pushed past him, zipping the fly of his jeans. He was smaller than the others, and they made room for him on the bench seat. He flopped down next to Connor.

'Who's this?' the short man growled.

'Are you Derek?'

'It speaks,' Connor smiled, and the other gypsies laughed.

'Yeah, I'm Derek. Who the fuck are you?'

'The name's Frank. Roy couldn't make it. I've got something for you.' Frank reached inside his jacket and Connor sprang to his feet. Frank was impressed by the large man's speed. Standing, he was taller than Frank and half as wide again. The shotgun looked tiny in his tattooed hands.

'Easy, lad,' Connor growled in a deep voice.

'He's not carrying, Pa,' the younger of Frank's escorts chipped in.

'Shut up, Mickey.' Connor's eyes never left Frank. 'Slowly. Two fingers.'

Frank withdrew the padded envelope from inside his coat and dangled it in the air. Another gypsy stepped forward and snatched it from him. Derek ripped it open, spilled the contents on the table.

'Sweet,' the Scot purred, flicking through the stiff new passport. Then he picked up the folded pages, a USB key drive.

'What's all this shit?'

Frank shrugged. 'Nothing. Personal stuff.'

Derek shoved the passport in his back pocket. 'So, what's the plan?'

'Roy got called in to work so I'll be taking you to the hotel, get you freshened up before your flight. Where's the boy?'

Connor retook his seat, the shotgun cradled across his lap. Amusement played at the corners of his mouth. 'Why?'

'We should take him with us when we go.'

'Is that right? Well, let me tell you something, *Frank*, until we get a phone call from Derek in Dubai, the kid stays here. Then we can negotiate his release.'

'Negotiate?'

'Kids cost money. I'll need compensating.'

Amusement rippled around the crowded bench seats. Frank smiled too.

'C'mon, guys, he's just a kid. He's got problems, special needs. His mom's really scared.'

'I told you he was a fucking retard!' Connor cackled, and the caravan rocked with laughter.

Frank grimaced, his fingers scratching his neck, reassured by the hilt of the hunting knife taped between his shoulder blades. Then his eyes flicked to the window, to the man in black disappearing inside the opposite caravan.

'That you, Riley?'

'Yeah—'

Roy coughed loud and hard to disguise his voice.

The woman was still where Roy had observed her through the window, her back to the door, cooking bacon on a two-ring stove. She had a mop of wild red hair, and two large hooped earrings dangled from her ears. She jerked the pan back and forth, bacon hissing loudly. Roy shut the door behind him and took a step towards her.

'I've had to gag that fucking kid,' she complained, turning around. 'Can't you stick him in a shed or—'

She froze, the pan still gripped in her hand as she looked Roy up and down. She seemed completely unfazed by the black clothing, the ski mask, and when she spoke there was no fear in her voice, only anger and suspicion. Roy felt distinctly unnerved.

'Who the fuck are you?'

Roy brought his hand up, the spray adhesive blasting into the woman's face. She screamed and swung the pan, missing Roy's head by an inch. Hot fat splashed across the walls. Roy rushed her, forcing the canister into her face, finger jammed on the button as she thrashed her head from side to side, her long nails flailing at Roy's eyes. He pulled his left arm back, punched her as hard as he could, the blow knocking her off her feet. He kicked her twice then fell on top of her, ripping the plastic cable ties from his pocket. He bound her hands behind her back, did the same to her ankles, then secured her hands to her feet. He pulled another ski mask over her head, back to front, restricting her vision, then taped over her mouth with a roll of electrical tape. He stood up, panting, nauseous.

The woman lay face down on the carpet, trussed like a Christmas turkey, her moans muffled by the adhesive, by the material of the ski mask.

Roy dragged his own mask off and splashed cold water on his face at the sink. He peered through a crack in the curtains. Outside, nothing moved. He searched the caravan, the floor creaking beneath his booted feet. Empty. He moved quickly to the last room, steeled himself. He shouldered his way through the door.

He froze.

Don't think, act.

He reached for the knife in his pocket, cutting the rope that tied his son's hands to the bedpost. He removed the blindfold, saw the eyes, red and raw, the cheeks pale and streaked with dirt and tears, his cries muffled by the rag still tied around his mouth. He removed that too and sat on the bed, rocking his son against his chest.

'It's all right, Max, Daddy's here.'

Max's sobs came in deep, distressing heaves. Roy checked his arms, his legs, and thanked God he was in one piece. He stood up, clutching his son, oblivious to the smells and stains seeping through his short trousers.

His only thought now was escape.

Josh's heart thumped in his chest.

He was now so close now he could almost taste the kill. He rode with his team in the Mercedes, moving south towards the trailer park, Eyes and Ears providing a constant update through the earpiece nestled beneath his helmet and Nomex hood. The hunter team sat in silence around him, locked and loaded, weapons cradled in their arms.

Josh smiled when he thought about Frank, his frame and gait so recognisable even through a thermal imaging camera. There would be no time for a dramatic confrontation, no lengthy victory speeches, just the emptying of rounds into Frank's body. He glanced through the windshield, saw the wipers beating off the rain, the tarmac ahead as slick as oil.

'Access road to the right, fifty metres,' Eyes reported over the radio. 'Target still inside trailer one, two Tangoes in stationary vehicle.'

'Roger.'

Villiers guided the Mercedes across the lane and blocked the entrance to the access road. The side door opened and the wind rushed in. Josh peered into the darkness, heard the sound of car doors slamming, the scrape and splash of approaching footsteps. Two figures sauntered towards the van, dark silhouettes against the distant lights, clubs held casually in their hands. Josh heard Villiers power down the window.

'Evening, lads. Can you tell me where Iver village is? I'm lost.'

'Fuck off,' barked one of the men.

'Wrong answer,' he heard Villiers say.

Suppressed gunfire chattered inside the Mercedes. Shell casings rolled and rattled across the floor. Then silence.

'Move.'

Josh climbed out behind his team. He waited as the bullet-riddled bodies were dragged from the road and dumped by the verge. Then he cocked his own weapon and led them beneath the trees in a silent column, the lights of the big trailer drawing him like a moth to a flame.

'Shush now, there's a good boy.'

Inside the caravan, Roy was struggling to keep Max quiet. The boy squirmed and sobbed, distraught in his arms. Roy hugged and kissed him, smoothing his hair until Max had calmed a little.

They had to go.

Right now.

He peered out the window, then eased open the caravan door. He stepped down and moved around the back, losing himself in the shadows. His escape route would take him in the opposite direction, away from the camp and towards the southern end of the lane where Vicky would—

The man appeared from nowhere, his face turned skyward, eyes squinting against the wind and rain. Roy froze in the shadows as the figure passed within six feet, conscious of his uncovered face, of Max's pale legs dangling from his arms. Roy held his breath, and then the man was gone.

He looked skyward.

That's when Roy heard it too.

Frank turned as the caravan door swung open.

Another man entered, scraping his feet on the thick matt, rain dripping from his heavy wax slicker.

'Can you hear that?' he asked, pointing to the ceiling.

'Hear what?

'The plane.'

'We're near the airport, ya idiot.' Connor's eyes settled back on Frank.

'No, this sounds more like one of those radio-controlled things. Right above us.'

Frank's heart quickened, adrenalin flooding his system. He knew what the 'plane' was, what it meant. The only question was, how would it play out? Every fibre of Frank's being pulsed with nervous energy, something he hadn't felt in—

Through the window he saw a trailer door swinging in the wind. Then he saw Roy, the boy held in his arms, charging through a distant cone of light.

His eyes met Connor's. The big man spun around, saw the retreating figure.

'Fuck!' He raised the shotgun, but Frank moved faster. He ripped the knife from his neck and grabbed the kid to his right in a single, explosive movement, slamming himself against a window. He held the blade against the younger man's neck, pressing on the carotid artery that pulsed beneath his tattoos. His other fingers found and released the window catch behind him.

Everyone jerked to their feet. Connor lumbered forward, barging the others out of his way. Liquor bottles crashed to the carpet. He held the gun up, the knuckles of his hands white, his face twisted in rage.

'Riley! Stevo! Go check on yer ma!' Connor watched Frank with malevolent eyes as two of the men bundled from the caravan. The big man took another step forward. Frank pressed the knife a little deeper.

'Pa!' the boy cried, and Connor held his ground.

'Don't do anything stupid,' Frank warned.

Derek stood up. 'Put the fucking shooter away, Jimbo. He's my ticket out of here.'

Connor spun around. 'Your flight's cancelled.'

He fired the shotgun, the blast lifting Derek against the window and dropping him back onto the bench seat. Blood poured from his chest and throat, and his hands scrabbled at his neck, at the gaping wound. He wheezed a few times, his eyes widened, and then his hands fell away and his head lolled to the side. Frank's ears rang from the blast, his nose filled with the stench of gunpowder.

'Your boss is a dead man,' Connor spat. Smoke from the shotgun drifted on the air. 'You can tell him this is war.'

Frank looked at Connor, then beyond him, through the window where the bodies of Riley and Stevo lay sprawled in the rain. Frank smiled.

'You have no idea of the concept of war.'

The lights went out.

Red laser beams flared across the windows.

Frank hurled himself backwards, crashing through the window and into the wet undergrowth as gunfire erupted on the other side of the trailer. He crawled along a drainage gulley, bullets ripping through the trailer's thin skin behind him in a storm of lead. He got to his feet, stumbling, running towards the woods that bordered the northern end of the camp.

Roy's escape wasn't going as planned.

Max was now in deep shock and lay like a dead weight in his Roy's arms. Any adrenaline he had left was being quickly displaced by exhaustion. He kept to his escape route, staggering through a copse of trees and out into a field. He'd only taken a dozen paces when he realised to his horror that it'd been recently ploughed. Now the rain had turned it into a quagmire.

He sunk to his calves, mud sucking at his boots, his legs, dragging them both down. He wasn't moving fast enough. His lungs heaved and he fell once, twice, scrabbling in the cloying mud, scraping it from Max's inert body. He looked over his shoulder, saw shadows near the treeline, heard a distant shout. He was dangerously exposed. His lungs burned. He clutched Max a little tighter, willed his legs to move.

He stumbled across the field towards the high hedge in the distance, a black wall that seemed so far away. Beyond, lay safety.

He kept his head down and kept moving.

Josh stepped into the trailer, pistol held ready, torch beam sweeping the scene. The walls were peppered with scores of bullet holes, the furniture splintered. He kicked over the bloody corpses but none of them were

Frank. He caught a movement and saw a civilian lying beneath the table bleeding out, moaning softly. Again, not Frank. Josh put two safety rounds into his chest.

He was surprised; his guys had eaten through their magazines but Frank had escaped. Josh was suddenly consumed by a rare bout of panic. Then his eye caught something, a small object on the table amongst the broken glass and blood. He scooped it up, inspected it under the torchlight. Then he waved the light over the table, snatched at the printed pages scattered there. The words leapt out at him; *Messina, Copse Hill, Cohen.* He stared at the USB in his hand again. It was the one. It had to be. And now it was in Josh's possession. His panic was suddenly replaced by a joyous, murderous intent.

'Primary target is on the move,' Eyes confirmed in his earpiece. 'Heading due north from your location, one hundred metres.'

The contractors were already on the move, flashing past the shattered windows, sprinting towards the far end of the camp and the trees beyond. The Mercedes splashed through the puddles and braked to a halt. Villiers climbed out, a pistol in his hand.

'Frank's on the loose!' Josh yelled above a long ripple of thunder.

He broke into a run, Villiers close behind him.

He'd waited until they were gone, his face buried in the mud, his body still.

He had no idea who they were but he knew he

was the only survivor. He crawled for ten yards along the stinking ditch, gasping in pain as he got to his feet, hiding in the shadows of the caravan until he was sure he was alone. Then he picked himself up, mindful of the bullet that was lodged in his side, the blood that soaked his trousers. He knew he should head straight for the nearest hospital, but that was only a tiny, logical part of his consciousness. The rest of him was consumed by pure, unadulterated hate, and it was hate that kept him moving towards the Range Rover parked beneath the trees.

Gritting his teeth he climbed inside and started the engine. He gunned the vehicle towards the main road. He slowed at the junction, caught the crumpled heaps of his clansmen, dumped in the mud and rain.

Someone was going to pay, Jim Connor decided.

In blood.

Frank heard the UAV buzzing somewhere overhead, the sounds of pursuit behind him.

He veered to the left, taking cover behind a thick tree, his chest heaving with effort. He looked up, searched the dark skies above, but he couldn't see the craft that tracked him. He heard movement, saw shadows darting through the woods. He ran, branches whipping his face, stumbling over brambles, nature in league with his pursuers. An angry insect zipped past him, then another, chipping splinters off the trees ahead. The tall wire fence came rushing out of the darkness as another bullet snapped through the undergrowth.

Frank went to work quickly, ripping off his jacket, soaking the small hole punched through the back with his own recently drawn blood. He draped it over the barbed wire on top of the fence, tugging and snagging it. He shoved the blood bag in his pocket and climbed, rolling over the rusted wire and dropping to the grass on the other side.

He ran forward in the mud, saw the pit, and threw himself in.

Roy collapsed onto the grass verge by the roadside.

Caked in mud, breathless, exhausted, he cradled his son in his arms. 'Nearly there, Max, Mummy's coming to get us.'

Max was mute, a rag doll. He had to get help.

Vicky was waiting in a layby a couple of hundred yards along the lane, but to Roy it might've been ten miles. Frank said no phones, so Roy had to move and move fast.

He got to his feet, heaving Max into his arms. He stumbled forward, battling against the wind, the road dark and wet. He'd staggered maybe fifty paces when the hedgerows lit up around him. He turned, shielding his eyes as the vehicle's full beam dazzled him. He hefted Max onto his left arm and waved as the car bumped to an unsteady stop against the grass verge. 'Thank God,' he wheezed. The driver's door flew open.

Roy hesitated.

It wasn't Vicky.

It was a man, a huge man, and then he saw the

machete gripped in his hand. Roy swore. He turned to run, his legs filled with water, each intake of breath like a knife in his chest. He heard the man behind him, cursing, gaining. Roy looked over his shoulder.

He wasn't going to make it.

He swung Max to the ground, pushed him away. 'Run,' Roy begged him, 'run, Max! Run away!' The boy staggered a couple of paces and then his muddy legs gave way. He plopped onto his backside, terror etched on his small, round face. He raised his little arms, reaching for Roy.

'No, Max,' Roy whispered.

The giant bore down on them. Roy turned, energy spent, tears of anger and frustration carving through his mud-splashed face. They'd almost made it.

He balled his hands into fists. 'You touch my boy, I'll fucking kill you.'

Ten paces away the giant swore, filthy, evil curses pouring from his mouth. Then he raised the machete. Roy felt a sharp wind, and a black object shot past him, colliding with the giant, sending him cartwheeling through the air. The Toyota slewed to a halt across the road. The door flew open.

Vicky.

She ran towards him, then past him, and fell beside Max. She scooped him off the ground and hurried back to the Toyota.

'Drive,' she ordered, dragging Roy by the sleeve.

Roy climbed behind the wheel and flicked on the lights.

'Go,' Vicky pointed, 'that way.'

Roy dropped the Toyota into gear and floored the accelerator. Ahead, the giant had somehow found the strength to get to his knees. He turned to face the oncoming vehicle, his clothes shredded, his face a mask of blood, a broken hand shielding his eyes from the glare of headlights.

'Don't stop,' Vicky said, her voice like ice.

Roy had no such intention, lining the gypsy up dead centre. He gripped the steering wheel, felt the thump of the impact, the big tyres dragging, then bouncing over the body in the road.

In the rear view mirror, road kill. Ahead, the narrow lane was clear.

Josh came to a halt by the fence, panting hard. He pressed his earpiece, frowning as he strained to listen to Eyes back in the command vehicle.

'He's gone to ground in the next field!' he shouted. He reached up, and was almost over the fence when he felt Villiers' hand on his coat, pulling him back. He dropped back down and spun around.

'Take your fucking hands off me!' he hissed, flipping his NVGs off his face.

The other contractors had reached the fence and were starting to scale it. Villiers waved them off. He pointed to a rusted sign further along the chain link: *Danger – Slurry Pit.*

'You fall into one of them and you're a dead man.'

Josh cursed. Wind and rain whipped through

the surrounding trees. 'He's close. The bird lost him somewhere beyond the fence. We go, now!'

He shone a torch through the chain link, at the muddy prints heading out into the darkness. Cutters snipped at the fence and Josh dragged Frank's torn jacket off the drooping barbed wire.

'He's hit,' Josh said, poking a crimson finger through a hole in the material. He led them through the freshly cut fence.

'Let's take it slow,' Villiers cautioned. 'Use your NVGs.'

The rank smell hit them hard, despite the wind and rain. Josh cuffed a sleeve over his nose and mouth as a large, dark rectangle of ground loomed before them.

'Lost the target right where you are now,' Eyes told Josh through his earpiece. 'You should be right on top of him.'

The rest of the team had fanned out in an extended line as Josh followed Frank's muddy tracks with his NVGs until he saw a final, desperate boot scuff on the concrete lip of the slurry pit.

Then nothing.

Except a wide, deep lake of animal faeces, urine and other farmyard waste. Villiers appeared by his side, a hand clamped over his mouth.

'See anything?'

Josh shook his head.

'If he went in there he's done.'

Josh knew Frank, knew what kind of man he'd once been. He swept the inky darkness of the pit, the perimeter fence, the ground beyond. Nothing moved. 'You think?'

Villiers nodded in the dark. 'Even Frank couldn't survive a fall in that stuff, especially if he's wounded. If the fumes didn't get him the shit will have dragged him down like quicksand. Very fucking nasty.'

He backed away from the edge and Josh did the same. 'Sweep the area,' he ordered into his radio. 'You see a heat source with two legs, I want to know.' Above him the Desert Hawk buzzed through the rain. He turned to Villiers. 'Take two guys and go around, make sure he didn't climb out on the other side.'

'The bird would've picked him up.'

'Do it anyway.'

If it was really over then it hadn't ended the way Josh wanted, but Frank drowning in a lake of shit would do the job just as effectively. And it was clean too. Frank's corpse would probably decompose completely before the farmer noticed he was spraying bones and rotten rags across his fields. It didn't matter anyway. The Transition would be underway before then.

Fifteen minutes later the hunter team had reassembled and gathered around him. No more tracks were found, no footprints, no trails of shit. If Frank went in, he never came out. Josh ordered Eyes to review the UAV feed. A few minutes later he got confirmation that Frank had taken the plunge.

'We should clear the area,' Villiers warned.

'Film it all, the fence, the signs, the prints, everything.'

Josh waited until it was done, watching the huge pool of filth, wanting to believe it was over. Frank was a resourceful sonofabitch, but no one was *that* resourceful, right? *Right,* he consoled himself. If the USB drive was the one from Copse Hill, if the bloodied jacket confirmed Frank's DNA, he'd write it all up and present it to Beeton and Lund. The UAV feed didn't lie. Frank Marshall was no more.

Job done.

Mission accomplished.

Twenty minutes later and Josh was satisfied they'd gathered enough evidence. He turned on his heel and led his team back through the trees towards the distant campsite, the buzz of the Desert Hawk still sweeping the ground behind them. By the time he reached the bullet-riddled trailers the reality was beginning to sink in. Whatever secrets Frank had possessed he'd taken them with him to the bottom of that stinking pit. He felt no remorse, no sympathy for the man he'd once considered a friend. The traitor was dead, and a shithole for a grave was the least Frank deserved. He climbed into the Mercedes. Villiers slid behind the wheel and started the vehicle.

'You did good tonight, Dave. You endorse my report, I'll send a jet for you in a month.'

'Consider it done,' Villiers smiled.

'Torch the trailers, the bodies, all of it.'

Josh powered up the window. He was eager to get back to Chelsea and file the report. Beeton and Lund would stand the G-Men down and close the book on

Frank Marshall. Then he'd be able to pack up and leave this damp, miserable country behind him for good. It things went as he hoped, he'd be congratulated on a job well done and welcomed back into the bosom of The Committee as a trusted acolyte.

After all, it was where he belonged.

Josh couldn't wait.

Chapter Twenty-Two

The rain had eased, the steady beat of the wipers the only sound that filled the vehicle. They were deep in the countryside now, the gypsy camp far behind them. Roy's eyes flicked between the rear view mirror and the empty road ahead.

'How is he?'

Vicky ignored the question. 'Take the next left.'

'What about the hotel?'

'Do it.'

Roy swung the wheel, steering the Toyota along another empty road. He was exhausted and nauseous and a dozen other things, but he had to shut it all out. It wasn't over yet. 'This isn't what we planned, Vicks.'

She jabbed a finger at the windscreen. 'There, on the left, the garden centre. Turn in there.'

'What? Why?'

'Just do it!'

Roy complied, turning into the wide gravel cutaway that fronted the garden centre. Its gates were closed and padlocked, its glass buildings shrouded in darkness.

'There they are.'

Roy saw it then, a dark-coloured minivan parked beneath an overhang of trees. A man waved as Roy braked alongside the Volkswagen. 'Jesus, is that Nate?' He spun around in his seat. 'Frank said no phones.'

'He didn't say anything about emails.'

Vicky climbed out, Max bundled in her arms. Roy

noticed two other men, one behind the wheel of the Volkswagen, the other helping Nate and Vicky. They were hard-faced and square-jawed, with curly earpieces trailing down their necks. Roy was hustled into the rear of the minivan.

'What about the car?'

The question was answered a moment later when orange flames bloomed inside the Toyota. By the time they were back on the road the vehicle was an inferno. Roy watched it until it was nothing but a red glow beyond a bend in the road.

On the seat in front of him Max was nestled between Nate and Vicky, her protective arms draped around him as she cooed in her son's ear and smoothed his muddy hair. In front of them were the two security guys, one behind the wheel, the other talking into a radio. Classical music played softly, dialling down the tension. Vicky had clearly made her own arrangements, and Roy felt relieved that the responsibility for their getaway had now been passed to others. He was exhausted, and both he and Max had been lucky to escape with their lives. He hoped Frank had made it out too.

They travelled for miles, mostly country back roads, then on to a busier trunk road, where they changed vehicles again, this time to a larger Ford. By the time they pulled through the tall iron gates of a secluded country estate over an hour had passed. Roy peered through the window as the wooded grounds gave way to open parkland and a large period manor house, its chimneys silhouetted against the night sky.

'Where are we?'

'Somewhere safe,' Nate said over his shoulder.

The Ford braked to a halt outside the main doors. Everyone got out, and Vicky disappeared inside with Max and a waiting man and a woman who Roy didn't recognise.

'Wait a minute—'

'It's okay,' Nate said. 'They're my family's physician and paediatrician. They're gonna take care of him.'

He ushered Roy inside the opulent entrance hall as the heavy doors were bolted behind them. Roy was impressed. 'Is this yours?'

Nate shook his head. 'My father's, owned by one of his offshore shell corporations. It's used for very discreet business gatherings. I've never been here, and neither has Victoria, so we can't be traced. The grounds are well protected and I've brought a team of professionals. We're quite safe here.'

Roy wasn't so sure—Josh had brought a team of professionals with him too. In fact, Roy wasn't sure if he'd ever feel safe again. Was this how former Prime Ministers and billionaires lived, he wondered, always surrounded by security, the constant threat of assassination and kidnap hanging over them twenty-four seven? Roy doubted he could cope with life as a human target.

'I want to thank you for what you did,' Nate said as he escorted Roy upstairs.

'He's my son. What d'you expect?'

Nate paused on the landing. 'I'm not looking for a

fight, Roy, I just wanted to express my gratitude. Victoria told me what you were up against tonight. What you did, for Max, for her, well, I think you showed a hell of a lot of courage. I admire that.'

'Yeah, well, you'd have done the same,' Roy mumbled, a little embarrassed. Nate eased open a door along the hallway.

'This is your room. Dump the clothes you're wearing in the bag provided. There are en suite facilities and fresh clothes in the closet. Victoria gave me your sizes. If you need anything else, the phone on the wall will patch you through to housekeeping.'

'Where's Max?'

'He's along the hall.'

Fifteen minutes later, after a hot shower and wearing new jeans and a T-shirt, Roy found Max's room along the landing. Vicky was seated by his bedside, still dressed in her black clothes, her hands clasped around Max's chubby fingers. His son was still, his face scrubbed and cleaned, his hair neatly parted, his cheeks showing a hint of their former colour. Stuffed toys surrounded him, a soft nightlight glowed in the corner, and nursery rhymes played from an iPod on a nightstand. Roy eased himself into the chair next to Vicky as the doctors retired from the room.

'How is he?'

'Better,' she said, her eyes never leaving Max. 'They've given him a mild tranquiliser to help him sleep. They're going to keep him sedated for the next few days. The period of trauma was comparatively short, so with a little luck it'll seem like a bad dream. In time he'll forget.'

Roy smoothed his son's hair with a gentle hand. 'That's good news.'

'I need to get out of these clothes. Meet me downstairs in thirty minutes.'

Roy was dozing when Vicky walked barefoot into the wood-panelled reception room over an hour later. He shifted in the surprisingly comfortable armchair, balling the sleep from his eyes. He was dead tired, his bones warmed by the fire burning in the grate, the logs crackling and spitting. Table lamps glowed around the room. Vicky was wearing loose white trousers and a baggy black top, her wet hair falling over her shoulders. Roy thought she looked beautiful.

'How is he?'

'Still sleeping. Like father, like son,' she smiled, flopping into the chair opposite him. Roy was glad she had the strength to joke, but the smile soon faded.

'So, how much of a threat is Sammy French to us now?'

Roy shrugged. 'We'll know in the next twenty-four hours, although I don't think Sammy is our biggest problem.'

'Where did you find him? Max, I mean?'

'It doesn't matter. The main thing is we got him back.' He waved a hand around the room. 'So, you told Nate, then.'

'Did you think I wouldn't?'

Roy shrugged, stung by a sudden barb of jealousy.

'No, I just thought—'

'Frank wanted us to disappear, go on the run. I wasn't comfortable with that so I told Nate. He set all this up, had the details emailed to an anonymous account. We're safe.'

Roy shook his head. 'No one's safe. Remember all that stuff Frank spoke about?'

'Of course I do.'

'The data, it's safe, right?' Vicky gave him a withering look. Roy held up his hands. 'Okay, I was just asking.'

'Now that Max is safe I need to take a look at it, see if any of what Frank says stacks up.' She crossed her legs, stared into the fire. 'I need to thank him for what he did. He'll be angry that we didn't follow his instructions.'

'Let's just hope he got away.'

'You don't think he did?'

Roy rose from the chair, stretched his limbs. He crossed to the window, pulled the curtain back, his eyes sweeping the dark grounds, the black wall of trees beyond.

'We don't know anything yet, Vicky. I guess we'll find out in the next few days.'

The minicab pulled into the empty bus stop two hundred yards short of Hatton Cross Tube station.

Frank paid the driver, adding a small tip, then eased himself out onto the pavement. It felt good to be out in the cold night air again, to wash away the antiseptic stench that clung to his skin. The rain had stopped, and somewhere beyond Heathrow's boundary fence an aircraft roared along the runway, climbing into the night sky. Frank saw its winking lights fade into the distance, saw the glow of the distant terminal buildings, and realised it hadn't been that long since he'd passed through Heathrow customs himself.

He was pleased with his night's work. He'd watched Josh and his team from beneath the lip of the steel grate, up to his eyes in putrid shit, the thin breathing tube snaking up into the rain gulley. He saw the torches sweeping across the festering lake, heard the boots above his head as they scoured the edges of the pit, and watched them reassemble on the other side and disappear back through the fence. He waited until he was certain they were gone, until the UAV had stopped criss-crossing the sky above. Then he waited a while longer, finally crawling out of the cloying morass and stumbling towards the woods beyond the farm. There he stripped, dumping his stinking clothes, the thin dry suit, the buoyancy aid and facemask, locating the holdall he'd stashed earlier that afternoon. He used the portable shower bag and antiseptic wash and scrubbed until it was empty then checked himself for cuts and scrapes. Then he'd changed into fresh clothes, crossed the wood until he reached the main road, and dumped his old clothes into a waste bin outside a darkened pub. Not long after that he flagged down a passing cab.

Now he watched that same cab drive away.

He started walking towards the nearby Tube station. Soon he'd find another taxi, hole up in a decent central London hotel for the night, call a private doctor, get a couple of booster shots. He ran events over in his mind, how he'd infiltrated enemy territory and executed his mission, coming through intact on the other side. Frank smiled; it was just like old times. Hopefully Roy and the kid had made it too. He'd find out soon enough.

He looked ahead, to his next mission.

With the Transition fast approaching they wouldn't be expecting him. He thought about the equipment he'd need, his route across Europe, the probability of mission success. It was almost zero, but that was okay with Frank. Lately the nights had become longer, the voices louder, his name whispered from the shadows. It would never end, he knew that now, but he would confront those beasts when he was good and ready. First he had to make sure that tonight's mission had succeeded, that the loose ends were tied up.

Loose ends used to be Frank's speciality.

He'd deal with one of them in the morning.

Chapter Twenty-Three

'Well, what d'you reckon?'

'My head says gangland,' the Detective Chief Inspector told his subordinate, 'but my gut says something else.' He fished a pen out of his pocket and scooped up an empty brass casing from the ground. It was one of hundreds scattered in the mud and concrete around the travellers' site where the DCI had been since the sunrise that morning. That sun had now climbed above the trees, glinting off the pools of rainwater that filled the potholes on the access road. 'See what I mean?' he said, offering up the spent casing. 'No head stamp. Untraceable.'

'Perfect,' the inspector grumbled. He stamped his feet, his breath fogging on the chilly morning air. 'Maybe we can fob this off onto Trident then?'

The DCI pointed to the charred remains of a large caravan a few metres away. 'You see any black kids in there? No you don't. What we *do* have are a dozen dead gypsies riddled with untraceable bullets, a hit and run out on the lane and a burnt-out Toyota five miles away.' He stared at the bullet casing for another few moments then placed it back on the ground.

He stood up, knees cracking in protest. The site was criss-crossed with police tape that swirled in the sharp morning breeze. White-suited forensics types combed the ground while more police officers erected tents over the two burned-out caravans. The DCI stood on the road between their blackened husks, noting the missing roofs and melted side panels, the bodies inside that were charred beyond recognition, the remains mangled and twisted into grotesque shapes.

'They used some sort of accelerant,' the inspector told him. 'It'll be a cast iron bitch to identify the victims.'

The DCI noted the pools of now-hardened molten metal on the concrete and shook his head. This wasn't normal for the travelling community. He knew that when gypsies wanted to settle something they'd normally do it bare-chested with their dukes up, surrounded by baying crowds in a field or a barn, with chunks of money changing hands on the side. Most gypsies were old school; automatic weapons and fire accelerants certainly didn't fit the profile. He poked a muddy rut with his wellington boot.

'What about these tyre marks?'

'Moulds have been cast and they're on the way back to the lab.'

'Witnesses?'

A head shake.

'You're kidding me? A bloody great fire fight and no one heard a thing?'

The inspector swept his arm across the horizon. 'Take a look around, guv. Nearest property is half a mile away, plus there was a big storm last night. Roads were empty, everyone tucked up indoors.'

The DCI shook his head. 'Jesus Christ, this is going to be one colossal bloody headache.'

The inspector nodded, made notes in his

pocketbook. He finished writing, tapped it with his pen. 'You know, there is a bright side. With this lot cooked the local crime figures should take a drop for a while.'

The DCI shook his head, zipping his coat up against the chill. 'You really are a wicked bastard,' he grinned.

Frank kept his finger on the buzzer until an angry voice rasped over the intercom.

'What?'

'I'm here to see Sammy. I'm a friend of Roy's.'

He stood back and waited, working the muscles of his upper body as he loitered in the doorway of the Putney club. He kept his back to the crawl of the morning traffic, his face obscured by a black baseball cap, the collar of his jacket snapped up against the wind. A minute later the door opened, and a skinny kid with long hair greeted him.

'Come in,' he waved. Frank stepped inside, his eyes adjusting to the gloom. The kid bolted the door behind him. 'Follow me, I'll show you up.'

'I know the way,' Frank told him, remembering Roy's roughly drawn floor plan.

'Good. I've got to bottle up.'

Frank jogged up the stairs, flexing his limbs, getting his heart rate up. When he reached the top floor a man beckoned him into the office. It was only when Frank got closer that he realised it was a woman.

Tank.

Frank's eyes flicked to her empty hands, the room

beyond, the gap beneath the door. No shadows there, no heavies waiting. He stepped across the threshold, ready for a sudden assault. None came. His eyes roamed the room, picking out the details from Roy's brief; the large windows overlooking the street, the palms, the expensive rug, the period oil painting above the desk.

The man behind that desk stared at Frank with baleful eyes, a moneyed looking dude with grey hair and a tanned complexion. A large newspaper was spread across the desk in front of him.

Sammy French.

Tank motioned him to raise his arms and gave him a sloppy pat down. Sammy waved him into a chair. He watched Tank close the door, then she moved somewhere behind him, out of his eye line. That was okay with Frank. She wore leather sneakers, and they creaked when she moved her feet.

'Haven't seen anyone favour a female bodyguard since Gaddafi,' he smiled. 'The Israelis have some competent operatives though.' He glanced over his shoulder. 'I doubt you're in their league, ma'am.' The woman didn't respond, just flared her nostrils.

'Now, now, that's not very nice,' Sammy tutted, folding his newspaper and tossing it to one side. 'People think Tank can't handle herself because she's a woman. Personally I think she can hold her own with just about anyone. I saw her break a man's neck once, a bloke about your size. He's buzzing around town in one of those little electric spastic chariots now.' Sammy laughed at his own observation. 'All right, enough of the banter. Let's start again, shall we...?'

'Frank.'

'You said you were a friend of Roy's, yeah?'

Frank nodded.

'Strange, I didn't think that little shitbag had any friends. Well, I don't know if he's told you, but Roy's in a bit of trouble, Frank. He was supposed to do something for me last night—'

'You mean the accessory to murder thing?'

Sammy paused for a beat. 'Roy's got a big mouth. Tell me, Frank, who are you exactly?'

'A friend. He told me about your plan, and as a friend I advised him to stay at home.'

'Really?' Sammy leaned back in his chair, his hands clasped behind his head. 'Probably not the best advice you could've given him.'

Frank shrugged. 'That's a matter of opinion.' He took off his baseball cap and ran a hand through his thinning hair. Tank's reflection watched him in the brass desk lamp. 'Nice picture,' he said, nodding at the Fusilier behind Sammy.

'So tell me, Frank, you're American, right?'

Frank nodded.

'How d'you know Roy then? What are you, a long lost relative? A boyfriend? Is that it, Frank?' Sammy laughed, hooking a leg across his knee. 'You know, it wouldn't surprise me if Roy was a shirt lifter.'

'Do you always feel the need to insult people?'

Sammy scratched his chin theatrically. 'Let me

see...actually, yeah.' He wheeled his chair closer to the desk, his arms folded in front of him. 'The thing is, I've got a terrible temper, Frank. Got me into a lot of trouble when I was a kid. I hurt a lot of people, mainly because I didn't know when to stop hitting them. It was the same when I first went to prison, everyone trying to give it the large one. They all came unstuck. I've calmed down over the years, but occasionally I get this terrible urge to do some damage. When that happens I try to control my emotions with a bit of levity.'

'Have I upset you?'

'I haven't decided yet.'

'Were you abused as a child?' Frank watched Sammy's eyes narrow and held up a hand. 'Hey, I only ask because I grew up in an orphanage, saw a lot of kids with a lot of problems. Many of them came from broken homes, dysfunctional families—all that can lead to feelings of guilt and anger, emotions that are usually expressed in the form of violent acts.'

'What are you, a fucking psychiatrist?'

Frank laughed. 'Hell no, but there's been times when I could've used one. You ever feel like that, Sammy? You ever feel like the whole world is against you, that not one living soul on this planet could ever understand the crushing guilt, the anguish that drives a man into black despair? The screams of a thousand tortured souls haunting you in the night?'

Sammy frowned. 'Jesus, you must be one fucked-up individual.'

'Oh, Jesus knows all right.'

'Come again?'

'I said Jesus knows. About my sins. My guilt.'

Now it was Sammy's turn to laugh. He peered under his desk. 'Tank, where did you put my tambourine and sandals?'

'Excuse me?'

The laughter faded. Sammy stared at Frank across the desk. 'Okay, let's cut the bullshit. Tell me why you're here.'

Frank's eyes flicked to the brass lamp, the reflection that had moved a little closer. He kept his hands in his lap, flexed his fingers, his feet braced beneath the chair.

'Roy Sullivan is an innocent man,' Frank said. 'He's lost his whole family before the age of forty. He's been tortured by the mystery of his missing brother for three years, a mystery that has cost him his marriage and a decent relationship with his son. He has nothing, and nobody.'

'I'm choking up already.'

'Listen to me, Sammy. You're done with Roy. He's suffered enough. Cut him loose.'

Sammy shook his head. 'Roy fucked up. He let people down last night. I'd made plans, spent money—'

'Derek's dead.'

Across the desk, Sammy froze. So did the reflection in the brass lamp. Sammy stared at Frank for several moments before he spoke. 'Say that again?'

'I saw him get cut in half with a shotgun last night. His friends at the trailer park, they're dead too.'

He watched the gangster's reaction, saw his

furrowed brow, his eyes scanning the neat row of mobile phones on his desk. He picked one up, thumbed its buttons.

'Derek won't be calling again.'

Sammy leaned back in his chair, his eyes clouded with doubt, a hand rubbing his jaw. 'You were there?'

Frank nodded.

'And Derek's dead?'

'Killed by a big guy with a tattoo right here.' Frank touched his cheek, just below his left eye.

'What happened to him?'

Frank shrugged. 'Dead too, most likely. So you see, you don't need Roy anymore.'

Sammy pointed to a TV in the corner of the room where a Sky News ticker trailed across the bottom of the screen. 'So tell me, Frank, why isn't it all over the news?'

'I don't know. Ask the cops.'

'Don't get smart,' Sammy warned, but his voice had lost its dangerous edge. The prospect of so many convenient deaths seemed to please him.

'You're in the clear,' Frank said. 'Just give me Roy's knife and the phone, then we'll be out of your life.'

Sammy shook his head. 'He really has got a big mouth, hasn't he?' He tugged open a drawer, produced the bloodstained plastic bag, the knife and iPhone inside. 'You mean these?' he said, holding the bag aloft.

Frank nodded. 'That's it.'

'Not a fucking chance.' He dropped the bag back into the drawer and slapped it shut. 'You think I'm going to let that little shit off the hook on your say so, Frank? I don't care if half of London is dead, Roy disobeyed orders. And instead of coming here to beg for my forgiveness, he sent some long streak of piss Yank to beg on his behalf. I can't let that slide, pal. So go back and tell Roy that I own him. Tell him I've got him for the rest of his naturals. And tell him I'll be seeing him very soon.'

He wagged a finger across the desk. 'As for you Frank, well, you can count yourself lucky you're walking out of here. You come to my place of business again uninvited and we'll be having a different sort of chat. Now get the fuck out.'

Frank stood, shoved the baseball cap in his pocket. Time to light the fuse.

'Don't be an asshole, Sammy. Just give me the bag and you won't get hurt.'

Sammy's face darkened. 'Last chance, Frankie. Leave. While you still can.'

'What's the matter? That pussy little temper of yours getting the better of you again?'

Sammy sprang to his feet, his chair slamming against the wall, the Fusilier wobbling above him. He snatched the bag from the drawer, pulled out the infantry knife, held it low by his leg. 'You want the knife, Frankie boy? Why don't you come and get it.'

Frank smiled. 'Like taking candy from a baby.'

Sammy snarled and came around the desk at speed.

Frank heard the creak of leather behind him.

He kicked backwards, sending his chair crashing into Tank's shins. The woman cursed, stumbled. Frank turned just as Sammy threw himself at him, the serrated black blade held high, then plunging down in a violent arc towards Frank's chest. Frank blocked the strike with his left arm and shot his right out, his extended fingers stabbing deep into Sammy's windpipe. Sammy dropped the knife and staggered backwards, his hands clutched against his throat. Frank spun around, just as Tank launched a roundhouse kick at his head. He ducked, the leg breezing the top of his skull, and moved in fast. Tank, younger and fitter, saw the move and spun past him. Frank picked up the brass desk lamp and hurled it at her. She twisted her body and the lamp crashed against the wall. Frank had underestimated her. She was fast, and tougher than he expected. There was no fear in her eyes, only the cool appraisal of a natural fighter looking for an advantage.

Swaying behind her, Sammy kicked the infantry knife at his feet. 'Kill him,' he wheezed. 'Spill his fucking guts.'

Tank scooped up the Gerber and came at Frank fast. She held the blade low and thrust it at his stomach, Frank twisted his body and caught the limb as she lunged. He locked her arm then elbowed her hard in the face, reassured by the sound and feel of crunching bone. Sammy reached behind him, pulled a pistol from his waistband. He wheezed and spat, his eyes streaming, the Browning swaying in his unsteady hand. Frank charged at him, using Tank as a shield. She cannoned into Sammy and the gun discharged, the noise deafening.

Sammy screamed.

The gun fell to the rug and Frank moved in fast, snatching it up, racking a new round into the breech. He spun around to face them. Tank swayed unsteadily on her feet, her nose splattered by Frank's elbow, the blood pouring down the front of her beige tracksuit. Sammy had sunk to his knees, his grey shirt and trousers soaked with dark blood, his hands shaking, his watery eyes pleading.

'Get it out,' he gasped. 'For fuck's sake, get it out.'

The knife was buried deep in Sammy's left side, just below the ribcage. He stared at it, shivering, his fingers dancing around the black handle, knowing he should pull it out but too frightened to touch it. Frank watched him turn very white, then topple onto his side.

Tank's eyes flicked from Sammy to the gun in Frank's hand. Frank could see the pain and confusion behind her eyes, yet there was something else there too—a seething anger, the frustration of a fighter denied the opportunity of hand to hand combat by the gun between them. Frank smiled, ejected the magazine, the round from the breech. He tossed the gun across the room and dropped into a fighting stance, his fingers beckoning.

'Okay, girlie, if that's what you really want. Let's see what you got.'

Tank pinched the bridge of her nose and expelled

blood and mucus in an angry snort. She stepped over Sammy's body to circle Frank, arms raised, fists bunched, chin tucked low as she bobbed her head from side to side. She closed the gap quickly, made her move, but Frank saw it coming. He dodged the kick, parried the punch and grabbed her arm, using her momentum to spin her around while putting a powerful lock on her elbow joint. Tank screamed in pain as Frank slammed her face onto Sammy's desk and applied even more pressure, bending the arm back and upwards until the elbow joint cracked, the splintered bone slicing through her tracksuit. Before she could scream again Frank grabbed the back of her head, his fingers finding purchase in her thick Mohican, and lifted it high, smashing her skull once, twice on the corner of the desk. He saw her eyes roll up into their sockets and let her body slump to the rug. He knelt down, checked her pulse. It was strong, steady. She was a tough broad. She'd live.

Frank ran to the door, pulled it open. No voices, no feet pounding up the stairs. Nothing.

He went behind the desk, saw a gym bag underneath. He emptied out the sweats and sneakers and slung it over his shoulder, taking every phone he could find, including Roy's bagged up iPhone and the one in Tank's pocket. He rifled the drawers, found a thick stack of fifty-pound notes. That went into the bag too. He traced the cables around the ceiling's cornice work, discovered the CCTV room next to Sammy's en suite facilities, ejected the discs from the recorders.

They went into the bag along with the cash and the phones.

Out in the office, Frank saw that Sammy had expired. He stood over his blood soaked body, pulled the knife from his guts. He knelt down next to the unconscious Tank, pressing the handle of the knife into her palm, rolling her fingers into the handle's grooves until the cops would be left with no doubt that she'd used the knife in at least two murders. Then he picked up the landline phone on Sammy's desk and punched three numbers in rapid succession.

'What emergency service do you require?' said the voice on the other end.

Frank waited a moment, until the operator had repeated the question, then whispered two faint words.

'Help me.'

He left the receiver on the desk, left the room. Loud music greeted him in the club downstairs. He saw the kid who'd let him in, stacking bottles of beer in glass-fronted fridges behind the bar, his body swaying to the thumping beat, back turned away from the room. Frank kept moving.

Three minutes later he was lost in the quiet streets of Putney, the sound of a single police siren wailing in the distance. Ten more after that he was striding along the towpath that ran alongside the River Thames, destination Hammersmith.

The river was empty, and the freshening breeze felt cleansing, washing away the stench of death and violence that lingered after his recent, brutal exertions.

His goal, however, had been achieved; Roy Sullivan was free, unburdened from the mystery of his brother's death, released from the debt of a dangerous criminal, free to escape the city, find sanctuary with his family before the Transition began. He should've felt good about it, his own guilt lifted, but he didn't.

The green iron span of Hammersmith Bridge soon came into view through the trees. He found a quiet spot in the bushes close to the water. He took the phones out of the bag, removed the SIM cards, and threw the handsets far out into the middle of the river. A nearby gaggle of brown-feathered water birds protested with angry calls and flapping wings. Frank moved on, snapping the DVDs into pieces, dropping broken SIMS into different waste bins.

Clouds crept across the sun. Back in Harlem he'd truly believed he could right the wrongs, absolve himself of his sins, but now he realised that that could never be. Even if he could stop the Transition, or save a billion lives, it would never wash the blood from his hands. Despair plucked at his consciousness, and Frank was scared again.

The sun came out then, bathing him in its warmth and light, and the fear melted away. It was another sign, he realised. He muttered a small prayer of thanks, that God had granted him the ability to save another, that He had watched over and guided him this far, leading him along His path towards his last, final mission.

The end was coming, and Frank smiled.

He was ready.

Chapter Twenty-Four

Roy saw the ivy-covered pillars looming out of the darkness and turned the wheel, steering the VW Golf through the iron gates and into the grounds of the manor house. He noticed Frank's suspicious eyes flick towards the wing mirror, to the shadowy figures that closed the gates behind them.

'How many?' he asked.

Roy shrugged. 'A dozen, maybe more. We barely see them but Nate says they're pros. Vicky's looking forward to seeing you,' he added, trying to change the subject.

Frank took in the extensive grounds, the dark woods that surrounded the estate's high walls. 'On the face of it this could be a good place to wait out the Transition. A little hard to defend maybe, but if there were enough of you...'

Roy touched his foot on the brakes, the Golf crunching to a stop on the gravel outside the main doors. 'To tell you the truth we haven't thought about it.'

'No?' Frank unclipped his seatbelt, twisted in his seat. 'This isn't a game, Roy. The Transition is coming. It can't be stopped.'

Roy turned off the engine. 'We can try though, right, Frank? Someone's got to try.'

Frank glanced past Roy to the manor house, where another shadow waited by the open door.

'Who else is here?'

'Me, Vicky, Nate, plus a couple of others.'

'Who?'

He took a breath. 'A politician. And a newspaper man.'

Frank shook his head. 'You're wasting your time.'

'Not everyone can be part of this bloody conspiracy, Frank. There must be some good people left.'

Frank remained silent, studying the manor house, the dimly lit hallway. 'How much do they know?'

'Right now they think it's a national security issue. Vicky set it up, swore them both to secrecy. She's been sitting by Max's bed going through your data for the last forty-eight hours. Have you actually seen any of it, Frank?'

'It doesn't matter. It won't make a difference.'

'Vicky thinks it can. She said she'd wait for you before she said anything. Please, Frank, come and meet them, tell your story. Jimmy died trying to uncover this whole mess. If it wasn't for him you wouldn't even be here.' Roy climbed out of the VW. 'C'mon, Frank. Please.'

Roy waited. The cooling engine ticked on the night air. He hoped he'd said the right things.

'What the hell,' Frank muttered, opening his door.

The security guard ushered them in, and Roy led Frank into a large, wood-panelled dining room. He saw Frank's eyes take in the gilded oil frames on the walls, the dark antique furniture, the heavy plum drapes shutting out the grounds beyond. Vicky and the others rose from their chairs around the large mahogany dining table. Before Roy could do the introductions Vicky stepped forward and greeted Frank by wrapping her arms around him. She held him like that for several moments, then took his hands in hers.

'Thank you, Frank.'

'How's the little feller?'

'He's doing okay. How about you?'

'Did Roy tell you?'

Vicky squeezed his hands. 'I've seen the news, Frank.'

Roy had seen it too.

Sammy's death had made the papers but there wasn't much more than a brief byline while investigations continued. The gypsy camp was a different story altogether. Details of that dark and violent night had consumed the media for the last couple of days, the red tops splashed with typically lurid headlines such as *Gypsy Camp Bloodbath, Traveller Terror* and *Big Fat Gypsy Massacre,* while the TV continued to broadcast the same aerial images of burned out caravans and country lanes blocked by police vehicles. Thankfully they seemed no closer to solving the mystery, hindered by a lack of witnesses and stonewalled by the travelling community itself. There was no word of Derek, the bodies so badly burned that they'd almost disintegrated.

Memories of his violent encounter with Max's hard-faced gaoler were still raw, her threats and curses, her painted nails clawing at his mouth and face. He remembered the smells in that caravan too, of furniture polish and cooking fat, knowing he'd never eat another bacon sandwich again without thinking of that night. He shook his head to clear his thoughts, catching the end of Frank's words.

'I tried to avoid violence,' he was saying. 'I didn't have any choice.'

'I don't care,' Vicky assured him. 'Max was in harm's way. You and Roy brought him home.'

'Is this conversation relevant to our meeting?'

All eyes in the room turned to the woman in the navy trouser suit and shoulder-length grey hair. Her presence here tonight was a result of Roy's journey to Selly Oak, near Birmingham, the day before. There he'd sat in the MP's surgery on the busy Pershore Road for over two hours, listening to the chatter around him, the complaints of littered pavements, of broken street lighting and speeding motorists outside the local primary school. He'd waited until last, when the final complainant had trudged off into the night, when her familiar face had invited him inside with that distinctive voice and a tired smile, still eager, after so many hours, to listen to the grumbles of her constituents. It was then that Roy knew he'd chosen well.

Her voice was strong and clear, and when she spoke, Roy was reminded of another time and place, the day the air was filled with noise, the streets with chaos, a day when that same voice had reverberated around that historic square. The day all this began.

It was Vicky who made the introductions. 'Frank, I'd like you to meet Anna Reynolds, Member of Parliament for Selly Oak. She also sits on the Home

Affairs Select Committee.'

'Mister Marshall,' said Reynolds, extending her hand.

'It's just Frank.'

The man standing next to Reynolds stepped forward and offered his own hand. 'My name is George Burnett. I'm the owner of the *West London Herald*.'

'George is my boss,' Vicky explained. 'He owns the *Herald* outright, Frank. No investors, no shareholders, no agendas, political or otherwise. One hundred per cent independent and objective. A champion of the free press, right, George?'

Burnett smiled with crooked teeth. 'Vicky flatters me but yes, we've managed to maintain that independence over the years.'

Roy could see Frank was wary. He moved past them to where Nate was standing at the head of the table. They shook hands.

'Your security detail, what's their brief?'

'Two teams of twelve, roaming patrols of the house and the estate.'

'Armed?'

Nate shook his head. 'They're private contractors, Blackstone Industries. Not authorised in the UK for firearms.'

'Blackstone, huh? They've got a good rep.'

'They should do,' Nate said, 'my father's on the board.'

Frank turned and addressed the room. 'Look, I don't know what you people expect to gain from this

341

little pow-wow but whatever it is, it's not going to matter. You're too late.'

'If time is pressing then I suggest we make a start,' Reynolds said.

'Anna's right,' Burnett echoed, his hands thrust into the pockets of his trousers. 'If you have a story that's in the public interest, we all need to hear it.'

Vicky pulled out a chair. 'Please, Frank. Take a seat.'

Roy took his place next to a reluctant Frank. Folders had been arranged on the table for the newcomers. He watched them study the neatly printed pages inside, the PowerPoint presentations and flowcharts. Reynolds was skimming through hers quickly. Burnett clicked a pen and doodled on a notepad to get the ink flowing. Vicky slipped into a chair next to Frank. She cleared her throat and addressed her editor and Reynolds across the table.

'The reason I've asked you both here is documented in this report. It's not comprehensive and most of it is unverified, but it contains information that will potentially impact every nation on this planet.'

She paused, tapping her own folder with a slender finger.

'There is a conspiracy underway, one that is as far reaching as it is deadly, and it has been in play for well over two decades. The people behind this conspiracy operate at the highest levels of every major industrial nation across the globe. They are billionaires, some well-known, most unheard of, but they are all tainted with the stain of their involvement. Frank has intimate knowledge of these matters. He knows names, dates, times and events—'

'Wait,' Frank interrupted, turning to Vicky. 'Who do you think you're going to convince with this?'

She held his stony gaze. 'My editor and Miss Reynolds for a start. If I can do that, then we have a chance.'

'A chance at what? I told you that the Transition can't be stopped. I told you to keep the data safe, so that future generations would know the truth.'

Roy turned in his chair. 'Frank, please—'

The American got to his feet, his eyes locking onto each of them in turn. 'Don't any of you get it? The Transition is like a runaway freight train—if you try to stop it you'll be crushed. If you go public with any of this, all you'll achieve is accelerating the speed of your own demise.'

He stabbed a finger at Burnett.

'Print and be damned, is that right? You'd be setting yourself against the power behind the global media, and as soon as they sniff this story they'll crush you *and* your little newspaper.'

He turned on Reynolds.

'As for a politician, well, no offence, ma'am, but you'll be an easy target. They'll find something on you and—'

'I can assure you, Mister Marshall, that I've lived a mundane and scandal-free existence.'

'Congratulations. In that case they'll make

something up. You'll spend every waking moment fighting a lie, and ultimately no one will care about you or anything you've got to say. They control the narrative.'

'Who are *they*?' Reynolds asked. She folded her arms on the table. 'Why don't you start from the beginning, Frank? Tell us who *they* are and why they cannot be stopped from doing something that all of you are clearly very concerned about.'

Roy laid a hand on Frank's arm. 'Tell them, Frank. Tell them everything.'

So he did.

It was midnight when Frank had finished with them.

Roy heard the sound of the grandfather clock in the hallway ring out a dozen soft, melodic chimes. He was dog-tired, slumped in a chair at the far end of the table, but he was determined to stay awake until he knew which way the wind would blow. He'd left the room twice, to use the toilet and to check in on Max, but for much of the evening he'd listened, watching the reactions of Burnett and Reynolds. Initially they'd been sceptical, well versed as they were in global politics and the workings of the media, but Frank slowly chipped away at their preconceptions. Reynolds had become particularly animated when Frank had revealed TDL Global's deep involvement, the crimes of her nemesis laid bare. But it didn't end there.

Frank told them everything, every detail he could recall, every installation he'd ever visited, every political and business connection he knew of, the players he'd met, every name he'd heard. Frank the confessor, the two priests across the table peeling back the layers, digging ever deeper, their faces paling at the enormity of his sins and those of his employers. Frank sat before them, collar open, shirt sleeves rolled to the elbows, undermining their faith in a system they'd believed in all their lives, and when they couldn't take much more of the truth Frank told them about Messina, bringing their carefully constructed world view crashing down around them. Finally, when the notepads were full and the coffee cups drained, Roy knew that Frank had convinced them. As he too had been convinced.

Burnett and Reynolds sat at the table for a long time, going back over their notes, a clarification here, another question there, but Roy could see it in their faces and it frightened him. They were defeated, crushed by the sheer weight of Frank's story. Now they sat in silence, troubled frowns creasing their faces, Burnett chewing his pen, Reynolds running a nervous hand through her hair. Across the table Frank watched them. There was no satisfaction in his victory, Roy could see that. He simply sat there, waiting.

It was the politician who moved first, getting to her feet and helping herself to something dark from the drinks cabinet in the corner of the room. She came back to the table with three glasses, sliding them across the polished wood to Frank and Burnett respectively. She took a small sip of her own and set the glass down.

'And the Transition will happen when?'

Frank shrugged. 'Soon.'

She looked beyond Frank, fingering the rim of her glass. 'I still can't believe it.'

The American necked his drink in a single swallow. 'Then don't. Either way, it's coming.'

Reynolds tipped her own drink back and pushed the glass to one side. 'Unless we stop it.'

'You can't.'

'Why not?'

'Haven't you been listening, ma'am? No offence, but you guys are seriously small fish in a sea of ravenous sharks. You'll get eaten the moment you swim in their direction.'

'There must be another way, Frank. What about the *direct action* you spoke of?'

'What do you mean?'

'You said you were going to bring the fight to them. You said one man wouldn't make a difference, yet you're going to do it anyway.'

'It's personal. I have a reckoning.'

'It seems we're all facing that same reckoning.'

Frank shook his head. 'I have to do this alone.'

'How will you find them?' Burnett said.

'I know where they're going to be. And when.'

Reynolds came around the table, took a seat next to Frank, pulling her chair close. 'Tell me, Frank, are you so disgusted with the world that you cannot bear to try and save it?'

'You don't understand—'

'I think I do. You talk about God and redemption, the need to make amends, and yet you think that applies only to you. I'm a churchgoer, Frank. I've sinned too. Don't *I* deserve the chance to change things?'

Roy saw Vicky and Nate enter the room. She gave Roy a nod, their signal that Max was fine, still sleeping. She eyed the glasses on the table.

'What's going on?'

'Frank's about to tell us how to stop the Transition,' Burnett told her.

'You can't stop it,' Frank scowled. 'An operation like that would be logistically impossible without government and military cooperation.'

'So indulge us,' Reynolds invited.

Vicky and Nate took seats at the table. All eyes were now on Frank.

'You want to waste your time, fine.' Frank pulled his chair a little closer to the table. 'The only way to neutralise The Committee would be to plan and execute an operation in total and utter secrecy. You would need authority at *the* highest level, with access to military hardware that can only be authorised on behalf of the President of the United States by the Secretary of State for Defence, and you can't ask him because I've seen him at the Eyrie in Denver. Do you get it now? Officially sanctioned action is impossible. Which leaves illegal action, completely off the books. And without political authority you're going to have to forget about the billion-dollar hardware you'd need to do the job properly and search for another solution. That would mean using small teams of experienced operators, willing to smuggle military-spec equipment and weapons across international borders and cross hostile terrain in order to engage with a well-armed and highly motivated paramilitary force. They would have to kill unarmed civilians without hesitation, putting their own lives and the lives of their families on the line, because if the plan fails, The Committee will hunt down every last man involved and kill them all. That's if the authorities don't arrest them first. Tell me you can do all of that, and I'll tell you how it can be done. Otherwise you've got nothing.'

Frank leaned back in his chair, spent. No one said anything for a minute or two. It was Reynolds who finally broke the silence.

'Surely Messina will provide that motivation? If people knew what the alternative was—'

'You're outta time.' Frank shook his head. 'My advice? Save yourselves and your loved ones. Prepare for what's coming.'

Roy felt another ripple of fear. He'd been experiencing them all evening, the cold fingers on the back of his neck, his thoughts slowly turning toward escape. Where would he go? Where would any of them go? He looked at Vicky across the table, saw Nate's hand gripping hers, saw that same fear reflected in Nate's eyes. Then he looked beyond them, to the antique sideboard against the wall, the silver frames arranged along its length.

He pushed his chair back, walked across the room, his finger tracing the framed photographs, of bow-tied men and well-heeled women, suits and dresses, formal and informal, the powerbrokers who frequented this impressive country retreat. But it was the larger of the photographs that had caught Roy's eye, two men standing side by side, their smiles wide, their hands locked together, one immaculately dressed in a tuxedo, the other clothed in the military splendour of a senior American officer, his chest bedecked with ribbons.

'Who's that?' Roy asked, tapping the polished glass.

Nate peered across the room. 'My father.'

Roy knew what Nate's dad looked like. His jealous fingers had searched the Internet way back. 'No, the other one.'

'That's General James Moody.'

Roy picked it up, studied it for several moments. 'They seem close.'

'They've been tight since grade school. Best men at each other's weddings, godfathers to each other's kids. They're practically brothers.'

Roy took the frame back to the table. He laid it down in front of Nate. 'This man is your godfather?'

'That's what I said. Bill's attended every major event in my life. He's family.'

'When did you last see him?'

'Thanksgiving. Mom and Dad flew down to the house in Tampa. I joined them for dinner on a layover. Why do you ask?'

Roy tapped the photograph. 'D'you think Bill would let you die?'

Nate's face darkened. 'Excuse me?'

'Roy!' Vicky protested.

Roy ignored her. Instead he looked at Frank and said, 'I want to see Max grow up, Frank. I want us all to go on and live normal lives.'

'You can forget that.'

'Bullshit,' Roy shot back. 'I'm scared, Frank. We all are. If this man is Nate's family then maybe he'll be scared too. Scared enough to help us.'

Frank sighed and got to his feet. He came around the table, picked up the photograph. He studied it carefully.

'A fellow jarhead, huh?'

Nate stood up. 'That's right.'

Frank drilled him with hard eyes. 'Everything we've spoken about—the Eyrie, the Transition, Messina— have you ever heard those words used in *any* of your dealings with your father?'

Nate shook his head.

'What about TDL Global? You do any business with them? Or Terra Petroleum?'

'I'm not familiar with Terra. I think we've brokered some investments for a TDL subsidiary. I'll need to check.'

'What about your personal diary? How does it look in six weeks? Six months? Any special family trips planned? Something out of the ordinary, somewhere remote?'

Nate shook his head. 'The family always gathers at the Hamptons for the summer. Dad likes to sail. This year's no exception.'

'What about the General? Senior career guys like him tend to fall into two categories. They either climb aboard the Washington merry-go-round or stay married to the Corps. Which one is Moody? Is he a politician or a patriot?'

Nate stared long and hard at Frank. 'Like you said, he's a Marine.'

'So was I. He's human.'

'Well, knowing Bill, if you had the audacity to question his patriotism he'd probably shoot you.'

Frank smiled. 'Oorah.'

'Right. In any case, he's not at the Pentagon. He's in Florida, McDill Air Force Base. He's CENTCOM commander.'

Frank raised an eyebrow. 'CENTCOM? Jesus.'

Roy spoke for the rest of the room. 'What's CENTCOM?'

'United States Central Command. It's a theatre-level combat command, runs operations across the Middle East and Afghanistan. CENTCOM's a big hitter. Huge.'

Frank fell silent. The clock in the hallway struck the half-hour. Frank's eyes remained fixed on Nate. 'So the General's a patriot, huh? You think he's got the stones to rip up the rulebook? To go rogue?'

'Bill's courage is not open for debate. I can't speak for his decision-making process.'

Frank stroked his jaw. 'He could still be dirty. Any approach would be risky.'

Nate bristled. 'My godfather is a man of impeccable

honour and integrity. No way would he be involved in any of this.'

'Honour or not, he's part of the machine. He's also in charge of a powerful combat group. When the Transition begins they'll be used to maintain order, and men of honour will be forced to do unspeakable things to their fellow countrymen in the name of freedom and security. And they'll do it because they'll be told it's the patriotic thing to do. The General's no different from anyone else.'

Nate shook his head. 'I feel sorry for you, Frank. You've been on the wrong side for too long.' He tapped the photograph with his finger. 'If you ever meet Bill you should ask him about his only child, Kyle. We were best friends in college, only Kyle didn't follow his dad into the military. He went MIT instead, computer engineering, a scarily bright kid. Bill and Kathy couldn't have been more proud.' He glanced at the photo again and said, 'On the morning of Nine Eleven, Kyle was a passenger on United Ninety-Three. The last call he made was to his dad, just before the plane went down in Shanksville. He was twenty-two years old. Bill and Kathy never got over it.'

Nate used the silence that followed to place the frame carefully back on the sideboard. Then he walked back around the table and stood before Frank.

'If I can get you in front of the General you can tell him your story. And when you're done, you can look him in the eye and ask him yourself if he has the stones to do anything about it.'

'I'll go one better,' Frank replied. 'You get me in front of the General and I'll tell him why there was never any plane crash in Shanksville. I'll tell him what really happened to his boy. And who was responsible.'

Roy registered the faces around him, Burnett and Reynolds's disbelief, Vicky's concern for her fiancé, a sudden and unexpected determination in Frank's eye. As for Nate, he already had a mobile phone clamped to his ear. In the silent wake of Frank's words, everyone could hear the distant ringing, the voice that answered the call.

'Yes, sir?'

Nate's eyes never left Frank's. 'Have the jet prepped for transatlantic, please, Robert. We're going to Florida. Tampa International.'

Chapter Twenty-Five

The air in the deep-level basement room was thick and stuffy, the silence like a lead blanket.

Roy fidgeted in his chair, ran a finger around his shirt collar. The grey linoleum floor beneath his shoes looked scuffed and worn, the drab green paint on the walls faded and peeling. The water cooler in the corner bubbled occasionally, the only other furniture four plain metal chairs, two of them now occupied by Vicky and himself.

Across the room shadows moved behind the frosted glass door as the meeting inside lingered into its second hour. Roy cocked his head again, but he couldn't hear anything. The briefing room was soundproofed, like the anteroom itself—even the sour-faced Military Policeman standing guard outside couldn't hear them. Roy shifted in his seat again. Like most government buildings the radiators were too warm, the air cloying, and the armpits of his shirt had become damp with sweat. He pulled his tie away from his neck.

'Are you all right?' Vicky whispered. 'You're sweating.'

Roy grimaced. 'What do you expect? We're stuck in a bunker fifty feet below ground and they've got the rads on full blast.' He dabbed his forehead with a tissue.

'Why did you wear a suit? It's not a job interview.'

'God knows. They sent a car for us, said we were going somewhere important. I wish I hadn't worn the bloody thing.'

Vicky smiled. 'Well, there's no chance of freezing to death, that's for sure.'

Roy fingered the plastic ID tag clipped to his pocket. 'What is Northwood anyway?'

'I asked Anna the same thing. It's a command centre for UK military operations.'

Roy grunted. His estranged wife looked infuriatingly composed in navy blue trousers and white shirt, a matching jacket draped over an empty chair. Her hair was tied in a neat ponytail, her make-up subtle, her skin already tinted by a few warm days of spring sunshine. She looked stunning, as she always did.

And she'd worked so hard lately, juggling her time between caring for Max and compiling a more detailed report from the information Frank had liberated, until the final document ran into hundreds of pages. Cohen's hacked email account had offered up a goldmine of intelligence, yet as he sweated in the basement, all Roy could think about were the human guinea pigs at Copse Hill, trapped in their own grisly dungeons. It was like something from a horror movie. He hoped they'd be in time to save some of them.

The door to the briefing room swung open. Roy sat a little straighter in his chair, knotting his tie. He heard Reynolds' voice rising as she crossed the threshold, deep in conversation with two other men, one in a smart, charcoal-grey suit and green tie, the other a military type with red epaulettes. The soldier murmured something and left the room. Roy watched him go, unsettled by his manner. He followed Vicky as she got to her feet.

'Sorry to have kept you waiting,' Reynolds said. 'I'd like you to meet Richard Cavendish, Permanent Secretary to the Cabinet Office and First Parliamentary Counsel. Richard will be the UK's political lead from here on in.'

'Thank you, Anna.'

Roy swallowed as he shook the man's hand, now thoroughly intimidated. The Permanent Secretary was one of those people who seemed to exude natural authority, tall, distinguished, a pair of silver-framed glasses perched on a long, thin nose. His voice was deep, cultured. He clutched a sheaf of papers in his hand.

'Well, we've made some progress since this crisis began,' he told them. 'A picture is building, and monitored conversations have repeatedly referenced this Transition event. The more we uncover, the more disturbing it gets.'

Roy looked beyond Cavendish, to the room they'd just vacated. There were maybe twenty people in there, men and women, uniforms and suits, all grouped around a large table bathed in bright overhead lights. Documents and maps lay scattered across its surface, pored over by some, while others stood in the shadows, locked in sober discussion. Roy could feel the tension leaking out and filling the dead air of the anteroom.

'The rabbit hole runs deep,' Cavendish continued, adjusting the glasses on his nose as he scanned the pages in his hand. 'We're talking captains of industry, media figures, politicians, even two Cabinet members.' He swept the glasses from his face. 'The intelligence you've brought us is quite staggering. Three events from our recent history—the death of David Kelly, the Iraq War, the Seven-Seven bombings—are all connected, but not in the way that we've been conditioned to view them. Doctor Kelly was right; dark actors were certainly at work. And that work has clearly continued.'

'What happens now?' Vicky asked.

Cavendish rubbed an eye with a knuckle and slipped his glasses back on. 'We all have to tread very carefully here. Since you brought this to us a small group of trusted individuals from government and defence has been formed. We're using the cover of a snap civil emergency table exercise; however, its duration and clandestine nature is beginning to raise eyebrows. Add to that the possible implication of our own Prime Minister and his connections to TDL Global...well, quite frankly we're in an invidious position. One leak, one word out of place, and it could get very messy. Everything depends on the Americans now. It's up to them to throw the first punch. All we can do is pray it lands clean.'

Vicky paled. 'What if it doesn't?'

Cavendish lowered his voice. 'I can't go into specifics. Suffice to say we have some very serious men and women in that room who are more than willing to sacrifice everything to stop this. A plan is being drawn up, a list of those involved. When the time comes, direct action will be implemented.'

Vicky frowned. 'Are you talking about targeted assassinations?'

Cavendish didn't blink. 'As I said, I can't talk about specifics. Technically we're committing treason, which is a rather anachronistic notion over here, but for General Moody and his team it means something else entirely. The Americans are fully aware of the consequences of failure, for all of us. We must place our trust in them.'

'What about the broader political issues?' Vicky pressed. 'The fallout from all of this is going to be unprecedented.'

Reynolds cleared her throat. 'Yes it is. If and when the dominoes start to fall we *must* be able to control the narrative, which is why you're here to head up our media campaign, Vicky. General Moody has his own source, a journalist from the *Washington Post* who's now embedded with his team. When the time comes you'll break your stories simultaneously, but only after we get the green light from the General. Here it'll come from the *Herald*, a source no one expects. George will help speed national dissemination.'

Roy remembered Vicky's boss at the manor house, the newspaper proprietor's initial fear turning to anger, his cold determination to break the story via a hundred trusted sources, the truth gaining momentum, spreading across the country, the continent, until it could no longer be ignored. Burnett was back in west London now, quietly making calls, and re-establishing old relationships. Preparing. Everyone had a role to play except Roy; he was out of the loop, and that suited him fine. He had his own mission.

'Everything we do now has to be documented accurately and objectively,' Reynolds continued. 'The citizens of this country, and the wider world in general, must know that what we do, we do to preserve our way of life and everything we hold dear. That's the role you'll play, Vicky. Whatever happens now, we'll have an account on record. Win or lose, the truth will remain.'

'I understand,' Vicky nodded.

Roy had a question of his own to ask. He found himself holding up his hand, like a schoolboy. 'Is there any word on Frank?'

'He's with General's Moody team,' Reynolds shrugged. 'I'm afraid that's all we know.'

Roy hadn't seen Frank since he'd disappeared with Nate into that Buckinghamshire night over two weeks ago. He wondered where he was now, what he was doing. If he was okay. 'How about my request?'

'It'll have to wait, until it's over,' Reynolds cautioned.

'We'll take care of it,' Cavendish added. 'The least we can do.' He cleared his throat, tapped the papers into his palm. 'Well, we should get back to it. I'll need you in the briefing room, Vicky. There are introductions to be made, protocols to go over.' He stepped to one side, held out his arm. Vicky picked up her bag from the chair. Roy smiled and gave her a nod. *Good luck.*

Vicky hesitated. 'Can you give us a moment?'

The officials shook hands with Roy and retired behind the frosted glass door. Roy dropped into a chair, loosening his tie. Vicky sat next to him. 'You should be in there. If it wasn't for you, we'd still be in the dark about all of this.'

'Rubbish. It's down to you, Vicks. I wanted to run and hide, remember?' He smiled and said, 'Don't put that bit in when you write all this up.'

Vicky chewed her lip. 'I'm scared, Roy. None of us knows what's going to happen.'

'True, but *they* don't know that we know. If it stays that way we've got a chance.'

'And if we don't, they'll unleash Angola.'

Roy shook his head. 'We can't think like that. In any case, Frank said they'll find the antiviral at Copse Hill.'

'That's if those lunatics down there cooperate. What if they destroy it? What if they alert The Committee?' Vicky glanced at the frosted glass door, lowered her voice. 'Nate's made plans, in case it doesn't work out. There's a plane on standby at Farnborough. We should all be together, just in case.'

Roy gave her hand a squeeze. 'That's good to know.' He tried to withdraw it but she held it tight.

'There's something I want to say, before I go in.' Vicky looked down at his hand, smoothing it with her own. 'I never really thanked you properly for saving Max. What you did that night—'

'What we both did.'

Her eyes locked onto his. 'No. What *you* did. You delivered on your promise, Roy. You brought our son back.' She blinked several times, shiny tears rolling down her cheeks. 'Damn, I'm not used to saying that.'

She rummaged in her handbag for a tissue, dabbed her eyes. 'You've changed, Roy Sullivan.'

'Roy two-point-zero,' he chuckled, but there was more to say. A confession to be made. 'You were right all along, Vicks. I pushed everyone away. I knew what I was doing, but I was angry, with you, with Jimmy, and I lost Max in all of that. I've been so bloody stupid.'

Vicky took his hands, held them tight. 'None of that matters now. The important thing is we're here, together. And Max is okay. The bad dreams have stopped and he's loving the Hamptons, playing on the beach. You should see him, Roy. He's blossoming.'

He had a sudden vision of Max, baggy shorts and chubby legs, splashing in the surf. Safe. Happy. He cleared his throat. 'I'm glad. He deserves it. You both do.' He let go of her hands and got to his feet. 'Best not keep them waiting, eh?'

'Best not.' Vicky stood too, slipping the straps of her handbag over her shoulder. 'What about the flat? Your job?'

Roy shrugged. 'I've not been back to either. The Fitzroy doesn't feel like home any more. I'm still off work—stress,' he explained, making finger quotes. 'Sooner or later I'm going to have to make a decision though. You think Nate would mind if I stayed on at the manor house until this is over?'

'Of course he won't.'

'Good. Tell him thanks.' He gave her arm a squeeze. 'Look after yourself, Vicky. Give Max a big kiss and cuddle for me. Tell him I'll see him soon.'

'I will.' Then she leaned forward and pecked him on the cheek. 'Take care. Don't be a stranger.'

Roy couldn't help himself. He reached out and held her. Vicky held him right back, and Roy was reminded of the girl he'd met on that hot summer night, the connection they'd made, somewhere in that unchartered place between the heart and the subconscious. He felt that familiar electricity surging through him once more, filling his chest. He leaned in close to her ear. 'I still love you, Vicky. I never stopped.'

'I know,' she whispered, her eyes moist, her lips soft on his cheek.

He squeezed her again then slowly, reluctantly, let her go. 'Maybe in the next life,' he said, brushing a stray hair off her face.

'Maybe.'

She crossed the room and opened the door, the low murmur of voices spilling out into the anteroom. She smiled at Roy one last time, then closed the door behind her.

Her shadow lingered beyond the frosted glass for a moment, and then she was gone.

Chapter Twenty-Six

He made the jump from a US Air Force C-130, stepping off the ramp at twenty-four thousand feet into the freezing night air high above the Swiss canton of Bernese Oberland. He'd made HALO and HAHO jumps many times before, when he was younger, a Navy Seal, fearless, immortal. Little had changed.

Frank fell from the sky.

He checked the altimeter strapped to his forearm, the GPS guidance system, the jagged peaks and inky black lakes below, correcting his body position, breathing steadily. He pulled the ripcord at just over three thousand feet, the black RAM Air canopy deploying above his head with a loud crack, the deceleration punching the wind from his body. He tugged his steering toggles, the parachute twisting in the air as he performed a visual check of the drop zone below.

At two hundred feet Frank released his combat equipment, watching it fall below him on its nylon lowering line. He hit the Dark Zone then, the ambient light suddenly lost, the ground a bottomless black hole. It meant only one thing—imminent impact. He yanked hard on his toggles, flaring the chute as the ground rushed up to meet him.

The impact knocked him off his feet.

He rolled once, twice, then slithered to a halt, the canopy drifting to earth a few meters away. He detached the chute and harness, removed his oxygen mask, his goggles, his black ballistic helmet. He drank in the cool night air.

He knelt in the long grass, controlling his breathing, his heart rate, watching, listening. The surrounding valley was silent, the tiny white pinpricks of the distant hamlet of Kallmunz the only visible source of man-made light. Everything else was God's own work, the towering, snow-capped peaks that climbed towards the star-filled sky, the pale half-moon that bathed the meadow in its ethereal glow. Nothing moved, save the tall grass around him and the treetops across the meadow that swayed before a gentle night breeze.

Frank remained motionless for several minutes, still, silent, until he was sure his insertion had not been detected by a nightwalker, a sleepless farmer or by the unmarked cars that patrolled the public roads for miles around the target. It had been a good jump, he decided. A pity it was his last. He moved quickly towards the forest behind him.

Deep inside the treeline he broke down his jump gear, piling it inside the parachute canopy and stuffing it between the low branches of a tree. There was no time to dig a hole; he was on a schedule, and the window of opportunity was minimal. He was dressed in camouflage gear, a digitised mix of whites, greys and pale greens designed for use in alpine and sub-alpine environments. He hefted his backpack over his shoulders. His weapon load-out included a small calibre Heckler and Koch UMP, a black Spyderco military lock knife in a harness on his right thigh, and a specially made garrotte wire that had been given to him by a smiling Navy Seal Master Chief back in Virginia. The gun was purely a defensive weapon; if he got into a firefight before the bird was flying the mission would've failed. After a final check for noise and movement, he headed up into the forest.

It took two hours to reach the ridge, another three to pick his way along the mountain goat trail and drop down into the steep-sided valley on the other side. By the time Frank reached his RV point, a cluster of prehistoric boulders just above the treeline, the morning sun had crept over the eastern horizon, bathing the valley in its pale yellow light. He settled into his hide and waited, his body squeezed between the rocks, a set of Steiner military rangefinder binoculars pressed against his eyes. His heart beat a little faster when he locked onto the hotel, a magnificent structure of dark timber and grey stone situated at the end of the narrow pass below him. He mapped the adjoining cinema block, the staff accommodation lodges, the security barracks, the sweeping drive that twisted through the landscaped grounds, stretching towards the thick forest that choked both sides of the single, discreetly guarded approach road. His covert reconnaissance told him what he needed to know; the advance party had arrived.

For the next forty-eight hours Frank watched them, the search teams that scoured the hotel grounds, the armed patrols that swept the surrounding forests, never climbing higher than the treeline where the winter snows still clung to the ledges and bluffs.

At the end of day three, as the sun dipped in the afternoon sky and a chill mist filled the valley, Frank set up the equipment, assembling it carefully so it pointed into the valley through a gap in the rocks. It was at the far edge of its operational range but a systems check concluded that it was still effective. Satisfied, Frank broke down his hide and packed up his personal gear. The mission brief now called for him to move higher, to activate the equipment remotely when the time came. Instead, Frank picked his way down towards the trees below.

It was the reason they'd wanted to send a team, a younger one, with more recent operational experience and unquestionable loyalty. Frank was a wild card, until recently a part of the problem, not the solution. But Frank had insisted, persuading an empathetic and vengeful General Moody that it had to be him. He wouldn't—couldn't—let them down.

Frank knew there'd be a window of opportunity, after the sweeps and the sniffer dogs, the thermal imaging and the carbon monoxide detectors, when the empty hotel would lie dormant, a sanitised zone, cold, silent. It was the twelve-hour window before the sun rose again, before the domestic staff arrived, the personal valets and assistants, the caterers, the chambermaids, the maintenance crews. That window was now open, and he was already moving through the trees.

His objective was the giant wall of grey rock that towered for several thousand feet behind the hotel, a place where the sun never penetrated, where the shadows were deepest and the air still froze, where the patrols were a little less frequent, where the entry points were few but unquestionably more accessible. He left the treeline, the mist wrapping him in its invisible cloak.

Frank's skin tingled. He felt the strong, steady beat of his heart, the adrenalin pumping through his system. It wouldn't be long now.

They were coming.

Ros Wyman's heart pumped with excitement.

The sun was shining, the sky clear and blue, stretching as far as the eye could see. Finally, after a long, cold winter, summer beckoned. She sang along to a song on the radio as she gunned her canary yellow Porsche Boxster around the country lanes to the Copse Hill facility. For the first time this year she had both the roof down *and* her sunglasses on, relishing the rush of wind as she sped through the Wiltshire countryside.

Up ahead she saw a familiar chicane in the road and she geared down, twisting through the tight turns and punching the accelerator once again, golden fields of wheat and barley stretching away on either side of the road. Her full-throated singing faltered as she slowed for a Vauxhall estate ambling along the road ahead of her. As she closed the gap she saw it was a family; mum, dad, the gurning faces of their offspring pressed up against the rear window. She waited for an opportunity to overtake them, frustrated by the appearance of several cars travelling in the other direction. She sighed and turned the radio down, but the delay wasn't enough to dampen the excitement that burned inside her.

The Transition was coming, as surely as the summer that lingered just over the horizon, and the thought of it filled her with joy. She imagined how it would be, the driving tour she had planned with several fellow motoring enthusiasts, the drive across a sparsely populated Europe, the cities devoid of jams, the autobahns empty, the sound of her Porsche—a new Turbo Cabriolet, she promised herself—echoing around barren mountain passes. What more could a person want?

But that was for much later.

Right now there was still work to be done. Angola had been signed off a week ago. All Wyman needed now was the green light from The Committee, and the Messina facility in Iraq could swing into full production. After that, Angola would be unstoppable, a global exterminator that would sweep away the past and create the conditions for a bright, shining future for mankind. Wyman's heart beat faster at the thought of it all.

She swung the Porsche into the private lane, the sun blotted out by the thick trees and the dark, overhead canopy. She clicked off her radio as she slowed for the recently replaced security barrier, her eyes flicking toward the security hut. Nothing moved behind the mesh-covered windows. She leaned on her horn. Her roof was down, her car distinctive; why weren't the idiots opening the barrier?

She was about the blast her horn again when she heard a car pulling up behind her. A black Range Rover, she noted in her mirror, not a Sport or one of those ridiculous Evoques, but the stylish Vogue SE. She punched her horn again to wake up the guards. Another security screw-up during an unscheduled VIP visit could prove more than embarrassing.

Still nothing moved. She heard a car door open behind her. She watched her mirror. A man approached, a large man with short, sandy hair, and wearing a dark rain mac. He smiled as he came alongside Wyman's car, held out his hand.

'Doctor Wyman?'

Wyman whipped off her sunglasses and returned the smile. He was good-looking in a rugged kind of way, but there was something unsettling about his eyes. She shook the proffered hand. 'And you are...?'

The man gripped it, firm, strong.

Squeezing.

'Look at me,' he hissed through gritted teeth. Wyman did as she was told, suddenly frightened. Her eyes flicked to the CCTV camera, the security hut. The man caught her look.

'Forget them, they can't help you.' He squeezed again, harder this time. Wyman winced. 'Have I got your attention, Doctor?' She nodded. 'Good. Listen to me very carefully.' He leaned forward, his hard eyes drilling into hers. 'In a moment the barrier will open. You'll drive through and we'll follow. You'll park your car and escort my colleagues and me into the facility. At that moment the power will be cut. When that happens you will stand perfectly still. Do not panic, do not move, because the building will quickly fill with armed men with extremely itchy trigger fingers. Have I made myself clear, Doctor Wyman?'

'Yes,' she breathed, not knowing what else to say, her fingers throbbing, her heart racing with fear as her wide eyes noted the large black gun beneath the man's raincoat. But what frightened her most was the latent anger of his voice, the steel in his blue eyes,

'Make no mistake,' he warned. 'If you try to run, if you try to raise the alarm in any way, you'll be the first to die. The place is surrounded, and the men who surround it have orders to shoot escapees on sight. Do as you're told, cooperate fully, and you'll live to see another sunrise. Make trouble, and you'll find yourself in your own incinerator by the day's end. Do we understand each other?'

'Yes,' she whispered.

The man let go and walked back to his vehicle. Wyman gripped the steering wheel, one hand throbbing, the other shaking, her eyes searching the surrounding woods for men with guns and orders to kill. She flinched as the security barrier suddenly rattled upwards. She dropped the car into gear and drove slowly beneath it, her mind a whirlwind of fear and confusion. She couldn't believe it was over, couldn't comprehend how they'd been discovered, how any investigation hadn't been detected by the all-seeing eye of The Committee. Why it hadn't been obstructed or quashed. Yet they *knew.*

Wyman realised she was on her own. There was no one to help her, no one else who could make a decision for her. Panic flooded her system, and she battled to control it. Her fight-or-flight reflexes had failed her. She was immobile, a rabbit caught in the headlights, unable to think or act. There were many things she could do; she could call ahead, have the facility locked down, initiate the emergency protocols that would wipe the servers, empty the filing cabinets and fill the shredders. The basement would be sealed, the flash-fire system triggered, incinerating everything and everybody in a white-hot blast of pure oxygen and superheated flame. She could do all those things—*should* do them—but realised she didn't have the courage. For a doctor such as herself it was irrational, yet she feared death more than anything.

She slowed the Porsche as the main building swept into view, steering the car into her reserved space. The Range Rover stopped alongside her. It was her love of humanity, her wish to end the cycle of poverty and starvation that had set her on this path. *That* would be her defence, she decided. Someone, somewhere, might just believe her.

She climbed out of the Porsche and walked to the main door on unsteady legs, now surrounded by the cold-eyed man and four others, their jackets flapping open, their hands ready. Wyman rummaged inside her handbag, pulled her ID card from her handbag and swiped it through the reader with trembling fingers. The light blinked green and the door clicked open. She felt a hand in her back, urging her onwards.

Doctor Ros Wyman took a deep breath.

Then she stepped inside.

'... and thereafter those that survive the Transition will have a choice: support the system and benefit from its benevolence, or reject it, and lose access to the control grid. Ultimately, the choice will be a simple one, and the survivors will soon come to realise that the dawn of a new era is upon them, one that will offer both life and purpose, an era that will shine gloriously across the New World that we will all build together."

The pyramid symbol on the huge cinema screen faded to black and the overhead lights came on, filling the auditorium with suffused light as a sustained applause competed with the rousing strings of a classical symphony piped through the cinema's sound system.

Like everyone else Josh was on his feet, thrilled by the moment, his hands pumping together as the standing ovation reached a crescendo. Standing next to him Villiers did the same, his face beaming with undisguised joy as he revelled in his newly acquired status. Josh watched The Committee vacate their seats and shuffle towards the exit. Like everyone else he was filled with a sense of awe at the mere sight of them, their solidarity, their sheer power. They were witnessing history.

They'd called it the Final Gathering of the Old World, as important as those first, legendary summits between the great and the good at Bohemian Grove in California decades ago. He watched the last of them file from the cinema, their oriental suits like a shimmering sea of blue silk beneath the soft overhead lighting. Behind them filed their ambassadors and emissaries all clothed in identical black attire, the rulers of the world followed by their courtiers. Josh saw Beeton's bald head amongst them, then the white-haired Lund, both trailing behind their masters.

When the VIPs had left, the audience began to filter towards the exit. Josh and Villiers shuffled amongst them as a palpable sense of anticipation crackled on the air, spilling from the glass-walled connecting walkway and out into the hotel's main lobby. A female voice on the PA system echoed around the vaulted ceiling, urging the congregation to return to their rooms. They made their way up the busy staircase towards the second floor of the east wing. The hotel was awesome, its Swiss owner a Committee member and head of a mutual fund worth four hundred billion dollars. As he headed up the wide staircase, Josh noted the numerous paintings of other stern-faced Europeans lining the walls, and was reminded of their own connections to past empires. The New World *would* look a little like Nazi Germany, he figured. There would be no Fuehrer of course, no single iconic leader, but the order that would rise from the chaos of the Transition would certainly last for a thousand years. The Committee would rule everything by consensus, like the Olympians presiding over the earth from their own Mount Atlas, one flag, one government, one defence force, one currency, the population bound together by order, by loyalty and servitude. It was the only way.

The crowd thinned. Josh bid Villiers goodnight and wandered along a hallway, whistling a nameless tune as he jangled the key in his hand. Everyone was banished to their rooms tonight, the hotel's facilities kept clear for The Committee's private banquet, and later the torchlight procession into the forest, ending at the stone temple where the effigy that represented the Old World would be burned. Josh's pulse raced. Maybe if he were lucky he'd catch a glimpse from his window. Good luck seemed to be with him right now.

On his return from the UK, Beeton and Lund had congratulated him, and then reinstated him to his former position at FEMA. The Committee was pleased by Frank's death, even more so by the safe return of Professor Cohen's data drive. No harm, no foul, as Beeton had smiled. It didn't suit him. Yet Josh had proved his worth, his dedication. Now he was reaping the rewards, his presence here in Switzerland the icing on his particular cake, invited not as part of his duties, but as a trusted acolyte, a witness to history.

The security, understandably, was intense. The hotel was heavily guarded, the innermost of a dozen security cordons that ranged in size and mission out to about twelve miles. Nothing could get anywhere near this special place tonight, and as an added precaution a diversionary conference had been organised elsewhere, a G8 mini-summit currently being held in Geneva, where the black-hooded anarchists had gathered with their placards and their smoke bombs. Josh knew it would also provide cover for the inordinate amount of private jets that had landed in Switzerland of late.

He finally reached his room, slipping the key into the lock and turning the handle. He locked the heavy door behind him, still humming a tune—

The explosive cloud of aerosol spray hit him in the face. Instinctively he turned away but already he could feel himself going down, his legs no longer functioning, catching a glimpse of a masked shadow in the unlit bathroom as he folded to the carpet. He tried to shout for help, but his tongue felt thick and limp, and saliva drooled from his mouth. He lay prone on the floor, his arms flapping, legs immobile, his mouth opening and closing like a beached fish.

Strong hands dug beneath his armpits, dragging him to the large double bed. He was thrown onto it face down, sucking a wedge of gold eiderdown into his mouth. The same hands bound his own with plastic flexi-cuffs, grabbing his feet and twisting him over onto his back. Josh's head lolled to one side, the saliva still running from his lips. He watched a man in maintenance overalls wedge a chair under the door handle, then drag another across the room and set it by the side of the bed. The man sat down, dragging the protective mask from his face, breathing heavily after his exertions. Josh was neither shocked nor surprised. He simply stared at the man who smiled at him, who ran a hand through his thinning red hair.

'Hi, Josh. How you doing, buddy?'

Josh couldn't reply even if he wanted to. His

useless tongue lolled in his mouth like a dog's. Then his eyes closed and the room went dark.

*

Frank checked his watch. Time was short but he made preparations anyway, just in case. He leaned against the walls on either side, his ear pressed close; TVs droned in both rooms, and Frank used the cover to pile furniture into the narrow corridor by the main door. It wouldn't hold an entry team for long but the improvised obstacle course, the incapacitating agent, and the Heckler Koch would sure help. Not that Frank needed them. The wheels were already in motion, but what he wanted more than anything now was time. Time to talk to his buddy Josh.

To say what had to be said.

He heard Josh moan, saw him struggle weakly, hands and feet bound. Frank sat in the chair next to the bed. He set the HK on the floor and pulled the Spyderco from his thigh sheath, lifting Josh's chin with the razor-sharp blade.

'I'm going to remove the gag,' he said. 'If you try to raise the alarm, I'll saw your throat open. Understood?' Josh nodded, his face powdered with green residue. Frank tugged on the handkerchief that plugged his mouth, wiped his face. The younger man coughed and spat. Frank waited until he'd regained his composure, until he uttered his first words.

'Why can't you just die like everybody else?' Josh croaked.

Frank pulled his chair a little closer to the bed. The TV was running a Swiss game show, the host badgering the grinning contestants in loud, rapid-fire German. 'I'm sorry to disappoint you, Josh.'

He stared at Frank for a long time. Then the inevitable question. 'How did you do it, Frank? How the hell did you get in here?'

'That doesn't matter. What matters is that we're together again. For the end.'

Josh trapped a strand of cotton with his tongue and spat it out on the bed. 'You can't stop it, Frank. No one can.'

'That's the trouble with you people. You've become overconfident. Arrogant.'

'You people? You're one of us, Frank. You've been with us right from the start.'

Frank shook his head. 'That's what I used to believe, but I was wrong. God showed me a new path.'

Josh moved himself up the bed until he leaned against the engraved wooden headboard. 'So it's true. Frank Marshall got religion. What happened, Frank? You see the light? Get struck by lightning?'

'Mock all you want. God is in each of us. We only have to look.'

Josh laughed, his cold cackle competing with the TV audience. 'Are you shitting me? C'mon, Frank, you know there's no God. There's only us, right here, right now. The rest is a crock of shit.'

'Oh ye of little faith.'

Josh flared his nostrils. 'Jesus, those priests in

Boston really did a number on you. What is this, some kinda delayed Catholic guilt trip?'

'I've been lost for years, Josh. A man in Harlem showed me the way.'

'Whoopdee-fucking-doo. You're not going to break out into song, are you, Frank?'

The older man frowned. 'It's disappointing how a declaration of faith seems to elicit ridicule in others. Besides, I can't sing, remember?'

Josh leaned forward, spite in his voice. 'I'll tell you what I do remember, Frank. I remember hiding the booze, cleaning up your puke, covering your ass a hundred fucking times. I remember begging you to get help, but most of all I remember you betraying me.'

Frank toyed with the knife, his thumb working the blade lock. He could see Josh's eyes flicking towards it, could see his forearms flexing, trying to work the plastic cuffs behind his back. 'That's why I'm here, Josh. You deserve to know the truth.'

'Why did you go to England, Frank? What was so special about that Sullivan kid?'

Frank leaned back in his chair, propping his feet up on the bed. 'Sullivan was the trigger. I thought he would bring me salvation. I was wrong.'

'The fuck are you talking about?'

Frank took a breath and exhaled, remembering the clear blue sky, the thick black smoke. 'It began a long time before that. The first time I felt something was in Jersey City, watching the North Tower burn. I got scared, nauseous. By the end of the day I was shaking like a leaf.

The panic attacks started after that, but I could handle them as long as I didn't dwell on things. I'd trained myself to avoid the triggers, the news stories about Nine Eleven, the endless documentaries. Then one day—some years later, at a motel in Newark—I caught a show on HBO about those poor bastards trapped above the fires, you know, the ones who'd jumped?'

Frank felt a familiar ripple of fear travel up his spine, the acid turning to ice in his stomach, the knuckles of his knife hand suddenly bloodless. 'I tried to switch that goddam TV off but a voice in my head dared me to keep watching. So I did.'

Josh smiled from the bed. 'Voices, Frank?'

He nodded, ignoring the taunt. 'The nightmares began that night. I found myself up there, clinging to one of those twisted metal ledges, smoke pouring out of the shattered office behind me, my clothes torn, flesh burned, gasping for air. But I was never alone. There were others around me, men and women, young and old, all crammed onto that narrow ledge a thousand feet above the sidewalk, clinging to each other, snatching at each other's clothes, cursing, screaming, buffeted by the wind, the roar of the flames behind us, until the only way out was to jump. And I jumped too, Josh, saw the tower flashing by, the others falling through the air around me, our screams snatched away on the wind, paralysed by the knowledge that certain death was imminent...'

Frank felt his throat constricting, his fingers trembling. Sweat soaked his underclothes. Then he heard Josh's voice from the bed.

'That's it? Nine Eleven fucked you up? After all the shit you've pulled?'

Frank tugged a handkerchief from his pocket, wiped perspiration from his face and neck. 'I started drinking after that. You know the rest. When they assigned us to Messina, when the Sullivan kid was killed, I knew I had to get away. I couldn't cope with any more death.' He rubbed his face, then fixed his gaze on Josh. 'There were times when I came close to telling you, Josh. You were a good kid, smart, loyal.' He tapped his chest with a finger. 'But there's nothing here. No soul. You talked about Nine Eleven like it was a ball game you'd seen on TV. You longed for the Transition. If The Committee knew I'd lost my way they would've ended me. And they'd have made you the trigger man.'

The TV droned on behind them, the arm of the game show host wrapped around the winning contestant.

'I wouldn't have done it,' Josh said. 'I tried to help you, didn't I? I respected you, Frank, covered your ass a hundred times. Come on, man, untie me. We can talk this over.'

'You still with SD?'

'FEMA,' Josh announced. 'Military liaison and coordination.'

'FEMA, huh?'

Frank knew the organisation well. When the public heard FEMA they thought Katrina and Sandy, tents and ready-meals. They knew nothing about the secret multi-billion-dollar budget, the powers that exceeded the President's, powers that included uprooting entire populations, seizing property, food supplies, transportation systems, and even suspending the Constitution. Controlling FEMA was always a major goal for The Committee—the agency was the perfect vehicle to oversee the chaos of the Transition and seize ultimate power.

'You nearly screwed it all up for me,' Josh snapped. 'I should've followed protocol, sent the dogs after you when you went MIA in Iraq, but I didn't. I knew you were fucked up, but I cut you slack, Frank, because I thought loyalty meant something. You caused me a lot of problems.'

Frank didn't blink. 'I'd hit bottom. I wasn't thinking.'

'Bullshit. You emptied your bank account, faked your own death. You even had your RFID chip removed. That wasn't spontaneous. You planned that shit.'

Frank switched the knife to his other hand, wiping a sweaty palm on his leg. 'Tell me about FEMA. What's the plan, when Angola breaks?' Confronting Josh was proving tougher than expected. He could feel that familiar tide of panic ebbing and flowing through his consciousness. He took a deep breath to calm his nerves. Josh saw it too.

'You okay, Frank?'

'Just tell me about the plan.'

'Sure. Why not?' Josh made himself a little more comfortable. 'We'll bide our time, adhering to standard FEMA protocols, until the crisis escalates and a national emergency is declared. That's when command

and control will relocate to Mount Weather. Soon after a steady stream of pre-prepared executive orders will authorise a national military mobilisation, followed by travel restrictions and curfews. Troops will be deployed to protect and preserve the nation's infrastructure. After that, martial law will come into force and dissenters removed to FEMA detention camps. That's where my focus will be.'

Frank could see the light burning in Josh's eyes.

'Eventually, after millions have died including most of Capitol Hill, executive authority will pass to the National Advisory Council.' Josh fidgeted excitedly on the bed. 'It's not too late, Frank. I could talk to them about you, tell them it's all been a huge mistake.'

Frank shook his head. 'Nice try, but I'm pretty sure my reappearance wouldn't be healthy for either of us.'

Josh's grin slipped. He twisted angrily, the gold eiderdown rumpled beneath his body. 'Goddamit, it doesn't have to be like this. We can work something out.'

'It's way too late for that.'

Josh shot a look at the knife. 'Don't do anything stupid, Frank.'

'Relax. I'm just waiting.'

'For what? No one can get anywhere near this place without us knowing.'

'I did.'

'You're a goddam freak,' Josh growled.

'Be nice.' Frank checked his watch. 'At least for the next few minutes.'

'Then what, Frank? The Swiss cops will show up?

Interpol?' He laughed, but there was no humour in the sound. 'You think any organisation on this planet can wipe its ass without The Committee knowing about it? You think they've spent decades and hundreds of trillions of dollars just so an asshole like you can drop a dime on them? You think it's that easy? You're one deluded son of a bitch,' Josh scowled. 'You've lost it, buddy. You're off the fucking reservation.'

'That's real nice, coming from a guy who's part Navajo.'

'Hey, I got an old Indian saying for you, Frank—kiss my fucking ass.' He glared at his former boss for a few moments, caught his breath. Then he said, 'you realise you're going to fail, right? You want to kill me, fine, go right ahead, because you can't stop them. We have to preserve what's left, you know that. People have to die, so the chosen can live. There's no other way.'

Frank shook his head and smiled. 'Pride goeth before destruction, a haughty spirit before a fall. That's Proverbs, chapter sixteen.' He checked his watch again, saw that time was short. He wasn't smiling any more. 'I know what this is, Josh. The Committee, they're all here. For the Gathering.'

Josh paled, his eyes searching Frank's. 'No, that's not true. You've fucked up again.'

Frank reached into his pocket, took out a card, flicked it into Josh's lap. Josh dropped his chin, stared at the gold-rimmed edges, the stiff white card with the small black pyramid symbol at its centre. Josh's jaw fell open.

'Where did you get this?'

'I found it on Cohen's desk, right after I killed him. I got sent the same invitation back in oh-one, two months before Nine Eleven. That Gathering was in Sweden.' Frank leaned in a little closer. 'They've been listening for weeks, my friend. They know all about The Committee, who they are, what they're doing. They know about Nine Eleven, about the oil, about Angola and Messina. They know who your people are in Washington, in London, Riyadh, Beijing—'

'You're lying.'

'Believe it.'

Frank picked up his backpack and placed it on the bed. 'I told them The Committee would be here. They cross-checked the private flight plans, put people at the airports, on local roads, the cyclists and hikers with their cameras and satellite phones.' He rummaged inside the pack, pulled out a small black box. 'They know it all, Josh. You've been compromised my friend.' He flipped open the toughened plastic cover, turned a switch inside. A green light flickered, then pulsed steadily.

'The fuck is that?' Josh's face was drained of all colour.

Frank checked the readout, set the remote unit down on the dresser, satisfied the laser designator was fully active. 'This is Samson, and he's going to bring this temple of evil crashing down around your ears.'

Josh began to struggle against his bonds, thrashing on the bed. Frank retook his seat. 'Don't waste your time, Josh. Accept the inevitable.'

'Cut me loose!' he yelled. Frank checked his watch; Josh could scream all he wanted now. The unit on the dresser sang to him.

'You fucking idiot!' Josh yelled. 'The world needs this. We have to move forward, we have to advance as a species. We can't do that if we've got ten billion fucking mouths to feed! We'll end up back in the Dark Ages, for Christ's sake!'

Frank heard knocking, voices outside. 'You remember back in oh-one, after the demolition teams had brought the towers down? The backslapping, the beers? I remember, Josh. I remember how you laughed with them. Thousands of people, lives, families, all destroyed. And you laughed.'

Josh bucked violently on the bed. 'Cut these fucking cuffs off!'

Frank spun around as the heavy door shuddered. He saw them in his mind, filling the corridor outside, their black leathery wings and scaly bodies pressed together, whispering his name, their talons gouging the door, carving through the wood.

His demons.

Finally they'd come for him.

Frank was ready.

He stood up, the chair toppling over. He scooped up the Heckler Koch and emptied the magazine through the door in one long burst. Cordite filled the room. Brass casings scattered across the carpet. He heard the moans of the fallen. Then alarms echoed through the building.

'What have you done?' he heard Josh wail.

He threw the weapon to one side. 'I'm doing God's work.'

He heard more beasts gathering beyond the splintered door, heard his name cursed, saw their red eyes watching him through the bullet holes. The frame rattled. The door shook. Bullets stitched the wall above the bed.

Josh tried to roll himself onto the floor. Frank pulled him down to the carpet.

'You've killed us,' he howled. 'You've killed us both.'

Frank knelt by the bed. He smiled, a final, tired smile. He was glad it was over.

'All of us will die, Josh. Today it's our turn. Pray with me, ask God for forgiveness. While you still can.'

Frank Marshall closed his eyes and began to whisper a final prayer.

Far above the snow-capped peaks of the Bernese Oberland, the *Spirit of America* made a final adjustment to its undetectable flight path and opened its bay doors. Moments later the billion-dollar B2 stealth bomber, an invisible black wing against the night sky, released the smart weapon from within its belly.

The huge metal cylinder dropped quickly, leaving the B2 far behind as it plummeted towards the narrow valley shrouded in darkness beneath it. Its on-board navigation package made several minor corrections to its flight path as it fell at terminal velocity towards the laser-painted target below. The sixteen-tonne weapon flew past the rugged mountain peaks and into the valley itself, rushing through the frigid night air, its approach undetectable from the ground, its target the largest of the buildings clustered at the far end of the valley. The weapon made a final correction, its aim almost perfect, the sloping roof bathed in reflected laser light, rushing up to meet it—

The thirty-seven thousand pound Massive Ordnance Penetrator GBU-57A/B punched through several floors of the hotel before it exploded in a searing white pulse of pure explosive energy that lit up the valley, obliterating the building in a detonation that thundered across the Swiss mountain range. The shock wave crashed into the towering peak behind the hotel, rolling up its jagged face, shearing off a million-tonne slab of rock and sending it roaring like a tsunami into the valley below, engulfing the shattered remains of the secluded complex under an impenetrable river of ice and granite.

When the dust had finally settled, when the last pebble had come to rest and the still of the night had drawn its blanket over the valley once more, the survivors, mostly security teams from the surrounding forests, made good their escape. As experienced operatives, they'd all agreed that the detonation was an extraordinarily large bomb, a smart one. A military one.

And that could only mean one thing.

The other survivors, those that were close to

the hotel yet had escaped the devastation, thought otherwise. They'd felt the hellish heat, had been deafened by the thunderclap that had echoed across the heavens, had watched a mountain cleaved in two, and yet had somehow—miraculously—been saved.

Those survivors came to a very different conclusion. God himself had intervened to save them, and it was God they thanked as they made their escape through the forest, leaving the rubble-filled valley of death behind them.

The Reverend Clarence Hays was at his desk when he saw a shadow pass by the barred window, followed by a knock on the alleyway door. He pushed his chair back and went out into the corridor, his sandals slapping against the soles of his bare feet. The man through the peephole wore the familiar brown uniform of a UPS guy and Hays threw the bolt, expecting something legal and threatening from New York State Electric and Gas. The long winter had proved costly, and the warm embrace the church had provided for the homeless during the worst of the winter storms had crippled Hays' finances. It wouldn't be long before he'd be forced to close his doors, and the thought of it crushed his spirit. It wasn't just his parishioners that needed the Lord's strength these days.

The UPS man smiled, bid Hays good morning, and handed over the package. Hays studied it, then realised he hadn't signed for it, but the UPS guy had already turned the corner of the alleyway and disappeared.

He bolted the door and went back to his office. Out in the church hall he could hear the distant chords of the battered piano as the choir began their morning practice, their harmonies soon filling the stillness of the corridor outside Hays' office. He sat down, turning the parcel over in his hands, curious. Hays' name and address were clearly visible, but there was no date stamp, no return address, no tracking number, nothing. Hays shrugged, reached for a pair of scissors and sliced the carton open. He flipped back the sides and dug inside. Loose foam packaging spilled over onto his desk. His fingers touched something familiar and he pulled the small, leather-bound book from inside the box. Hays frowned for a moment, and then he realised it was the travel Bible he'd given Frank Marshall a while back.

Frank Marshall.

Hays felt a momentary rush of guilt as he realised he hadn't thought about Frank for some time. These days he could barely keep up with the demand for his ministrations, yet he remembered Frank well, a deeply troubled man, his desire to right a dreadful wrong more powerful than most. Hays wondered what had become of him, hoping that the parcel would fill in a few blanks.

He reached inside once more, his fingers finding a hard block of plastic, his eyes widening as he turned the object over in his hand. He reached in again, produced another. Then another. Hays stood up, turned the box over and shook it, spilling everything out onto his desk. He flopped back into his chair, his eyes unable to comprehend what he was seeing. Then he found the letter. He ripped it open and began to read.

It was from Frank, and it was brief. It was an explanation of sorts, his short journey along the path to righteousness. It spoke of the guilt that had plagued him, of his quest for redemption that had finally saved others, and of the nightmares that would never leave him. But most of all he wanted to thank Hays for the strength he'd given him to complete his journey, and to say a final goodbye.

Frank was never coming back.

Hays arranged everything neatly on his desk as the sound of the choir echoed along the corridor. His hands reached out, sought physical confirmation of what his eyes refused to believe, touching each one in turn, the two dozen vacuum-sealed, four-inch-high packs of one hundred dollar bills that would enable Hays to continue God's work for many years to come.

He took a sharp breath, emotion building inside him, in sync with the unseen choir as they climbed towards their vocal heights.

He leaned back in his chair, winded. Then he did something he hadn't done in many, many years.

Clarence Hays began to cry.

Epilogue

Roy turned his face skyward.

Far to the west the sun had already dipped below the horizon, painting the endless sky in glorious hues of blue and soft pink. To the east night beckoned, the first stars dusting the heavens with their faint light. It was a poignant moment, and he was glad that the quiet ceremony was taking place at the stern of the *Ocean Viking*. He took a final look at the stars then stepped to the rail and dropped the wreath overboard, where it slapped onto the calm waters of the Persian Gulf.

'Bye, Jimmy,' he whispered.

On the deck behind him the Dutch captain intoned a few words about souls being consigned to the deep, followed by a chorus of *amens* from a small contingent of the ship's Filipino crew. Roy gripped the rail as the wreath bobbed on the surface, watching it as it began to drift away from the anchored ship.

He didn't know if this was the spot where Jimmy's body was sent to its watery grave. The men who were responsible, and those that might've survived the assault on the Terra Petroleum compound, were being held by the Americans at an undisclosed location. Still, it was as good a spot as any, the lights of the Al-Basrah Oil Terminal glittering on the horizon far behind them, surrounded by the empty waters of the Gulf.

The wreath had already drifted some distance away, and Roy wondered where it might finish up.

Probably on some Iranian beach, flung like a Frisbee between laughing kids, and he smiled because he thought Jimmy might find that pretty funny. In the end it didn't really matter. What was important was the ceremony itself, arranged by the new administration in London and overseen by the men who stood a short distance away, the British Embassy representative and the Chief Financial Officer of TDL Global (UK) division who'd ordered the ten-thousand-tonne support ship to be placed at Roy's disposal.

He remained at the stern rail for a while, remembering Jimmy and watching the distant wreath until the shadow of night stretched across the water and claimed it for its own.

When he finally turned away the hovering officials stepped forward. The embassy man, Bradshaw, was dressed in khaki trousers and a pressed white shirt, the much heavier Cooke sweating copiously in a blue suit. Together they thanked the Filipinos in a round of smiles and handshakes and the crewmen retired behind a rust-streaked bulkhead door, leaving them alone on the open rear deck.

'That was very nice,' Bradshaw smiled. He was a small man, dapper, his sandy hair neatly parted to one side.

'Jimmy would've liked it,' Roy said. 'So, what happens now?'

'We'll head back shortly. They've laid on a late supper at the embassy.'

'The least we can do,' Cooke insisted. He was

older than Bradshaw, with large bags under his eyes and a puffy red face that was damp with sweat. Roy wondered if it had less to do with the balmy temperature than the fact that the blameless Cooke had survived a brutal cull of TDL's senior management.

'Your brother was a TDL employee and as such we have a responsibility to our employees' next of kin,' Cooke continued. He reached inside his jacket. 'I hope that this isn't an inappropriate moment; however, time is pressing and we've been afforded a little privacy.' Roy saw a large damp patch of sweat beneath the man's armpit as he produced an envelope from his pocket. 'This is a settlement, in sterling, for your brother's estate.'

'Estate?' Roy took the envelope. It was made of expensive paper, thick and creamy, with the TDL logo embossed in one corner.

'Correct. As you know, your brother worked for us for some years. His monthly salary was automatically credited to a TDL holding account from which he withdrew a small stipend each month. Fiscally, your brother was rather prudent,' Cooke observed.

Roy extracted a single sheet of paper from the envelope and smoothed it open, his eye drawn to the bold-typed and underlined figure at the foot of the page. 'Jesus Christ,' he whispered.

'As I said, rather prudent,' Cooke reiterated. 'Your brother also had the foresight to take out a very generous life insurance policy. You'll see we've matched that figure and added a compensation package of our own. I hope you'll find it satisfactory.'

Roy's eyes switched from the expectant gaze of the TDL accountant to the life-changing sum at the foot of the page and back again. 'Is this for real?'

'Absolutely,' Cooke nodded.

Roy stared at it again. It was a huge chunk of money, sure, but Jimmy was gone. He weighed the statement in his hand and said to Cooke, 'I'd give twice that for one more hour with my brother.'

A look of horror passed across the rotund accountant's face. 'Yes of course,' he blustered, 'I didn't mean to—'

'It's fine, I'm just saying, that's all. I appreciate everything you've done.' He held out his hand and Cooke pumped it gratefully.

Roy folded the statement and slipped it into the pocket of his shorts.

Bradshaw laid a hand on Cooke's arm. 'Would you mind giving us a moment, Steven? A couple of personal matters I need to discuss with Roy here.'

'Of course, of course.'

Cooke retreated towards the bulkhead door, slamming it behind him with a loud clang, and Bradshaw led Roy towards the stern rail. Beneath them the sea slapped gently against the hull of the ship. When Bradshaw spoke it was in low tones, his arms resting on the rail.

'I've been authorised to give you a limited debrief, Roy. It's off the record, you understand. You can't repeat it.'

Roy felt his hands gripping the rail a little tighter. He'd existed outside the bubble for weeks, completely in the dark, the little contact he'd had with Vicky minimal and devoid of specifics. Maybe now he'd get some answers.

'Just tell me one thing—is it over?'

Bradshaw nodded. 'Most of The Committee perished in Switzerland but there were a handful who were too old or infirm to travel. Some have since committed suicide and three have disappeared. The others are being interrogated at a detention facility in the States. I would imagine their human rights are being violated in some distinctly imaginative ways.'

'What about Messina?' The very mention of the word still sent a chill down Roy's spine.

Bradshaw glanced over his shoulder, checking they were still alone on the open deck.

'The site has been neutralised by American Special Forces, that's pretty much all the information anyone is getting right now. A special UN Resolution has been passed and an assembly formed to ensure that the threat is completely eradicated. I'm guessing that that task might take many years before every thread of this ghastly conspiracy is discovered but for now the immediate danger has passed. We mop up as best we can, get things back to normal as quickly as possible. Well, about as normal as they ever get.'

Roy looked out to sea, where the blues and pinks of dusk had finally been erased by the inky blackness of the night sky. The stars were brighter now, reminding him of another night not so long ago, crouched in the mud of a Buckinghamshire field. And the man who'd led him there.

'What about Frank Marshall? D'you know where he is now?'

Bradshaw shook his head. 'I'm afraid I'm not familiar with the name.'

The PA crackled and a voice echoed across the deck in a language Roy didn't understand. He heard a bulkhead door creak open and several crewmen in oily orange overalls appeared on deck. The *Ocean Viking*'s powerful diesels rumbled into life. Roy looked down, where the waters beneath the stern were being churned to white foam. The ship began to move. A warm offshore breeze plucked at his loose shirt.

'So it's over.'

'Pretty much,' said Bradshaw. He checked his watch. 'We'll be back in Kuwait in a few hours. With a little luck you should be in London by tomorrow afternoon.'

'Thanks, Mister Bradshaw.'

The embassy man—Roy thought he was probably SIS—headed across the deck and disappeared inside the ship. Roy stayed at the rail, feeling the quiet vibration of the engines, enjoying the sensation of movement, his eye drawn to the phosphorous wake that trailed behind the vessel. The truth was he was glad to be going home. Two days cooking in the heat of the Gulf wasn't exactly a holiday and there was much to do when he got back to London.

With Jimmy's money he'd be able to leave the Fitzroy for good. He'd only been back once, to sift through the wreckage and salvage a few belongings. It had been a creepy experience, alone in the flat, the ghosts of Derek and Sammy still haunting the empty rooms.

He'd closed the front door behind him and loitered on the balcony, listening to the steady thump of music from next door, the shouts echoing across the estate. He knew then that he'd never return. All of his memories, of Mum and Dad, of Jimmy, Vicky and Max, would stay with him forever, no matter where he was.

As the *Ocean Viking* began its journey toward the distant port at Kuwait City, Roy felt strangely in tune with the vessel. There was something symbolic at work, a tangible sense of leaving the past behind, sailing towards the promise of a better life. He thought of Vicky, her future as bright as the stars overhead, and Max, how he longed to see him again, to hold him in his arms. *Soon*, he promised himself.

A cool breeze lifted off the dark waters. He took a deep, cleansing breath, exhaling as his eyes roamed the emptiness of the Gulf. He wondered where Frank was then, the man who'd briefly entered his life but had changed it immeasurably. Not just for him, but for everyone. Roy hoped that wherever he was he'd found the peace he'd craved. Maybe someday, when things got back to normal, their paths would cross again. Maybe.

He tilted his head and looked far up into the night

sky where distant stars and cloudy galaxies littered the heavens. It was so beautifully infinite, so awe-inspiring, that Roy wondered if Frank was right, that perhaps there really was a God, a heavenly kingdom. If so, then maybe Jimmy was up there right now, looking down on him, smiling. Laughing, probably.

He touched the St Christopher around his neck and closed his eyes, the sound of his brother's voice echoing inside his head, those familiar gravelly tones, the humour that laced his words.

'You did it, Roy. I'm proud of you, kid. Who would've thought it, eh?'

In the shadows of his mind's eye he saw Jimmy waving to him, a wide grin splitting his handsome face. Then the image faded, and Jimmy was swallowed by the darkness.

He'd found peace, Roy realised, and that made him smile too.

He didn't think he'd ever hear his brother's voice again.

Breathe.

Breeaaathe...

The anger, the rage, began to subside.

The first time he'd felt it was a couple of days ago, a barely controlled fit of temper that caused him to drive his combat knife into his mattress over and over again, until his body was bathed in sweat and his usually boundless energy spent. He couldn't remember what had triggered it, only that it had been a difficult choice between skewering the mattress or his buddy's chest. The truth was, his memory was getting decidedly hazy lately.

He remembered the operation though.

He remembered he was a D-Boy from the 1st Special Forces Operational Detachment Delta, and the Messina op was his first as a fully-fledged Operator. He remembered being selected for the infiltration team, that the target had been surrounded for a week, their communications compromised, their movements tracked by long lenses, by high-altitude UAVs and real-time satellite reconnaissance. Even the air itself was monitored for contamination.

He remembered the HAHO jump, drifting in a tight stack on the light desert winds for twenty miles before touchdown deep in the Iraqi desert. He remembered advancing toward the abandoned drilling platform, the power outage, the metal stairs that took him underground, gun barrel sweeping left and right, the loud beating of his heart, the quiet commands in his headset. He remembered his first contact, the suppressed weapon rattling in his hands, dropping targets in the tight and bloody corridors of the complex. He remembered being pumped with the adrenalin of invincibility. He remembered the order to hold position, then ignoring that order as he pursued a fleeing shadow beyond the glass wall of the laboratory.

That was his first mistake of the mission.

He remembered the shadow lunging at him from the darkness. He remembered the fight, his assailant bigger, stronger, knocking the rifle from his gloved hands, his flailing limbs smashing equipment and sending flasks and vials crashing to the floor. He remembered the NVGs being twisted off his face, the brutal fight in complete darkness, the soundproofed walls soaking up his breathless grunts as he thrashed around the floor with his attacker. He remembered his fingers finding the butt of his pistol, firing several desperate rounds, the corpse rolling off his chest. He remembered fighting for breath, removing his Nomex facemask, gulping lungfuls of strange tasting air.

He remembered resuming his original cover position in the corridor outside. He remembered cursing himself. He remembered the blood running down his leg where the shattered glass had cut his butt open, where the unknown chemicals had soaked his combat pants. He remembered the feelings of dread, of his off-mission brawl being discovered, his expulsion from Delta, a promising career in ruins. He remembered the exfil, and lying to the medics who'd screened each operator for injuries.

That was his second mistake.

He remembered keeping his mouth shut, praying the decontamination units would wash away the sins of his misadventure and cleanse the wound on his ass cheek hidden beneath a flesh-coloured dressing.

He remembered sitting inside the Chinook as it came in low above the neon wash of Baghdad. He remembered crossing the Tigris, the floodlit walls of the US embassy, then running barefoot across the embassy grounds, filing through the inflatable porch, passing through the chemical mist of another portable decontamination unit outside the maintenance shed. He remembered drying himself with paper towels and padding naked to the accommodation block. He vaguely remembered the team debrief in the early hours of that morning.

He remembered all of that.

He could still remember his name—Vann Jackson—and he thought he might've been from Cheyenne, Wyoming, though he couldn't remember ever being there.

Alone in his room, he realised everything else was becoming fuzzy. He could no longer remember where he'd been born, or where he'd gone to school, or even the name of the high school team he'd played quarterback for.

He opened his locker door, stared at the picture taped there, a pretty redhead with a fat baby on her lap. A week ago he'd known them. Now they were strangers. He tore it up and threw it in the trash. He sank onto his disembowelled mattress. He was tired, irritable.

And his butt ached.

He stood up again, dropped his fatigues around his ankles, inspecting the wound at length. It had finally stopped weeping that weird fluid, but the skin around it had turned a bluish colour, spreading across his left buttock and the back of his thigh. Looking at it made him angry. He ground his teeth together, tasted blood in his throat. He balled his fists, consumed by an overpowering urge to break something or someone.

Then he felt something else.

He yanked his fatigues up and staggered into the corridor. He made it to the bathroom just in time, retching loudly, violently, into the sink, his final heaves ones of panic — dark red blood painted the shiny aluminium, the faucets, the mirror above.

He ran a shaking hand over his face, the skin as white as snow, grey circles beneath his eyes. His heart pounded and sweat pimpled his temples. Blood dripped from his beard onto the thick matt of his dark chest hair.

The nausea passed.

He fingered the blood in the sink, the strange yellow gobbets of Christ-knew-what mixed in with it. It wasn't food. He hadn't eaten in days. He let the cold faucet run, washing it all away.

The bathroom door swung open.

Another operator entered, whistling a tune and wearing a towel around his waist. He stood at the urinal behind him, still whistling as he shook himself, before crossing to the long row of sinks. He washed his hands, flicked the water from his fingers and wiped them on his towel. He glanced at his fellow D-Boy in the mirror and frowned.

'Dude, are you okay? You look like shit.'

Vann Jackson stared at the intruder in the mirror, trying and failing to remember his name. It didn't matter. He was done with names.

He swiped a lingering streak of blood from the

sink, a fake smile plastered across his pale features, the radically mutated Angola virus still coursing through his veins, dividing, multiplying.

Infecting.

'Me? I'm good, man. Never better.'

To be continued

**For more information
about DC Alden please visit
the official website at:**

www.dcaldenbooks.com

Also by DC Alden

Invasion
The Horse at the Gates

CPSIA information can be obtained at www.ICGtesting.com
Printed in the USA
LVOW11s1748310816

502664LV00009B/802/P